BLACKBIRD
Excalibur

by
Martin Schiller

Author of "Blackbird: A Warrior of the No-When",
"Blackbird: A Green and Pleasant England",
"Blackbird: White Tiger of the West"
and Other Works of Wonder and Imagination

Printed with the Express Permission of the Masters
PANTARI PRESS
Seattle, Washington, United States of America
Second Universe, 21st Century
2020

Published by Pantari Press
© Copyright 2020 Martin Schiller. All Rights Reserved.
ISBN-13: 978-0-578-63094-6
ISBN-10: 0-578-63094-X

DEDICATION

For Hypatia

PROLOGUE

In which I behold the ravages visited upon Nazca. Then I learn of a new home for our squadron and realize that something is amiss with Ms. Meier. After this, we travel through the Jump Worlds to the City of Hw'ii'kk.

The shattered domes of Nazca were the perfect mirror of my funereal mood. The base looked just as broken and forlorn as I myself felt.

Nor was I alone in my grief. Blackbird too had been affected, for in their attack, the Lyrans had destroyed the Control Tower, and with it, her artificial friend, Amica. Only my reassurance that a copy of the AI had been saved to the friendship ball had kept her from going completely to pieces. That, and the promise that when the chance arose, I would see it installed in our garden at last.

And as for me? I had only hope to sustain me; that somehow Elizabeth would be restored to my company. It was a thin, and threadbare thing, and in complete opposition to the odds, but still, far preferable to despair.

I shall find you, my love, I vowed as I guided my Phaseship earthwards, *wherever and whenever you are.*

Presently, I set down on a section of tarmac that had not suffered overmuch from the bombing. My squadronmates were awaiting me, and to the last, their expressions were as darksome as mine.

"Whither is the fight?" I asked as I strode up to them. Just then, I relished the possibility of combat, if only to turn my anguish into anger and deal the Lyrans some great and grievous injury.

Hamilket 1 disillusioned me though. "For now, there is no battle, Penelope. We are consolidating our forces at a new base. This one will no longer serve us, and it shall be demolished."

Glancing past him, and beyond our line of timeships, I could see that groups of mechanica were already starting in on this unhappy task. They were already hard at work pulling apart the remains of a dome and setting the pieces aside in a great pile.

Soon, Nazca would be returned to what it had once been before the Masters had claimed it, I reflected, a lonely windswept plain with only the occasional condor to populate its sky. I had become quite accustomed to it, and now, it would no longer serve as my second home.

Another precious thing lost then, I thought dolefully. "What is our destination, sir?"

"The city of Hw'ii'kk," he answered. "The Saurii have agreed to assist with our relocation. We will of course, be using the Jump Worlds to make the journey."

Stifling a groan of displeasure, I nodded in acquiescence. Thanks to the memories of former lives, and my own experience, I was as familiar as any Chrononaut with this disagreeable method of travel. It utilized naturally occurring temporal nodes just as a puddle jumper might, but in worlds situated outside of the nine universes.

These strange realms, governed as they were by entirely different physical laws, allowed them to function as what 20th century physicists had dubbed 'worm holes'. By passing through them, hundreds of thousands of years could be bypassed, and the relative flight time shortened considerably.

The only disadvantage was the fundamental nature of the worlds themselves; many were quite hazardous and presented great challenges for a time pilot. Still, they were vastly preferable to the alternative of weeks, if not months of flying, and everyone understood this.

As one, we all turned and headed for our respective vessels. In the process, I could not help but notice that Ziva seemed to be in a particularly foul mood which did not appear to be entirely related to the Jump Worlds. Something else was bothering her.

Moreover, Manfred also seemed distressed, and he was keeping a careful distance from his lover. Worse, when she and I exchanged glances, the look that she gave me was distinctly frosty.

But this was neither the time nor the place to puzzle it out. Despite the temporal shortcut that the Jump Worlds offered, we still had a very long and demanding flight ahead of us. In fact, it would take us from our present location in 2000 BCE to a point 205 million years in the past.

My readers might well wonder, just as I did, at our choice of destination, for there are many other historical periods that would have been perfect for a new base, and none of them quite as remote. Yet, the decision was not mine to make, but that of the Masters, and I therefore contented myself with the knowledge that once we arrived, the reasons for such an arduous trip would be made clear.

And here, I must divagate from my tale in order to tell another and beg the clemency of my audience. I am no author like Paul Laske, and perforce my account will be far less artful. I must also apologize for its content, for some among my readership might find what I disclose to be rather unsettling, especially those who harbor rigid theological views concerning the special place that mankind allegedly holds in the eyes of God.

You see, we humans tend to suffer from a great conceit. We believe ourselves to be the very summit of life, and the only intelligent species that has ever existed on the Earth.

Yet as any Chrononaut understands, this is not so. Our planet has hosted many other beings, who like ourselves, learned to walk upright, mastered fire, made tools and weapons, built structures and eventually, created entire societies. Not mere offshoots of the human race, such as the giants, the Chuchniya, or the Neanderthal, but born of an entirely different genus altogether.

Long before the first mammals were anything more than rat-like creatures, the dinosaurs had ruled supreme, and it was from among this mighty group, that a race of intelligent predators had arisen to become the masters of their world.

We who came after them, call them the Saurii, and it was to their city, set on a gentle Jurassic savannah, that we were bound. I shall describe these people, for even though they are not human, they are certainly people in their own right, but later, and in greater detail. For now, though, it is enough that they have been introduced to those who took their place on the stage of history.

Our first Jump World was situated in the 10th universe, which we reached by way of a transit from the 2nd to the 9th, and from there, through a node positioned over the deserts of Tasmania (where the natives had long believed that a doorway into the Dreamtime existed).

This Jump World was a place of fantastic beauty; a glittering forest of crystalline spires that had always reminded me of earthly trees. Yet they were not but made of pure silicon, and the cobalt-tinted sky above them was composed of cyanide and a mixture of other toxic gases.

This was not the principle danger of the place, though. That hazard came from the spires, and in the form of tiny crystals that arose from their branches like a reverse rain shower the very instant that we drew near enough to agitate them.

Almost immediately, these particles attached themselves to Blackbird and the other ships, and then began to accumulate at an alarming pace, so that they soon threatened to encase our hulls and hampered our ability to remain airborne. In reply, our ships sent charges out along their energy fields that repelled the crystals. But despite this measure, more replaced them.

As fantastic as this diamond woodland was, it was death to stay in it for any length of time. Thus, we were all of us gladsome when we spotted the next node sparkling in the late afternoon sunlight and made our escape into the next Jump World.

It was just as strange as its predecessor, for it was naught but a roiling mass of scarlet clouds that seemed to rise into eternity itself, interlaced with massive bolts of green lightning. There was no evidence of solid land anywhere, and the pressure around us increased exponentially.

We were in fact, travelling through the upper layers of a gas giant very like Jupiter, and just as unwelcoming. Again, the energy fields around our Phaseships preserved us, keeping the crushing atmospheric forces at bay and shepherding us onwards to our next node.

Rain met us in the third Jump World. It came at us in great sheets and was accompanied by hurricane force winds which we were compelled to compensate for. Unlike the cloud-world, there was land, but it was a dismal sight, battered as it was by the downpour and where it met the ocean, flooded by terrific waves.

Nothing lived in this place, save in the seas, and I strongly doubted that even the fish (or whatever they were) were enjoying their existence overmuch. It was a world of eternal storms and the node that was stationed there was more welcome than any lighthouse.

Yet the fourth Jump World was no safe haven either. It too possessed an ocean, but one composed of an oily black substance that was not water at all, but something else.

Something that was alive. Something that sensed us and tried in vain to leap up and pluck us from the sky. Here, our chronoguns had good effect, vaporizing the liquid tendrils as they rose.

Next, we entered a Jump World spanned by a Dantesque city of pure fire. It was populated by beings made of plasma who writhed in agony and seemed unaware of our presence.

This in turn was followed by another world of ice and desolation, and then, one where the Earth itself did not exist. In its place was naught but great fragments of floating rock that we were compelled to avoid---and this was followed by another place that was just as unsettling, and so on.

Finally, after ten hours of this ordeal, we returned at last to the River of Time and thence entered the Jurassic. As terrible as the creatures that inhabited this time were, they were as nothing compared to what we had just flown through, and the sight of their realm came as a relief.

Our arrival was not without astonishments though, for even as we entered free air and made to descend, Blackbird detected something that neither of us had expected.

"Penny," she advised, "the airspace around us seems to be populated by unknown aerial lifeforms. I am altering course to evade them."

"It is?" I queried. To my eyes, the skies were free of everything but clouds, the occasional pterodactyl, and something that every time pilot becomes familiar with; rods, or as some call them, 'skyfish'.

These odd creatures, that originate from the fourth dimension of reality, are little more than a slim, headless cylinder with an odd membrane which enables them to fly along at great speeds.

Curious and playful by nature, they tend to be attracted by anything--especially if it is in the air. But they are so common that I knew that Blackbird was not referring to them at all.

"The creatures that I am detecting only register on infrared," she informed me, changing the display to provide a view. It plainly showed that they were all around us, and of enormous proportions.

Closely resembling the *Cyanea lamarckii*, or Bluefire Jellyfish of Scotland and the North Sea, the smallest of them were five times our size, whilst others would have dwarfed a zeppelin in mass. More importantly, these airborne invertebrates did not seem to harbor any hostile intent and were doing their best to avoid any collisions.

"I believe that I have located a file concerning them in my data banks," Blackbird said at last. "It was compiled in the 2nd universe, and their 21st century. There, they were categorized as Ebani, or *Entidad Biological Anomalous No Identificada,* unidentified biological entities."

"No doubt 'debunked' by government agencies?" I asked with no little acerbity. That very thing had occurred to the skyfish, and only after the American Shadow Government (itself a puppet of the Illuminati), had managed to capture some of them and breed them as biological surveillance assets. The effort which had subsequently been expended by their legions of pet scientists to play them off as nothing more than camera artifacts, had been a true masterpiece of disinformation.

"No Penny," she corrected. "These beings remain unexplained and nothing indicates that they should exist in this age. However, given the fact that the jellyfish they resemble predates the dinosaurs themselves, it does make perfect sense."

"Yes, it does at that," I allowed, wondering at how they might have evolved and what their means of sustenance and reproduction were.

The Professor must be positively agog with interest, I mused. *When time permits, I shall have to ask him to share what he might have learned about these strange aerial invertebrates.*

Sleep however, was of greater importance to me just then. That and navigating our way around these gentle giants.

Our new base, dubbed Saurii, after our hosts, was located on a wide grassy plain some distance from the city of Hw'ii'kk. In anticipation of our arrival, the mechanica had managed to create a series of dirt runways and moreover, several domes were already in place. While it was a far cry from what Nazca had been before the attack, it still seemed serviceable enough to my eye.

Dozens of Phaseships were already parked on the largest runway, and we landed in the nearest available space and disembarked. Again, as we walked towards the closest dome, Ziva maintained her attitude of coolness towards me and made no attempt at conversation.

What troubles her so? I wondered. I could not account for her unpleasant mood, but I was compelled to set the matter aside in favor of Hamilket 2.

"Your quarters have been recreated," he announced. "They will be located in the same places that they were before Nazca was expanded, and at the moment we have only one conference room. Drop your gear at your lodgings and report there for a briefing."

The thought that I would be occupying a space that would only remind me of Elizabeth, and what I had lost, compelled me to speak.

"I cannot accept that, sir," I said. "I would prefer instead a simple chamber with only a cot and a shelf for a few books. Until Elizabeth is returned to me, I require nothing more."

He nodded, slowly and with understanding. "Very well, Penny. I shall see to it that you are assigned more--spartan--accommodations. What books would you like brought to you?"

"None save those that Major Singh might approve of," I replied. "My readings must consist only of material that addresses the business of war. I wish nothing frivolous to distract me from that endeavor."

This earned me a significant glance from Major Sixkiller and several of the others, but I paid it no heed. Until I had my lady love back in my arms and had seen Mr. Grey and his filth laid low, I did not deserve, nor require any extravagance. Mine would be a soldier's existence, with only the prospect of victory to sustain me.

CHAPTER 1: Codex Dæmoniorum

Wherein I am dispatched by Special Section to retrieve vital records concerning Elizabeth from a secret library. Then the Professor pleads his case, and Ziva remains cool and distant towards me.

Owing to the speed with which the mechanica worked, my new quarters were ready for me by the time I approached the door. Opening it, I found that everything within was precisely as I had commanded; a simple seamless chamber with a small but serviceable bathroom.

The furnishings were equally as plain; a utilitarian bed suited for one person only, a small reading desk and chair, and a diminutive bookshelf set into the wall.

Putting down my travelling bag, I took a moment to inspect the contents of the shelf and found that their titles satisfied my requirements exactly. Sun Tzu's *Art of War* was there, along with *Strategy: A History* by Lawrence Freedman, *The Direction of War: Contemporary Strategy in Historical Perspective*, and similar works.

In sum, it was the perfect setting, and having nothing else to examine, I left my possessions where they were and went directly to the conference room. Charles Woodsworth had stationed himself at the entrance and he bore a small tray. It contained cotton buds and test tubes filled with a preservative solution.

"We are taking samples from everyone," he elucidated. What he did not add was the reason for this measure; with the destruction of our stores in Seattle, it was the only way for us to replenish our stock of clones.

"Of course," I replied, dutifully opening my mouth and allowing him to swab it.

"Thank you," he returned, carefully inserting the sample into a tube and sealing it. "And as soon as you have the chance, we'll need you to make a refactor recording."

"Consider it done," I assured him. This said, I entered the chamber.

Kára Grímsdóttir, Colonel Ambrose, Lady Anne, and Sigrun were already in attendance, but as I took my place among my sqaudronmates, none of them made to speak. Rather, they sat quietly on their side of the table and allowed the Hamilkets to initiate the proceedings.

"Your mission will be to travel to the 2nd universe in the 20th century," Hamilket 1 advised, "and there, insert yourselves into a secure library at the *Abbazia di Montecassino*. It is 142 kilometers outside of Rome and located near the town of Cassino in the Province of Frosinone."

I recognized the name immediately for it was well known in several universes, mine included. Founded in 529 CE, Monte Cassino had weathered earthquakes, bombings and the depredations of invading armies.

Its principle claim to fame was not its endurance however, but its library, which at one time had been the very repository of all written knowledge in the Western world. In fact, Europe owed it a great deal, for had it not been for the efforts of its Benedictine monks, humanity would never have successfully emerged from the Dark Ages of the 2nd universe. Even my timeline had benefited, for it had been its Zerodian clerks who had been responsible for the preservation of Hypatia's writings and the other treasures rescued from the Library of Alexandria.

"What is the objective?" I asked. In answer, the Wing Leader looked to Sigrun.

"No less than to penetrate the most clandestine repository of information in that entire world," she informed us. "The *Archivum Secretum Vaticanum*, the secret archives of the Vatican. We would have sent one of our regular Teams in for this, but at the moment, those resources are otherwise engaged."

Although I appreciated the necessity of sending us, our destination puzzled me, for it was at odds with what I knew, and Manfred voiced the question that was being aborn within me.

"Isn't that archive in Rome, in Vatican City?" he inquired.

The Finn shook her head. "No. The Secret Archives were moved from Vatican City in the 18th Century and quietly relocated to Monte Cassino. From that time onwards, the Holy See maintained the myth that it was in Rome in order to send the curious searching in the wrong direction, and it has proven to be a beautiful strategy. Only Special Section and the Lyrans know the truth."

"Yes," Ziva interjected, "but wasn't the Abbey bombed during their Second World War?"

Sigrun nodded. "It was, and with the help of the Lyrans, the archive was temporarily stored in special vaults in the Apennine Mountains. Then, just as soon as the conflict was over, everything was returned to the Abbey."

"Why do the Lyrans care about the Archive a'tall?" Major Sixkiller queried. "I'd figure they'd have all the info they'd need without it."

"For one," Lady Anne volunteered, "it is the home of many valuable artifacts, whose mere existence gives them sway over the population. For example, they can offer alchemical manuscripts that detail the means to prolong life and reverse aging, or the means to acquire great wealth through the agency of the Philosopher's Stone."

"Yes, but the Lyrans could easily share their own technology in that regard," I observed. "It is far superior to what some medieval text might contain."

The transmutation of lead into gold was a fine example; it was nothing more than a simple matter of rearranging a few atoms here and there. Mere child's play for either the Masters, or the Lyrans.

"It is, and they could," she agreed. "However, they are miserly in nature, and would rather barter lesser secrets whenever they can. And even when they do part with their knowledge, it tends towards the inferior. Do you not recall the saucers that they allowed the Nazi's to possess? They were all subpar models, yet the Nazis were glad to have them."

She was completely correct. The flying disks that the Lyrans had gifted the fascists with had been nowhere near as deadly as the ones that they themselves flew. In fact, they had been mere rubbish by comparison.

"Moreover," she added, "the Lyrans also use the archive to *conceal* knowledge. Knowledge that if revealed, would challenge the sovereignty of their human puppets.'

"The bones of alien races are hidden there, along with documentation concerning the true lineage of Jesus Christ, as well as the unedited prophesies of the Lady of Fatima. There is even a simple Chronoviewer that a monk constructed to gaze back in time with."

"Incredible," I remarked. "It seems quite the collection then." But in truth, none of it appealed to me. My only interest was in whatever might lead me to Elizabeth and Mr. Grey.

"It is at that," Colonel Ambrose agreed. "Our objective is a trifle less fantastic though. We are after a specific book, the *Codex Dæmoniorum*. Among other things, the code concealed within its pages reveals the identity of certain 'sleeper agents' scattered throughout the centuries.'

"It was written by another Lyran agent, who like myself, was about to defect to the Masters, and before the Triskelion Order began to suspect her loyalty. Thankfully, I discovered the key to the cipher, and in turn, recorded it in the file that we retrieved in Morocco. So, it all boils down to a matter of locating the Codex and deciphering it."

Elizabeth's name might be listed in those pages, I thought with dread, and then I amended myself; *Or not.*

Then Hamilket 2 announced the specifics of our assignment. "Ms. Steele, Hauptman von Knectenberg, Captain Meier and Major Sixkiller, you will form the core of our Team and once you arrive, you will be under Ms. Nälkäinen's command. Please equip yourself accordingly and report to the tarmac."

"Yes sir," we answered in unison.

Both hopeful and terrified at what the Codex might reveal, I returned to my quarters straightaway, and there, donned the black combat suit that Special Section's Action Teams favored. Once I had checked everything and verified the status of my weaponry (which consisted of a truly gargantuan knife, a chronopistol and a suppressed submachinegun), I returned to the hall, and met my companions.

When Ziva beheld me, she frowned in displeasure before looking away, and Manfred pointedly avoided my eyes. Whatever the reason for this behavior, its cause was quite serious, I knew. Yet I was still not in any position to uncork the bottle and determine the nature of its contents; the mission came first. Consequently, I held my tongue and accompanied them in an uncomfortable silence.

Which was as well, for as we passed the office that the Hamilkets occupied, I discovered that we had another matter to contend with altogether. The Professor was there and pleading with them quite earnestly.

"Sirs," he was saying, "I know that I am no Chrononaut, nor any member of Special Section, but I beg to be included in this endeavor! Surely, my special knowledge of antiquities will prove to be an asset."

"Professor Merriweather," Hamilket 1 replied patiently. "I deeply appreciate your desire to take part, but you are not properly trained to face the hazards that the Team might encounter."

Merriweather was not about to be put off so easily though. "Wing Leader," he persisted. "I am willing to face the danger if it will afford me the opportunity to visit the Archives. The material contained within it is utterly priceless and the insights that it might lend me will surely serve the Masters. Surrounded as I would be by experienced agents, I should be safe enough."

It was Sigrun who settled the matter. "He is correct, Wing Leader," she said from the doorway. "The Professor's knowledge could in fact be of great assistance. He may observe things that we would otherwise miss and give insights that would never occur to us. Provided that he will agree to follow *all* of my instructions—and make certain that he makes a refactor copy of himself—I see no harm in bringing him along."

The Professor turned to her, beaming with gratitude. "I have already done so, madam. Rest assured that my clone will be fully functional and ready to serve should worse come to worse."

"And we shall do our best to see that its services will not be required," she quipped wryly. With a final glance at the Hamilkets that brooked no dissention, she nodded to Merriweather to accompany us.

"Oh, this is truly marvelous," he exclaimed as he took his place alongside me. "The *Archivum Secretum Vaticanum*! What wonders await us! I can hardly contain myself."

Despite Ziva's unfriendly mood and Manfred's gloom, I was moved to smile at him. The poor fellow was like a little child anticipating his first trip to the circus.

Let us just hope that it will not prove to be a jaunt inside of the lion's cage, I reflected darkly. Given the significance of the Archive, I had little doubt that unpleasant measures had been put in place to deter trespassers.

Again, we employed the Jump Worlds to make our journey and perforce, the trip was far longer than it had been from 2000 BCE, and when at last we arrived in the 2nd universe, we had been in flight for some fifteen hours. Thus, we were compelled to afford ourselves a day to recuperate from the stresses we had been subjected to. This we did on a remote island in the Caribbean and once recovered, we made for Italy.

There, and mindful of the likelihood that sensor arrays were in place in and around the Abbey, we took care not only to cloak ourselves, but made landfall near the town of Ceprano, some 35 kilometers away.

Further, we made a point of flying at a very low altitude and using the terrain to conceal ourselves, or what Major Sixkiller referred to as 'nap of the earth' flying. We also kept a weather eye out for the presence of any Lyran disks patrolling the area. Mercifully though, none made any appearance, and by and by, we reached our destination entirely unmolested.

The Abbey itself proved to be a great cluster of Romanesque buildings, perched atop the mountain which had engendered its name, and as we assumed orbit over the basilica, it was easy for me to appreciate why it, and its predecessor, a temple of Apollo, had been constructed there. It occupied the whole of the summit, dominating the surrounding countryside and commanding the eye.

Yet I was not as ensnared as I might have been, for the gravity of our errand overrode any sense of awe or admiration. Instead, only a grim determination to see our mission through filled my spirit.

Presently, a message appeared on my main display. It was an encoded burst transmission, warning me to make ready. It also included the result of our passive scans.

Based on this data, the Archive was some 200 meters below the Abbey, and deep in the heart of the mountain itself. Only a single elevator linked it with the outside world, and it was a given that access through it was both encoded, and closely monitored.

A moment later, the coordinates for our first jump-point appeared. I saw that they would deliver us into a machine room of some sort, and accordingly, I opened up my puddle jumper and set the dials.

The figures for the second jump came after this, and I made a point of memorizing them. These would take our group from the machine room and into a wide gallery, and from the many corridors and lesser chambers, I deduced that this was the Archive itself. I also noted that there was a guard station positioned just outside the gallery, and that it was currently manned by two fellows, presumably members of the Vatican's elite protective force, the Swiss Guard.

Further, an additional contingent occupied what appeared to be a barracks and command station, but as vaunted a fighting force as they were, I felt no cause for alarm. Our plan, which we had discussed mid-flight, would see to them neatly enough.

Then another message arrived, signaling me that the time had come. I gave command of the ship over to Blackbird, then counted down thirty seconds, took a breath, and engaged the puddle jumper.

Just as intended, our group materialized in the machine room. and without any conversation between us, we set our puddle-jumpers for the second point and activated them.

When we reappeared, we were in the gallery. Unlike the serene, medieval ambiance of the Abbey above it, it was a sterile place, all metal and strip lighting. In truth, it strongly resembled the halls of the NSA Data Center in Utah, with nary a nod to the aesthetic sensibilities of its visitors.

This is not to say that it was devoid of contents though, for the very opposite was the case. Clear display boxes or vitrines, lined its walls. They contained all manner of items, ranging from ancient manuscripts to precious archeological treasures. One particularly large enclosure even held an object that looked suspiciously like the Ark of the Covenant as it had been described in my readings of the Christian Bible (though I could not be entirely certain).

While I wondered at this, I heard a polite cough, and turning, saw that the Colonel had a pocket watch in his hand, though my readers will surely guess that it was no normal timepiece.

And here, I must profoundly apologize for a terrible oversight on my part. After all that I have written thus far, I have come to realize that I have quite forgotten to disclose its proper name. So, in order to rectify this grievous (and embarrassing) error, I shall finally do so.

The device that he held is properly referred to as a *kiriket*, or in the Queen's English, a 'cricket'. It is so named for when it is activated, 'the world around it sleeps whilst the cricket sings'.

This said (and again with my deepest regrets for neglecting my responsibilities as an author), I shall endeavor to describe the particular model that he possessed, for there are actually several versions, and the differences are quite significant.

The first, with two winding stems and a third hand, is the one which my readers have already become acquainted with during my visit to Studio 'S', and they will surely recall that it permits its user to enter a pocket dimension which is quite separate from its larger neighbor.

The Colonel's version however, had *triple* winding stems and a *fourth* hand, and this extra control made it possible for the user to remain in their local reality, but to completely suspend time within it for a distance of half a kilometer. Thus, one could physically interact with the world around them whilst everyone else was temporally frozen and unaware of their presence—unless they possessed crickets of their own, of course. Being as handy as such a device would be to anyone intent on mischief, its distribution, was by necessity, highly restricted, and this was the first time that I had been given the opportunity to employ it.

It had only one significant limitation however; though it can freeze time, it can only do so for 30 minutes, after which, a lengthy recharge is required. Therefore, we all of us understood that we would need to be quick about our business and not waste a single, precious moment.

And for his part, the Colonel did not tarry. With a devilish wink, he handed me my cricket, and then produced several more from his backpack, which he passed out to every member of our party.

"Pull the third stem partway out," he instructed, "and then set the fourth hand to two minutes past three. Then, in exactly ten seconds, pull the stem all the way out, beginning--now."

Even as he said this, I could hear the sound of running footsteps drawing nigh. Our presence had been detected, and right at the 10 second mark, the Swiss Guards burst into the chamber, attired in their archaic blue uniforms, but wielding very contemporary machine pistols.

"*Non muoverti!*", one of them barked. "*Mostraci le tue mani!*"

Alas, neither he, nor his partner, were afforded the opportunity to fulfill their obligations as guardians of the Archive. As one, we pulled our stems, and for half a second, the face of our watches glowed as they recognized one another and synchronized. A brilliant flash followed this, momentarily stealing away my vision, and when it cleared, the guardsmen were frozen in mid-stride.

In a way, I felt sorry for the poor blighters, for as long as our temporal alteration held, we had the full run of the place and there was nothing they could do about it whatsoever.

"We have exactly thirty minutes before those chaps come 'round," the Colonel reminded us. "Best that we be about our business then, eh wot?"

Meantime, the Professor was already inspecting the nearest display cases. One in particular arrested his attention and he stood stock still before it, his jaw gone slack with amazement. Wondering if we had already located the object of our quest, I went over to him.

"Incredible," he declared in a hushed, reverent tone. "The very contract that Vlad Țepeș signed with the Devil to become a vampire—and in an archaic form of Romanian that only exists in one other document *anywhere* in the Nine Universes! It is even written in the Impaler's own blood! I simply *must* have it!"

Before I could remind him that we had far more pressing things to attend to, he opened the case and carefully put the document away in a large satchel. Until this moment, I had paid this accessory of his scant attention, but now it's purport became abundantly clear; scholar though he was, he was plainly not above robbing the Archive of its treasures. I did not hold this against him though. It was the least that the Lyrans deserved.

"Sir," I urged as he made to open another case, his eyes alight with avarice. "We must needs be away. Our time here is short."

"Yes, yes, but—" he began to say. Then he thought the better of it. "Yes, of course my dear, you are quite correct. Lead the way."

This, however, was the very problem. Whilst every corridor had a placard positioned above it, none were marked with anything more than numbers, and these were in Lyran digits!

Nor was there any data terminal or a physical map for us to consult. Clearly, visitors to the Archive were expected to arrive armed with the knowledge of which passage they needed to follow— or like ourselves, had not been invited and could therefore remain ignorant.

"This is certainly a problem," Merriweather observed. "Though not insurmountable. If the Archive's collection is anything like other repositories, then objects which are like unto one another will be stored together by class."

"A logical deduction," Sigrun agreed. "I suggest that we break off into pairs and each team explore a hall. Whoever finds the area dedicated to books and manuscripts will signal the rest and we will converge there." She looked to Kára who immediately took her place beside her.

The others then paired off just as one might have expected them to. Lady Anne teamed up with the Colonel, Manfred with Ziva (though he did not seem to be overly thrilled by the prospect), and Major Sixkiller joined the Professor and I.

"Twenty-five minutes remaining," the Colonel warned. Glancing at my watch and seeing that this was so, I inclined my jaw to my compatriots, and we fell into step together. Our corridor, which had been labeled simply as number 2, went on for some length before we came to the first set of chambers. These also bore numbers; 2.1 and 2.2.

Room 2.1 contained taxidermy, but of such a bizarre nature that I scarcely believed my eyes. What looked to be a dragon out of myth had been mounted on a large pedestal, with its wings spread wide. Its neighbor was a unicorn, and this in turn, was companioned by a large specimen jar containing either a genuine mermaid, or a fabrication so perfect that I failed to detect even the slightest flaw. But perhaps the most shocking exhibit, and which turned my stomach, was none other than a collection of humans and humanoids, and among them, a Chuchniya posed in a lifelike manner.

There was more besides, yet I could not bear to remain and urged my friends to step across the hall to the other chamber. They complied without dissent and seemed just as disturbed as I at what we had just beheld.

Room 2.2 proved to be a collection of alien artifacts. There were the skulls of races that I could not identify, strange plaques inscribed with enigmatic characters, devices whose purpose was thoroughly unguessable, and at the very center, a large ebon sphere that floated above the floor without support just as a Phaseship might.

Moving on, we came to 2.3, and here we were briefly cheered, for the space was filled with bound volumes and boxes of paper files. Yet, as I peered at their labels, I saw that they concerned *"The Assassination of John F. Kennedy"*, *"The Roswell Incident,"* and many other subjects that were equally as mystifying.

To me, Kennedy was a total unknown, and Roswell merely a remote point on the map. More importantly, neither these files, nor any of the others, concerned the Codex, and accordingly, I made to leave the room.

But Major Sixkiller had paused at the box concerning Kennedy, her eyes aglitter with interest. "I've just gotta know," she explained. "It's one of the biggest mysteries in the 2nd universe. Heck, they even wonder about it over in the 5th."

Then, without further ado, she reached in, withdrew a manila file and opened it. What she read within its pages made her eyes go wide in astonishment.

"Oh no," she cried, shaking her head in disbelief. "*Them? They* did it? Penny, I'm takin this with me just to read it again." At that, she stuffed it into the Professor's pack.

"Are we quite done here?" I asked her.

"Yep," she replied. Then to herself, "Who woulda thunk? Damn!"

"Pray tell, who did the deed, Cassie?" Merriweather inquired.

"Sugar-O Donuts," she replied. "They got mad when he visited Dallas and wouldn't come t' visit their store. 'Course, I can kinda understand. Disrespectin Sugar-O is like disrespectin the *entire* South—but now—I'm not sure I'll ever eat one again. *Damn!*"

"I had no idea that your people took confections so seriously," he admitted.

She then proceeded to explain the whole matter of donuts and their integral place in the fabric of Southern society, particularly where it concerned something called 'sprinkles', however, I did not award it much attention, being more concerned with the contents of Room 2.4.

This was the home to all manner of arcane bric-a-brac such as alchemists and sorcerers employed. Given the title of the Codex, the *Book of Dark Spirits*, it seemed likely that the volume might well reside within its precincts, and when I gave voice to this, my companions agreed, and we searched the room with great vigor.

Sadly, and although there were many texts that concerned the business of magic and demonology, none of them proved to be the volume that we sought. Not that our failure prevented the Professor from adding to his collection though; in the process of our inspection, he purloined several books for himself, and each one only seemed to increase his delight.

"Marvelous," he declared, stuffing the last of them into his satchel. "Simply marvelous. I now have the original notes written by Rabbi Loew showing exactly how he created his golem to protect the Jews of Prague. Think of it, Penny; a formula to instill animation into lifeless clay!"

Nodding indulgently, I glanced at my cricket and saw that we had only fifteen minutes remaining in which to search (whilst pointedly ignoring a large mirror whose glass was populated by rather disquieting—*things*).

"There is one final room in this hall," I reminded my friends. This was Room 2.5, and situated at the very end of the passage. "Let us check there."

This proved to be a very fortuitous decision. The chamber was rather spacious, and contained a large number of books, along with various weapons of different sizes and purpose. It also boasted a large space in the center which had been reserved for individual reading tables. Moreover, we discovered that the books themselves were stored in alphabetical order which greatly facilitated our efforts. At length, it was the Professor who found the item that we had so hoped to retrieve.

"Eureka!" he declared triumphantly, holding it up for us to see. "The Codex is ours."

I was just about to notify the others about our success when we were very rudely interrupted. Men in black appeared before us, straight out of the ether, and brandishing their sinister wands. Had I the luxury, I might have wondered at how they were capable of transcending the effect of our crickets, save that there was no opportunity to do anything more than register their presence.

I was not alarmed though. The Tigress had arisen within me, and she and I smiled at them. There were fifty of the biorobots in all, and to the two of us at least, these odds seemed almost fair. They actually had a fighting chance--but only that.

Then the nearest biorobot raised its wand and pointed it straight at me. Out of reflex, I sent myself into a roll so as to evade injury, but my maneuver proved unnecessary. The device did not discharge and even as I came back up onto my feet, I realized that the qualities of our shared reality were somehow preventing it from functioning.

A puzzled look came over the creature's face as it comprehended the same thing, and then it cast the wand aside and grasped a sword from a nearby wall. Its fellows did likewise, arming themselves with whatever was at hand; maces, spears and other medieval weapons. Then as one, and at what must have been a telepathic signal from their leader, they advanced on us.

"Professor, Major," I cried, not taking my eyes off my enemies, "retreat to a safe corner and remain there!"

Then I too seized up a weapon. It was a halberd, although not the Chinese *qinglong-ji* that I had learned to wield in my former life. Rather it was the heavier, European version, topped by a cruel looking axe with a long spike at its apex, and flukes that were intended for pulling a rider from their horse. There was nothing graceful about it at all, and yet as I hefted it, I was satisfied that it would prove to be serviceable enough.

Baring my fangs and hissing, I brought the thing to the ready position. *Come on then, you bloody bastards,* I thought.

In turn, these very same bastards obliged me, surging forwards in unison. The foremost of them received my spike in its throat, causing the biorobot to stagger and drop. Another, who had made to outflank me, received the butt end of my weapon (which was also equipped with a sharp metal spike) directly into its chest, fatally piercing its sternum.

Yet a third discovered that a swipe of my axe was quite capable of separating it from its right foot, Unable to support itself, the thing toppled to the floor like a bowling pin.

Had they been human, they would have been dissuaded by all this carnage, but they were not. Instead, they continued to press their attack.

Dodging slashes and strikes, I jammed the top edge of my axe into the bridge of a fourth creatures' nose, whilst putting my body weight behind the strike. What followed was a thoroughly satisfying 'crunch' as the cartilage and a goodly portion of the surrounding bone collapsed. Even as it staggered backwards, pawing at the ruin of its face, a fifth biorobot was attempting to thrust at me with his sword blade.

I parried and used the flukes to pull the weapon from its grip. As it flew away, I stepped in, bringing the axe down onto its chest. Here,

23

the sheer mass of my weapon prevailed, cleaving deeply, and opening its entire torso wide.

But still they came. One rather unsportsmanlike fellow attempted to seize my halberd by its shaft, however it did the creature little good. Retaining my hold with one hand, I merely drew my long knife with the other, rushed in and buried the blade deep into the side of its neck. Suddenly preoccupied with a much greater problem than controlling my weapon, the thing let go, and I was able to continue on with my business unimpeded.

It went on and on like this, the halberd creating a field of death and devastation in its wake, and through it all, I laughed. I laughed heartily, and as if I had consumed an entire bottle of wine. Rather than feeling fear, or rage, I was mad with joy at the unbridled destruction that I was unleashing.

In the face of this, is it any wonder that when at last, the battle was over, that I stood alone amidst a field of corpses with none left to oppose me? Or that beyond feeling a bit winded and covered from head to toe with gore, that I had only a nick or two as a souvenir? My only regret was that the body of Mr. Grey was not among the mangled remains lying at my feet.

Then my disappointment was interrupted. Two additional figures had appeared. They were not Lyrans though, nor biorobots, but none other than my sister Caroline, and her companion, the Chuchniya. This time, she was dressed in a medieval gown, complete with a hennin, and she looked about her with a calm, unflustered expression as if the corpses were as normal as the sight of picnickers taking their ease in Hyde Park.

As was her custom, she did not speak, but I heard her thinking to the Wild Man just as clearly as if she had.

"Look!" she told him, "She wields Rhongomyniad and Carnwennan with equal vigor. She is nearly ready for her great task."

In reply, the Chuchniya merely shrugged, and made a rumbling sound that I took for an acknowledgement. And before I could ask either of them what they meant by this exchange, they turned, walked two steps, and dematerialized.

Naturally, neither the Professor or Major Sixkiller had been privy to this visitation, for they made no remark about it. Instead, their comments were reserved for the battle which had preceded it.

"Damn girl," Sixkiller exclaimed. "I've heard've openin up a can of whoopass, but ya'll just let go with a whole *six-pack!*"

"A truly amazing display of martial prowess," the Professor added with equal admiration. "Had I not witnessed it with my own eyes, I would have scarcely believed it."

"Thank you," I returned, wiping some of the blood from my face and tossing the halberd away. "That is a great compliment, sir. But I think that we should locate our fellow Chrononauts and depart before enemy reinforcements force me to provide you with another demonstration."

"Quite so," Merriweather agreed.

Ever the stoics, neither Kára Grímsdóttir or Sigrun commented upon my blood-spattered appearance. Nor did they display any great exuberance over the procurement of the Codex. Instead, they merely accepted the news with curt nods, and then saw to it that our team reassembled and prepared itself for extraction.

"Not bad," the Colonel remarked when he and Lady Anne rejoined us. "My watch shows two minutes still remaining. Anyone care to take a final stroll before we take our leave?"

Lady Anne awarded him a gimlet stare. "I think that we should avail ourselves of the surplus time that we have instead."

"Oh very well," he sighed gustily. "Set your puddle jumpers for the machine room and jump on my mark. Five, four, three, two, one—now."

Once in the machine room, we jumped again to our respective Phaseships—and not an instant too soon. Scarcely a second later, I saw that the entire Archive had gone into alarm, and that the elevator system was now locked down.

Too late, I thought with no little amusement. We had our prize in hand and there was no help for it.

Pleased, I trailed after the others as we left the Abbey behind for a transit into the No-When. It was only when we were on our way to the first Jump World that I dared to relax—and to consider the issue of Ziva and Manfred. For that, I knew that the best source of information would be Manfred himself.

"Hauptman?" I asked on a private channel, "May I speak with you for a moment?"

There was a long pause during which he considered my request. Then he replied. "Yah."

"Manfred, Captain Meier seems to be quite cross with me, and I have also noticed that your mood is none too cheerful either. Can you enlighten me as to the cause?"

"She is angry with you," he explained. "She doesn't think that you should have let those people in New Berlin go free. And she is angry with me as well for agreeing to it and making my peace with Ernst."

"Whyever for?" I queried, now thoroughly mystified. "Allowing those civilians to depart was the only moral thing to do, and Ernst *was* your brother after all."

"Yah," he answered. "I know all that. But she sees it as a betrayal."

"A betrayal?"

"Yah," he sighed, sounding very worn. "A betrayal of her people and all that they have suffered at the hands of the Nazis. I tried to explain the situation to her, but she would not listen to me."

"Then she would have preferred that they all *died?*" I demanded. "Even the women and the children?"

Although I could not see him, I could readily envision his weary shrug. "She has no mercy in her heart for anyone associated with the Nazis—even the innocent. I am sorry, Penny, but I can do nothing to change her mind. All I can do is hope that time will heal things between us."

"Perhaps if I spoke with her—" I suggested.

"It would do no good," he put in. "She is a very strong-willed woman, and she will not change her mind until she is ready. If she is *ever* ready."

"I see," I answered, not at all pleased. But I did not regret my decision; I had resolved the matter of New Berlin in favor of justice and sheer decency, and though I hated the idea that I had slighted a friend in the process, I refused to believe that I had erred.

And as much as I loathed the idea, I also knew that Manfred was correct. Time would have to suffice, and forcing the matter would only exacerbate the situation.

CHAPTER 2: The Living Sky

In which I visit the city of Hw'ii'kk and there, suffer some distress. Then, I am compelled to accept the return of my implant. After this, the Masters negotiate a solution to the Jump Worlds, a disturbing vision haunts my sleep, and I serve as a test pilot. Afterwards, I learn about modern art.

Again, the Jump Worlds exacted their toll upon us, and by the time we reached the Jurassic, we were well and truly exhausted. Fully aware of our sorry state, the Hamilkets kept the debriefing short, and then added in a bit of welcome news.

"The Masters are negotiating with certain parties to provide us with a less demanding means of travel," Hamilket 2 announced. "If all goes well, we will no longer need the Jump Worlds to reach our objectives, and our flight time will be considerably shortened."

This elicited a collective sigh of relief, and we were hastily dismissed. For my part, I made straight for my quarters, and there, went directly to bed.

Some twelve hours later, and having enjoyed a deep, dreamless slumber, I reawakened only to discover that no missions were awaiting us. The day was mine to do with as I wished, and as the weather was fair, and I was in no mood for reading (or brooding in my chamber), I elected to engage in some sightseeing.

My destination required little consideration; I decided that a visit to the city of Hw'ii'kk was in order, and there, I intended to avail myself of the chance to observe the Saurii in their natural habitat.

Since they were now our allies, I was rather curious about them. Better still, their city was close by, being but a twenty-minute walk along a simple dirt road and over gentle terrain. Accordingly, I broke my fast with a light meal and left the base on foot.

At this juncture, I should make mention that I did not undertake my stroll without ensuring that I was properly equipped, for in addition to a decent sunhat, there was the matter of breathable air to consider.

As it happens, whenever one travels any further than 30 million years in the past, oxygen and CO_2 levels become an important concern. For example, if one desires to observe Paleozoic Trilobites at play, they will find that the level of atmospheric oxygen is only 4-5% of what it is in the 20th century.

If instead, they fancy the giant dragonflies of the Carboniferous era, they will shortly discover that it is 35% higher. Worse, if they simply cannot do without a tour of the Late Permian, they will encounter the aftereffects of a super volcano, and truly appalling levels of CO^2.

All of which begs the question of the Jurassic. Though mild in comparison to these other epochs, it is still no paradise for modern lungs. Here, breathable oxygen tends to range from 12% to 13%, with anything below 19.5% considered to be deficient and injurious to one's health. Accordingly, whenever anyone such as I ventured outside of the domes, a proper breathing apparatus was the only effective means of ensuring an agreeable excursion.

Fortunately, the Masters had long since addressed this irksome problem, and had provided us with simple face masks which were neither bulky, nor required any special air tanks (having as they did, an ultraminiaturized supply system and the means to filter and manage the air). While it was not terribly flattering, it was a necessity that one became accustomed to, and thus, I made certain to affix such a unit to my mouth and nose.

Of course, there was also another protective measure to take into consideration; the Jurassic is justly famous for its fearsome predators, and some form of effective physical protection is simply *de rigueur* for the well-dressed prehistoric explorer.

In my case, this meant wearing a chronopistol (which is proof against even the hardiest Allosaur). However, I do not wish my readers to assume that my sidearm was the only guarantee of my safety, for our base was surrounded by defensive energy fields, and our hosts had also taken steps of their own.

These consisted of rather ingenious windmills, whose sole purpose was to emit ultrasonic sounds that the local wildlife found to be disagreeable, and yet did not discomfort the Saurii themselves. In addition, the area had been well-planted with flora that deterred predators, either by means of their scent, or their physical features (these being thorns and other unfriendly attributes).

In sum, the entire neighborhood was quite safe and when I stepped onto the road and began my journey, I was able to enjoy the scenery without the distraction of any monster attempting to make me into its meal.

Halfway to my goal, I was pleasantly surprised to encounter the Professor. He had seated himself on a small, grassy hillock adjacent to the road, and was engaged in sketching something on a large pad. Like myself, he wore a sunhat and his breather mask, but also a pair of electronic spectacles which resembled the combat monocles that I had used during my foray to Highgate.

I stepped off the track and joined him. "A good morning to you, sir. Please do forgive me if I am interrupting."

"No, no," he replied, waving this off. "You are not imposing in the least, my dear. In fact, I was just about to take a break."

"Might I ask what you are sketching?" I queried.

"The Ebani in the sky above us," he explained, turning the pad around so that I might see. "But I am afraid that I am not much of an artist."

His drawing depicted one of the creatures in great detail, set against the landscape before us. According to this, his subject was perhaps a dozen or so kilometers away and of tremendous proportions.

Then, remembering himself, he handed me his spectacles and when I donned them, I discovered that they allowed their wearer to perceive the infrared and therefore, the creatures themselves.

"They are incredible beings," he commented, adding a few final touches to his illustration. "Did you know that they are not limited solely to the Jurassic? In fact, they are known throughout the Nine Universes, and in many centuries, though it seems that they prefer this era above all the rest."

"Do they indeed?" I asked, watching as a flock of much smaller beings that I took to be juveniles arrived, and then flitted playfully around the adult.

"Quite," he returned. "Beyond the fact that they are invisible outside of the infrared spectrum, they are also rather unique in another respect. They are trans-dimensional beings, and according to the file that you retrieved from the Black Knight, the Ebani are capable of moving across time and space without being subject to its limitations. In fact, they can fold the very fabric of the universe so as to reduce the distance between any two points to zero."

"So, they can travel instantly, and anywhere," I deduced.

"Precisely," he confirmed. "Just as we believe the Wild Man and others like him are able to. I should also add that this is the very reason why we relocated ourselves in this remote period in history. If the Masters can convince the Ebani to come to our aid, then the Jump Worlds, and even using the River of Time, will become entirely unnecessary."

Though I felt a small pang of regret at the thought of abandoning the River as a means of travel, it was still very welcome news.

"Tell me," I asked, "what do the Saurii call the Ebani?"

"Our hosts refer to them simply as *Ke'tzz'a,* or Gods," he answered, taking in the heavens above us with a wave of his hand, "and their realm as the *Koo-ka'a-an,* the Living Sky."

"Gods?" asked I, returning his spectacles.

"Yes. The Saurii can perceive infrared light, and they have always held the Ebani to be divine beings.'

"Then, approximately 10,000 years ago, their great savior figure, the prophetess *Coo'coo'ma'tz* appeared. She declared that one day, and if they lived virtuous enough lives, they would become just like the Ebani, and exist as creatures of the air.'

"A rather remarkable vision when you consider that it will eventually come to pass, and that their distant progeny will be the very birds that you and I so love and admire."

This impressed me greatly. Coo'coo'ma'tz 's vision had been truly prophetic, or *would be*, given a few million years here or there.

"Her story does not end with this far-seeing proclamation," he added. "It is said that she was gifted with miraculous powers; she could heal the sick, raise the dead, and many other miracles besides. She was even credited with the ability to appear to her followers, though the distance between them made this impossible.'

"Unfortunately, she also made many of the priestesses of the time jealous, and in turn, they convinced the Great Matriarch, the Ma'haa, to condemn her to death. According to the legend, Coo'coo'ma'tz went to her execution promising that she would not truly die, but live forever, and that all those who believed in her would do likewise."

"It all sounds very like the tale of Jesus," I observed.

"That it does," the Professor agreed. "It seems that no matter the time nor the place, the same divine drama plays itself out—even in the Jurassic."

At that, he stood, dusted himself off, and stowed his drawing supplies in his pack. "Are you on your way to Hw'ii'kk perhaps? I was of a mind to go there myself and could do with some company."

I nodded. "I am sir, and I too would welcome the companionship."

"Excellent!" he beamed.

Falling into step with one another, we returned to the road, and as we walked along, our confabulation centered on the books that he had pilfered from the library, and especially the Codex. Alas, I learned that Colonel Ambrose was still in the process of deciphering the damnable thing, and this frustrated me greatly. Of course, there was nothing to be done for it, and I had to let the matter go and concentrate on other subjects, lest my impatience drive me to madness.

At length, and just as we were coming into view of the city, we had the occasion to meet our first Saurii. There were three of them; two of which were on foot and the third that was riding in a simple wagon pulled by a species of dinosaur that I took to be an herbivore.

Like ourselves, they walked upright on two legs and possessed hands that were equipped with four clawed fingers and that great tool of any advanced species, a thumb. Here though, any resemblance between us ended, for the creatures were quite short in comparison to ourselves, with the tallest of them being no more than 1.2 meters in height.

Moreover, they did not wear any garments, but were covered instead by small feathers. These shimmered brilliantly wherever the light caught them, and as I would later learn, it was the males who were the most flamboyantly colored, with the females being somewhat drab by comparison.

Another feature that differentiated them from humans were their eyes, which were quite large and possessed brilliantly colored irises. These would 'flash' or 'pin' depending upon their emotional state and in much the same manner as the birds of my era. As for their faces, they were narrow, and featured a protruding nose and mouth that suggested the beak that it would one day become.

Seeing us approach, the nearest of them bobbed his head and uttered a greeting. To the unaided ear, it might have sounded like nothing more than a nonsensical combination of clicks, chirps and rumbles, but the Professor and I had both taken the precaution of wearing our communications earpieces. These were linked to the base and the Phaseships, making it possible for us to understand the creature quite clearly.

"Well met!" the Saurii greeted. "may the skies look down upon you in favor."

"And may the Gods bless you from on high," the Professor returned politely, aided by the speaker set in his earpiece. His words were well received, and the creature's companions added in their own salutes as we passed one another.

Eventually, we achieved the city's outskirts and entered it. As might be expected, Hw'ii'kk was quite unlike London, or my old Seattle. Its streets were naught but hard packed earth, and the buildings which lined them were constructed of adobe covered with plaster, and seldom more than two stories tall. Nor were there any doors to bar entry. Rather, the entrances were hung with elaborately beaded curtains, or colored cloth.

And, just as we had seen on the road, the Saurii preferred to walk, or employ carts drawn by beasts. This they did in great numbers, for Hw'ii'kk, being a major settlement, was a bustling place, however not so much so that we went without notice. We did after all, tower over them and they could not help but stop and remark upon our exotic appearance or exchange friendly gestures.

Of course, we also attracted a horde of children who followed us out of sheer curiosity (or at least until an adult intervened). In all, it was a very genial situation, and despite the unfamiliar nature of its people, I found myself feeling at ease in their society almost immediately.

After a short while, we happened upon a marketplace, and it was here that the Saurii demonstrated their level of artistic and technological achievement. Because of their eye structure, they were particularly sensitive to the color red, and according to the Professor, were capable of differentiating upwards of 2,000 variations of this color, far exceeding what our inferior mammalian senses could detect.

They also employed this keen appreciation to great effect, creating dyes that ran the full spectrum of the color's possibilities. Even with my visual limitations, the end result, which was expressed in pottery and textiles, proved to be utterly breathtaking.

So, and despite my resolution to cleave only to the practical, I found myself becoming desirous of a particularly glorious wall-hanging and an equally exquisite example of local pottery.

"Oh, Elizabeth would love this!" I declared. Then realizing what I had just said, my mood darkened with the swiftness of a storm gathering on a summer's day.

"Elizabeth *will* love this," the Professor insisted. "She will not be named in the Codex, and wherever she is, we will find and liberate her. I am certain of it."

Tears of desperation welled up in my eyes, and he quickly offered me his kerchief and then gathered me in, heedless of our Saurii onlookers.

"I hope so," I bawled into his shoulder. "I do so hope it."

When at last, I had managed to compose myself, he stepped back and gently cupped my chin.

"Buy the pottery and the wall hanging," he suggested gently. "Display them in your quarters as a promise and a vow of better days to come, and when they do arrive, give them to her."

"Yes," I replied, still teary-eyed. "You are right, and I shall."

The problem though, was the matter of money. Neither the Professor or I had come bearing any local currency, which proved to consist of bits of metal and polished glass.

Given our paucity of funds, and the fact that I was in no mood for any further exploration, we subsequently agreed to return to the base. It was during this journey, that a shadow fell over us, and shielding my eyes against the sun, I saw that several disks had just appeared in the sky.

Yet I felt no cause for alarm, for they did not prove to be Lyran machines, but of the kind that the Greys piloted. Moreover, they did not land at the base, but instead, flew straight to Hw'ii'kk following the road. Because of this, I instantly guessed at their purpose. Ambassadors of the Masters, (if not my mother herself) were likely aboard, and the negotiations that Hamilket 2 had promised were about to begin.

Wishing them all the luck, my companion and I walked on. By and by, we reached the central dome, where we were met by Charles Woodsworth.

"Hello Penny," he greeted. "So very good to see you again."

"And you Charles," I returned, for as ragged as my mood was, I could not help but feel cheered by the sight of him.

"Has there been any progress?" Merriweather inquired.

"Yes sir," he answered. "And I daresay that you will both want to see the results for yourselves."

The Professor explained. "Charles has been continuing with our analysis of the implant that you received aboard the Black Knight."

With all that had transpired since that seminal event, I had all but forgotten about the little device, or its connection with Excalibur, and to be frank, I was eager for anything that distracted me from my concerns about Elizabeth.

"Yes," Charles stated. "We have learned a great deal about it. Did you know that it is half machine and half organic? Deucedly clever that—can't really tell where one leaves off and the other begins. It is nothing at all like that dreadful Lyran cyborg, but a fully seamless marriage of the two opposites."

"Fascinating," I replied, for it was at that.

Brimming with eagerness, he led us down the hall and into the Professor's laboratory. Although the space did not prove to be nearly as grand as what my mentor had enjoyed at Nazca, when I entered and looked about me, I was still heartened by the fact that despite their depredations, the Lyrans had failed to impede his work in any significant degree.

Just as before, there were several experiments in progress arranged about the chamber, and among these, was the implant itself, floating in a containment field. A holographic projection was on display beside it, depicting a schematic of the device's innards, along with strings of data that I could not even begin to decipher.

The Professor paused, and peered at the hologram, carefully examining the information before taking out his pipe, and lighting it. "I should think that I can guess at what you found, Charles," he ventured. "Was it as we suspected?"

"Yes sir. I double-checked," Charles nodded. "and there can be no doubt about it."

"About--*what?*" I asked the both of them, unable to conceal my impatience.

Merriweather took a puff from his pipe and turned to me. "It turns out that that implant is more than a mere storage device. It also serves another function."

I raised in inquiring eyebrow at this. "Which is?"

"As a key," Charles supplied. "Or more correctly a transponder."

"A transponder, you say?"

"Yes," he answered. "We believe that it allows its user to safely unlock X'Kallabar."

"Safely?" I asked.

"Yes," Charles answered. "Without it, the weapon would prove quite injurious to anyone attempting to interface with it. In fact, the passage that we deciphered indicates that even to touch it without the transponder would result in immediate immolation and death. Rather unpleasant, I'd say."

"Yes, quite," I agreed, now glad for the fact that Caroline had intervened when she had. I also realized exactly where all of this was leading. "So, you intend to re-implant that thing into me?"

"We do at that," Merriweather disclosed. "Of course, we cannot force you to cooperate, but I would beg you to consider this; it was given to you and you alone. Naturally, we cannot presume to know the motives of those who created the Black Knight, but I would venture to say that they were not well disposed toward the Lyrans and wanted us to have custody of X'Kallabar instead."

Although I did not relish the idea of having the device put back into my arm, I readily apprehended his point.

"Oh, very well," I sighed, offering out my limb. "Let us have done with it then."

And so, the implant was returned to its place beneath the skin of my arm. The little nanobots within me, combined with the expertise with which it was introduced, made certain that the entire affair was a relatively painless one, and that I healed so speedily that stitches were wholly unnecessary.

This did not prevent a side-effect though; despite every effort, once it was nestled beneath my epidermis, the damned thing itched terribly and I was compelled to exert a goodly portion of my will not to scratch at it, and more besides to ignore the blemish that marred my otherwise perfect physique. Still, I told myself, if it helped us to triumph over the Lyrans, then it was well worth the discomfort, if not the imperfection.

When I made to rise, Charles laid a hand upon my shoulder, forestalling me. "There is one other thing," he advised.

"Not another implant," I pouted.

"Not quite," the Professor explained. He had a syringe in hand, filled with a clear, but slightly yellowish fluid.

I thought that I recognized the solution; it had the same appearance as that which was used to convey nanites into the bloodstream.

"Nanites?" I ventured.

"Only one," he told me, already finding a vein and swabbing it with alcohol. "A bit of technology from the year 2900, and courtesy of our friends in Atlantis."

Then he injected me and stepped back. "The nanite that is now swimming about in you is very specialized. It replaces our ear-coms by seating itself in the brain. There, it allows the user to communicate by thought alone with their Phaseship. A vast improvement on the old system, wouldn't you say?"

I had to agree. "Yes, it is at that. Tell me, however does it work?"

He held up a finger bidding me to wait and consulted his pocket watch. At last, he nodded to himself in satisfaction.

"Good. It should be in place. Now, to answer your question, just think of Blackbird. Give it a try, won't you?"

Closing my eyes, I did as he bade. *Blackbird?*

In answer, I heard her voice in my consciousness. It came to me just as clearly as if she had spoken aloud.

Yes, Penny?

To add to my amazement, an image appeared in my mind. It was of the area immediately around my Phaseship, as her exterior cameras would perceive it.

By the great Nothingness, I am seeing her camera feeds. Put mildly, I was deeply impressed.

"Special Section has had its operatives using this device for some time," Merriweather expounded, "but given the recent unpleasantness with the Lyrans, the Masters decided to distribute it to our pilots."

"I shall have to extend my thanks to my mother when next I see her," I replied.

By now, dear reader, you should be well acquainted with my difficulties at attaining a restful sleep, beset as I am by troubled dreams, and I would not burden you with the details, save that such visions often tend to be of a significant nature.

As it happened, that evening, and after laying down, I was beset by a nightmare. In it, I found myself travelling through space. It was not the empty void of the No-When mind you, but the starry expanse that circumambulates every Earth in all of the nine universes.

After but a breath, I had left our planet far behind me, and arrived at a point somewhere near the great ringed world of Saturn. While some might have found the spectacle of its rings to be magnificent, I felt only a growing sense of dread that increased the nearer I came.

Moreover, as I did so, I spotted several objects that were not part of the rings, but positioned near them, and their presence caused my trepidation to soar to even greater heights. Whatever they were about, I knew that it was something truly devilish in nature.

"You will die here," a voice proclaimed. I recognized the speaker as the Sibyl, and I knew her words for truth. This was where I would meet my end. Whether it would be a true death, or merely a transition to another cloned body I could not say. Only its finality was a certainty.

Understandably, I awoke bathed in a cold sweat and looked about me for the oracle's presence. Yet, she was nowhere to be seen, and it was some while before I could convince myself that it had all been naught but an evil fancy, borne of stress, and perchance, the aftereffects of the implant.

Eventually, I recovered, and formulated my plans for the day. I fully intended to return to Hw'ii'kk, and there, make good my promise to the Professor. And this time, I had the currency to make my purchase.

It had come to me courtesy of our small, but serviceable fabrication facility, and consisted not only of bits of polished metal and glass, but also some excellent facsimiles of proper English coinage. While I thought it unlikely that the merchants of Hw'ii'kk would accept the Empire's specie, it still lent me the reassurance that from this point forwards, I would not be without funds (and that if by chance it *did* manage to pass for legal tender, that it would not only secure me my goods, but send any future American archeologists into fits of extreme apoplexy).

Just as before, my trip proved brief, and when I was within the city's confines, I had no trouble at all finding my way back to the marketplace, where in short order, I made my purchase. Of course, this was not without experiencing some unpleasant emotions, and it was as struggle not to let my worries overtake me. Still, I managed, vowing that my new acquisitions would be just as the Professor had suggested; a symbol of my lover's redemption and rescue, to be carefully preserved until that very day arrived.

With my treasures in hand, I decided against going back to the base, but chose instead to venture deeper into the city. Which was as well, for my steps eventually brought me to its central plaza, and the stepped pyramid that served as Hw'ii'kk's main religious shrine.

A great crowd had gathered before it, and at its summit, a group of priests were exhorting their listeners to greater acts of piety and devotion, promising that the vision of Coo'coo'ma'tz would inevitably come to pass.

On any other day, I might have considered this to be nothing more than a variant of the same sermons that the Saurii had likely heard for thousands of years. Yet, I could not ignore the mood of the crowd around me; even though their body language was wholly alien, it was plain from their agitated squawks and cheeps that they had been stirred to excitement.

Something very special was about to occur.

Nary a minute later, it happened. One of the saucers flown by the Greys rose majestically from behind the pyramid, floated over to where the priests were waiting, and extended its egress ramp. When it touched down, three figures alighted, and despite the distance, I instantly recognized them as my mother, Sigrun Nälkäinen and Major Sixkiller.

Seeing this, the Saurii went wild with a religious fervor that was terrifying in its intensity, chanting their prophetess's name over and over. "Coo'coo'ma'tz!" they cried. "Coo'coo'ma'tz!"

This great outpouring of pure, ecstatic emotion had not come about because of these visitors however (for the novelty of our kind had largely worn off by this point). Rather, it was elicited by what Cassie and Sigrun had brought with them.

The first, supported by the Major, was a rather curious creature, bedecked with sable feathers, that at first, I took to be a *Corvus corax*, a common raven. However, after a moment, I realized that it was in fact an Archaeopteryx, hailing from the late Jurassic period and some 50,000,000 years in the future.

The second creature, borne on Sigrun's arm, was the largest golden eagle that I had ever beheld. Agitated by the crowd, the magnificent raptor gave out an imperious cry, and flapped its great wings, which in turn, caused every Sauriian to drop to the ground and piously avert their eyes.

As the women and their birds descended the pyramid with the priests in train, an appreciative smile came to my lips. Though the eagle and its proto-avian partner were no more than winged predators to me, to the Saurii they were the very embodiment of everything that their great seeress had foretold; the Archaeopteryx symbolizing the transition that their far-flung offspring would one day undergo, and the eagle, its ultimate outcome.

It was a truly masterful piece of showmanship.

Later, and at dinner, I was joined by the trio and their avian companions.

"Howdy, Penny," Major Sixkiller greeted, holding out her Archaeopteryx for me to inspect. "This here's Archie. I'd let him pay his respects t'ya'll, but the little shit has a mean streak a mile wide, and a nasty-ass bite t'match."

Indeed, I remarked upon the fact that the creature was wearing a sturdy leather muzzle, and from what I recalled about his species, it prevented him from making use of his rather small, but extremely sharp teeth.

"And this is Anchin," Sigrun informed me, inclining her jaw to the eagle perched on her gauntleted hand. "Her name means 'hunter' in Mongolian. She was given to me as a present from a tribal leader who disagreed with the warlike policies of the Great Khan."

For her part, Anchin regarded me with a queenly hauteur.

"She is remarkable," I said admiringly. "They both are."

"Yes," my mother agreed. "They were perfect for what we had in mind here. Not only are they the physical proof of Coo'coo'ma'tz's prophesies, but they also represent a tangible offer of immortality."

I set down my fork. "Immortality?"

"Yes," Sigrun supplied. "We plan to sponsor a number of bird sanctuaries throughout the nine universes, and any Saurii who offer up their aid will receive a session with the refactor and have a sampling of their DNA collected. These in turn, will be taken to the sanctuaries and infused into the birds that are bred there. Thus, our allies will be absolutely assured a life in the future as denizens of the Living Sky."

This seemed to be a rather sensible exchange to my ears. We would have all of the ground crews and service personnel that we could ever require, and the Saurii would achieve Godhood as they reckoned it.

"There is more," my mother added. "we will also enjoy the intercession of their priests, who call themselves the *K'iin Ke'tzz'a*, the Speakers of the Gods. They will convince the Ebani to lend us their services and once this is secured, aid us in directing the creatures."

"And how exactly will the Ebani convey us through time and space?" I inquired. This seemed an important detail, which up until now, had gone unmentioned.

Lady Anne's answer was quite surprising. "By allowing our Phaseships to pass through their outer skins and then reside within them during the journey. Then, at the other side, we will simply exit and go on about our business. The concept is somewhat like that of a 20th century aircraft carrier, save that our carrier is alive."

I must say that I found this to be somewhat unsettling. I had never imagined that one day, I might allow myself and my Phaseship to be ingested by a giant *Cnidarian*, but when I considered the alternative, it was far preferable to the Jump Worlds (though the arrangement vaguely reminded me of the tale of Jonah, absent any divine punishment, of course).

"Very well then," I responded. "Thank you for enlightening me."

"My pleasure," she said. "Now, let us discuss your role in this important endeavor. You and your Phaseship have been chosen to be the first to test this new method of travel."

"Of course," I replied. "We shall certainly do our utmost to see it to a successful conclusion."

"Just so," she smiled. "You will also be accompanied by one of the Saurii Speakers, and once inside of the Ebani, she will provide the creature with directions and interact with it as required."

On cue, a lone Saurii entered the room. She was small, even for one of her kind, and I briefly wondered if she were a juvenile, but then discarded the notion. The Speakers were all uniformly adult, and female (for they believed that only females, like the great Coo'coo'ma'tz herself, possessed the divine mandate to communicate with the Ebani).

And although we were of a different species, I could also tell that she was nervous in the presence of Archie and Anchin, and bobbed her head deferentially in their direction as she came up to the table.

"Her name is H'reep," my mother stated.

Reflexively, I extended my hand to her, and when she did not take it, my progenitrix explained.

"Their customs are not like our own, my daughter. They do not shake hands in greeting, for that is the equivalent of extending a wing, and signals a request for attention rather than a formal acknowledgement. Better to recognize her with a bow and with your head held up as you do so."

So corrected, I turned to the Saurii and did this very thing. In return, she reciprocated.

"My name is Penny," I told her.

H'reep cocked her head, making an odd clicking noise as she considered this. Then her irises expanded as comprehension dawned, and she canted her head towards me.

"B-enn-ee?"

"No, no," I corrected, "*Penny.*"

"B-b-eh-n-ee," she quavered.

"They have some difficulty with the consonants 'p' and 'l'," my mother advised. "Better to leave off."

"Very well," I agreed. "Benee will simply have to do."

"Benee," H'reep repeated, clearly pleased that the issue had been resolved in her favor.

Presently, my mother turned to her, and communicated without the aid of a com, and in what to my untrained ears sounded very like fluent Saurii. In reply, she received a squawk of affirmation.

"H'reep says that she is ready to leave whenever you are."

41

"Then I shall meet her on the tarmac," I responded. Awarding the Saurii Speaker another careful bow, I left the chamber and headed to my quarters to change into my flightsuit. Ten minutes later, I had finished and was showing her aboard Blackbird.

As we had only one command station, I was compelled to improvise and arranged for H'reep to take her place in the nearest guest seat, with a holographic projection to provide her with information throughout the flight.

I must say that as I watched her take her place, that I admired the little Saurian's courage, for although everything about my Phaseship was entirely foreign to her (and perchance more than a little frightening) she maintained a calm facade.

The only exception was when we lifted off and she realized that we were leaving the ground far behind us, which caused her to give out an excited chirp. For her, this was nothing less than an ecstatic religious experience, even if it were facilitated by a machine, and she promptly began to recite a prayer of praise to the Gods of the Living Sky. Out of deference to her beliefs, I waited until she had finished with her devotions before I reminded her of our mission.

"Which of the Ebani--the Ke'tzz'a--are we to be flying with?" I asked, for just then, there were several of them in our immediate vicinity.

"The nearest," she chittered, extending a clawed finger towards her hologram. I saw that it was by far the largest of the creatures, and as I altered our course, it began to drift lazily in our direction.

Meanwhile, H'reep had begun a chant of sorts, consisting of a deep throated hum that rose in intensity as I closed the distance. In response, the Ebani answered it with a great thrumming call that I felt in my very bones, intermixed with eerie cries that strongly reminded me of whale-song.

Accordingly, I increased our thrust. "Well, as the Major would say, *'Here goes nothing'*."

The Phaseship's hull made contact with the skin of the Ebani a moment later, and then passed through it with only the slightest resistance. Inside, it was as if we had submerged ourselves under the ocean; the outside world, while still visible on the displays, was wildly distorted by the gelatinous medium that filled the creature, and ribbons of sunlight caught by the denser portions sparkled all around us like fairy-lights.

"We have docked with the creature," I reported, wondering at what would come next. Meanwhile, H'reep's crest had raised and she spread her arms wide, her chanting increasing beyond the level of my hearing.

In turn, the sunlight began to flicker and dance before my eyes. At the same time, my body felt as if a low voltage charge were passing through it, whilst my thoughts began to race. Memories began to surface in my minds' eye in much the same manner that random images might appear to someone on the verge of sleep, lacking any rhyme or reason for their appearance.

Of a sudden, I saw the man with the hand torch from my childhood, running down the street with the Bookmen hard on his heels. Then, I was in Elizabeth's arms for the very first time, until that too disappeared and I stood in the City of the Giants with my mother. After that, another image arose, and more besides, and I finally comprehended what was occurring. Somehow, the Ebani was sorting through my very consciousness, and in the process, learning what it could about me.

The same thing was happening to Blackbird, though for her it was far less pleasant. "Oh Penny!", she cried. "It is inside of me. Oh, it hurts! It hurts! Please make it stop!"

Concerned, I turned to H'reep, but she did not seem to notice me, nor Blackbird's distress, caught up as she was in her rapturous interaction with the Ebani. Then and there, I very nearly abandoned our mission, yet I was mindful of the importance of what we were attempting and resisted the urge.

Instead, I fought my way past the churning parade of memories and sent an order to my ship that I had never imagined I might ever give. I commanded her to shut down her higher functions and place herself in hibernation.

At once, Blackbird's distress ceased.

Mine however, had only just begun. By this stage, I could scarcely entertain a single rational thought so intense were my recollections; of every meal I had ever eaten, every laugh that had ever graced me, and every tear, every joy and every pain.

Nor did this imagery confine itself to my present life. Some I recognized as coming from former iterations of myself, whilst others were a complete surprise. These were lives that I told myself I had never lived, and yet somehow, I knew each and every one of them to be utterly real, and a legitimate part of my past, however inexplicable they seemed.

In one, I saw myself growing up with Caroline, and in another, I pursued an entirely ordinary existence in my old Seattle, having never rebelled against the Bookmen. In yet another, I lived a life of quiet contemplation on Cyllene, wholly alien and separate from anything I had ever known on Earth.

But stranger still were the memories that claimed to be from lives that I had lived before my very first iteration, indeed, before my mother had even existed. In one, I was a young Welsh woman hefting a spear and bracing myself to defend my village against Viking raiders. Then I was a man studying alchemy in the Renaissance, and this was followed by the life of a Gallae--a transvestite priest--serving in the ancient temple of Cybele in Ostia.

Then the future revealed itself, but here, the images were fragmentary, and slipped out of my grasp like quicksilver. I saw myself confronting Elizabeth and Mr. Grey at last, but the resolution of that meeting refused to reveal itself. Next, I was holding X'Kallabar in my hand as the planet Saturn grew large before me and someone said, *"There is no more I can do for you my sister. What remains is in your hands alone..."*

It was then that I too wanted to scream for help just as Blackbird had, yet I knew that I could not direct this appeal to H'reep, nor expect rescue from any other quarter. Finally, unable to bear it any longer, I struggled out of my pilot's chair, staggered past the entranced Saurii to our medical stores, and there, took hold of a pen-injector filled with a powerful tranquilizer. It was intended to render a patient temporally unconscious whilst a mechanica performed emergency surgery.

Without pausing, I jabbed the thing deep into my thigh, ignoring the pain of the needle. The drugs that it delivered took effect right away, affording me only a few precious seconds to resume my seat before I could no longer remain erect. Then, as my vision went gray, the memories ceased, and oblivion replaced them.

In due course, and when I had at last returned to consciousness, I found that we were no longer inside of the Ebani, but floating near it in empty space. And below us, I could see the Earth.

Though groggy, I was still able to operate my console, and determined that I had indeed arrived at my destination. According to the temporal readouts, we were in the 8th universe, its first century and the year 5 AD. Moreover, the total elapsed flight time registered as no more than 9.86960440109th of a second.

Then the significance of this hit me. *The sum of Pi squared,* I thought. The literal--and supposedly impossible--mathematical expression connoting the squaring of the circle--but here, made manifest where it concerned time. And although I did not know it then, this same figure would remain a constant no matter how long one voyaged within the Ebani.

Shaking my head to clear my mind, I sent the command for Blackbird to reawaken. Like myself, she was initially disoriented, but soon came 'round.

"Penny? Did we make it? Did we arrive?"

"Yes. We did, my dearest," I reassured her.

The only question was how we would manage to withstand the return trip. I, for one, did not feel up to another mental drubbing, and I did not have to ask Blackbird what her position was. The only workable solution seemed to be another shut-down of her higher functions, and a second dose of the tranquilizer.

But as it happened, I was not obligated to see this plan through. Instead of subjecting me to another kaleidoscopic parade of memories, the Ebani left us both unmolested and merely folded space to deliver us back to our starting point. Though I puzzled at this pleasant surprise, I certainly did not object, and concentrated instead on the business of delivering us back to our base.

There, I found that my entire squadron was awaiting us, eager to hear my account of the experiment. Once I had shared the tale, my mother led H'reep away to consult with a small delegation of her fellow Speakers. Then after some minutes, the Sauriians departed and she returned to us with important news.

"You need not be concerned about suffering any further mental intrusions," she stated. "Having never interacted with our kind before, the Ebani were merely curious as to our nature. Penelope, it seems, was our unwitting ambassador, and we were not found wanting."

"Why thanks a bunch, Penny," Major Sixkiller grinned, patting my shoulder. "Mighty generous of ya'll."

"Perhaps the next time that we interact with an alien species, you shall be so honored, Major," I replied tartly. Given what my

45

consciousness had endured, the title of interspecies representative was not one that I ever wished to bear again.

I was afforded the luxury an entire evening in which to relax before Lady Anne informed me that another mission had been scheduled. This time, I was to accompany her to the 2nd universe, its 21st century and the city of New York, in America.

To my disappointment, our adventure was not to be a direct strike against the Lyrans, but instead, a clandestine affair conducted on behalf of Special Section. Nonetheless, I kept my disgruntlement to myself and with H'reep's assistance, conveyed us into a waiting Ebani.

Exactly as promised, the creature employed its miraculous powers to convey us to our destination without incident. Thus, we experienced no travel time (save the enigmatic 9.86960440109th of a second) and arrived over the city.

While it was not as lovely as Victorian London, or my old Seattle, New York City of the 21st century was still a wonder to behold. A great collection of glittering towers that rose to incredible heights, it boasted a staggering 8.5 million souls. That a gaggle of rustic colonials had managed to establish such a megalopolis boggled my mind, yet achieve it they had, and this earned my grudging admiration.

Nor was I alone in my appreciation. Seeing the city laid out before her, H'reep chirruped in excitement. "Is *that* the city that you humans come from?" she asked. "Oh, it is so beautiful!"

"No, H'reep" said I. "It is but one of our cities, and nowhere near as wonderful as the one that I call my home."

As H'reep pondered this, Lady Anne spoke.

"We shall land in Central Park, and then take a cab to our destination. H'reep, I must apologize, but you cannot accompany us on this expedition. The people of this timeline are not accustomed to non-human sentient beings and your appearance would surely alarm them."

H'reep's crest flattened and her head drooped in unhappiness, but after a moment, her eyes pinned, and she clicked reluctantly in acceptance. "Yes Annee, I will remain."

"There's a girl," Lady Anne grinned. "We shan't be overlong."

For my part, I felt sorry for H'reep, but Lady Anne was correct. There would be no way of concealing her from the populace, nor preventing the panic that would certainly result.

"Blackbird can provide you with interactive files," I offered. "They will allow you to explore the city's particulars while you await our return."

"Thank you, Benee," H'reep said with an unmistakable tinge of sadness. "I will content myself with that."

With the matter settled as best it could be, I concentrated on finding us a landing site. As with all things American, the park proved to be of truly gargantuan proportions, and after circling it once, I finally discovered a suitable location at the edge of the expanse, and near a roadway.

The moment that our engines had powered down, Lady Anne directed me to change out of my flightsuit and into clothing that was more suited to the time-period. This proved to be a black evening gown that in the 1890's would have barely qualified as an undergarment, and a risqué one at that. Her own attire was little better, and I must admit that as we left H'reep behind and stepped out into the evening air, I was more than a little self-conscious of my near nakedness.

Our 'cab' proved to be a garish yellow motorcar, with its driver speaking something that vaguely resembled English. Nonetheless, he managed to comprehend Lady Anne's instructions well enough, and in a trice, we were off.

The ride that followed was far worse than any 19th century hackney might have inflicted; a brutal affair that was conducted at truly terrifying velocities. More than once, I was absolutely certain of our impending doom, but probability favored us, and we were delivered wholly intact (and relatively unscathed) to an art gallery located in a fashionable neighborhood.

"In addition to our mission here, I also intend to teach you a very valuable lesson," Lady Anne advised. "This is how a seasoned time-traveler can accrue great wealth for themselves, and how Special Section derives some of its funding."

"From the sale of art?" I inquired, not quite certain that I had heard her correctly. By and large, artists in my century tended to hover eternally on the edge of starvation, and those who brokered their work fared little better. It was not a lucrative field by any means.

"Oh, not just *any* art, my dear," she replied. "What is called 'modern art', and perhaps the greatest swindle in all of history. But come, see for yourself."

Intrigued, I followed her from the cab, and the very instant that I laid eyes on the gallery's collection, I became completely befuddled, for I could not see anything that might have been called art. Instead, the nearest 'piece' (if one could even call it that) consisted of nothing but a canvas completely covered with crimson paint, as if the artist had simply grown tired of the color white and had brushed it over with the nearest alternative.

Its neighbor was naught but a pair of cardboard boxes that had been well shellacked, and firmly affixed to the wall. A group of patrons stood before it, carefully considering its merits and talking amongst themselves.

"What a profound statement," one man declared. "The artist has managed to express the transient nature of all existence, and in the most primal terms possible. It is the anguished howl of the modern soul, longing for freedom."

"Yes," a woman agreed breathlessly, "and the play of light and shadow on the piece definitely stresses the struggle between the thirst for group acceptance and the inner drive for individuation."

This vacuous proclamation earned her enthusiastic nods of approval from those around her. I however, was not one of them.

"What utter tosh!" I declared in Atlantean. "Are they entirely deluded? That is nothing but common trash."

My hostess chuckled and answered me in the same tongue. "It is, and well I know it. I collected those very boxes from an alley near here, and then had my fellow work them up a bit. Xavier is a true genius when it comes to converting rubbish to riches, and he receives a tidy cut for his efforts. So, tell me, what do you think it is worth? Be honest."

"A farthing?" I ventured acidly, though even that sum seemed rather much.

Again, she was amused. "Hardly, my dear. When it goes to auction, it will sell for over £200,000, and that first work that you saw will bring in £1,000,000, give or take a shilling."

To have called me stunned would have been an understatement. As I gaped at her, she took two glasses of white wine from a passing server's tray and handed one over to me. I promptly imbibed, and then with the wine to fortify me, spoke my mind.

"This is insanity," I declared. "Not art!"

"Penny," she gently corrected, "in this age, the prevailing philosophy is that *anything* can be considered art, and with the right marketing, what you or I would rightly consider to be unfit for the rubbish bin becomes a treasure. Better yet, no one dares to call it what it is for fear of being judged ignorant and unsophisticated."

"But--", I stammered. "Whatever happened to beauty? To culture?"

She waved her hand as if she were banishing them away. "Gone. Replaced by modernism. By *'form following function'*. You see, my dear, this era has no time for real beauty and has abandoned all standards in favor of bland conformity and utilitarianism."

"Then I say that they are dead inside," I opined, my gaze falling on a particularly appalling sculpture. It consisted of a ceramic commode painted over with garish patches of opposing color, none of which appealed to the eye.

"They are," she conceded. "but they are also quite gullible and *extremely* wealthy. Have no fear though; this epidemic of soullessness will not last. In 2050, a coronal mass ejection twice as large as the Carrington event of 1859 will wipe out all of their precious technology. Then, and only after a period of utter chaos, will they be forced to reconsider themselves. In the process, beauty will once again become fashionable.'

"But that as they say, is tomorrow's news. What matters for the here and now is that 'modern' art is one of the great sources of my income. In fact, I own this gallery, and several others besides, and they bring in fantastic sums that I then convert into gold. Gold that I exchange for pound notes back in the 19th century—and with the help of certain bankers working for the Fellowship."

Despite my repugnance for the gallery's exhibits and what they represented, I had to admit that hers was a clever scheme indeed.

There was more that she had to disclose though.

"Another source of capital is investment in burgeoning young firms," she stated. "Thanks to my ability to know exactly which companies will become successes, and which will fail, I own significant shares of stock in many of the largest corporations in this timeline.'

"Real estate ventures are also quite lucrative. I buy up a patch of worthless farmland in the 1st century for a mere pittance, and by the 20th, and when cities have sprung up all over it, it is worth millions. This was how I became the owner of Charlotte Place, by the way. In the days of old Londinium, it was naught but a failed pig farm. Yet, in the 19th century, it is the very height of elegance."

As I tried to reconcile the mental image of my beautiful home with that of an ancient pig sty, she guided me past more unspeakable monstrosities, and through a door into the back of the establishment. There, a group of empty display cases stood by, waiting for their contents. Finishing off her wine, she carefully placed the empty glass inside one of them, and then stepped back to admire her creation.

"Perfect!", she declared. "We will feature this in our very next exhibition. But what to call it?" She stroked her chin thoughtfully and then her eyes lit up.

"How does 'In Vino Veritas' sound?" she asked me. "The fact that the glass is entirely empty should engender some *extremely* interesting discussions—and fetch a rather nice sale price, eh wot?"

I simply could not bring myself to reply, for I was too disgusted by the whole affair.

"Penny," she suggested soothingly, "you can console yourself with some of the proceeds of tonight's affair and then buy some *real* art to adorn your London home. But before then, I must remind you that we still have our errand for Special Section to attend to."

This said, she took me into a small office, and there, opened up a wall safe. It proved to contain a simple velvet sack, and when she revealed the contents to me, I saw that it was coinage. Peering more closely, I determined that it was of Roman origin, and from the reign of Tiberius Caesar, but with one glaring exception; both the silver *denarii* and golden *aurei* were as new as if they had been minted just the day before.

"Modern reproductions," she explained. "Again, courtesy of my friend Xavier, but so accurate in detail that no one will ever discover the forgery. Now, we must be away. We have an appointment to keep at a very important historical event."

Mystified, I watched as she transferred the currency to a metal briefcase, and then, after she had snatched up an additional travel bag, I accompanied her through a rear exit, and from there, into the back of another cab.

Just half an hour later, we had left New York, with all of its terrifying 'cabs' and its ghastly notions of art, far behind us.

CHAPTER 3: Greater Love Hath No Man

Wherein I meet Jesus of Nazareth and witness his death. In the process, I once again play my unwitting part in history. Then, I glimpse Elizabeth and Mr. Grey, and after giving chase, confront Colonel Ambrose and demand the truth.

Rather than travel back to the Jurassic, Lady Anne had H'reep direct the Ebani to take us to the 1st century, and the year 30 AD. There, I was instructed to fly us to Palestine, and the city of Jerusalem. This time though, it was no Ottoman possession, nor British, nor even Israeli, but Roman, and part of the province of Judea.

"Might I ask what brings us here?" I inquired.

"A very special man," Lady Anne replied mysteriously.

"What is his name?" I asked as I began to search for a landing site.

"Yeshua ben Yosef," she revealed, "and a carpenter by trade. Really Penny, after all your studies of religion, you should well know who *that* is."

Jesus, I thought. *No less than Jesus of Nazareth.*

"What business do we have with him?" I queried.

"That, my dear, is up to you," she stated. "There is already an operation under way here to forward the aims of the Masters, but your mother wanted you to play a pivotal role in the final direction that it will take. Hence, we are to head to the following coordinates; 31.7793° North, 35.2398° East. There, you will disembark, and speak with Jesus in person."

I was flabbergasted, and as one might imagine, felt rather unprepared for such a momentous occasion. In all my temporal ramblings, I had met only two great figures from history, Tesla and Hitler. Tesla had proven to be an illusion, generated by the Black Knight, and Hitler, only a target for my bullets. Jesus would be of an entirely different order altogether.

"Whatever are we to converse about?"

"Whatever you wish, my dearest," she responded. "Perchance you can even manage to convince him not to go to his death. Think on it; that would change *everything* in this timeline."

"My mother would really wish for that?" I asked. As fundamental as his crucifixion was to the Christian narrative, its gruesome nature had always repelled me, and I had often wondered if there might have been a better alternative.

"She only wishes for this meeting to serve as a learning experience for you," Lady Anne advised, "and that it thwarts the aims of the Lyrans. As it is, they have already made one attempt to kidnap him, but we intercepted their 'black bag team' before they could pull it off. Apparently, they were going to use a refactor to transform Jesus into a drunkard who had renounced his faith."

"So, my aim is to prevent him from losing his ideals then?" I probed, not at all sure that my weak understanding of Western religion would suffice. I was certainly no theologian.

"Again," she sighed, "that is up to you, Penny. Just as at New Berlin, the choice has been left entirely in your hands, come what may."

The coordinates that I had been provided with took us directly over a location marked on our charts as the Garden of Gethsemane, and the place where Jesus had been betrayed. Though it was evening, my instruments penetrated the shadows with ease, and I could see that it was dotted with ancient olive trees and further, that four figures were present. One was standing and the others were lying on the ground.

Jesus and his apostles, Peter, John and James, I thought.

In addition, I also detected the presence of several oculons that were undoubtedly keeping watch for any Lyran mischief, and several mechanica as well. They were hidden nearby, and running at minimal power levels, but clearly ready to spring into action if the need arose.

Since I had already taken the precaution of placing Blackbird into full stealth mode, I had little concern as I brought her into a hover. For all intents and purposes, we were naught but a faint distortion set against the stars and easily missed by anyone who happened to gaze heavenwards.

"Time to change costume again," Lady Anne announced.

As it happened, the travel bag that she had brought with her contained these very garments; an ankle length chiton, a himation with a decorative border, a long tunic and some jewelry to offset it all. Seeing this, it was plain that I was intended to portray a woman of means, but also a foreigner to Judea.

"If he asks," she suggested, "tell him that you are from Syria and specifically, the city of Palmyra. That will explain your fair hair and eyes, for it is a trading city and there are many there who have their roots in Macedonia."

I nodded. "The land of the yellow haired Alexander, called the Great. And the rest?"

"As I advised, the rest is up to you," she reminded me. "Choose your words wisely."

So directed, I inserted a com-bud into my ear and instructed Blackbird to land, and assume a hover 'till I called for her again. Then I made my way into the garden's precincts. and positioned myself behind one of the ancient trees (for I wished to gather my thoughts and take in Jesus's measure before I engaged him in conversation).

It happened that Yeshua ben Yosef was not at all how I had envisioned him. For one, he was not light skinned, nor fair haired as he had been depicted at St. Paul's. Nor did he have blue eyes such as I. Instead, he was somewhat short of stature, with dark hair and an olive complexion, and although he was bearded, his whiskers were not long, but trimmed closely in the Roman style. So too was his hair.

Overall, he seemed like any common laborer, with a muscular build that suggested a life of hard work (which made sense, given that he was by profession, a carpenter). Moreover, his clothing was not the pristine drapery of classical imagination, but a short, knee length chiton and a himation. Both were made of rough, undyed wool, and he had only a pair of simple leather sandals to protect his feet from injury. Had I not known better, I might have easily overlooked him in a crowd as being of no importance whatsoever.

Yet, he *was* important, I reminded myself, for from him one of the world's great religions would eventually spring, with all of its blessings, and all its evils.

Presently, I watched as he went over to the sleeping men, and roused them from their slumbers.

"Couldst thou not keep watch with me for one hour?" he asked them. "Watch and pray so that thou will not fall into temptation."

Then he sighed to himself and added, "The spirit is willing, but the body is weak."

In turn, his apostles earnestly apologized, and promised to remain awake, but it was not long after Jesus had departed, that their eyelids grew heavy again, and they lapsed back into sleep.

Rather than return and rebuke them, Jesus walked over to an empty corner of the garden. For a long while, he simply stared up into the night sky, and then I realized that he was weeping.

"My Father, if it is possible, may this cup be taken from me," he entreated. "Yet not as I will, but as thou wilt."

I do not know if he received a reply or not, but at last, he lowered his gaze, and looked back over his shoulder, directly at me. "Thou canst come out now. I know that thou art there, and I know who and what thou truly are."

He thinks me an angel, I thought with no little alarm. My studies of Christianity had mentioned that such a being had paid him a visit, and I immediately made to correct this assumption.

"Sir, I am no heavenly messenger," I said, my com delivering this to him in Aramaic. "I am merely a traveler from Syria who has come to hear you teach."

He smiled knowingly. "No, methinks that thou art far more than a simple traveler. Forsooth, thou art a being from another world, and another time. Indeed, thou camest here in a chariot that can travel through the skies. Even now, it is above us, cloaked from the sight of men and listening as we converse."

To prove this, he inclined his jaw upwards—right to where Blackbird was hovering in her stealth field. I was amazed, but not so much so that I lost sight of my intentions.

"Then if you know all that," I challenged, "then you also know why I am here. I have read your words at length and appreciated their wisdom. I beg you now to reconsider what you are about to allow."

Jesus smiled at this. "For that, I would call thee Satan and tell thee to get behind me. But I shall not, for I can also see that thou art sincere in thy concern."

"But you are going willingly to the slaughter," I protested. "Surely there is another way!"

He shook his head. "If thou didst read my teachings as thou claimest, then thou knowest better. What must be, must be. And why wouldst thou, of all beings, protest? Did thee not die at the hands of another, and yet become reborn, and more perfect than ever?"

"And what of thy friend Pishqu, who went just as willingly to her own end so that she could become like unto thee? My way is no different than thine, save for one thing; I am willing to die so that *all* men can be saved, for without this sacrifice, they are surely doomed.'

"I admit that I doubted my role, like any man would, but I have God to thank for sending thee to test me one final time. Though thou would deny it, thou art an angel sent by Him, but methinks a very stubborn one."

Frustrated and not a little dismayed that the situation had gone so awry, I persisted. "But I can get you away from here! I can take you somewhere safe. No one will ever have to know the truth—we will simply make them believe that you were taken up into heaven and save you all of the agony."

"But God will know," he countered, "and I. A lie must not play a part in this thing, traveler. It must be as it is intended to be.'

"There is one more thing that I must tell you. It is this; other sheep I have which are not of this fold. Them also I must bring, and they will hear my voice. There will be one flock, and one shepherd."

"I do not understand," I confessed.

"No," he agreed. "Clearly, you do not. Or not yet at least, but mayhap your little friend, the bird, will help to enlighten you. For the present though, there is one small boon that I would ask of thee, oh angel."

"What is it that you wish?" I replied, wondering at how he knew about H'reep.

"To be there, at the end," he said. "That is all. Now away with thee. The betrayer comes!"

He waved his hand, and to my astonishment, I was conveyed back to the helm of my Phaseship. I could see Jesus on my displays, gazing up at me and waving farewell. I also knew that any attempt to return to the garden would result in another involuntary transportation. Thus, I was forced to watch as events unfolded, and he was taken away by the soldiers.

As it happened, I was not the only one who was distressed by this fateful meeting. H'reep too, was just as upset as I, if not moreso.

"Coo'coo'ma'tz!" she declared, her crest raised in alarm and agitation. "They have taken her away! We must help her!"

"Who?" I asked, genuinely puzzled.

"The Great One!" she cried. "She is in danger!"

I looked to Lady Anne in my confusion, and in turn, she interceded with the Saurii.

"Coo'coo'ma'tz will be well," she promised the distraught creature, "It is all part of a great ritual and they cannot harm her."

H'reep calmed—slightly---but it was plain that it would be some time ere she would fully be able to master herself.

Still mystified, I addressed Lady Anne "What is she going on about? Coo'coo'ma'tz was not present. Jesus was."

"Coo'coo'ma'tz *was* present," my clone insisted. "As was every other prophet figure that has ever been known. To you, he seemed like Jesus, but to our friend here, it was her race's great savioress. In truth, what you interacted with was beyond all human comprehension."

"Then you are telling me that he was not real?" I asked. "That I treated with some form of illusion?"

Lady Anne shook her head. "No. I assure you that Jesus of Nazareth is a very real man, composed of flesh and blood, and that you *did* speak with him."

"Forgive me then, for I am utterly at sea here," I responded.

"Yes, I imagine so," she acknowledged, stroking her chin pensively. "While this is a matter best explained by our mother, I shall endeavor to do my utmost, though mysticism is not my forte."

I inclined my head for her to go on.

"Do you perchance recall what you experienced aboard the Black Knight?"

"I do. Vividly," I responded.

"That same ineffable source sometimes chooses certain *special* beings to serve as its vessel so as to communicate with the rest of us," she elucidated, " Jesus is one such, Buddha another, Coo'coo'ma'tz yet another, and so on.'

"Whenever this occurs, it is It, and not they, who are speaking, and also the reason why, when one compares the teachings of all the great prophets, that they are so alike to one another. After all, they ultimately spring from the same font--even if it appears to each of us in a different guise. Does that clarify the matter somewhat?"

"Quite," I said, now fully appreciating the veracity of H'reep's claim.

"Very good," she declared. "Now, we are off to Golgotha and mustn't keep Jesus waiting."

Knowing what was about to transpire, H'reep was of great concern to me, but Lady Anne had a solution in mind. She immediately ordered Blackbird to cut the feed to the Saurii's com, thereby depriving her of a translation, and spoke to the AI in Atlantean.

"Whilst we are attending to our business in Jerusalem, I wish for you to keep our friend here occupied with whatever diversions you have at your disposal."

"But I *like* H'reep," Blackbird answered, "I think that we shall become great friends, and I would not want to keep anything from her. That would be wrong."

"This you must conceal," Lady Anne warned. "If you consider her a friend as you say, then you must do her the favor of sparing her any upset. That is what true friends do for those they care for; they sometimes protect them from unpleasant truths.'

"Do you understand me? Keep her occupied and do not allow her to witness what transpires—and if she asks, tell her only that her prophetess was let go and ascended to heaven. Nothing more."

"N'che Sedem," Blackbird responded, plainly unhappy with this instruction.

"Capitol! Now, if you would, please return the feed and take us to the city. Then orbit until we call for you."

Blackbird complied, all the while doing her utmost to divert H'reep's attention. "While Penny and Lady Anne are gone, you and I will have great fun!" she promised her. "There are *so* many stories that I can tell you about humans—and there is music as well. You will surely love that!"

Not long after, we were delivered to the outskirts of Jerusalem, and once Lady Anne had donned a costume of her own, we left H'reep in Blackbird's care. It took us but a few minutes to find the crowd that had gathered outside the city gates, and no one took any special note of us as we joined the throng.

Thus, I was afforded the opportunity to witness one of the greatest moments in history, and without doubt, one of its most terrible.

The people around us were in a cruel mood, and as Jesus went by, crowned with thorns and bearing the marks of the scourge upon his body, they pelted him with all manner of missiles. In fact, they did this with such malicious glee that the Tigress began to arise within me. Just then, she greatly wanted to repay them in good measure for all of their wickedness, and I was of like mind.

He is one of you, I thought, tasting bile and feeling my fangs growing out. *How can you do this?* Such a naked betrayal was beyond all tolerance.

But before I could fully transform, I felt something cold and metallic on the back of my neck, and the touch of Lady Anne's hand on my arm. Simultaneously, the Tigress was forced to subside and my eyes, ears and teeth resumed their normal configurations.

"Now, now, Penny," she chided, "I apologize, but it simply would not do for you to tear these people to shreds. What must be, must be, and I remind you that this was what *he* desired.'

"Moreover, we are not the only representatives of the Masters here. A number of agents, working for Special Section, are also in the crowd and have been tasked with preventing any last-minute Lyran interference. Surely, you would not wish to add to their concerns."

With great displeasure, I realized that she had just used a restraining device similar to that which Mr. Grey had once employed, and although I gave her a searing look, I knew in my heart that she was entirely correct. The tragedy unfolding here would have to play out without the involvement of a white tiger bent on murder-- especially if her actions might involve any injury to our agents. Accordingly, I stood by in furious silence as Jesus endured his punishment.

After many minutes, he arrived at last at the foot of the hill called the Skull, and there, I was forced to endure the sight of the soldiers lashing him to his *patibulum*—the cross beam, whilst several others went aside and callously gambled for the possession of his cloak.

Once Jesus had been secured, the legionnaires then began the gruesome process of pounding in the great nails through plaques made of olive wood, and I was forced to look away, for it was too terrible a thing to behold.

I must also confess that being unable to fight, I would have gladly chosen its alternative and fled the place then and there. But again, Lady Anne restrained me.

"We must remain," she said. "We are here to the very end."

So, unable to depart, I abided and watched as Jesus was hoisted aloft and the crosspiece was joined with the *stipe,* the upright, creating not the Latin cross depicted at St. Paul's, but a Tau.

Then came the final nails to his legs. They were pounded in just above his ankles and firmly pinned him to either side of the upright.

Too add further insult, the soldiers had also placed a sign above his head. It was written in Greek and declared him to be the King of the Jews. This title elicited much laughter from the crowd, and only compounded my thirst for their violent deaths.

Yet, I could do nothing.

Save yourself! I thought. *You had the power to eject me from the garden. Use that same ability to liberate yourself.*

That such an action would have been in direct contravention to his stated wishes, mattered not. I was simply too overwhelmed to care about anything but seeing this shameful spectacle brought to an end. Nor was I alone in this, for my sentiments were echoed by a common thief who had been chosen to die alongside him.

"Save us," the man pleaded, "save yourself."

But Jesus did not do so, and instead, suffered in silence.

The hours passed, broken only by a brief darkening of the skies, and an earthquake, that to my immense delight, panicked both the mob and the soldiers. But neither of these were enough to forestall the event, and at last, I broke away from Lady Anne and approached one the Roman soldiers.

"Take this," I insisted, stripping off my gold bracelets and holding them out. "Have some decency man, and put him out of his misery."

"Lady, methinks that he is already dead," the soldier opined, but still, he took my offerings.

"Make certain," I demanded, "and finish this."

The legionnaire eyed me uncertainly, but a nod from his commander decided him. Hefting his long pilum, he went up to Jesus and thrust the spear deep into his side. But instead of blood, what came out of the body seemed more like liquid wax to me, though the result was the same. Jesus was dead.

"Well done, Penelope," Lady Anne commended when I had returned to her. "As always, and despite yourself, you have managed to stay true to history, though I feel sympathy for that poor Roman soldier. Longinus will have much to ponder in the years that still remain to him."

By now, I had reached the very limits of my temper. "Are we quite finished then?"

She nodded, wholly unfazed. "Yes. We are at that. The Lyrans had hoped to prevent Jesus's crucifixion, but clearly, they failed."

"And I should *rejoice* at this news?" I replied acidly.

"Yes," she answered. "you should. Had they succeeded, there would have been no Christianity, and perforce, no monks to preserve knowledge after the fall of Rome. In turn, their true target, and the one that they have always desired to destroy, the Renaissance, would never have come to pass. Instead, the Dark Ages would have become the Dark Eternity.'

"You can thank our visit to New York for the part it played in our victory, by the way. The thirty pieces of silver that we brought with us proved to be the perfect bribe for Judas Iscariot."

"Then you are saying that the traitor worked for us?" I quired.

"No," she replied with an airy wave of her hand. "He was a fanatic who had hoped that Jesus would lead an uprising against the Romans; a dupe who unwittingly served our purposes. Nothing more."

"And the gold?"

"It helped our agents to sway Pilate and some of the more 'lenient' of the Pharisees to condemn Jesus. A sound investment in the future, I should say."

I did not tell her what I thought of all this, but I was certain that she knew. Despite all that had been at stake, I was sickened.

Leaving the summit and the body of Jesus behind us, we walked down to the bottom of the hill. There, she finally removed my restraint, but not without issuing me a warning.

"I advise you to remain in control of yourself," she said. "These people, however revolting they might be, are not to be harmed, and if you act out, I shall be forced to take severer measures."

I answered this with a feral growl, but I did not test her resolve as we entered the gates of Jerusalem. Instead, I confined myself to rewarding anyone that we passed with murderous glances. To my satisfaction, a goodly number of them blanched in terror and stepped aside in great haste.

Presently, we entered an area filled with small shops and bisected by narrow streets. Then I caught a glimpse through the crowd of a pair of figures, and gasped. Though they were costumed to appear like everyone around us, there was no mistaking either of them. It was none other than Elizabeth and Mr. Grey.

"They are here!" I declared. Lady Anne turned 'round at this and saw what I meant. Simultaneously, Mr. Grey took Elizabeth by the arm and pulled her around a corner.

"Elizabeth!" I cried, drawing my chronopistol from beneath my robes and breaking into a run. That Lady Anne called after me, warning me to wait for our agents, scarcely registered. My mind was awhirl with the desire for Mr. Grey's death and Elizabeth's rescue--or her end if she proved false.

A heartbeat later, I reached the spot where I had seen them only to find myself confronted by another claustrophobic thoroughfare. But neither of them were in sight, and I immediately deduced that they had used a puddle jumper to effect their escape.

What had I seen in Elizabeth's eyes? I wondered. Had it been fear? Or the earnest hope that I would be her deliverer? I could not say for certain.

"They must have been part of the Lyran team," Lady Anne said as she caught up.

I barely acknowledged this and contacted Blackbird. "Check the area for any temporal anomalies," I ordered.

After a moment, my AI came back with her results. "There were two signals, Penny. The first leads from your location to a wine shop 100 meters away to the north. The other occurred at the shop itself and has no end point that I can determine."

A transtemporal bolt-hole then, I mused. This meant that Mr. Grey and Elizabeth were gone. Pressing on was pointless.

"Do we have any further business here?" I asked Lady Anne.

"No," she answered. "Our mission here is complete. The timeline remains intact."

"Then I am of a mind to return to Saurii straightaway," I told her. "Colonel Ambrose and I need to converse--*at length.*"

In the Jurassic, I left Lady Anne and sought out the Colonel. He was exactly where I had expected him, ensconced in a corner of the Professor's laboratory, and brooding over the Codex with a pot of tea and a sandwich. Seeing him thus, my desperation boiled over.

"I saw her!" I exclaimed. "Tell me what you have learned! Tell me all. Is she a sleeper agent, a clone, or is she bewitched? Please, I must know the truth."

Without quite realizing it, I had grasped him by his lapels and only the few shreds of reason that I still retained prevented me from shaking him vigorously.

"Just today I satisfied myself about her, and I was about to send word to you." he answered calmly.

"And?"

"And she is not named in the Codex and is therefore not a sleeper. I am also certain that the Lyrans have not cloned her, or at least not yet."

"How can you be certain?" I asked.

"I had some of our agents investigate the base that she helped destroy," he disclosed, gently prising my fingers loose from his garment. "They found some samples of her hair."

"What does that prove?"

"Exactly what I stated; that she has not been cloned," the Colonel repeated, smoothing out his jacket and leaning back in his chair. "Every time a copy is made, its DNA is imprinted with unique markers that identify what iteration it is. Hers was the same as it was before she was kidnapped and taken to Moberly. What you saw therefore, was the Elizabeth that you know, and none other."

All at once, my strength went out of me and I sat down heavily in the chair next to his. "Then--then--she has been—conditioned--to serve the Lyrans? Or did she choose to do so willingly?"

"I do not think it likely that she is a willing accomplice," he replied. "Think on it, Penny; she would have no motive whatsoever for betraying us. Nor did she spend time in the company of any Lyran agents who might have persuaded her to change her allegiances.'

"Are you sure?" I challenged.

He patted the Codex with his hand. "Quite. This book positively identified those Lyran operatives who are amongst us, and none of them were ever in contact with your beloved, even for a short while."

"Then you *did* find spies?" I inquired. "Who are they?"

He wagged his finger at me. "That is something that will be disclosed at the proper time and place. What matters for the moment is what I told you; Elizabeth is no turncoat."

"Which leaves us with imprinting," I concluded.

"Precisely," he said. "Mr. Grey must have done it to her while she was his prisoner at Moberly. Further, it seems clear that his alterations were intended to remain dormant until the time was right for them to arise and take control of her personality."

"Then, she did not know that she had been changed?"

"I seriously doubt it, my dear," he responded. "Had she been conscious of the imprinting, the Lyrans would have run the risk of her inadvertently betraying herself. This way, we were unable to detect anything until it was too late. Quite brilliant, really."

At this, he poured us both some tea and then added in a splash of brandy from his flask. I took mine with shaking hands and drank deeply.

"Now, as to the business of her cure," he continued. "I have it on good authority that a treatment is available, but I must warn you that there is no absolute guarantee of success."

"And what if it should fail?"

He hesitated. Then, "In that eventuality, we would be forced to create a new clone and imprint it."

"Which would condemn her present iteration to what?" I demanded. "Death?"

"That might be our only choice," he advised cautiously. The very thought of having to put her down like some kind of maddened animal filled me with dread.

"Then we must succeed!" I avowed, setting my teacup down with such force that its ear was broken off.

"Yes, we must," he answered, eyeing the damaged cup speculatively. "In the meantime, rest assured that Special Section will make every effort to locate her and then see to her treatment."

"There is no other course of action," I replied firmly. "None."

He shrugged. "As you say, Penny."

"I also wish to see the recordings," I put in. "The ones that show her actions at the Seattle base." Up to now, I had avoided viewing them, or even making any inquiries.

"I can arrange for that," he agreed. "But are you certain that that would be for the best? They will only serve to disturb you."

I rose. "I am. And I assure you that they *will* disturb me--but not because of her. Because of *him*. I would see what he did to her and hate him all the more for it when we meet again." My fangs had come out at last, lending this no little emphasis.

Ambrose nodded sympathetically. "The mechanica have managed to construct a small theater in your absence, for recreational purposes. I will see to it that you can use it in privacy."

The flicker that I viewed had none of the glamour, nor the artistry of productions such as the *Thief of Baghdad,* yet it was no less riveting. As I watched, I saw my dearest Elizabeth enter the base companioned by Mr. Grey and a squad of Lyran commandos.

They encountered no resistance, undoubtedly because of Elizabeth's presence, and in short order, began their sabotage, throwing grenades and other devices into the various rooms. All through it, she seemed to be perfectly at ease, and even smiled as she contributed her own explosives to the mayhem. It was at once, a terrible thing to behold, and also quite surreal, for a part of me could still not grapple with the reality of her actions.

The worst of it came when the marauders reached the great circular room where all of my clones, and those of so many others, resided within their crystalline coffins. With careful precision, the commandos moved among them, setting groups of explosives where they would do the greatest damage.

Then, with their fiendish work complete, they exited together.

What followed was the result of their maliciousness, as the incendiary charges went off in sequence, setting the whole room and all of its sleeping occupants ablaze. Overcome by the intense heat, the coffins shattered, and the clones themselves ignited like so many grisly candles. The only mercy was that none of them roused during this hellish conflagration, for I think that had any of them done so, I would have shrieked aloud and run from the auditorium.

After a minute or so of this awful spectacle, another feed presented itself (for it had clearly been edited from multiple sources for my viewing). It was nowhere near as hideous, displaying only the great garage that the commandos had used to make their entry, yet it still contained one element of horror. This was where Mr. Grey and Elizabeth paused and looked directly upwards into the camera itself, and I knew that they were seeing not it, but me.

As Mr. Grey smiled, my beloved spoke. Though there was no audio, I could still make out her words clearly enough, and they cut me to the bone; *"Penny, you were always a fool."*

Had I not known what I now knew, that Elizabeth was in truth only a Lyran puppet, this would have been the very *coup-de-gras* to my spirit. As it was, it still stung deeply and I felt my anger rising, just as I knew it would, towards the very source of that hurt.

"I shall kill you," I vowed to Mr. Grey's image. "I will do so in such a manner as to make the Devil himself recoil in dread."

Then I smelled musk and heard a voice in my mind. *I have a question for you, sister.*

Looking around, I discovered that Caroline and the Chuchniya had joined me. They were seated off to my left and but a row behind. This time, Caroline was costumed in the uniform of a Chrononaut, though her universe and century were obscured.

"Ask it," I replied, brushing away the tears of anger and sorrow that had gathered at the corners of my eyes.

Now that you know she is innocent, would you do anything to save her? Would you pay any price for Elizabeth's salvation? Even trade your own life?

"Yes." I answered unhesitatingly. "I would."

"Then perhaps you begin to understand," another voice interjected. It was my mother. She was to my right and three rows back, along with the Sibyl and her companion, Maggie the Blind Girl.

"But not nearly enough," Maggie observed.

"No," the Sibyl agreed. "Soon though."

"Are you certain of this?" my mother asked her.

The Sibyl smiled and nodded.

I stood up and turned to face them directly. "What are you all going on about?"

However, no one was there to reply. Save for myself, the theater was now entirely empty.

Confused and upset, I did not seek out any human company when I departed. Rather, I searched for, and found, Old Fred.

"I wish my quarters to be changed," I instructed. "Make them as they were when Elizabeth was still with us, but with one change; see to it that the vase and the tapestry I recently purchased is ensconced in a place of prominence. When she is returned to me, I want those to be the first things that she beholds."

"N'che Sedem," the mechanica answered, his eyes going green for a moment.

At this, I left him to his work and went to the mess hall. Just then, I needed a place in which to abide and collect myself.

As it happened, I was in the midst of picking at a bowl of chocolate glacé (with no real enthusiasm) when Major Sixkiller strode in.

"Howdy Penny," she greeted. "I just heard that ya'll went on a mission and met Jesus."

"I did," I answered, trying to lend my voice some semblance of vigor.

"Jesus Kee-rist, Penny," she exclaimed--and then she hastily crossed herself. "I—mean darn—you didn't even ask him for an autograph?"

"He was somewhat preoccupied," I replied. "The man was after all, going to his death. I should think that asking him to sign a copy of the New Testament would have been a bit crass at such a juncture."

"Yeah, I guess I can see that," she agreed. Then, she noticed my mood. "What's botherin ya'll, Penny?"

So I told her all.

At the end of my narrative, she took my hand in hers and gave it a gentle pat. "We'll get her back, Penny. And if she's all messed up in the head, we'll set her mind t'rights. I know we will."

As much as I wished it were otherwise, I was not as certain as my companion.

Not long after, I returned to my quarters. They had been refurbished just as I had instructed and they were now the exact duplicate of what Elizabeth and I had occupied in Nazca, even down to the attendance of my virtual maidservant, Mrs. Schrödinger.

"Welcome back, mu'um," the hologram said, giving me a ghostly curtsey. "I'm certain you'll find everything to your liking."

"I am sure that I shall," I replied, struggling to maintain my composure. Though the reproduction was perfect, it was impossible for me not to notice my lover's absence, or the lump that had formed in my throat.

Soon, I promised myself. *Somehow.*

"There is one other thing, mu'um," Mrs. Schrödinger added. "Your mother happened by earlier today. She couldn't stay, but she sends you her best wishes and will try to visit when time allows. She also left you a parcel."

Of course, I thought. *Mother always leaves me strange presents.*

Looking past my maid (or to be more accurate, *through* her), I spotted it immediately, for it was sitting in plain view and wrapped in brown paper and twine. I also saw that a card had been included and I picked it up.

It read; *"The Ladder to Heaven is filled with trials, and only self-examination and sacrifice will see you safely to the summit."*

I must admit that I was tempted to leave the package unopened, but after my experiences with the irascible box of tarot cards, I knew better. It was simply a given that if I ignored it, it would somehow manage to unwrap itself, and there was even the chance that it would, like the box, attack me out of sheer supernatural pique.

Better to get it over with then, I decided, and with a sigh, I tore the paper away. The contents proved to be a framed reproduction of William Blake's *"Jacob's Ladder"*.

However, unlike other graphic accounts of this tale, the ladder was depicted as a spiral staircase ascending heavenwards into the sun itself. Nor was it empty, but populated by ethereal beings dressed in graceful, flowing robes. Some sported long wings, which identified them as angels, whilst others appeared to be flightless.

In addition, a number of these ethereal messengers bore trays of food and drink, or led children up to the summit. Further, a man who I presumed to be Jacob himself, lay on the ground at the very base of the stair, his head resting upon a rock and his eyes closed in sleep.

Overall, it was a rather lovely piece, even if it was a certainty that it concealed some hidden message or possessed extraordinary powers.

I turned to face Mrs. Schrödinger. "Please summon one of the mechanica and have them hang this for me. I should think that the space between the bookshelves near the fire will do nicely."

She rewarded me with another curtsey, and then proceeded to communicate with the nearest robot. Satisfied, I returned my gaze to the print and what I saw there startled me.

The image of Jacob was gone. In his place, and positioned exactly as he had been, was a perfect rendering of none other than myself, lying asleep as the angels went about their heavenly business.

"How curious," I remarked, wondering at its import. Nothing further occurred though, and in due course, the mechanica arrived and installed it in its new home.

I must confess that afterwards, and as my evening progressed, I kept glancing towards the print, wondering if it would undergo another transformation. Yet, beyond the figure of Jacob, it remained unaltered.

More to the point, it was not making any effort to annoy me as the box of Tarot cards had done, and this was a blessing in and of itself.

Unlike my slumbering image, true sleep proved a struggle of Herculean proportions. My thoughts were only of Elizabeth and what the future might bring for us. But in the end exhaustion won out, and in the middle of my troubled cogitations, I slipped into unconsciousness.

Some while later, I was overtaken by another vision of Saturn, coupled with the terrible dread that accompanied it. This time though, it did not end where it had before, but went on until I was drawn to the very edge of those frightening rings. I was still too far away to make out what was at work there, but somehow, I knew that it had everything to do with the Lyrans.

I also became certain that if I were forced to abide in this terrible place any further, that madness would not be long in coming for me, followed by oblivion. Worse, I heard the sound of children laughing, and I recognized them immediately. The Sibyl had returned, and now she was accompanied by her new companion, Maggie.

Then someone else joined us and turning in space, I beheld my mother.

"What a positively dreadful place," she remarked. "Yet you and I must speak at length and without distraction, so I shall remove you from this nightmare."

In the next instant, I was conveyed to a lovely garden. It was located indoors, and as its ceiling was made of glass (or some similar substance), I was able to determine that I was now on Cyllene, the home world of my race, for the pink sky above was laced with turquoise clouds and Saturn had been replaced by its gentler twin. Moreover, I beheld delicate spires rising up to meet these incarnadine heights, not only confirming my surmise, but providing me with an exact location. I was in the city of the Masters itself.

As for the garden, it followed a circular plan, with the ground level dominated by a large pool filled with colorful fish--or things that looked very like them. In the center of this, a great pillar rose up from the waters to the very summit of the chamber, lending its support to the glass.

Moreover, the entire length of this column was dotted with terraces which reminded me of large stone window boxes. These held all manner of plants and hanging vines, and their flowers glowed with a lambent light, whilst waterfalls of the purest liquid fell from other containers in graceful cascades.

Even the very air of the place seemed enchanted, filled as it was with the heady scent of unknown blooms. The sunlight too played its part in this bewitchment; caressing the scene with long, golden fingers, that in turn, engendered dozens of rainbows, and gilded the wings of small flying creatures with an aureate glow.

In sum, it was the very antitheses of what I had been enduring only a moment before, and my mother allowed me a long moment to drink it all in and rejuvenate myself. Then, when she perceived that I was ready, she led me to a walkway that encircled the pond, and we fell into step together.

"This is my favorite place," she stated. "Like yourself, I adore gardens, and I think that there is none finer than this one in all of the nine universes."

I certainly could not disagree, though I wondered at why I had been brought there.

"Have you ever asked yourself how it is that I can travel without the aid of a Phaseship, or any other contrivance?" she inquired. "Or for that matter, how the Sibyl manages the trick?"

Point in fact, the question *had* occurred to me, but I had been so caught up in other matters that I had never had the occasion (or the presence of mind) to inquire.

"I suppose that I have," I finally confessed.

She held out her hand and one of the little flying creatures landed upon it for a moment before taking off again. "The answer, my daughter, is that we are Dreamers."

As I am sure my readers will fully appreciate, I did not know what to make of this extraordinary disclosure.

"What mean you, madam?"

"I mean that we Pleiadeans--and yes, even the Lyrans—have managed to master far more than mere technology. My ancestors, and yours, realized that any true science is more than the mere understanding of circuits and gears, or chemical combinations. Those comprise only one half of the equation, and there is another component that is equally as vital."

"And what is that?" asked I.

"Mastery of the mind," she supplied. "For without this, there is no wisdom, and therefore no limits to the monstrosities or mistakes that might otherwise be committed. In the end, any science that fails to grasp this, and favors only the material, will never be more than that of stunted barbarians, forever denied the chance at achieving any real greatness.'

"But wisdom is not the only gift that such a mastery brings, Penelope. It also imparts abilities that technology alone cannot ever hope to rival. One of these is the incredible power of our dreams."

Once, when I had been a scientist, I would have raised the banner of logic and laughed at this statement as so much stuff and nonsense. But since that time, I had become acquainted with the formidable powers of the Masters and still bore the scar that Caroline had dealt me in the grotto of X'Kallabar. Perforce, I pushed aside what few shreds of skepticism I still possessed and attended to my mother's words.

"The story begins many centuries ago," she began, "when some of our greatest thinkers realized that dreams could be harnessed to serve the will of the dreamer. That they could be shaped into whatever form one desired and rendered as clearly as the waking state.'

71

"At first, this discovery allowed us to exploit the time that we normally wasted in sleep, and we used it to further our researches into the mysteries of the universe and the Self.'

"Then, as our research progressed, we learned that dreams could also be shared. We came to understand that they were not merely individual fancies, but a whole and separate reality. In turn, this gave us the ability to actively collaborate with one another, no matter the distance between us, or the physical limitations.'

"What followed after this was an even more profound discovery. From time to time, and quite without intending it, these same experimental dreamers would appear to others in the waking world. To the dreamer, it was a dream, but for those who encountered them, they were like ghosts. Ghosts who were not of the dead, but of the living.'

"From this, our researchers realized that we had discovered a gateway that opened up onto enormous power. Thus, we combined the technology of our computers and bioplasmic amplifiers with the natural abilities of the dreamers themselves. So equipped, they were soon able to walk among the waking at will. Better yet, when they did so, they were able to influence the very realities of anyone that they encountered, drawing them into visions that had been fashioned by the dreamer's desires."

Having reached a small stone bench, she paused, and waved for me to seat myself whilst she remained standing.

"It did not end there though," she advised. "As time progressed, something even more momentous transpired. The dreamers became capable of true bilocation. They learned how to will their very bodies to travel with them, wherever and whenever they so wished. Further, they discovered that the technology which had allowed them to progress this far was no longer necessary, and even an impediment."

I found my tongue at last. "So, in the end, they became exactly like the Chuchniya, and Caroline? They became Walkers Between the Worlds?"

"Yes," she responded. "*Exactly* like them--and as humans will one day become, provided that they are afforded the opportunity to do so. This is the very sum of all Lyran fears, and why, whenever they are in power, they strive to discredit the mind and the spirit in favor of gross materialism. As long as human beings are swayed by doubt and lured into the pursuit of meaningless baubles, they will remain enslaved."

"The stunted barbarians that you referred to?" I queried.

"The very same," she nodded. "But this condition will not last. We have foreseen it. One day, humanity will complete the journey that it began eons ago and then become our equals.'

"The indications of this can be found everywhere in its history; in the *tulpas* that the Tibetan lamas can generate through focused will, in the *Upanishads* and Indian yogis who can teleport themselves, in the *egregores* created by western mystics, and among the many holy men who have appeared to their followers over great and impossible distances. You even had the privilege of making the acquaintance of one such man."

"Jesus of Nazareth," I guessed, recalling my studies of the Christian Bible. At the time, I had considered his supernatural manifestations to be nothing more than mere allegory. But now, I was the wiser.

"None other," she confirmed.

"And what of me?" I inquired. "Will I become like you some day? Like the Sibyl?"

She sat and took my hand. "You are already more like us than you realize, my daughter."

Even as she said this, the garden faded away. It was replaced by the halls of my base.

"We will talk again," my mother promised. "Till then, rest you well, for challenges await you upon the morrow."

With that, she disappeared, undoubtedly intent on returning to the peace of her extraterrestrial garden. Such tranquility, however, was not to be mine.

Nearing my quarters, I happened to encounter H'reep, who was travelling in the opposite direction. Seeing me, the little creature chirped with excitement and immediately threw herself to the floor, averting her eyes and uttering prayers.

Nonplussed by this rather eccentric display, I passed her by and entered my chambers. Being a dream, I did not bother with the door, but simply passed through the wall.

Once within, I caught a glimpse of myself lying asleep, and this was enough. A powerful force grabbed hold of me and I was pulled back into my body as if by an invisible riptide. In a trice, I was sitting up in my bed, and very much awake.

This was not all though. When I decided to break my fast and went to the mess hall, I once again crossed paths with H'reep.

"Coo'coo'ma'tz!" she squawked, pointing hysterically in my direction. And as before, she prostrated herself and refused to meet my gaze.

Then I realized what the problem was. Somehow, she had seen me with my mother, and now considered me to be divine.

"You silly creature!" I snapped. "I am no occult entity. Get yourself up and stop this nonsense immediately!"

H'reep however, did not comply, but remained right where she was, chanting more prayers of praise to her savior figure. As my readers will fully appreciate, it was most embarrassing.

Fortunately, Professor Merriweather had also chosen to dine in the hall that morning, and seeing the commotion, hurried over.

"Here now," he crooned, kneeling next to the prone creature. "This is not what you think it is. Not at all. Come with me and let me explain it to you."

His words had no effect however. H'reep remained right where she was and kept on with her incessant invocations.

Realizing that he was making no headway, the Professor looked up to me. "Penny," he suggested, "perhaps you should remove yourself, at least until I can manage to talk some sense into her."

I was only too glad to accommodate him, and taking my plate with me, retreated to the peace and quiet of my quarters. Some minutes later, the Professor joined me.

"I think that I have managed to mitigate the situation," he advised. "If so, then there will not be a repetition of today's performance."

"I should hope not," I replied. "Whatever did you say to her?"

"Merely that our kind is capable of the feat that she witnessed, and that for us, it is nothing remarkable. Further, I assured her that though this makes us similar to her Saviouress in that one respect, we are by no means deific. Though I had to repeat this to her many times over, in the end, I believe that she took it to heart."

"That is good news," I told him. "I was concerned that I would be forced to endure an endless barrage of genuflections. You have my profound thanks, sir."

But in truth, a part of me was just as in awe as H'reep had been, for I now knew exactly what my mother's print had been attempting to convey; that I was Jacob the Dreamer.

"This place shall be called Bethel." he had declared. The same biblical passage had also stated that his God had changed his name to Israel, and that his would be an enduring legacy.

What will my legacy be? I wondered. *What mantle of responsibility is about to be placed upon my shoulders?*

Sighing at my lack of insight, I made for my bookshelf, intent on engaging in some recreational reading. In the process, I happened to glance at the Ladder print and noticed that several more figures had been altered.

The angel nearest to my sleeping form had become another representation of myself, but dressed as I had been on the night of my death in the Professor's laboratory. A third angel further up the spiral pathway now portrayed me as a shapeshifter, and was actively morphing back and forth from human to tiger. And yet another was dressed in the white robes that I had worn during my ill-fated trek to Kanchenjunga with Brother Lobsang.

It was all a replay in miniature of my adventures to date, I mused.

None of them were the equal of the fifth angel though, for here, the depiction was clearly of something that I had yet to encounter. Although it was quite blurry in comparison to the others, and faded in and out of existence, I was dressed in shining armor and wielding a sword!

But though I searched for it, I could not see any angels that represented Elizabeth, and I did my best to find comfort in the fact that the ladder was still filled with many other holy messengers that might transmute themselves. That, and the knowledge that although my journey was far from over, hope still existed.

CHAPTER 4: Eye of the Falcon God

I visit the Temple of Horus and there, my fellows and I are tasked with a great mission and fight a desperate battle. In the process, Pishqu is shot down and I go to her rescue. Then, the Great Flood and a mysterious disappearance.

The Professor's words to H'reep proved efficacious. Though she still tended to avoid my eyes and seemed uneasy in my presence, we managed to conduct our affairs in a businesslike manner.

Which was as well, for the Masters had decided that the time had come for us to move against the Lyrans in a significant way. Accordingly, all of the Saurii Speakers who served aboard our Phaseships, including H'reep, were summoned to the largest conference room and briefed on the details.

We pilots however, were not included, and yet we did not feel any offense, for we appreciated the need for compartmentalization more than ever. Just that morning, Special Section had arrested several individuals that the Codex had identified. These included a number of pilots from El Dorado and Avalon, and most surprisingly of all, Khentetka's Assistant Wingleader, Peseshet, who had made a full confession of her treason.

So, we abided in the mess hall, clothed in our flightsuits and whiled away our time. As one might expect, this involved a great deal of gossip and speculation, but I did not engage in any of it. It was enough for me that the traitors had been found out, and that just as the Colonel had reported, Elizabeth had not been so named.

Unfortunately, this gladsome news was offset by the fact that I was seated near Ziva 1, and she did not converse with me, but only awarded me the chilliest of glares. Knowing the cause, and certain that I could convince her of my innocence, this frustrated me greatly, and I was sorely tempted to confront her. But a warning glance from Manfred was enough to dissuade me from taking such a course. She was not ready yet, and I told myself that I would simply have to tolerate the situation until this changed.

Fortunately, Major Sixkiller 1 and Hamilket 2 happened by at this unhappy juncture, and their presence was enough to provide me with distraction. In short order, they had managed to engage me in a conversation about the merits of a camera safari in the forested valleys east of Hw'ii'kk. Here, I was told, was the best opportunity to view the great Allosaurs that hunted the area, and their prey, the herbivorous Brachiosaurs. The idea was so attractive, that I was able to temporarily put aside my concerns about Captain Meier and agree to their proposal.

We were in the midst of negotiating a time and date, when Sigrun Nälkäinen and Major Singh entered the room.

"All pilots will report to the tarmac and prepare for take-off." Major Singh announced. "Your destination will be revealed to you upon your arrival."

Immediately, those of us who were eating took a final bite of our meals, or finished off our beverages, and as one, we took up our helmets and headed for the lifts. The very air seemed electrified with our anticipation.

In short order, we were airborne and making our rendezvous with the Ebani, and after a brief interchange with the Speakers, the creatures folded time and space. When normal reality reasserted itself, we found that we had been delivered to the 1st universe in its 4th century, and from there, Sigrun directed us to the continent of Africa, and thence to the area occupied by Egypt. Here, we assumed stealth mode and were able to proceed undetected.

This was not the ancient kingdom that many of my readers might suppose, but a thoroughly modern realm (being as it was, a close ally of Atlantis, and the beneficiary of much of their advanced technology). The airspace that we entered was dotted with jet aircraft, both great and small, and Egypt's capitol, Cairo, proved to be a gleaming metropolis of many millions of souls.

However, it was nothing compared to the sight of the Great Pyramids at Giza. These were covered in pristine limestone and crowned by golden capstones that shone so brightly that the structures seemed to glow. Moreover, the Nile proved to be a bustling place, filled with boats of all sizes, and a high-speed rail system ran beside the mighty river, which at Sigrun's direction, we followed at some length.

Then at last, when my instruments indicated that we had reached the city of Edfu, I beheld another marvel; the Temple of Horus. Like the pyramids, it was no relic, but in perfect condition, being as it was a thriving religious center. Not only did the rail system serve it by way of a modern station, but scores of electric omnibuses and private motorcars sat in the shadow of its massive pylon gate.

Further, as we circled overhead, I caught a glimpse of the peristyle court within, and saw that it was filled with tourists and pilgrims who had come to pay homage to the God of the Midday Sun. Of all the places for us to undertake a mission against the Lyrans, it seemed the least likely of any that I might have imagined, which I reasoned, was perhaps why it had been chosen. Like Studio "S", no one would have suspected it of serving such a clandestine purpose.

As it was, we were not the first arrivals. Scores of Phaseships were already present. They were parked in groups upon the sands and cloaked from casual view by their stealth fields. Some were of the Falcon variety, whilst others were Gamels, and at Sigrun's direction, we set ourselves down beside them.

Then we disembarked, and after but a moment, one of the omnibuses came up from the car park and we were directed to board it. From there, we were conveyed to the verge of the pylon gateway, and Sigrun walked down the aisle of our bus, passing out kirikets of the most common variety to one and all.

Suffice it to say, that once the crickets were activated, the crowds ceased to be a concern. We emerged from the omnibus encased in a separate bubble of time, and the people around us had assumed the quality of phantoms. The only exception was a white-clad priest of Horus and Wing Leader Khentetka, who met us in the courtyard.

"Welcome," she greeted. "Please follow us."

Falling into step behind her, I overheard the conversation between herself and our leaders.

"I was saddened to hear about Peseshet," Sigrun offered.

"Her disloyalty was a terrible blow to me," Khentetka replied with noticeable pain. "And when Special Section decided to relocate Mission Command, I suggested this place. I wanted to demonstrate to everyone that not all who are born of Kemet are as deceitful."

"No one ever thought such a thing," Major Singh assured her. "The people of the Black Land have a well-deserved reputation for integrity. Peseshet was merely an aberration. Nothing more."

Though she made a polite sound of acceptance, it was obvious that it would be a long while before she would forget her hurt, or let go of her sense of accountability.

The Lyrans ruin everything, everywhere they go, I thought bitterly, and I could not but empathize with the woman. After all, I too, had been betrayed by someone that I loved, but in my case, I now had reason to feel a cautious optimism. Khentetka had no such solace to cling to and I pitied her.

When our group reached the end of the court, we passed through the *pronaos* and came into the hypostyle hall. Normally this area was reserved for religious rituals, and I recalled that in ancient times, none but the Pharaoh and the temple priests had been allowed to enter.

This however, was modern Egypt, and the area had been opened up to visitors. They were all around us, and a sign in Egyptian and Atlantean proclaimed that services would soon be held to honor the god, for it was approaching midday. The scholar in me was fascinated by the prospect of witnessing such a rite, but I knew that this was not to be; we had come here on a serious errand and did not have the time to sightsee.

The priest who led us, hurried us along, till we entered the Hall of Offerings and then he guided us into what in normal time would have been the sanctuary, and the home of a solar barque. But for us, in our minute-between, no such ritual vessel existed.

Nor were there any chapels to subdivide the space. Instead, we found ourselves entering a spacious chamber, with only stylized stone pillars and a great statue of Horus to remind us of the Temple that existed just one reality removed.

Like Studio "S", this space was filled with control stations and technicians. Moreover, it was equipped with an enormous holographic projector stand, around which scores of Chrononauts and their Wing Leaders had already gathered. An image of the moon which orbited the earth of the 4th universe hovered before them, with portions of it marked out, and certain craters highlighted.

Seeing this, and the grave demeanor of the assembly, I knew in an instant what we were about. Without question, our targets would be no less than the moon-portals that the Lyrans used to travel from one universe to another. It was also equally certain that we would face some stiff opposition when we challenged them.

"Ah, *bueno*," a woman said as she noticed us. "Everyone is here, so we can begin."

The speaker was a short, dark-haired figure, with eyes as piercing as those of the Falcon God himself. She was El Dorado's Wing Leader, Juana Garcia de Arintero, (who my readers may recall, was a personage that I had met once before, albeit briefly).

"Our mission," she began, "will be to deprive the Lyrans of their moon portals and therefore impair their ability to travel. To accomplish this, the Gamels will lay mines in each portal and the Falcons will protect them and respond to any enemy retaliation.'

"Because we cannot know how many disks our enemy will field against us, nor at which of the nine moons, a reaction force will be on standby. They will respond using their Ebani when and where they are needed.'

"Further, each raiding group will take only a single Speaker with them, who will ride in one Phaseship designated as a stand-off craft. This ship will not participate in any combat but stay in reserve so that the group's Ebani can be in readiness should the reaction force, or another raid group, require its assistance."

Hearing this, I found myself hoping that Pishqu would be awarded this task. In my estimation, this did not seem the kind of fight that she belonged in.

"What kind of mines will we be laying?" This had come from one of the Gamel pilots.

De Arintero smiled wolfishly. "Something *muy especial*. They are designated *Anka* after a mythical bird of fire. Anything coming within their field will be pulled into a timeline where the sun has grown so old that it has swallowed the moon. There is no return from such a journey."

It was a gruesome use of time as a weapon, but I had to admire its brutal efficiency.

De Arintero continued. "One particular area of concern during this operation will be attack from land-based units. We know that the Lyrans have established bases in the equatorial regions of Earth to facilitate their flights to the moons, and our intelligence indicates that they may launch attacks from there. So, be mindful of anything coming up from the surface. As to your individual assignments, your Wing Leaders will provide them to you. *Que Dios te cuide y nos conceda la victoria.*"

She crossed herself, and several others joined in. It was at this point, and as I made my way over to Hamilket 2 with my squadronmates, that I happened to look upwards into the eyes of the Falcon God's statue. Almost as if the god himself had whispered it to me, I suddenly understood the deeper reasons behind Khentetka's choice of this place.

Horus, I recalled, was not only personified by a falcon (and therefore symbolically linked to Phaseships such as mine) but was considered to be a god of the sky, whose left eye was the sun and the right, the moon. Moreover, a tale that I had encountered during my studies of religion came to mind.

According to legend, a great war had taken place between Horus and his rival, Set. The stakes in this conflict had been no less than dominion over all of Egypt, and the battle had been a fierce one, costing Set his testicle, and Horus, his right eye. But in the end, Set was vanquished to the open desert, and ibis-headed Thoth fashioned Horus a replacement for his missing orb.

It was because of this that the priesthood of Horus annually held a ritual that they called *The Return of the Moon*, wherein they celebrated the full restoration of the god's powers and his victory over his divine opponent.

In our own small way, this was exactly what we were attempting to accomplish, I realized. By denying it to the Lyrans, we were returning all of the nine moons to mankind, and I was certain that the Falcon God was pleased with our intentions.

Whether his blessing would ensure our victory was another matter though. So was the question of how I would respond if I were forced to face Elizabeth in battle. I had no ready answers, and the mental image of the *White Rose* flying alongside Lyran disks haunted me all the way back to my Phaseship.

Leaving Egypt behind, our force divided, with each group entering an Ebani and departing for its assignment. My squadron travelled with a trio of Gamels, and we were charged with attacking the moon portal of the 4th universe.

To my frustration, I also learned that Pishqu had not been assigned to serve as the stand-off ship. Instead, an even less experienced pilot from El Dorado had been tasked with the chore. But I kept my reservations to myself and decided that when the battle was joined, that I would endeavor to keep a close eye on the Nazcan girl and intervene if it became necessary.

The journey itself was unremarkable, and we encountered no opposition; the earth-base that Special Section had identified at Alcântara, in Brazil, remained quiescent. And save for the remains of several lunar landers, and installations which had long since been abandoned by the Anunnaki and Andromedans, the moon itself seemed wholly untouched and entirely untenanted.

It was only when we reached its northern pole and were within sight of our objective, the Pförtner crater, that the situation changed. A dozen Lyran disks rose up from the area around it and came straight at us. Immediately, I found myself engaged by two such disks, each launching their missiles.

"Initiating counter-measures," Blackbird announced, even as I returned fire. The enemy projectiles went wild, spiraling off into space, or sending up plumes of grey dust and rock as they slammed into the lunar surface, but many of my missiles also suffered the same fate.

One however, managed to hit its mark. Though silent, the explosion that this produced was spectacular; the Lyran machine was completely obliterated, and pieces of it flew away in all directions. Its partner was undeterred however, and brought their energy weapons to bear, missing my Phaseship by only the narrowest of margins.

In answer, I pulled up hard and then spun sideways before the enemy pilot could catch me at what would have been the zenith of my loop. Then I employed a tactic that Major Singh had taught me; I reversed my thrusters and, in the process, retarded my ship's forward movement.

Of a sudden, my pursuer overshot me, and before he could react, I slid in behind him, bared my fangs, and fired. Unlike the Lyran, I did not miss, and my chronoguns cut the disk across its equator as neatly as if it had been riven by a sword. Even as the two halves went off to meet their separate dooms, I pitched to starboard and went after another machine that was engaging Ziva 1.

"I have him," I told her. "Break left!"

Unaware of my presence, the Lyran attempted to stay with her and only managed to present me with the perfect target. There was no time for the rotter to respond to my missile when I launched it, and then, nothing left of him but an expanding ball of gas and debris.

Ziva however, did not express any gratitude for her salvation, but went to the rescue of one of the Gamels, saying nothing. I did not let this vex me though, for the Lyrans were hard on the transport's heels and this was no time to nurse a petty hurt. Instead, I took my place beside her and we attacked in tandem.

Together, we managed to destroy our targets, but not before my quarry dealt a death blow to the Gamel. Cursing as the transport lost control and crashed into a crater, I took out my anger on another Lyran, sending him to his own lunar grave but an instant later.

We were now reduced to only two Gamels, and although all our Falcons had survived the fight, Manfred 1's craft had suffered significant damage, as had Sixkiller 2's. Where our fast reaction force was, I did not know, but I reasoned that they were occupied with another emergency elsewhere. For the present at least, the success of our mission was entirely in our hands.

"We will have to seal this portal as soon as possible," I urged Hamilket 2. "More of the enemy may well be on their way."

"My thoughts exactly," he responded. "Gamel Leader, initiate your run. The rest of you, follow me." Moving with him, we flew by the transports, and arrowed towards the crater.

Which was as well, for a force of six more disks had just emerged from there. One of these we destroyed immediately, and another was damaged enough that it changed course and fled.

The odds had become even, and we pressed the attack. In but a handful of seconds yet another Lyran was down, and at this, his remaining comrades lost all heart, turning away and making for the Earth as fast as they could.

While the Tigress and I were sorely tempted to give chase, we did not do so, and neither did any of my fellows. Our mission was not yet fulfilled and none of us had any wish to discover what weapons the Brazilian base possessed, or if other disks lay in wait.

So, we remained, and stood watch over the Gamels as they dropped into the crater, opened their cargo bays, and let go of their mines. Given the moon's lower gravity, these did not fall quickly, but fall they did, passing through the hologram that concealed the entrance to the portal, and then straight into its maw.

When they activated, there was little to herald the event save for additions to my display showing their positions and detection radius, and for a moment, I was certain that this would be all. But presently, my instruments warned that more enemy machines were rising up from the moon's interior to challenge us.

In this, they did not succeed; the machine leading the pack entered the field surrounding one of the mines, causing a brilliant flash of light, and I briefly bore witness to the disk being dragged through time and space straight into the heart of a future sun. Another, close on its heels, suffered the same terrible fate, and the remainder, realizing what was in store for them, turned about and headed back into the depths in full retreat.

Though it had come at a cost, we had succeeded. The men and women of the downed Gamel would be revived in new bodies, and for the peoples of the 4th universe, the moon would no longer be a source of oppression. Rather, it would once again serve as the light by which they could live their lives in peace and freedom.

It was on the heels of this lofty reflection that my mother appeared in the cabin.

"The group that is attacking the moon of the 6th universe is in dire straits," she announced, and I realized that she was addressing not only myself, but my entire squadron. "Our reaction force is already there, but more Phaseships are required. Make haste!"

With this, she vanished, and I and my comrades set our course for the stand-off ship and the Ebani.

The scene that I beheld several minutes later was unlike anything that I had ever witnessed before. The space above the moon was filled with Phaseships and Lyran disks, and in greater numbers than in any other battle I had yet experienced. Plainly, this was where the outcome of our struggle would be decided, and both sides had committed every craft that they could muster to tilt the balance in their favor.

"Penny *darling!*" I heard a voice on the com exclaim. It was my clone, Louise. "We seem to be in a bit of a dust-up here. Do be a dear and help us sort it all out, would you?"

I needed no such invitation though (and especially not from the likes of a reprobate such as her), and increasing thrust, threw myself into the fray. In but seconds, three Lyran machines were coming for me, unleashing a barrage of energy bolts.

In reply, I spun, returning fire and corkscrewing away. Undeterred, the trio changed course and followed me, and in the process, came under the guns of Manfred 1 and Sixkiller 2. One Lyran machine was destroyed, and the other two hastily separated.

"I shall take the one on the right," I informed them, coming about as I made this declaration.

My target went into an evasive roll, and I changed course to stay with him, attempting to score a hit with my guns. Although he managed to avoid my fire, he flew straight into the shots coming at him from an Avalon pilot, forcing me to break way so as to avoid the wreckage.

Even as I did so, another Lyran came down from above, trying to take advantage of my situation. It was most unsporting of him, and growling as only a Tigress could, I turned hard to port and then went after him as he dropped past me.

Yet, just when I was certain that I had him, I detected another disk sneaking up from behind. Right away, I broke off, ascended and went to port. A stream of energy bolts flew by, and although I twisted and turned like an eel, the blighter stayed with me.

But of a sudden, he was no more. Ziva 1 had come to my rescue and shot him down.

"Many thanks," I said, but of course, she did not reply and went off in search of another enemy.

Meantime, a dozen Lyran disks where coming out from the moon-portal to join the fray, and among them, was a single Phaseship. I did not need to magnify the image to know whose craft it was, for no other could have flown alongside them unscathed.

Exactly as I had feared, Elizabeth had arrived.

"Hamilket!" I exclaimed. "Do you see? It is Elizabeth. Please, I beg you, do not allow anyone to fire upon her."

This of course, was born of pure emotion and devoid of any tactical sense whatsoever. I knew as well as he that she constituted as much a threat to our forces as any of the Lyran machines. Yet, I could not allow her to be harmed. Not without at least attempting to reach her, and perchance, interrupt the spell that held her in thrall.

Perforce, I did not wait for the Wing Leader to reply and instead, broadcast directly to the *White Rose*.

"Elizabeth my love! It is I, Penelope. Do not fight us! I know that Mr. Grey's conditioning is not so complete that our love cannot overcome it. Please, I forgive you everything! Abandon the Lyrans and come with me."

There was a long pause, and then, as my targeting systems positively identified the *White Rose*, Elizabeth spoke, but in a voice so filled with contempt that I almost did not recognize her.

"Our *love?* "she spat. "Love is nothing but simpering weakness. Mr. Grey opened my eyes to the truth; there is nothing greater in the nine universes than power itself. I have no need for love, or its pathetic twin, compassion, and I spit on your forgiveness."

I was so shocked by this rebuke that it took me a moment to understand that she had just chosen a target for herself. She was diving at Pishqu's craft, firing as she went.

Perceiving the danger, the Nazcan girl made every effort to evade her, but Elizabeth stayed behind her, sending bolt after bolt in her direction. Worse, no one else was near enough to lend any aid, save for myself.

Immediately, I descended and added thrust. "Elizabeth!" I cried, "In the name of the Great Nothingness, stop!"

My plea had no effect however, and nary a second later, she landed a decisive hit on Pishqu's rear thrusters. Suddenly lacking power, the Phaseship pitched downwards and spiraled towards the portal crater with the *White Rose* hard on its tail. It was plain that my estranged lover meant to finish the poor girl off.

There was no choice left to me. It would either be Elizabeth's life, or Pishqu's. Forcing back my anguish, I performed the hardest task that I have ever undertaken; I sent the command and launched a pair of missiles at the *White Rose.*

They streaked across the space between us, and just when I was certain that I was about to witness her demise, Elizabeth initiated countermeasures, and veered away. Though I admit that it was a betrayal of my duty to the Masters, and to my comrades, I cheered at her narrow escape.

But even as she managed this feat, she came under another attack and from a new quarter. A pilot with the Avalon detachment had joined us and launched missiles of his own.

Again, she avoided the projectiles, and again he fired upon her. Worse, two additional Chrononauts from Shamballa arrived and lent their support. She was now grossly outnumbered and mere moments from being destroyed.

Run damn you, I thought desperately. *Give up and flee.*

Someone or something must have overheard my silent prayer, for presently, she did that very thing. With the rockets closing in on all sides, she performed a transit, and in a burst of light, vanished into the No-When.

It was only then that I finally released the breath that I had been holding in the entire time--and then I remembered poor Pishqu. Though I looked about for any wreckage, I could see nothing.

"Wing Leader," I said, endeavoring to suppress the lingering emotion in my voice. "I believe that Pishqu has gone down into the portal itself. We cannot mine the entrance and forsake her."

"We must," Hamilket 1 asserted. "That portal has to be sealed before more Lyrans can arrive."

"Then allow me to go after her and seal it behind me," I entreated. "Once I locate her, I will find another way out for us, perhaps through the Jump Worlds."

By this point, the battle had turned in our favor. The Lyran reinforcements that had accompanied Elizabeth were either gone, or taking flight, and most of the icons on my display were friendly assets. Hamilket could surely spare me.

"Penelope," he replied. "You cannot attempt such a thing alone. Not with the possibility of encountering enemy reinforcements. You will take along Captain Meier 1, Major Sixkiller 2 and Manfred 1."

"Of course, sir."

It took but a few seconds for the Wing Leader to transmit the order and for my compatriots to assemble around me. Mercifully, none of them made any mention of my recent encounter with Elizabeth, and for that I was immensely grateful. At present, the subject was far too painful to entertain. Instead, they limited their conversation solely to the mission, and we moved out as a group towards the portal crater.

The Gamels had already positioned themselves there and they waited as we went into the shaft that led to the portal itself. Once we were well away, they deployed their munitions, and these armed themselves immediately.

Now, there would be no turning back for us, and I kept a close eye on my screens for any indication of Lyran disks or the wreckage of Pishqu's craft.

We encountered neither though, and as we continued our descent, the passage became lit with streaks of phantasmal light that became more intense the deeper we went. Then at last, the portal itself came into view. It was just as I remembered it from my trip with Mr. Grey; a candescent ball of white light interspersed with rainbow-like scintillations.

"Penny? Do you know how *dieses verrückte Ding* operates?" Manfred asked judiciously. It was a fair question, and one that I had no ready answer for.

"You simply pass through it and come out the other side," I responded, simultaneously realizing how glib I sounded. "That was how Mr. Grey did it."

In hindsight, I should have added that I had been rather enraged at the time and more interested in causing the man's murder than with the technical particulars.

"Yah," he replied with obvious skepticism. "Yah, sure. Okay."

"Penny," Blackbird put in, "he is right about being cautious. This is after all, a piece of alien technology."

"That it is," I observed. "Yet we do not have the time to study it in detail, and perforce, we must press onwards."

So, in we went.

Once inside the cosmic gateway, my displays became filled with a light so intense that they strained to compensate for the glare. Concurrently, my navigational systems and the temporal readouts became utterly incoherent. According to their data, we were effectively nowhere, and existing at a moment beyond any time at all.

When at last, my screens dimmed and the readouts had regained their sanity, I determined that we had somehow become separated from the other Phaseships. Exactly how this had transpired, and where they had gone to, utterly eluded me.

What was clear, was that we had come out into the 2nd universe, the year 2807 BCE and specifically May the 24th. Moreover, I was detecting a distress signal coming from the Earth. It was located in what would eventually be called the Outer Banks of North Carolina.

But what I beheld was not the gentle planet that I was accustomed to. Instead, virtually its entire surface was covered by fierce storms, and I counted at least a dozen hurricanes, all of which were truly monstrous in size. Had I not known better, I would have assumed that I was gazing upon a Jump World.

"What has happened here?" I asked.

"A cometary event and a great flood," Blackbird responded. "According to my files, on May 10th, a comet composed of rock and ice 4.8 kilometers in diameter struck the Indian Ocean, just off the coast of Madagascar. This resulted in a tsunami over 183 meters high which ravaged most of the world's coastlines, and its effects were felt hundreds of kilometers inland. '

"The impact also spewed tons of particulates into the atmosphere and created world-wide hurricanes of category 5 strength, and higher. On the basis of this, I believe that we may encounter some significant turbulence on our way down."

It happened that Blackbird had not been exaggerating about the force of the winds in the least. Although it had been two weeks since the cosmic collision, the gusts that we encountered taxed my skills as a pilot to their very utmost. It was as if I were battling against a living thing, pregnant with malice, and determined to swat us out of the sky.

Despite this vicious onslaught though, I kept a firm grip on the control sticks, and Blackbird did her utmost to lend me her aid, so that after a few minutes we managed to leave the tempest behind and entered into a relatively calm layer of air.

There, I was able to behold the state of the world in the aftermath of the comet. Darkness reigned and massive storms raged everywhere, discharging enormous bolts of lightning. They stabbed at the lands below them like fiery daggers, and the light cast from their hellish assault brought the extent of the disaster into stark and sickening relief.

While there were places well inland that had clearly been spared, only death existed near the sea. There, great tidal waves had scoured everything clear, leaving naught but grey mud and devastation.

The toll for both animals and humans, must have been severe, I mused, spotting the remains of what had once been a settlement and then, a little further on, the carcasses of a pod of whales.

Blackbird confirmed this. "According to my files, what you are witnessing is the genesis of every tale about the Great Flood that has ever been told. Eighty percent of the human population of this time has been wiped out, and the event itself will be forever etched into the memory of the survivors.'

"Eventually, 175 different narratives will arise and among widely separated groups of people, but all of them will agree on the scope of the disaster. Of these, the Epic of Gilgamesh and the story of Noah in the Christian Bible, will become the most well-known. Would you like to hear either of these accounts?"

"No! No thank you," I said, rather more sharply than I might have intended. Just then I did not wish to dwell on the historical or religious implications of this event. Pishqu's rescue was all that I wanted to concentrate on, and increasing our speed, I flew us as directly as the weather allowed towards the distress signal.

Finally, and after ten minutes had gone by, I located her Phaseship. It had washed up upon the shore, its bright yellow pontoons deployed all around it. Even though one set had deflated and was lying on the sands in shreds, the remainder had held fast and the craft itself seemed reasonably intact, save for a badly damaged left wing and its ruined thrusters.

"Pishqu," I called over the com, "Can you hear me? Please answer."

When no reply came, I circled the wreck, searching for any sign of life. "Blackbird, can you make contact with the AI?"

"No Penny," she answered. "It appears to be offline, although I cannot diagnose the problem, or get it to reawaken, which is very strange. The damage that the Phaseship sustained is not consistent with such an outage."

"I see," I replied pensively. "And what of the mechanica?"

"It appears to be dormant, and in its cradle," she responded.

That IS odd, I thought, landing us just above the surf line. Then I rose from my seat, pulled a medical kit from our stores, and summoned Old Fred.

"Come with me. I may have need of you."

The robot unlimbered itself, and followed me down the egress ramp onto the sands, wherein we made for the stricken machine. All the while, I called out to Pishqu.

"Pishqu! Pishqu, can you hear me? Are you there?"

But save for the hiss of the wind over the sands, the distant rumble of thunder, and the sound of the waves striking the shore, all was silent. Now becoming well and truly concerned, I closed the remaining distance and made my way up into the Phaseship's cabin.

90

No one awaited me there however. Except for a few empty ration packs littering the deck, the space was entirely untenanted. Stranger still, a word had been etched into the bulkhead with some type of sharp object. It was scribed in Atlantean characters and read, "C-R-O-A-T-O-A-N."

Bewildered, I also noted that the survival kit remained within its niche next to the dormant mechanica. Wherever Pishqu had gone to, she had done so alone, and without any equipment.

"Blackbird," I said over my ear com. "Can you detect any human life nearby?"

"No, Penny," my AI returned. "You are the only human within 20 square kilometers. Nor do I detect any other lifeforms except for marine creatures."

I exited the cabin and looked about me in perplexity. Then I spotted a set of human footprints.

They bore the mark of our standard footwear and led away from the Phaseship in a purposeful manner. When I made to follow them though, I discovered that they terminated after only 30 meters and although I searched for more, my efforts proved fruitless. It was as if Pishqu had been plucked up into the very sky by an unknown force.

Frustrated, I re-boarded my timeship. "Blackbird, try to access the ship's records. Let us see what the log discloses."

There was the briefest of pauses before my AI reported the results. "According to the log, they came down in the ocean and floated here. Then after a few days, Pishqu was contacted by someone and departed. However, I do not have all of the data. Except for the cabin footage, everything else appears to have been erased."

"Play the part where she receives her visitor," I instructed.

My AI complied and the fragmentary file played out on my center screen. It showed Pishqu rising from her pilots' seat and speaking with someone that the camera's angle could not capture. Then, pausing only long enough to engrave her cryptic message onto the bulkhead, she descended the egress ramp and walked out of view, showing no signs of distress whatsoever.

"An indigene perchance?" I ventured.

"I do not know," Blackbird answered. "My files only indicate the contact. After that, all they contain are variations on a word; croatoan."

"What does it mean?" I asked her, thinking that perhaps it was the location of a settlement, or the name of a tribal group.

"I have no idea, Penny," my AI confessed. "Although my records indicate that croatoan will one day be the unofficial name for a nearby island, I have no indication that it is inhabited at this point in history."

"We shall soon see," I replied, hopeful that it would prove to be Pishqu's ultimate destination.

However, when we flew to the place, it proved to be just as lifeless as everywhere else. Accordingly, and with no other alternative, I returned us to the crash site, and proceeded to search the general vicinity from the air.

Two hours passed without any success, and then Blackbird informed me that my squadronmates had finally caught up with us. Like myself, they too had been thrown into separate centuries, and only after ascending into the No-When and tracing one another's engine signals, had they been able to regroup and find me.

I wasted no time, quickly appraising them of the situation, and they promptly added their numbers to the search. Alas, this proved to be no more successful than my solitary effort, and it soon became obvious to one and all that we would never find the girl. Pishqu had vanished without a trace.

"What should we do now?" Manfred asked. "We certainly cannot remain here indefinitely."

"Blast it, I know that!" I snapped, unwilling to admit defeat.

"Penny," Sixkiller put in gently. "We also can't leave that ship just lyin around for anyone to find. I say we nuke it and leave some supplies and a rescue beacon. If Pishqu comes back, she could fire it off and we'd know about it."

Though I dearly desired it to be otherwise, I could not find any fault with her suggestion. "Yes," I conceded tiredly. "We must needs do what is necessary."

Perforce, we landed, gathered up food, medicine, and survival gear (including the portable beacon) and created a cache for it above the surf line. Then, and after we had re-boarded our vessels and ascended, I sent the command for the Phaseship's self-destruct sequence.

In seconds, Pishqu's ship vaporized, and the only signs that anyone had ever visited the place were a small pile of rocks marking the cache, and our footprints.

Having no Ebani to call upon, we were compelled to utilize the River of Time in order to return to the 6th universe, and there, finally reunited with our forces. Unfortunately, this afforded me a surfeit of time with which to ruminate about Elizabeth, and by the point that our squadron came within sight of our base, I had managed to make myself well and truly miserable.

After facing her in combat, it seemed utterly impossible to me that my lover could ever be restored to her former self, and it should come as no surprise to my readers that the instant that I landed and we had been debriefed, that I sought out the Professor in the hope of receiving some measure of reassurance. I found him in his quarters and taking in my state, he received me immediately.

"How can you be certain?" I asked him as he showed me to a chair near the holographic fireplace. "How do you *know* that we can ever overwrite the damage that Mr. Grey has done to her?"

"By the simple fact that Mr. Grey succeeded," he answered. "Until now, such a thing was only theoretical—at least as far as the Master' science was concerned. Her transformation establishes without any doubt that the refactor can be utilized to completely rewrite a personality. All that remains is to do the same thing in reverse.'

"Of course, before we can do that, we shall have to take her into custody, for as you yourself proved, she will not willingly submit herself to such an ordeal."

"And to do that, she will have to be found, and then cornered like an animal," I observed disconsolately. "Tell me, does Special Section have *any* idea as to her whereabouts?"

He shook his head. "Not yet, my dear. However, both Lady Anne and the Colonel have assured me that they are marshalling every resource for the hunt."

Seeing my doubt and my pain, he added. "Penelope, I know in my heart that she *will* be found—and that we *shall* succeed."

I nodded and brushed away a tear. "Yes," I said in a small voice, "we shall." Yet I was nowhere near as sure as he, and for all the power that the Tigress and my martial skills lent me, I felt quite helpless.

The following morning, and just as I had expected I would, I was summoned back to the conference room to follow up on the matter of Pishqu.

The Professor was in attendance, as were the two Hamilkets and Louise. My caliginous mood was immediately replaced by sheer astonishment (and disgust), as my clone toasted my entrance with of all things, a Marmalade Cocktail!

Ignoring her salute and her manifest lack of propriety (for one simply did *not* imbibe so early in the day), I seated myself and the Professor began.

"Your Phaseship was correct about Croatoan," he informed me as he lit his pipe. "It is classified as a barrier island and was later renamed Hatteras."

As he discarded his match in an ashtray that a mechanica offered him, he gestured for a hologram to appear. It showed the island and its immediate neighbors.

"However, this is not the only reference to this term. I learned that it also appears in connection with the colony of Roanoke, which was the first attempt in the 2nd universe to establish a permanent English settlement in the New World. In the very first year of its founding, its leader, John White, left for England to gather more resources and manpower, but when he returned three years later, the 115 settlers that he had left behind had all vanished without a trace."

My eyebrows rose at this enigmatic disclosure, and I daresay that my blood thrilled.

He went on. "The only clue as to their fate was the word 'croatoan', which was found etched into a tree. Whilst some scholars suggested that they had simply fallen victim to disease or had succumbed to attack by hostile natives, others postulated that they had joined with the indigenous population and interbred, thus explaining later reports by explorers who claimed to have encountered blond haired and blue-eyed natives living amongst the local tribes."

"Fascinating," I remarked. "But I was unable to find any living inhabitants in the year that I visited. More the like, I think that

Pishqu was met by another time-traveler, or perhaps even captured by the Lyrans."

"That is certainly possible," he allowed, "though you should know that 'croatoan' is connected to a number of other mysterious disappearances in the same universe. For one, the word was written in the logbook of the *Carroll A. Deering* which washed ashore with its entire crew gone missing. For another, it was scribbled in the notebook of the aviatrix Emelia Earhart, who also vanished without a trace. Then there was the case of the famous highwayman Black Bart, who etched it onto the wall of his cell and was never seen again. Even Edgar Allen Poe plays a cameo role in this strange affair."

This caught me unawares. "The poet and mystery writer?"

"The same," he answered. "Apparently, it was the last thing that he uttered on his deathbed. So you see, 'croatoan' is a term which is enshrouded in mystery."

"Unquestionably," I acceded. "Though I vastly prefer my theory. It at least, offers up some chance."

Our meeting concluded at this juncture, and rather than return to my quarters where I would only be surrounded by uncertainties, I elected to embark on a constitutional around the perimeter of the base. Eventually, this brought me to a lovely little pond bounded by a grove of cycads.

To be sure, it was no Hyde Park, but still, it allowed me a place in which to enjoy the shade and admire some truly impressive examples of the giant dragonfly, *Libellulium,* While they were not the monsters of the Carboniferous era, they were still large enough to deal out a rather painful bite, thus compelling me to activate the repeller field from a device attached to my belt. Once within its protection, I was then afforded the opportunity to enjoy their presence without concern for my safety.

The species that called this area their home were quite lovely, being colored the most amazing and perfect shade of blue that I had ever beheld. The sight of them caught my breath and lent me the equanimity that I had so hoped to obtain.

Perhaps, this was what she had been waiting for, for after a moment, the dragonflies halted in midair and the world went still. I knew immediately that my mother had just joined me.

"Pishqu will not be found," she stated, coming to my side.

I turned to regard her. "How do you know that for a certainty? What has happened to her?"

My mother smiled. "I know it the same way that I know anything else, my daughter. As for the 'what', I shall tell you, for it is yet another important component of your learning. Croatoan is not an island, nor the name of an aboriginal tribe—though they adopted it out of respect for what it truly was."

"And what was that?"

"The Unknowable itself," she said. "That which is undefinable. Some have called it the Nagual, while others described it as a thing which is beyond the ability of any language to adequately convey.'

"Croatoan is a force that exists at the very border between all of the worlds. It is the knife edge between dreams and waking--a living doorway--that chooses when and where it will open. And once inside of it, there is no return. All who enter are irreversibly changed. I tell you that Pishqu is no more; she has become part of It, and It, of her."

"Then you are saying that she is dead," I concluded.

She shook her head. "No. She is simply not Pishqu any longer, but *It*. That is not the lesson though.'

"What is, is this; the only ones who can survive such a thing, and emerge intact, are those who can direct their consciousness past what they believe themselves to be, to what they truly are. They must embody that which is beyond all mundane conception of beingness in favor of their higher self, and divorced from all worldly concerns. The Spanish have a saying that applies here. It is *'Ser en el Mundo, pero non del Mundo', 'To be in the world, but not of the world.'*"

I shook my head. "I do not understand you, mother."

"Alas," she observed sadly. "You do not. Suffice it to say, that there are things in the nine universes that cannot be adequately described, and yet still manage to exist. Croatoan is one such."

"Then do you intend to create another iteration of Pishqu?" I inquired.

"No," she told me. "Though the Phaseship detachment at Avalon could surely recreate her, she will not be reborn."

"Whyever not? Surely we still need pilots to fight the Lyran menace."

My mother nodded. "We do at that, and we will obtain what we need. Pishqu however, will not be among their number. Her case is a unique one; we need her exactly where she is now, and for reasons that will become plain at a later date. For now, suffice it to say that at this juncture, friends in the right places are just as important to us as fighters are."

I blinked, utterly mystified.

"But come," she invited. "Enough of Pishqu. Are you not more interested in Elizabeth?"

I straightened. "Yes! I am. What of her? Have you news?"

"Not I, but the Ladder," she answered. "The answer that you desire is there. Seek out its council."

This said, she dematerialized, and time resumed its normal stride.

The Ladder, I thought. Without hesitation, I turned and sprinted for my quarters. There, I found that a sixth image had changed.

Originally, it had depicted two angels, standing together and embracing one another. But presently, it seemed as if I could see myself and a woman that closely resembled Elizabeth, but although I tried, I could not be absolutely certain.

Suddenly weary beyond all endurance, I dropped to my knees, clenched my hands together, and looked up to the ceiling and thence, to God.

"I still do not know what I should call you," I whispered, "but I beseech you; cease playing with me. Return my love to me. Bring her back, safe and whole and well."

CHAPTER 5: The King of Mars

Wherein I revisit the Bermuda Triangle. Then, a journey to Mars and a worrisome discovery at Candor Chasma. After that, the defeat of the Lyrans, a meeting with American royalty, and I learn the sad fate of the New Berliners. I am then compelled to deliver terrible news to Manfred. and to remain sane, fulfil my promise to the Tigress.

That evening, I received a blessing of sorts (in that it afforded me the opportunity for a distraction). Manfred 1 arrived at my rooms to collect me, with news that a new mission had been assigned to us.

Again, operational security dictated that the Speakers were briefed in camera, and once this was complete, we took off in the moonlight, uncertain of our ultimate destination.

This proved to be in the 5th universe, and there, we joined three other wings and descended to sea level over the Gulf of Mexico, just west of Florida. We were also ordered to assume stealth mode.

"Having denied the Lyrans their moon-portals," Hamilket 2 told us, "we are now going to challenge their access to another means of transportation. Penelope, you should know this time and place quite well."

I did in fact recognize it. Having checked my screens, I had discovered that we had arrived on the exact date and time that Major Sixkiller and I had assisted the Confederate Navy in destroying the *Monitor*. Further, I could detect the presence of two Phaseships, which registered as none other than my Blackbird and the Major's vessel!

By the Great Nothingness, I thought, stunned by the implications of this. *I am in the same time and place as my doppelganger.*

Immediately, a conversation that I had once had with the Professor came to the forefront of my mind. It had occurred shortly after my Awakening, and our confabulation had centered on the nature of reality.

"The actions of parallelity and alternality work together to create the multiverse," I had proclaimed. *"Alternate timelines automatically come into play, and the two opposing forces never collide. An analogy would be a pair of oncoming trains that switch to separate tracks at the very last moment. The conflict simply cannot occur."*

"So, in summation, we could use broad terms and state that the multiverse preserves itself through the process of constant expansion and branching?" he had inquired.

"It does," I had stated.

And here was the undeniable proof of my assertion. Though there were two of me here, no great cataclysm had occurred. The universe had simply accommodated our joint presence and had gone on with its business while whistling a merry tune.

There was one feature of this event that found me at sea though; how it was that the 'other' Blackbird and Major Sixkiller's ship had not noticed an entire squadron of Phaseships. Even though we were cloaked, I knew that we were not invisible to machines of our own faction. When I gave voice to this, Hamilket promptly enlightened me.

"Prior to their mission, the AI's of both Phaseships were instructed to ignore our signatures," he explained, "and in anticipation of this very temporal intersection. So, we will allow them to do as they did, and not involve ourselves until the proper moment."

Thus, we watched in silence as my twin chased the Lyran. It was only when the disk had abandoned the *Monitor* to its fate and entered the vortex, that we were given permission to proceed.

"Follow them through the tunnel of fog," Hamilket instructed, and we did as he ordered, keeping well back from the Lyran, "and set your temporal fields to match mine."

We all did as he instructed, and the passage before us elongated, drawing itself out into infinity. And far ahead of us, the disk hurtled onwards, with my double and the Major in hot pursuit. However, it was not overly long before they became lost and the Lyran was alone—save for us, and we kept well back.

"A little something that we learned from our interrogation of the traitors, and from certain other clandestine assets," the Atlantean explained.

"The Lyrans still believe that we do not know how to use the Triangle vortex to travel as they do. But as you can see, they are quite incorrect." The satisfaction in his tone was quite plain and I daresay that I shared it.

But whiter are we bound? I wondered.

In due course I received my answer, and with it, a surprise. We came out of the fog into the 2nd universe, and the year 1952. However, we were not above the Earth at all, but well on our way to Mars.

After but a few minutes, the disk passed Phobos, the larger of the planet's two moons. There, I discovered that some sort of installation had been built on the surface of the satellite, though I could not hazard a guess as to its purpose.

Meantime, our quarry had descended into the thin Martian atmosphere, and was making for the great canyon system of Vallis Marinaris. It was not long before I apprehended its final destination; Candor Chasma, and the base that the *Thule Gesellschaft* had built and then abandoned.

As my readers will recall, this had been where we had delivered the population of New Berlin to begin a new life for themselves. And quite without willing it, my thoughts immediately turned to Ernst von Knectenburg, Greta, and the children that I had befriended.

Had the Lyrans discovered them? It seemed so, and I worried greatly over their fate.

At length, the disk landed and, in the process, I saw that the Martian base had undergone many changes. The last I had seen of it, it had been a rather smallish affair, no more than a central dome united to four 'L' shaped wings that together, formed a rather dusty swastika.

Though all of this was still in evidence, more domes and other pressurized structures had been added. Additionally, I observed communications towers and several batteries of anti-aircraft missiles, as well as what appeared to be energy-based weapons. In short, nothing that the former citizens of New Berlin would have ever desired, or constructed.

Out of caution, Hamilket ordered us to land on an unoccupied mesa, and once we had done so, launched his remote probes. These were not the fist-sized affairs that I was accustomed to, however. Rather, they were ultraminiaturized versions developed by Special Section, each one being only slightly larger than the head of a sewing needle.

Despite their diminutive size however, they proved to be the equal of the larger versions in every respect, delivering a perfect video feed as they flew along. Nay, it is more accurate to state that they were in fact superior to the standard oculon, coming equipped as they did with tiny stealth fields, and communicating with us by way of encrypted micro-burst transmissions.

Thus, they were completely invisible to our opposition, and I found myself becoming enjealoused of the Wing Leader and those operatives who worked for Special Section. Compared to these 'nanoculons' as they were called, my own reconnaissance robots now seemed hopelessly out of date, and painfully clumsy.

It was not overlong before the little robots sent us their first images of the complex. Or more precisely, of what they had encountered at the external airlocks. Here, warnings and instructions had been prominently posted.

What was peculiar about them was that they were in multiple languages, not merely German. There were also directives in Russian, English, and the script that I recognized as being Lyran, making it obvious that the base was inhabited by a multilingual group—and one that appeared to be friendly to our enemies.

My earlier sense of alarm only increased in magnitude at this discovery. I was now absolutely certain that something truly terrible had happened to the Antarctic refugees.

More minutes passed, and then our clandestine survey revealed what appeared to be a large underground mining facility. It was situated near the base, and it was here that I gained my first glimpse of the inhabitants, although the term 'inmates' would have been more appropriate.

Just then, the nanoculons were overflying a group of them as they exited from a large elevator. To the last, they were dressed in bulky green pressure suits, yet even so, I could not mistake the exhaustion in their gait, or their dejected air.

Nor could I ignore their guards. These figures were attired in grey pressure suits, marked out with white triskelions. They stood singly, or in small groups, watching the procession as it filed past, sometimes waving impatiently for its members to hurry up, or in one case, employing the butt end of a weapon to prod the unfortunate into compliance.

From their tall stature, and imperious demeanor, I knew that I was gazing at Lyrans. But a moment later, this was confirmed when a nanoculon came close enough to reveal the features of one guard through his faceplate.

His blond hair, and cold blue eyes were unmistakable, and he was beautiful in his masculine perfection, but in the same way that Lucifer the fallen angel had also been beautiful. His was an aura of utter pitilessness and casual cruelty. How it was that beings such as he, and Pleiadeans like myself, happened to enjoy a shared bloodline boggled my mind. Despite our outward similarities, we had nothing whatsoever in common.

Next, the nanoculon flitted to one of the people wearing the green armor, allowing me to see them just as clearly as I had their captors. The individual in question proved to be no demi-god like the guard, but a mortal, and quite human. Sheer weariness defined her; her cheeks were hollow, her skin pallid, and her eyes beheld only endless servitude. She was a slave in the purest form, lacking any hope of liberation from her toils save that which death might grant.

Is it any wonder, that I was immediately reminded of Tibet? Of my great error there? Or its horrific result?

In the interim, and having seen enough, Hamilket interrupted my ruminations with an announcement. "Special Action Teams are currently en route, and once they arrive, our mission will be to support their effort as they assault and capture the base. Until then, we are to standby, and continue to observe the enemy."

Perforce, all that I could do was abide in my cabin, while my darksome thoughts pricked at me like the pitchforks of medieval devils.

Mercifully, the Gamels were not long in coming. They arrived just after the advent of the Martian sunset and landed at the edge of the central mesa, fully cloaked. A second group did likewise at the mine.

The commandos that disembarked from these transports were attired in special armored pressure suits similar to that which the Lyran guards wore, save that they were black in color, and afforded them the ability to cloak themselves just as a Phaseship might. Thus, when they activated this feature and moved away from the Gamels, they were entirely invisible to the naked eye. The only indication of their presence came from the digital markers on my displays.

These men and women did not hurry, but moved with care and precision across the rocky ground until at last, they had positioned themselves at the airlocks and the anti-aircraft emplacements. Seeing them taking their places, the Tigress within me grew restive, aching to accompany them and share in the excitement of the impending battle.

This of course, was impossible; during our sojourn, Hamilket had assigned each of us our own targets, and all of them were to be attacked from the air. Therefore, the part that the Tigress and I were destined to play was quite limited in scope, and displeased with this restriction, she attempted to assert herself.

I, in turn, exerted my own will, forcing her back and insisting that she content herself with her lot. Our struggle was a brief one, and despite having forced a partial transformation upon me, she relented—albeit with great reluctance and no little protest.

Once this is over, I shall have to take us hunting, I resolved. *By way of apology, and as compensation.*

It had been far too long since she and I had gone off in search of adventure together, and both of us needed the respite. But the Jurassic, with its huge predators, was completely unsuited as neither of us had any wish for us to become someone else's dinner. Somewhere else would have to do.

Presently, Hamilket's voice came over the com. "All pilots; lift off and prepare to engage your targets."

Mine was a communications tower, and I followed my orders and ascended. After this, everything transpired very rapidly; the commandos sprang into action, detonating charges that rendered the anti-aircraft batteries inoperative, whilst the teams stationed at the airlock breached the doors and moved inside. I myself made short work of the tower, cutting its mast in half with my chronoguns so that its instrumentation fell away like a topped tree.

After that, it was all a matter of strafing and destroying what disks were parked on the mesa, and then assuming an overwatch. We also made a point to minimize our com traffic so as to keep the channels free for the Action Teams.

Their conversations were a replay of what I had heard during the operation to take Moberly, Missouri, filled as they were with shouted orders, calls for assistance, and gunfire. Yet I could tell from the progress of the icons on my screen, that our forces had managed to achieve complete surprise and were aggressively pressing their advantage.

For their part, the Lyrans offered up a stiff resistance, but slowly, their images winked out, one by one, 'till at last only ours remained. Then the "All Clear" was announced. After only a few minutes of ferocious fighting, the base was ours, as was the mine, and according to a secondary feed, the mysterious installation on Phobos had also fallen.

Here, I feel compelled to pause, and offer up some commentary. Many of my readers might be amazed by the speed of this assault, yet those with genuine combat experience will not be surprised in the least. They know, as well as I, that in any fight, the objective is *never* to prolong a battle, but to hit the opposition hard enough, and with enough force and speed, to subdue them before they can manage to respond effectively. Long, drawn-out duels are the stuff of melodramatic fiction, and not reality. Having said this, I shall now resume my tale.

Shortly after the Lyran holdings were taken, the Gamels returned, this time uncloaked, and instead of commandos, teams of specialists exited from their cargo bays. Their mission was to gather whatever useful intelligence they could, which in turn, inspired me to contact my Wing Leader.

"Sir," I said, "Since it is in our hands, I wish to enter the base. I should like to know what became of the New Berliners and render what aid I can."

I did not add that I also harbored the desperate hope that I would find some clues regarding Elizabeth, or perhaps, even the woman herself.

He took a moment to consider my petition, and then another to confer with the leader of the commando teams. Finally, he responded.

"You may do so, but the Team Leader insists that you be accompanied at all times. Although we control the base, there is still the possibility of encountering hidden dangers."

"Naturally, sir," I agreed.

"I'm of a mind t'go along with her," Major Sixkiller piped in.

Again, our leader contemplated the request, and weighed it against our operational requirements. "You may do so," he told her.

"Thank ya kindly," she replied.

We promptly left our orbits and landed near one of the breach-points. Given that our flightsuits were designed to function in the absolute vacuum of the No-When, the only preparation that we required was to seal our helmets and exit through our small airlocks.

A trio of commandos were awaiting us, and they escorted us inside the base. As it happened, most of the installation was still pressurized, so that after only a few meters, and a transition through a sealed interior door, we were able to remove our helmets.

"Have you found any of the citizens?" I asked the leader of our bodyguards. He was a huge Ostlander with a shocking head of red hair, and by the name printed on his armored suit, I deduced that he was called Thorsson.

"Not here," he answered. "Right now, the citizens are in their barracks at the mine. The only people that were here when we breached the locks were the Lyran *skiderikken*.

Though I did not understand the Danish term, it was impossible to miss the contempt in the Ostlander's tone and knew it for a vile insult.

"Then this is a barracks for the Lyrans then?" I questioned.

Thorsson nodded. "Yah, and also where they have their clones."

My heart leapt. *Elizabeth could be here,* I thought, *encased in a crystalline coffin.* "Take me to them."

The big commando shrugged and led us down a number of corridors. Some of these were wholly untouched, whilst others bore soot marks, bullet holes, and rust patches that bespoke of the recent firefights. And on more than one occasion, we were compelled to step over, or around the bodies of the dead Lyran defenders.

In my previous existence in the 3rd universe, sights like this would have disturbed me, but since becoming a Chrononaut, I had gradually become inured to such things, especially where the fallen were my enemies. The Major reacted likewise, merely accepting what we encountered without emotion.

But when we passed a number of plastic containers that had been neatly stacked against the wall, it was a far different matter. They were labeled, "Federal Emergency Management Agency", and I myself thought nothing of them. The Major though, reacted most vociferously.

"FEMA!" she swore, "I always knew those Yankee bastards were up t'no good! This fuckin cinches it."

Unfazed by her outburst, our escort was moving on, and not wishing to be left behind, I urged Cassie back into motion. Though she regarded the boxes with an expression of contempt (and muttered angrily under her breath), she complied.

Eventually, her fury dissipated, and we arrived at a passage whose sign announced that it led to the clone storage area. Despite a quadrilingual message warning that access to the area was restricted, the portal, which otherwise guarded it against intrusion, stood ajar, having been blown forcefully off its hinges.

Inside, groups of specialists were busily examining the containers and the clones within them. These were all Lyran, and I was gladsome that they were so imprisoned.

"Is there any more to see?" I asked our guide. He nodded and took us to a side chamber. It was labeled "Transshipment" and its door had also been breached. Stepping past him, I entered, hoping that this would be where I would find my lover at last.

The room itself proved to be small and held only six containers. But none of them housed any Lyrans, nor Elizabeth. Instead, they were occupied by six human males.

The nearest I recognized with immediate distaste; it was none other than a copy of Adolph Hitler. His neighbor was also familiar, being Napoleon Bonaparte.

The others however, were complete mysteries and I endeavored to read their labels. Though I failed to decipher the Lyran portion, the English and Cyrillic parts were quite clear.

According to the placards, a third coffin contained a rough looking Asian fellow named Atilla the Hun. His neighbor was listed as being John Wayne, and next to him was a mullato, who was simply referred to as 'Prince'. But it was the sixth man, Elvis Presley, that caused Major Sixkiller to become quite animated.

"My God, Penny!" Sixkiller exclaimed, pointing towards him emphatically. "Do ya'll know who this is?"

Gazing at the figure, I shook my head in negation. "I am certain that I have no idea."

"Why this's the *King!*" she informed me, as if this fact should have been patently obvious.

"The *King?*"

"Yes!", she said. "The King. And that's the Duke and Prince!"

They were royalty of some kind, I realized. Then, in a flash it came to me; they were also Americans. *American nobility*.

I immediately rounded on her. "Ah hah! Clearly, you Colonials finally saw the light of reason and set a proper monarchy to rule over you. It certainly took you long enough."

"No," she corrected laughingly. "Ya'll don't understand, Penny. Not *that* King or that kinda Duke. *The* King. *The* Duke—and well, Prince. They're all here—and as close to alive as anyone could be in a set-up like this."

She walked up to the American King and gazed rapturously at him. "Elvis! And here we all thought he was dead and gone. Come on—we gotta get him out."

Without waiting to see if I concurred or not, she began searching for some form of release mechanism. Not knowing what else to do, I joined her, and in the process of our hunt, she explained his true social status as the 'King of Rock and Roll' (whatever *that* was) and then the standing of Mr. Wayne and Mr. Prince. To my shock, I learned that they were not blue-bloods at all, but mere commoners. Entertainers in fact!

If anything, this made Sixkillers fervor to liberate King Elvis all the more inexplicable. In my century, and also in the 19th century of the second universe, performers of any kind, while providing welcome diversions from the vicissitudes of life, were not considered to be members of polite society, much less persons of any stature, or political influence. Rather, they occupied a lower class all their own, and were generally regarded as people of loose morals and doubtful virtue.

The idea that the American culture had elevated such figures to be the equals of their wealthiest and wisest men—nay, even to award them a place *above* them—was positively mind-boggling (and only emphasized the depths to which the Colonies had sunk after their so-called War of Independence).

Presently, we located the controls to Elvis' chamber and the Major entered the commands. After a moment, the container opened, King Elvis blinked, looked about him, and sat up.

"Elvis? How're ya'll feelin?" Sixkiller asked, sounding more to my ears like a breathless teenager than a grown woman.

The King regarded her uncomprehendingly, and then at last, he answered. "Lord almighty, I feel my temperature rising. Higher and higher, it's burning through to my soul."

By this, I took him to mean that he felt unwell, and I turned and shouted to the corridor. "Medic! We require a medic here!"

"Girl, girl, girl," Elvis continued, "You gonna set me on fire. My brain is flaming. I don't know which way to go. I'm just a hunka hunka burnin love."

"I am certain that you are, Your Majesty" I assured him. "I am also equally convinced that once the medics have had a chance to examine you, that your condition will be rectified posthaste."

The paramedics arrived right on the heels of this, examined the King, and found him to be sound, at least as far as his general health went. The status of his mind however, was very much in doubt.

"Penny," Sixkiller ventured, "I think somthin went wrong with his deep freeze."

"I should say so," I agreed. Just then, he reminded me of King Ludwig of Bavaria; an amiable enough gentleman, but as mad as a hatter.

"What about the others?" she asked.

I was about to tell her that they could wait (especially where it concerned Hitler and Napoleon, who could stay frozen forever as far as I was concerned) when we were joined by none other than Lady Anne, Colonel Ambrose and oddly, my clone, Louise.

The trio paused briefly before the case containing John Wayne, and then moved on to Hitler, eyeing him with great interest.

"I see some potential value in this copy," Lady Anne commented. "Perhaps an idiot version to disrupt things in 1940?"

Her companions nodded, and after some whispered discussion amongst themselves, finally deigned to notice us.

"King Elvis will be looked after," she informed us. "In the interim, you should make for the mines, Penelope. Your presence has been requested there, and I think that you will greatly appreciate the Major's company before your visit is complete."

Even as she said this, a new set of medics arrived, and gently escorted the befuddled King away.

What we encountered at the mine, or more correctly, the quarters housing the mineworkers, is hard for me to describe without difficulty, even now. They consisted of large pressurized modules, linked together by access tubes, and contained great communal spaces. These were surrounded by catwalks and observation stations which looked down upon row after row of metal beds stacked two high.

The only decoration in the chamber that we visited was a motto, painted on a wall where all could see it, and in stark black characters as high as an average-sized man. It was in German.

"Gehorsam ist Arbeit," it exhorted. *"Arbeit ist Leben. Das Leben ist Gehorsam,"*, "Obedience is Work. Work is Life. Life is Obedience."

This was no living space, but a prison dormitory of the lowest order. The air which assaulted my senses reeked with the sour odor of unwashed bodies, fecal matter and urine.

The inmates themselves were a wretched lot, universally attired in green jumpsuits that hung off their thin bodies like rags on abandoned scarecrows. Despite the fact that I wore the uniform of a Chrononaut, and smiled in reassurance, my resemblance to their former captors made more than a few of them shrink away. These people had learned the true meaning of terror, I apprehended, and mere expressions of friendliness could not erase this legacy.

Some though, were beyond any capacity for dread. They lay quietly on their thin mattresses, too weak to move, and their eyes filled with the acceptance of their own impending doom. One thing was absent from this grim tableau, however; I saw no children among the prisoners, nor any of the elderly.

Cold fingers went down my spine at this, and then a medic walked up. "Ms. Steele? Major Sixkiller? We were told that you were coming. She's been asking after you."

"She?" I inquired.

The man nodded. "Yes. She said that she knew you back in New Berlin. She wants to see you."

Before I could make any further inquiry, he turned and took us to a space between the lines of beds that seemed to serve as a common gathering area. There, the medics had established an aid station of sorts, and were ministering to the internees as best they could. A crowd had gathered around them, and it was from this mass, that a figure detached itself.

Even though she was but a malnourished shadow of what she had once been, I was still able to recognize her. It was Greta. In New Berlin, she had been the caretaker of a pair of orphaned children.

"You came," she said tonelessly. "At the beginning, I prayed every day and every night that you would come for us. Then I gave up asking God for help, and now, you are finally here."

"The children?" I asked, already afraid to hear the answer.

She looked to a point somewhere over my shoulder, seeing not the barracks, but the bitter past. "They are gone," she answered. Her voice was that of a woman who had endured so much misery that she hadn't any emotion left to spare.

"When the Lyrans came, they took all the little ones, all the old people, anyone who could not work, and shoved them out of the airlocks."

I could scarcely ask my next question. "And Ernst? Major von Knectenberg?"

Greta shook her head. "Dead. They killed him when he demanded that we be treated humanely."

Her gaze shifted to a point on the floor not far from where we stood. It bore a dark stain that I instinctively recognized as old blood, a mute testimony to the murder that had been done there.

"He died right there," she stated. "They made an example of him for the rest of us to see."

"I did not know," I said, my voice and my will finally faltering, "Had I been aware…"

Major Sixkiller placed a comforting hand upon my shoulder. "Ya'll couldn't've known, Penny. This isn't your fault. It's the damned Lyrans. Ya'll did what you thought was right."

Impulsively, I grabbed at the sleeve of a nearby medic. "I beg you, do what you can for these poor people."

Then to Greta, "I am so terribly, terribly sorry."

"There is something else," she stated. "It was Ernst's, and we kept it hidden from the Lyrans."

Without verifying if I was following, she turned on her heels and made her way down a row of beds, halting when she reached what I presumed was her sleeping place. There, she pulled and twisted on one of the metal pipes that made up its headboard until it popped off. Then she reached into the cavity with her fingers. When at last, she found what she had been searching for, she drew it out for me to see. It was a knife, carefully wrapped in plastic.

"He would have wanted you to have this," she told me, thrusting it into my hand. Of course, I took it, and before I could ask her any questions about it, or offer up more apologies, she walked away without ever looking back.

Unable to bear another moment of this dreadful place, I sought out the exit. Escape however, was not an option, for as I neared it, I encountered H'reep and several of her fellow Speakers.

They had paused there and were looking about them in shock. Though I had not known that their kind were capable of it, tears as profound as any human's were streaming down their feathered faces.

"Benee," H'reep asked, her chirps tremulous. "How is it that your kind can do this to one another?"

We are monsters to her now, I thought with no little dismay. Worse, she was correct. We *were* monsters.

"I cannot account for the evil that lurks within our hearts," I told her," be it Lyran, or Pleiadean, or Human. It is simply there, and we must struggle against its temptations every day of our lives. In the end, some of us are simply too weak to resist."

"It is a terrible thing, this evil of yours," H'reep observed. "And I wonder if someday, your kind might visit it's like upon us."

"I would never let that happen," I vowed, but knowing the sad history of humankind, and the Lyran inclination towards barbarity as well as I did, my words were delivered without any real conviction.

Utterly ashamed of all who were like me, I could say no more, and pushed my way past her and out of the barracks.

I retreated to the solitude of an unused storage chamber, and there, agonized over what I had just witnessed. *This is my fault,* I told myself. *My mistake. It was my choice that led to all this.*

The sound of someone clearing their throat interrupted my self-castigation, and looking up, I beheld Major Singh.

"I know what you are telling yourself," he said. "You are blaming yourself for this."

"Yes!" I snapped. "I am. This is all my doing. Had I not sent these people here, this never would have happened. None of it!"

He nodded. "I understand. And I was once in the very same situation."

"You were?"

"Yes. It was in Burma, and before I became a Chrononaut," he explained. "We received word that a Japanese motorized column was headed for the Sittang river, and we scrambled our fighters along with the bombers.'

"What we did not know was that our reconnaissance had been wrong; the Japanese had no such vehicles, and the men that we were sent to attack were actually part of the 17th Indian Division. The casualties that we inflicted on them were terrible, and it was only when we returned to our airbase that we learned the truth."

"How awful," I sympathized.

"For a time, I blamed myself for the deaths of those soldiers. But eventually, I came to understand that I had only acted upon what I knew, and that the fault lay elsewhere.'

"But that is not the lesson that I would teach you today, Penelope. Instead, it is this; despite my misplaced guilt, the very next day, I arose from my bunk, and took to the air once again. I shouldered my burden, and carried on.'

"*That* is what a true warrior does. And why? Because these people, and many others like them, depend on stalwarts like you and I to remain strong, and to fight for them, for they surely cannot fight for themselves."

This said, he turned, and left me. For a time, I pondered his words, and although I could not free myself of my sense of culpability, I appreciated his wisdom. Accordingly, when Major Sixkiller found me at last, and informed me that my presence had been requested for a briefing, I straightened my uniform, and followed her with resolute steps, determined to do my job as best I could. It was the least that I could do for Greta and her people. As for absolution, it would have to wait.

The Major showed me into what had once been a conference room for the Lyrans. Their disgusting triskelion insignia had been unceremoniously ripped from the wall, and Lady Anne and her companions sat beneath the blemish, facing us as we came in.

She addressed Major Sixkiller first. "Major, you have an assignment. Your task will be to transport King Elvis from here to the city of Las Vegas, where you will meet with members of the Fellowship, and once you have done turned him over to them, you will return here straightaway."

"What's gonna happen to him?" the Major asked.

"His memories of this place will be erased, and he will be comfortably ensconced in a new life," she informed her.

Sixkiller nodded. "Yes, ma'am."

"Very good," our hostess said. "You are dismissed. Penelope, you are to remain. We have business to discuss."

Cassie and I exchanged glances, and she shrugged, as if to say *'darned if I know what's up'*.

When she had departed, Colonel Ambrose steepled his fingers together and smiled at me. "Because you are in training to become one of the Masters, it was decided that you should play a larger role in the operational side of things. By necessity, this entails a greater disclosure of the facts than what the average Chrononaut might be privy to—even one as steadfast as the Major. I am sure you can understand our reasoning; operational security must always be of paramount importance."

"Go on," I invited.

"First, there is the matter of King Elvis, and the other entertainers. While we were perusing the Lyran database, we were able to determine the reason for their incarceration. Apparently, Mr. Presley, Mr. Wayne, and the man known as Prince Rogers Nelson, were all involved with the Illuminati, who saw them as useful tools for manipulating the public."

I was caught entirely unawares by this. "The Illuminati? Did we not defeat them in the 19th century?" It had certainly seemed so at the time.

"No", he sighed. "Only the London toffs. The organization itself managed to survive, and eventually, established itself in the heart of the American entertainment industry. You see, my dear, their Lyran masters taught them a lesson that they took very much to heart; it is that perception, not knowledge, that is the key to power, and those who can control perceptions, control society."

"I see," I replied. "Then those men are all Illuminati agents."

"No," Lady Anne corrected. "They are all *ex*-Illuminati agents. Each one, and for different reasons, became disaffected with the organization, and either threatened to expose them, or earned themselves a reputation for unreliability.'

"This was certainly the case with another would-be turncoat, a Ms. Marilyn Monroe, but unlike her, they were not murdered to ensure their silence. Rather, their deaths were staged, and they were brought here."

"To what end?"

"To discover the qualities that made them so appealing to the masses," the Colonel supplied. "and with an eye towards creating new celebrities who would achieve the same lofty heights, yet never betray their masters."

Again, I was struck dumb by the level of influence that entertainers had been allowed to wield in the latter part of the 20th century (and equally gratified that my era had been wise enough to discourage this practice).

"What of Mr. Wayne and the Prince then?" I queried. "What will be their fate?"

"As they have no intelligence value to us, they will be treated in the same manner as King Elvis; they will have their pertinent memories erased, and then be relocated to new universes where they won't be able to cause anyone any trouble."

I merely bobbed my head. This seemed a sensible solution.

"Now, to weightier issues," Ambrose continued. "Specifically, the matter of Mars; according to what we were able to discern, the Lyrans and their American and Russian partners, arrived here some two years after the New Berliners took occupancy of the base."

At this juncture, I was sorely tempted to ask to be excused. The subject matter was still too fresh for me to confront. But I did not, and reminded myself of my recent vow. *Carry on,* I told myself. *Carry on.*

So instead, I asked, "In 1949? I thought that they did not land on Mars until the 1960's. That is what Mr. Laske's book indicated."

"Disinformation," Colonel Ambrose explained, "created to distract anyone who might have otherwise learned the truth, including poor Mr. Laske. I must confess that I myself, believed the same lie --until the records proved otherwise, which just goes to show that any of us can be gulled by a clever enough deception.'

He shrugged in self-deprecation, and added, "As it is, the only genuine landings that humanity has ever managed to pull off without any assistance were on the moon, and those were only allowed to go forwards to distract the public from the real show. Like the space shuttle, they were pure theater."

"Colonel?" Lady Anne interrupted, "mightn't we return to the main subject?"

"Yes, quite right," he hastily agreed. "As I mentioned, the Lyrans and their allies invaded Mars in '49. Of course, the New Berliners were no match for them, and once subjugated, they were used to build the barracks and dig the mines. Because of the harsh treatment that they received at the hands of their overlords, no more than 4,000 of the original 100,000 settlers remain alive today."

Hearing this, my hard-won self-control began to slip away, and I felt my fangs growing out. *'Why?!* What could this place and these people offer them?"

"Cheap labor for one," he said, "and natural resources that could be gathered well away from any prying eyes on Earth, which in turn could be used to construct...this."

He pushed a small plastic envelope across the desk to me. It contained a tiny square, scarcely 5 millimeters wide, and composed of a milk-white substance. It also had a length of wire depending from it that seemed thinner than a human hair.

"And *this* is?"

"An ultraminiaturized microchip," Lady Anne stated. "Built in their factory on Phobos so as to take advantage of its perfect vacuum. Its purpose is to be united with a device that will not exist for another sixty-six years, though I think that you will be quite familiar with it." With this, she reached into her tunic and produced a common smart phone.

She was quite correct. I had first become acquainted with this dubious technology when Bookman Pierce had taken me to the Seattle of the 20th century. Since then, I had come to regard it with a certain measure of revulsion. While it provided many entertaining diversions, and allowed for easy communications, it had also contributed to the erosion of human interaction and the inexorable decay of their society.

"Married to this chip, the smart phone and other internet devices, become a transmitter which can send its signal to those parts of the human brain that govern imagination, and free will. It can then override them with whatever message that the NSA, or other allied agencies, care to broadcast. Though at this stage, precisely what those messages might consist of remains a mystery that we intend to ferret out."

At this juncture, I felt compelled to interpolate. "Madame, I was of the belief that this objective had already been accomplished through the use of modified vaccines. At Auschwitz, Mr. Grey boasted that by the end of the 20th century, the human population would be completely dominated though this means. Is this not so?"

"Not entirely," she responded. "Though he and his Nazi chums did achieve a great deal, their results have not been quite as grandiose as he claimed. The man *is* given to a certain amount of puffery after all.'

"In truth, while the vaccines that they created will weaken the human spirit and seriously degrade its capacity for innovation, they will not completely overcome all segments of the population, due in part to varying reactions to the sera.'

"*This,* however, is far more effective, and it will not face resistance from any portion of society—even the so-called anti-vaxxers. By 2020, *everyone* will simply *have* to have a smart phone, and as a result, 75 percent of the world's population will become connected.'

"And that number will only increase annually, 'til at last it reaches 100 percent. Then, the combination of doctored vaccines, and devices equipped with these little chips, will virtually ensure Lyran victory."

"Unless something conspires to overturn their efforts," I growled, determined to be this very 'something'.

"Quite so," she grinned. "There is already an effort under way to develop special 'apps' that will defeat the Lyran chips and render the phones harmless."

When she saw the ignorance writ plain on my face, she added, "Software, my dear. Composed so as to block the chip from making any transmissions, but without impairing the phone itself."

I nodded. "Is that it then?"

"For now," Colonel Ambrose replied.

I however, was *not* finished. Having endured this meeting as I had, I felt entitled to some recompense.

"Then *I* have something to discuss. I should like to know what you discovered about Elizabeth. Did you find anything in the database concerning her whereabouts?"

Lady Anne answered. "We know that she visited here with Mr. Grey, and based on this and other sightings, it would seem that they are working together on a fairly regular basis. There were also some location references that we are still puzzling out, and if they are what we think they are, then we may—I say *may*—be able to determine the location of his lair."

"Tell me the moment that you learn anything."

"Of course," she agreed affably.

Without bothering to excuse myself, I promptly left the room, glad to be shut of it. The events of the day had left me utterly drained, and all I desired just then was sleep. Restful, healing sleep.

Accordingly, I returned to my Phaseship, and once there, reclined my chair and closed my eyes.

My mind however was not inclined towards unconsciousness, and I soon became embroiled in a mental review of all my problems and self-recriminations. After an hour or so of this inner torment, I finally resorted to a draught of laudanum, wherein I was transported at last into the comforting realm of utter nothingness.

My unknowing bliss continued 'till at last, I began my return to wakefulness, and there, the nightmares, having patiently lain in wait for me, came in full force.

I saw myself walking among the bunks in the mineworker's barracks, passing the dead and the dying, yet not as a Chrononaut, but in the grey armor of a Lyran. Worse, I soon met with another such as I, and to my shock, I realized that I was looking upon Elizabeth.

As I cried out and reached for her, she brought down the polarized shield on her helmet, blocking my view of her features so that I was left with naught but a reflection of myself and what was behind me.

It was not the barracks though. Rather, it was an image of Saturn's rings as seen from space, and as is the manner of dreams, I was instantly conveyed to that very location, and then felt myself being pulled towards the nameless evil that resided there.

But I never reached it. Instead, I awoke, feeling no more refreshed than I had when I had first laid myself down. And although

117

the Sibyl had not made an appearance during this vision, I was certain that she had had a hand in the disturbance.

When will she put an end to this, and reveal her true purpose? I wondered tiredly. *And when will I finally be allowed to enjoy my share of peace?*

Hours later, Major Sixkiller returned from her assignment, having conveyed King Elvis to Las Vegas in the year 1979, and some two years after his ersatz death. By her account, plans were in progress to establish him as, of all things, an 'Elvis Impersonator'.

While I had no idea how lucrative such an endeavor might prove, she was quite sanguine about his prospects and greatly satisfied with the outcome.

This said, she and I remained at the Martian base for another two days. During this interval, we assisted our forces with whatever tasks they set for us, which included ferrying in medical supplies and food.

I also summoned up the courage to examine the dagger that Greta had given me. When I did so, I discovered that it was not a Nazi weapon at all, and mystified, I sought her out, hoping that she could explain its provenance to me. But she refused to converse on this, or any other subject, and I was compelled to seek out one of Von Knectenberg's former comrades for the details.

From him, I learned that the weapon actually hearkened back to a time before the First World War, and had been a symbol of honor among the members of the *Bayerische Automobil und Flugzeug Club*, the Bavarian Aero and Automobile Corps.

Moreover, he disclosed that it had originally been owned by none other than Von Knectenberg's father, who had served as a pilot, first in the Corps, and then in the Great War itself. It had been he who had encouraged his son's interest in flying, steering him first to gliders, and then into joining the Luftwaffe. And when he had come of age at last, Ernst had inherited the blade.

Given all this, it was easy for me to appreciate the inspiration behind Ernst's love of flying, and why the blade had been so precious to him. So much so in fact, that according to my source, he had eschewed the wearing of the SS Dagger in its favor, thus compounding the enmity of his fascist superiors.

To be completely candid, I *had* seen it on his belt during our meeting in the Antarctic, but at the time, I had simply presumed it to be nothing more than another bit of National Socialist frippery, and thus, had ignored it in favor of more pressing issues. But now that I knew the truth, I took pains to give it the honor that it deserved by adding it to my own belt.

I also took the time to visit his grave, and that of the others who had perished under Lyran rule. The makeshift cemetery had been located some ways away from the mine, and on a rise that overlooked Candor Chasma.

It was a dismal place, with markers improvised from discarded pieces of plastic piping, and the names of the deceased had been etched onto their surfaces with crude metal tools. But Von Knechtenberg's final resting place had been made as grand as his people could manage, having affixed an extra sheet of plastic to the PVC cross.

This bore the legend; *Major Ernst von Knechtenberg, our guide across the wilderness of space and beloved leader. 5 May 1917-14 June 1949.*

That I wept when I read this simple epitaph should come as no surprise at all to you, dear reader. Nor that I worried greatly at how the news of his brother's death would affect Manfred when at last he heard of it. I also dreaded being the bearer of that awful message, but although Lady Anne and the Colonel had indicated their willingness to relay it for me, I had refused them.

It was my burden, and mine alone.

In the interim, there were larger issues that transcended my small tragedy, and they concerned those New Berliners who had managed to survive the Lyran occupation. While their condition remained dire (and would be for some time to come), a substantial effort had been made towards improving their situation.

Moreover, on the day that the Major and I departed, it was announced that they would be receiving regular aid from the Masters, and that their community would be under our protection from this point onwards, first by veteran forces, and later by a special, dedicated squadron.

Mars would become off-limits to the Americans, the Russians, and especially, the Lyrans. This in no way compensated the New Berliners for their suffering, but it did offer the promise of a brighter future, free of molestation.

The Saurii Speakers however, were another matter altogether. Their visit to the barracks, and the conditions that they had witnessed there, had left them all badly shaken, and only the most earnest of efforts by Lady Anne and the Colonel had managed to convince them to remain with us.

H'reep however, was the sole exception. She had had enough of our kind, and had announced that she would be leaving our service to return to her home forthwith.

Although another Speaker would take her place (for there was still no shortage of volunteers), I made a point of requesting that I be excused from the responsibility of partnering with them.

Despite what Major Singh had said, I still felt that the disaster that was Mars had been due to my actions, and I had no wish to be responsible for inflicting any future traumas upon another innocent. I had done more than enough of that already.

For once, I was not grateful for the Ebani's ability to deliver me instantly to the Jurassic, for it only meant that I would have to face my unhappy chore all the sooner.

Fortifying myself, I exited Blackbird and walked resolutely into the main dome. There, I did not allow myself to tarry, knowing that if I did so, that it would be a titanic struggle to convince myself to resume my journey.

When at last, I stood before the door to Manfred's quarters, I briefly contemplated simply turning around and petitioning the Hamilkets for aid, but immediately reproved myself for such naked cowardice. So instead, I drew in a deep breath to fortify my nerves and rapped upon the portal.

It was Manfred 1 who answered. "Penelope? You are back from your mission then?" Behind him, I could see Ziva 1, regarding me with undisguised loathing.

"Yes," I said. "May I come in?"

He looked over his shoulder at his mate, and although she crossed her arms to indicate that I was not welcome, she turned and walked out of the room.

"Yah," he replied. "For a moment."

"You may wish to seat yourself," I warned. "I have some terrible news to deliver."

"What is it?" he asked, his expression anxious.

"Please, I beg you, seat yourself." He complied, taking his place in a large armchair.

"It is about your brother, Ernst."

"What about him? Has something happened?"

I nodded, suddenly finding it hard to form an intelligible sentence. "He is …no more…the Lyrans…"

Manfred's eyes misted over as comprehension dawned. "He is dead then?"

"Yes," I replied. "I am so terribly sorry…"

But Manfred just sat there, saying nothing. Then, he slowly lowered his head and began to sob. As I went to him, hoping to offer up what comfort I could, Ziva reentered the room. She immediately interposed herself and shoved me back into the hall.

"Go away," she snapped. "All you ever bring us is pain, you Nazi bitch!"

Before I could make any reply, she slammed the door in my face.

Of a sudden, my entire world seemed to go into a spin, and my head felt as if it were about to burst wide open. Everything; my worries over Elizabeth, all of the terrible things that I had witnessed on Mars, and now this, came crashing down upon me in one great, black wave that threatened to overcome me.

I have to get out of here, I thought desperately. *I cannot take any more of this. I simply must go somewhere to think! To breathe!*

I had reached my absolute limit. Turning away from Manfred's quarters, I headed directly for the Hamilket's office.

"Sirs," I said when I entered, "I must have permission to depart. I—I cannot remain here. I find that I require---that I require—some--time for myself. Right away."

"Ya'll'd better let her," a voice suggested from behind me. It was Major Sixkiller, and I knew that she had witnessed the exchange betwixt myself and Ziva.

Hamilket 1 rose from his desk. "I have heard about Manfred's brother. You cannot blame yourself for that, Penelope. Perhaps the chance to talk with someone would help—the Professor, or perhaps a trained councilor. Special Section could provide you with--"

"No!" I snapped, knowing as I did so that I was beginning to transform. "I simply need time away from all this! I beseech you, let me go! I cannot abide here for one more moment."

My Wing Leader looked to the Major as if for support. But she said, "It'd be better if we did it her way."

He considered this. Then he acquiesced. "Very well. I will unlock Blackbird, but you will take the Major with you."

"No!" I shouted, dragging a clawed hand across the desk and leaving deep gouges in the wood. "*Alone!* I must go alone."

"Alone, Hamilket," Cassie maintained. "Blackbird'll make sure she returns safe n'sound. It'll all be fine."

He took in the damage that I had just inflicted on his desk and prudently nodded. "Yes, alone then."

Without thanking him, I turned on my heels, went to the tarmac and thence to Blackbird. Realizing that it was I, she opened the egress hatch and I stormed up the stairs.

"Away!" I cried. "Take me away from here."

"Where should we go, Penny?" she asked.

I blurted out the very first thing that came into my fevered mind. "The 2nd universe, by way of the Jump Worlds. I will decide the rest once we have arrived."

Our subsequent journey into the No-When and then the Jump Worlds themselves, was as harrowing as my readers might well imagine, yet its unpleasantness proved a welcome distraction in the same manner that a scourge might have eased the mind of a medieval monk. Thus, by the time we had reached more modern times, and had transitioned across the River of Time from the 10th to the 2nd universe, my madness had largely receded.

"Destination?" Blackbird inquired.

Without summoning it, the vow that I had made to take the Tigress hunting came to mind, and with it, a tremendous sense of longing.

Yes, I thought. *The thrill of the hunt, of wild spaces, unencumbered by any human concerns. That is what I require! That is where I will find my solace.*

"Siberia," I told her, "and as far away from Mankind as we can possibly manage."

"What year?"

I pondered this carefully. Though the region was one of the most remote on any of the nine Earths, it still had its share of problems.

Accordingly, I called up a file that provided me with a summary of historical events.

To my disappointment, I learned that in the early 13ᵗʰ century, the Mongols had invaded the area and subjugated its native peoples. Then later, Ivan the Terrible and his forces had made a nuisance of themselves in their insatiable lust for sable. After that, the Communists had arrived, bringing with them the despicable system of gulags.

In sum, there were only a few points in the record that were relatively free of conquerors, and their violence. I chose the best of these.

"The 12ᵗʰ century," I announced. "Somewhere along the Amur River."

At this stage in the timeline, I knew that the region would be sparsely populated, and only by local indigenes, particularly the Nanai and Ulchi peoples. These were a simple folk, earning their living from what the forests and the great river could provide. More importantly, they embraced a shamanic religion that venerated nature, and especially the spirits of *Doonta* the Bear and *Amba,* the Tiger. Hence, I was confident that I would have no trouble from them, and all the solitude that I desired.

"Very well, Penny," Blackbird assented. With this, the Phaseship banked and began its descent into the River of Time.

Not long after, we arrived in the century and landed in an open space among the trees. There, I left my pilot's seat and shed my flightsuit.

"Remain concealed until I call for you," I ordered, now entirely naked. "I cannot say how long I shall be."

"N'che Sedem," my AI responded. "I will await your call."

With our business attended to, I opened the egress hatch and stepped out into the Siberian winter, taking in a deep breath of the forest's perfume, and then, with the same ease that I had just shed my garments, I let the Tigress take custody.

In but a second, I had fully transformed, and without so much as a backwards glance at my Phaseship, I ran on all fours for the tree line, eager to begin the hunt, and for a time, enjoy the opportunity to leave my human life, and all of its complications, well behind me.

A full week followed, and the seventh night found me well sated. But an hour earlier, I had brought down a deer, and although it had been a bit thin, the taste of it had still seemed finer to me than the choicest *Filet Mignon*. Nor could any human dining experience rival the sheer pleasure of breaking its bones in my powerful jaws and licking out the tender marrow, itself tastier than any goose liver paté.

I do not expect my human readers to appreciate this, but those who are shapeshifters like myself, will fully grasp the pleasure that I derived from this simple repast, and perchance, long for the same thing. To these worthies, I extend my heartfelt good wishes for a successful hunt, and an equally wonderful dining experience.

But of course, I have digressed again, and beg my audience, both human and *were*, to overlook my meanderings and remain patient with me as I resume my tale, for there is still much of it to tell.

Well-fed as I was, I left what remained of the carcass and prowled a stand of birch, stopping every so often to rub against a trunk, and then add a splash of urine so as to stake my claim upon the place.

You see, I had found this location to be very much to my liking, and perforce, I was not inclined to share it with any other tiger. As a rule, felines both large and small do not subscribe to the human notion of 'sharing'. What was mine, was mine--and just to underscore the seriousness of my claim, I also took the time to leave deep scratches in a few of the larger trees with my claws.

Confident that others of my kind would grasp the significance of this visual message, and stay well away, I moved on, hoping to find myself a tasty little mouse to serve as my dessert. Though the snow around me was deep, I could see their tiny tracks, and I knew that if I persisted long enough, that I would have my treat.

But the scent of a fire interrupted my search. It had come on the shoulders of the breeze and comingled with that of another smell. A human was nearby, and the fire had been of their devising.

Curious, I padded forwards, my paws making no noise on the snow as I advanced. Then I heard a sound, and pausing, realized that whoever this was, they were singing in a soft voice and beating gently on a drum.

Who could this be? I asked myself. *Who would be out in such a lonely place at this hour of the night?*

In a few more steps, I spotted the flames of a small campfire and the man sitting before it. He was not a Russian, but decidedly Asiatic in appearance, and his garments were made of thick and well worked fish skin. It resembled conventional leather (save for the imprint of the scales), and likely provided him with excellent protection from the cold and the damp.

He also wore a circular breastplate fashioned from the same skin. It bore strange symbols on its face, and was suspended from his neck by a thong, itself liberally decorated with beads and feathers. However, these items were not half as striking as his headdress, which seemed to be made from the fur of a bear and was long enough to reach well past his shoulders.

As for the drum that I had overheard, it was naught but a round piece of rawhide stretched across a wooden frame, and to coax the sound from it, he used a simple piece of wood as his drumstick.

One of the Nanai, I decided, *and most likely a shaman.* Though the uncertain light of the fire colluded with the shadows of his headdress to conceal the upper half of his features, he still seemed somewhat familiar. It was as if we had met somewhere, though I could not place the time nor the event.

Now more fascinated than ever, I moved closer, knowing that as I did so, that he would see me. And after a moment, I was proven correct, for he ceased to play on his drum and smiled in my direction.

Then he spoke, first in his native tongue, and then in Russian. "*Bachigoapu puren ambani.* Tell me, are you a spirit in the shape of a tiger? Or are you carrying a spirit in your tiger's body? No, wait--I can sense it now; you are *both* a spirit *and* a tiger."

Of a sudden, he switched languages again, and I was shocked to hear Atlantean coming from his lips.

"I know you! You and I have met before, and a long time ago. You were a woman then, and blond like a Russian. Welcome, Tiger Sister."

Suddenly, it came to me. Back when I had been a newly minted Chrononaut, I had ferried this fellow from the 6th universe to the 7th. He had been an agent of the Fellowship, and playing the part of an itinerant Shaman.

His mission had been to influence the mythologies of the local tribes in favor of the Masters, and Time Pilots in distress. He had also been accompanied by the Chuchniya and had been the first one to introduce me to that strange being.

So surprised was I by this that I resumed my human form. Oddly, I was not ashamed when I realized that I was standing naked before him. It was as if the animal in me had not entirely fled, so that I was wholly unburdened by the strictures of any human modesty.

The Shaman however, *was* upset, though not by my unclothed appearance. He was instead, vexed by the result of his actions.

"Oh, just look at what I have done!" he declared. "I have startled the tiger and made her go away! Please accept my humble apologies, Tiger Sister."

Hastily, he grabbed up a great, furry blanket and covered me over, for now, I was becoming not a little chilled by the wintery air.

"No offense taken, sir," I said, my teeth chattering and my breath misting before me. "I was simply caught unawares is all."

Inviting me to sit beside him, he pulled a leather bladder from its place near the fire, poured some tea into a cup fashioned from reindeer horn, and handed it to me. Nodding my thanks, I took it and sipped. While it was not on par with Earl Grey or Darjeeling, it was still very refreshing and most welcome.

"Tell me, "he asked. "Do you often change your shape and hunt in the forest like this?"

"No," answered I. "And do you often treat with shapeshifters in the middle of the night?"

"Not often enough," he answered. "That is the curse of this modern age. That which is truly important tends to be neglected in favor of the non-essentials. I blame the smart-phone for this distraction."

I laughed (now able to do so without being affected by the cold), for the device he had just mentioned was still 793 years in the future, when IBM would unveil its Simon Personal Communicator, and begin humanity's downward spiral.

We sat conversing like this for several hours. In the process, I learned that my companion was called Bamba, that he had been recruited by the Fellowship in his 20's, and had served the Masters ever since. Though he tended to ply his trade in his native Siberia, he had travelled throughout the length and breadth of Asia and in all of its iterations in the nine universes.

This vast experience, and his abilities as both a communicator and a storyteller (for these were the perquisites for a Shaman such as he), also made him the perfect listener. Perforce, it was not long before I was pouring my heart out to him, and revealing all of my cares and concerns.

Just the opportunity to speak of them freely, was extremely cathartic. In this, Bamba proved better for me than any councilor that the Hamilkets or Special Section might have ever provided.

Then at length, and after I had finished, he took up his drum and began to chant softly. When he finally spoke, his voice possessed a faraway quality that told me that he was seeing into the future. I listened to his words with every fibre of my being.

"I see your tracks in the snow, Tiger Sister," he said. "and I see where one who was lost to you returns to travel by your side."

My heart leapt, but then, just as quickly, I felt the sharp knife of disappointment cutting my joy away, for he had more to tell.

"I also see a place where there is blood upon the snow. Much blood."

"Whose blood is it?" I pressed, my breath catching in my throat for fear of the answer. "Is it hers? Or mine? *Or both?*"

"I cannot say," he replied. "The spirits refuse to tell me. But I see more tracks after that, though whose they are is not clear."

Overcome by this dire announcement, I brought my hands to my face and cried my heart out. Out of pity, Bamba set his drum aside and brought his arm around me.

"I have some advice for you, Tiger Sister," he said gently into my ear. "It does not come from the spirits, nor even a Shaman, but from a man who has spent many years in this world, and others.'

"It is this; our path through the forest is filled with hardships, and happiness is only a fleeting thing at best. All that we can do is to cherish what joy comes our way, and face adversity with bravery and a noble heart. And if the Fates demand it, we must make whatever sacrifices are required of us in the name of those we love, and for the greater good."

I wiped my eyes and looked up to him. "And Elizabeth?"

"I think that your two paths are intertwined," he offered. "You and she have become separated in the forest before, but you have always found one another in the end. Why should it be any different now, Tiger Sister?"

I nodded, hope once more arising within me. "I thank you for your wisdom, Brother Bamba."

"May good fortune follow you, Tiger Sister."

Standing, I looked up to the starry sky. Then I sent a thought to Blackbird through my nanite.

Blackbird, can you hear me?

After the briefest of moments, she answered. *Yes, I can.*

It is time for us to return home, I told her, instantly receiving a mental image of her engines spinning up, followed by the footage of her rising, and then the trees rushing by beneath her hull as she headed unerringly in my direction.

Save for what the spirits had deigned to share, I had no idea what awaited me, but whatever it proved to be, I was determined to do exactly as Bamba had counseled, and face my challenges as courageously as possible.

CHAPTER 6: Project Blue Beam

In which Project Blue Beam is thwarted. Then, Elizabeth's whereabouts are finally discovered, and she is rescued from the clutches of the Lyrans. After this, her recovery begins.

My voyage back was by necessity, a circuitous one. I did not utilize the Jump Worlds, but instead, flew along the River 'till I found the 1st universe and the century where the Avalon detachment had based itself.

There, I was able to procure a ride on an Ebani, that as luck would have it, was headed my way with a load of fresh pilots who had been temporarily assigned to my squadron. As always, the trip itself was instantaneous, and as soon as we arrived, I saw that our compliment of Phaseships had quadrupled in number. Moreover, Saurii ground crews seemed to be everywhere and were hard at work, loading ordinance or providing last minute maintenance.

Something terribly important was in the offing, I decided.

Finding myself a space, I landed, and walked to the main dome, where I encountered Hamilket 2. He was in his flightsuit and carrying his helmet.

"Welcome back, Penelope" he greeted.

I awarded him a respectful nod. "Wing Leader."

"We were about to send for you, but Fate has favored us with your timely return." he smiled. "We are mobilizing for another operation against the Lyrans."

"So, we are off to Egypt then?"

"Yes," he replied. "Several of us, including yourself, are to leave for the Temple of Horus within the hour. The rest of the squadron will follow at a later point."

"Good," I said, conjecturing that it would likely involve a classified briefing. "I simply have to attend to a brief errand, and then I shall be ready to depart."

He inclined his head in assent and bade me goodbye, and I went thither to my quarters, where I planted myself before the Ladder print. As I had so wished, another change had come over it in my absence, and I let out a great exhalation of relief.

The couple that had been embracing one another had finally resolved into a coherent image, thus confirming Bamba's prophecy, and leaving no doubt whatsoever as to their identity, One figure was undeniably myself, and the other, Elizabeth, and better still, we were smiling joyfully at one another.

Elated by this, I dropped to my knees and looked heavenwards. "Thank you," I declared. "Thank you, God, for this most welcome sign."

Then I stood, and returned to Blackbird, eager to do whatever I could to help make the Ladder's promise a reality.

It was well after dark when we arrived in the 1st universe, and over the Temple of Horus. A great full moon shone down upon the complex, and the car park, which during the day had been filled with buses and private vehicles, was now completely deserted, save for a single electric motorcar. Even as we landed, it came out to collect us, and we were immediately conveyed to the pylon gate where Khentetka and a priest stood by.

After a brief exchange of pleasantries, they escorted us through the temple and into the sanctuary. There, we were issued our crickets, and entered the hidden command center.

Just as before, it was filled with a contingent of specialists, and glancing upwards at the holographic displays, I remarked upon an image of the planet Earth surrounded by thousands of objects in orbit all around it.

Khentetka did not explain the significance of this but instead, waved for us to follow her to the entrance of a small conference room.

"Would any of you wish for refreshments?" she offered, "We have coffee and tea."

The two Hamilkets accepted her invitation, though I refrained for I was not thirsty, but keen to begin the operation. Accordingly, and while they were helping themselves to the contents of a nearby cart, I stepped into the chamber to take my seat, and encountered Louise.

She grinned broadly at me, and toasted my arrival with of all things, a glass of pink champagne!

"Penny, *darling!*" she drawled, "So *good* to see you again."

"Yes," I replied without bothering to mask my displeasure. "I can well imagine."

That was when I took stock of what was in her other hand. It was, of all things, a 21st century smart phone. Even as I apprehended this, she winked salaciously, took a sip from her drink, and then pecked at the phone with her thumb, clearly pleased with what she saw on the tiny screen.

"Whatever are you looking at?" I demanded, for as annoying as I found her, I could not contain my curiosity.

"One of the 'apps' that we developed to counter the Lyran mind-chip," she stated, never taking her eyes off the image. "They call it 'Pokago-Go', and it is a game involving a rather charming group of odd little creatures. It is really quite engaging and *very* popular in the 21st century. Did you know that there is actually a gym located in the Jurassic?"

"No, I was quite unaware of that," I replied, not caring at all what her game used a 'gym' for.

"Well, there *is*," she asserted. "Oh, and here is another app that we developed; *ChattyKat*. It allows cats to speak to one another over the phone, and it even comes with subtitles.'

"You would be *amazed* at what our feline friends say to one another--and the level of their insolence is absolutely astonishing. I daresay that I have been introduced to an entirely new dimension of rudeness. Oh, and lest I forget, there is one other which is equally worthy of mention, '*SXXiChat*'."

Before I could respond, she turned the screen around so that I could see the program in action. The image that it displayed immediately caused me to color to my eyes and I hastily looked away. The animated graphic left nothing whatsoever to the imagination. In fact, less than nothing.

An instant later, the Hamilkets and Khentetka entered the chamber, and giggling heartily at my discomposure, Louise set the phone down on the conference room table, and then awarded me another salute with her glass.

I pointedly did *not* acknowledge her.

"Colonel Ambrose and Lady Anne should be with us shortly," Khentetka advised, "as will Sigrun and Ms. Grímsdóttir."

Accordingly, we waited together for several minutes, 'till at last the quartet arrived and took their places.

"Good evening everyone," Colonel Ambrose began. "Our mission will concern itself with an ongoing Lyran operation taking place in the 2nd universe. The Shadow Governments that work for them have dubbed it *Project Blue Beam'* and a rather courageous fellow, one Serge Monast, revealed its full details. In retaliation, the Lyrans had their proxies in the CIA murder him. They also abducted his children and their whereabouts are currently unknown."

This was certainly on par with what I knew of our opposition, and I pulled an unhappy expression as an image of a jet aeroplane discharging some kind of mist, materialized over the conference table.

"To date, Project Blue Beam represents a concerted effort to control the human population," he continued. "Initially, the idea was to seed the upper atmosphere with various chemicals, and specifically aluminum, so as to create a gigantic projection screen. This aerial 'screen' was intended to display holographic images of all the world's great savior figures, which were then to combine into one enigmatic personality."

"A Lyran, no doubt?" I asked.

"Indeed," he grinned. "The belief was that this would goad humanity into embracing a world-wide religion tailored towards obedience to a global State."

"Yes, but certainly not everyone would have gone along with that," I countered. "The atheists among them would have certainly questioned it, not to mention the resistance that would come from world religious leaders and also the very devout."

"Quite," he returned. "And this was where the purpose of the little chips that we discovered revealed itself. Rather than impose a generalized state of obedience as we had originally supposed, they were in fact intended to generate the proper levels of religious belief and thereby override all doubts. But, thanks to your efforts, we put the kibosh to this. Congratulations, by the way."

I accepted his accolade with a nod, though I did not feel terribly heroic; it had all been mere happenstance and none of it mitigated what the New Berliners had suffered.

"So," he went on, "failing in this endeavor, our opposition was forced to take another tack altogether. One that did not involve the smart phones or any deep mental conditioning, but instead, relied purely on fear to achieve its ends."

I sat up. "Fear?"

This was Louise's cue, and she drained her glass of champagne, lit a cigarette and elucidated.

"Why, by instigating a phony alien invasion of course," she said, waving her ridiculous cigarette holder in the air. "Since the chemtrail program is still ongoing, all the Lyrans have to do is change out the holograms, and then use their disks to blow a few things up here and there, and *viola*, we have something that *everyone* will be afraid of. Just like in *War of the Worlds*."

My blood curdled, for I knew this great work of fiction intimately, having read it in London. Though it had been serialized in 1897 by *Pearson's Magazine*, I had still been able to obtain a copy in 1890, courtesy of Blackbird's data files, and it had thoroughly terrified me.

It was also quite obvious what the result of this ersatz invasion would be. Eager to survive, humanity would rally around the banner of the Shadow Governments, and then the Lyrans would scoop up whoever they wished in the guise of the invaders, or alternately, pretend to intervene as earth's alien saviors, and thus engender willing recruits eager to fight alongside them.

It was absolutely fiendish.

"Whence do these holograms originate from?" I inquired, for this seemed to be the very key to thwarting this bit of Lyran rascality.

"From satellites primarily," Sigrun supplied, and here, the jet plane was replaced by the same image of the Earth that I had encountered on my way in.

"Every satellite launched into orbit since Sputnik contains a small library of secret holographic files," she informed me. "In addition, ground-based and air-based assets play an important role in the Blue Beam network, not only providing further imagery, but also broadcasting conventional sound effects and sonic wavelengths capable of producing high levels of anxiety in the human brain."

"So, what are we to do then?" I asked.

"That question is the very purpose of this meeting and the reason for our presence," Lady Anne stated. "Let us get on with it then."

Over the next several hours, we did just that, combining our efforts and formulating a plan. While the finished product certainly possessed its share of flaws, I was confident that like the invasion envisioned by Mr. Wells, that this one would also fail. Not through the agency of disease though; instead, the Lyrans would be brought low by the actions of a few lion-hearted Chrononauts and the righteousness of our cause.

I was also equally certain that one of my seniors would be leading the briefing, but in this, I proved to be quite mistaken. Just as we made to leave the conference room to face a command center now filled with newly arrived pilots, Lady Anne informed me that it was *I* who would be presenting the material!

"Have no fear," she soothed, "I am certain that your grasp of our strategy is flawless. Besides which, if you are to play a larger role in this conflict, you simply must accept the responsibility that comes with such an elevation in status."

I was so stunned that I could not articulate a reply. The burden that she had just placed upon my shoulders was as daunting a challenge as facing any enemy pilot in combat. I had never had any public speaking experience and trepidation seized me up in its talons. In a word, I was terrified at the prospect.

"A little liquid courage perhaps?" It was Louise, and she proffered me a flask filled with spirits.

Tempted though I was to accept, I pushed it away with wintry disdain. "I should think not."

"Well," she answered impishly, "At least you won't be asked to sing and dance."

Shooing her away, Lady Anne leaned in to whisper in my ear. "Choose one person in the crowd," she counseled, "and speak directly to them. Then find another, and do the same, and so on.'

"Make your address seem more like a normal conversation between two friends than what it truly is. That way, you will remain focused and build up a rapport with your audience. Now, off with you."

Armed with this wisdom, I stepped up to the holographic projector, made eye contact with a pilot from El Dorado, and gave it my all. I began by briefly explaining the general nature of our enterprise, and then, turning to the Wing Leaders, detailed the specifics.

When at last I finished, and had answered a few questions here and there, I realized that despite my apprehension, I had actually managed things quite well. In fact, when I stepped away from the projector, both the Colonel and Lady Anne came forwards to congratulate me.

"Well done, Penelope," Colonel Ambrose said. "Very succinct and to the point. Had I not known better, I would have assumed that you were a veteran speaker."

"Quite right," Lady Anne agreed. "You did a fine job of it. All that remains now is to see our plan through to the end."

Exactly as intended, and with the help of the Saurii Speakers, the Ebanis delivered our entire contingent to a point in space 36,000 kilometers above the Earth. This was just beyond the geostationary orbit of the satellites that were involved in the Blue Beam network.

Here, we found them already engaged in their deviltry; an image of a gigantic spaceship, painted with the Lyran triskelion, was being projected into the upper atmosphere, and terrestrial communications channels, both military and civilian, were jammed with panicked conversations. Some concerned the so-called 'alien mothership' whilst others relayed the details of smaller craft making appearances all across the globe.

In addition, the Secretary-General of the United Nations was making an appeal to the planet's population to form a unified front against the threat, marking him as an asset of the Shadow Government. Predictably, the entire world was in a state of absolute chaos.

We, however, were not duped in the least, for our instruments clearly revealed that every one of these alleged invaders were in fact nothing more substantial than focused laser light, or Lyran air assets.

And we shall soon banish them all, I vowed.

Even then, our forces were separating into attack groups with some of the Phaseships going after the satellites themselves, whilst others (including my own squadron) entered the atmosphere and descended towards our ground-based objectives.

The one that Major Sixkiller and I were tasked with eliminating was the High Frequency Active Auroral Research Program, or HAARP facility, located in Gakona, Alaska, and I fully expected to encounter opposition on the way down.

Oddly though, nothing rose up to offer a challenge, and back behind us, my screens showed the satellites disappearing one by one as my fellow Chrononauts brought their missiles and chronoguns to bear. It seemed as if a very one-sided victory was in the offing.

However, as we neared our destination and leveled off for an attack run, Blackbird advised me of an abrupt change in the weather.

"Penny," she warned. "There is a powerful stormfront ahead of us. I cannot explain it—it was not there a moment ago."

Looking to my displays, I saw that my artificial companion was reporting correctly. What just minutes before had been a clear, peaceful sky, was now filling with angry thunderheads, dark with the promise of rain and flashing with lightning.

"Major?" I asked, contacting my companion, "do you think that this weather has anything to do with HAARP?"

"I sure as shit do," she replied. "The boys in the tinfoil hats always said that it was made to control the weather, but I never believed them before now. Seems like they were right."

More importantly, the issue of how the facility had managed to detect us vexed me greatly. We had followed our usual protocol and come in stealth mode, but somehow, this had not deceived our target, and I shared my concern with Major Sixkiller.

"Can't rightly say how they spotted us," she responded. "But it's something that the Masters'll sure wanna hear about."

"Quite so," I agreed, sending out a brief encrypted message to all the Wing Leaders advising them of this development.

The storm meanwhile had swelled to truly monstrous proportions. While it was nowhere near what I had encountered during my ill-fated attempt to rescue Pishqu, it was still quite formidable, and its winds buffeted our craft as we flew into it.

Hail came next; not the small bits of ice that I was accustomed to, but huge chunks larger than my fists. Blackbird's energy field repelled them of course, and in response, they grew in size till they rivaled soccer balls in magnitude.

"Whoa," Major Sixkiller exclaimed. "That's almost as big as what they have down in Texas! *Sheei-tt!*"

More lightening flashed, and nary a moment later, it pummeled my Phaseship without mercy.

"Ouch!" Blackbird declared when a particularly powerful bolt struck her field. "That hurt!"

"Hang on my dearest," I urged, seeing that the strike had severely taxed her energy levels. "Major, I strongly suggest that we climb above this tempest, and then descend upon our target."

"No arguments from me," she replied. This was followed by sounds that indicated her craft had just been struck.

"Godfuckit! That was a hell of a hit! I think this storm might be even *worse* than Texas!"

Together, we ascended heavenwards, rising above the clouds, which by now had lost all of their grey and had become wholly black in color. Though we were beyond its reach, the lightning still tried to follow us like the claws of some diabolical beast.

I paid them no heed though, but consulted by displays. According to them, we were now directly above the HAARP facility. Thus, I pitched the nose downwards and began my attack, with the Major following in train. Our return into the storm was accompanied by more wind and even fiercer lightning.

Yet Blackbird compensated for this assault, and in but a few moments, I could see the facility itself. It sat in the midst of a cleared space in the forest; a huge square filled with antennae aglow with a strange, purplish light.

I had already armed my *Bennu* missiles and targeted the very center of the installation. A moment later, my instruments indicated that I had acquired a lock, and I fired. But not before HAARP made one final attempt to defend itself. To my surprise, heretofore unknown batteries of energy weapons activated, spewing bolts of violaceous fire. One of these hit the starboard wing, and Blackbird cried out.

"Oh Penny, I am hit!"

Immediately, I launched a second rocket and spun away. My first shot had been intercepted by the beams, and my second suffered the same fate, but Major Sixkiller managed to succeed where I had not; her missile streaked to earth and a massive fireball erupted. The shockwave from the blast flattened the trees for miles in all directions and set them ablaze. As for HAARP, nothing remained, save a great cloud of dust and cinders. The skies meantime, had begun to clear.

"That was one hell of a ride," the Major remarked. Already, we were changing course and flying north. Our next target was the Poker Flat Research Range in Chatanika.

"Let us hope that we have a quieter time of it at this target," I said, monitoring the progress of Blackbird's nanorobots as they repaired the breach in her wing.

"I won't argue with that," Sixkiller concurred.

In the interim, the situation above us in space had changed. Several flights of aerospace fighters, classified as *Aurora*, and piloted by United States Air Force personnel, were counterattacking, companioned by Lyran disks.

Further, several ground stations were responding as well, especially the Jindalee Operational Radar Network, in Laverton, West Australia. It had long been suspected that some form of anti-space battery was positioned on this continent, and now, we had our confirmation. Though it was not terribly accurate, a very powerful energy weapon was firing at us from what the Aussies called the Outback.

As for our part in all this, when we drew near enough, the Research Range demonstrated that it too could detect us, and its concealed energy gun batteries did their level best to blast us from the sky. Having anticipated this, we did not suffer any damage however, and carried on with our business. One Bennu missile was all that was required to transform the Range into a charred duplicate of the HAARP facility.

"What's next on the list?" Sixkiller asked as we pulled up and away.

I called up our list of prospective targets. "The MU Radar in Shigaraki, Japan."

There were other sites located in Eastern Europe and in the Americas of course, but these were being handled by different strike teams and were too far away to consider.

"I'd rather be upstairs," the Major said, giving voice to my own sentiments.

"Let us complete our work," I proposed, "and if there are any hostiles left over, we will ascend and join the fight."

Naturally, she groused at this, though not overmuch, for I had given us both something to look forwards to.

As it happened, the Gods of War took pity on us (though now that I pen these words, I do not think that the term 'pity' is actually a part of their vocabulary). We had just left Alaska behind us and were soaring out over the Bering Sea, when my instruments indicated that a trio of machines were coming our way. One was identified as a Lyran disk, and the other two were American Auroras.

"Well, Major, it seems that the fray has found *us*," I observed dryly.

"Hot damn!" she cried.

Presently, the two Auroras broke off to the left and the right, whilst the disk came straight at us. Accordingly, we separated and launched missiles.

Watching the Auroras dropping chaff and making to come around, I recalled something that I had perceived the very first time I had ever laid eyes on one. It had been on the occasion of my visit to the Black Knight, when one of them had been sent out to destroy it.

This was the realization of the Aurora's major weakness; designed as it was for high speed, it lacked agility, and by necessity, its turns were quite wide. This made it an extremely poor contender when it came to air-to-air combat, especially up against a Phaseship.

I also found that I had no desire for the deaths of these American pilots, and neither did the Tigress. This was partly the legacy of my misadventure in Tibet, but also the fact that they posed no real threat to us. Therefore, killing them seemed rather mean and not a little unsporting.

The Lyran disk however, was another matter. Its pilot deserved no quarter whatsoever. Consequently, I concentrated on removing it from the equation and spoke to Major Sixkiller.

"Major, "I said. "Keep the Americans busy, would you? Do not slay them, though. Once I have dealt with the disk, we shall work out their fate."

Sixkiller answered this with a quick wag of her wings and then went after the nearest of the Auroras. Though it was able to fend off her rockets, she managed to get on its tail as easily as I had anticipated, and then bracketed it with her chronoguns. And, just as requested, not a one of her shots landed, but even so, the inferior machine was hard pressed to evade her.

To his credit, the second Aurora pilot tried to come to the rescue of his countryman whilst attempting to line up on Sixkiller's tail, though without any success; she was able to slip away every time and continued to harass the first machine. I must admit that although the situation between them was deadly serious, there was a comical aspect to it, so outmatched were they.

I, meanwhile, was engaged in a spin-for-spin *gavotte* with the disk, with the both of us attempting to anticipate the other's next move and counter it. Yet in the end, the Lyran made the wrong decision and I caught him as he inadvertently came into line with my guns. It was only for an instant, but it was enough for me to score one hit, and then, as his craft wobbled unsteadily, another. Finished, he tumbled downwards till he hit the water and there, disintegrated.

Now I addressed the Auroras. "American pilots; your Lyran ally is no more. Leave the battle or we will be compelled to destroy you. We do not wish this, for you are merely unwitting dupes, but we shall if we must."

Realizing that the odds were now decidedly against them, and equally certain of our resolve, the fighters turned and headed for the Kamchatka Peninsula as fast as their engines would allow. In but moments, we were alone with nothing but the empty sky and the opens seas for company.

"Well, that was short," Sixkiller pronounced, "but kinda fun. I imagine that they'll have to spend some time hosin out their cockpits. Ya'll owe me by the way."

I chuckled. Though vulgar, her statement was rather apt. Near death experiences tend to incite the most embarrassing bodily responses, and this day, these poor fellows had had them aplenty.

"I promise to compensate you, Major," I replied. "I will send a message to the strike team tasked with Australia and ask that they attend to the radar station in Japan. Then you and I shall go 'upstairs' and join in on the festivities. Does that satisfy?"

"Yep," she answered. "That suits me just fine." In her own way, the Major was just as ferocious as any weretiger, and just as eager for the hunt.

Once 'upstairs', we found that the space above the Earth had changed for the better. Gone were the counterfeit motherships, and the airwaves were no longer filled with panic.

Instead, puzzlement had replaced it, as the human race struggled to understand the cause behind its sudden change in fortunes. There were also many who wondered at why the alien invaders had chosen to destroy obscure weather research facilities, and climate monitoring satellites, rather than military targets.

Of course, the answers would never be provided to them. Nor would we receive any thanks. It was enough that we had done our jobs and saved them from enslavement by the *real* invaders.

The cost though, had been heavy, especially for the Lyrans and their allies in the Shadow Government. Here, the Auroras had done no better than they had over the Bering Sea. A goodly number of them had chosen to fight rather than flee, and to the last, there was nothing left of them save bits of orbiting wreckage.

As for their masters, the Lyrans had committed nearly all of their local assets into the fracas, and the contest between our two forces had been a fierce one. In the end though, we had managed to vanquish the lot of them, but in return, they had done us some injury as well; three Chrononauts had been killed and twice as many had been injured.

For me, this was no sterile set of statistics, for I knew one of those who had died. It had been no less than Captain Ziva Meier 1 herself. And although I was fully aware that the Avalon detachment still retained a fully functioning cloning facility, and that she would soon be returned to us, the news still saddened me, if only for Manfred's sake.

Death, however temporary, is always a hard blow to bear, and I knew that this event would only compound his grief over Ernst's demise. I also accepted the fact that once again, the task of delivering this tiding would fall upon my shoulders, although this time, I agreed to accept the assistance of both the Major and Hamilket 2.

Accordingly, when we returned to the Jurassic, we sought out Manfred together. He was, as one might imagine, saddened by my message, but being a clone, the announcement did not cut him near as deeply as it might have a normal human. He had after all, the promise of her resurrection to cling to.

Yet, I had the impression that something deeper was troubling him that this hope had not banished, and a day later, and when the opportunity arose, I broached the subject.

By this point, our base had grown enough in size that we now possessed a small sanctuary as part of our recreation area. It was not dedicated to any single belief system (for our pilots hailed from far too many diverse situations to limit it in such a manner), nor even a truly religious space, but instead, had been set aside for meditation and contemplation.

This was where I found him, seated at one of the padded benches, and staring up towards the simple seven-pointed star that adorned the far wall. Just from the set of his shoulders alone, I could see the strain that he was under.

"Manfred?" I queried gently. "May I join you?"

He looked over his shoulder and nodded to me in invitation. I in turn, took my place beside him.

"What is it, Manfred? What bothers you so?"

At first, he did not answer, but then at last, he spoke. "It is about Ziva," he confessed. "I am afraid."

"Of what? Avalon just sent word; a new iteration of her has been decanted, and she should soon be back with us."

In fact, the very moment that the Avalon pilots had returned to their base, they had gotten their technicians straight to work on replacing all of the lost Chrononauts, including Ziva.

"I am afraid," he repeated. "I know that there are some things that she will recall immediately, but there are others that she will have to struggle to recover."

"Yes, of course. It was that way with me," I replied. "Yet I *did* manage to recall them."

He faced me; his eyes filled with a childlike desperation. "But what *if*—what if she doesn't remember that she loves me? What if she feels nothing for us? What do I do then?"

Blackbird had once uttered the same fears, and although I had recovered most of my memories, I still wondered from time to time at what I might have lost along the way. Worse, in the most private corner of my thoughts, I too fretted over my lover and wondered at how Elizabeth would feel towards me once she was found, and her conditioning reversed.

Pleiadean or not, I was prone to the same frailties as Manfred, or any human for that matter, and doubt was certainly one of these. But I was not about to add any fuel to this particular fire.

"Manfred," I said with all of the conviction that I could muster, "if anything can survive death, it is love. She *will* know you, and she will care for you. I am certain of it."

Captain Meier did indeed return to us, and nary a week later. She was immediately given over to Manfred's care, and he spent every waking moment in her company. Though I often saw them strolling together outside the base, or sitting in the Mess Hall, I maintained my distance out of the concern that my presence would only aggravate her. And from what I could observe, Manfred's misgivings about her continuing to care for him had proven baseless; they seemed as close as ever, and this in turn, lent me some optimism with regard to Elizabeth.

It was on the tenth day of Ms. Meier's recovery that a rather surprising turn of events transpired. I had been detained by the Professor for an examination of my implant, and thus, had missed the pair when they consumed their lunch. Perforce, when I was finally free to consume my own meal, they had departed the Mess for their quarters, and I supped alone.

My repast was not terribly appetizing; a bisque made from a local decapod. It was nowhere near as flavorful as a *Eurypterid* or *Homarus Gammarus*, the European Lobster of my century, and the mechanica had added far too much sherry for my liking.

Eventually, my thoughts drifted from my meal to Elizabeth and the Ladder print. Since its last transformation, there had been no other changes, and I wondered at when it might choose to reveal another portent, and what it might be.

It was in the midst of this somber rumination that Hamilket 1 entered and walked up to my table.

"Ziva is asking for you," he advised.

"For me?" I inquired, hardly believing my ears.

The Atlantean nodded. "Yes. She has specifically requested your presence."

I set down my spoon, and rose, worried at how I would be received. But I could not refuse the invitation, nor my Wing Leader.

So, I departed the mess hall forthwith and went to straightaway to her quarters. When I knocked, it was Manfred who answered, and I could see Ziva beyond him, seated on the couch in their living area. Though I searched her eyes for any warning of what was to come, I failed to discern her intent, and entered with great trepidation.

"Ziva?" I asked carefully. "Are you well?"

"I am," she answered, patting the chair next to her. "Would you sit with me?"

Seeing this as his opportunity, Manfred rose and hastily left the room, earning him an unhappy glance from my quarter.

Damn you Manfred, I thought. *Do not leave me to face this struggle alone.*

But leave he did, and of a sudden, Ziva and I were the only ones in the room. Then, to my utter surprise, she reached out and took my hand in hers.

"I knew very little about my last life when I Awoke," she began. "Then I started to remember things. About the Nazis and what they did to my people. About what you did in Antarctica. I hated you then."

I looked away, unable to meet her eyes and tried to withdraw my hand, but she clenched it tighter.

"Then I remembered my mother. She was a very angry, bitter woman. She held many grudges against her family and her friends, and she went to the grave with all of that resentment blackening her heart.'

"I always thought that she was a fool, and that she should have found it within herself to forgive her loved ones, especially in her final days. But she never did."

I made no reply to this, but simply listened, afraid that anything I uttered would ignite another tragedy between us.

"In my last life, I was becoming just like her, Penny. Just as unforgiving. Just as hard. Just as cruel. I can see all that now that I've been reborn, and I don't want to repeat my mistakes. I have the chance for a better life now. I guess that's the one benefit of dying and coming back."

Unable to contain myself any further, I spoke at last. "Ziva, I meant you no harm. I simply could not condemn innocents to suffer for the crimes of their leaders. Not after what I did in Tibet."

"Yes," she replied. "I understand that now. In my former life, I was too angry with you to see *why* you did what you did. I was too filled with my hatred for the Nazis.'

"But now, I know better; what you did was the only right thing to do, Penny—the only just and moral thing, and I would like to think that I would have done the same had I been in your place. I forgive

144

you. I was being a fool, and I hope that you will find it in your heart to forgive *me*."

"Oh Ziva," I said, my eyes misting over. "I do, and I profoundly apologize for all the pain that I ever brought to you or Manfred. I never wished to visit such heartache upon either of you."

At this, she embraced me, and I in turn, reciprocated heartily. It was only then that Manfred dared to reenter the room, and in moments, we had gathered him in.

After this, we three spent the evening together in their quarters. At Ziva's request, our meal was brought to us by a mechanica, and as we sat and enjoyed it, we reacquainted with one another as friends. It was the close of a sad chapter between us, and one that I had not dared to hope for.

At length, and as we were nearing the end of our repast, there was a knock at the door. It was Major Sixkiller 1, and she was quite out of breath.

"Cassie" I said, rising. "Whatever is the matter?"

"Elizabeth," she gasped. "We've found her! We know where she is."

In that instant, all else in the universe dwindled to insignificance. "Take me!" I exclaimed. "Take me to Lady Anne and the Colonel straightaway."

As it happened, they had already been headed in our direction and we very nearly collided in the corridor.

"You have heard the news, I see," Colonel Ambrose remarked as he and his companion pulled up short.

"I have," I said, breathless with excitement. "Tell me, what plans are underway to rescue her? And how might I take part?"

"Come," Lady Anne invited. "We will discuss all that in the conference room." Then she noticed the Major. "This is a Special Section matter. I am afraid that you cannot accompany us."

"*Bull*-shit!" Cassie protested. "I'm comin along. Penny here's been drivin me nuts ever since Elizabeth ran off, and I'm not about to miss out now. Ya'll'll have to get a mechanica to stop me."

"Oh, let her come," I implored. "She is my dearest friend, and she should be included in any effort to rescue my lover. I beg you, make an exception here."

Lady Anne considered my petition, and answered. "Very well. She may accompany you—but with one stipulation; she is to follow the raid leader's instructions to the very letter."

We nodded in enthusiastic unison, and then fell into step behind the pair as they led us to the conference room.

There, Colonel Ambrose began the briefing. "It took quite a bit of poking about, but we have determined that Mr. Grey has based himself in the hollow of a dead volcano, located on the island of *Motu'o'le'oti* in German Samoa, in the 4th universe, 21st century. The name *Motu'o'le'oti* translates to *Island of Death,* and unsurprisingly, the locals consider it to be cursed, and therefore tend to avoid it rather assiduously."

To me, it sounded like a truly dreadful place, but Major Sixkiller snorted in derision. "Oh *puhleeze!* Really?"

Bewildered, I cocked my head towards her. "What is so humorous about that?"

"Penny," she replied. "Island of Death? A volcano lair? Is that the best you 19th century folks can come up with? Heck, even an underwater bubble-base is more original."

"Well, I happen to think that it is *quite* original," I protested, feeling somewhat miffed, "*and* diabolically clever. After all, who would ever think of seeking him in such an uncongenial location?"

"Well, James Bond for one," she retorted. "Jeeze, it's a trope, girl. I'll bet when we get there the guards'll all be runnin around in hard-hats and totin' machine guns."

"I should expect them to be so equipped," I maintained. "After all, such a place must have its fair share of overhead hazards, and automatic weapons would simply be *de rigueur* for the hired help."

At this, she burst out in uncontrolled laughter, and I reddened. "Okay, Penny, whatever. But I get to push the big red self-destruct button."

Red self-destruct button? I wondered. Who—even an evil villain like Mr. Grey--would ever allow such a thing to exist, much less situate it were an enemy could gain access to it? The idea was positively ludicrous.

"Of course, Major," I promised. "rest assured that when the time comes, the honor will be entirely yours."

As for who this James Bond fellow was, I decided that I would certainly inquire about him when time permitted. It seemed likely that he was a member of Special Section, and it is always wise to know something about an individual before one is formally introduced.

Presently, Lady Anne disclosed the finer details of our mission. "Due to the ability of the Lyrans to detect our Phaseships in stealth mode, we will not be inserting by air. Instead, we will be conveyed to the location by way of an Imperial German *Unterseeboot*."

I noticed her use of the term 'we' and raised an eyebrow. "'We', madam? Is it your intent to accompany the team?"

"It is," she said. "Given the importance of this endeavor, I feel that I am obligated to assist. Further, ours will not be the only group to assault the island, for we shall also have the services of three *Kommando Spezialkräfte* teams to call upon.'

"As for the submersible, the U-476 is a nuclear-powered vessel and employs the latest hydro-jet engines, making it almost completely silent. The captain should be able to deliver us to within sighting distance of the shore without discovery, and from there, we and our teams will make landfall using rubber boats--again courtesy of the Imperial Navy.'

"Once ashore, we will then travel to the base of the volcano and a ventilation duct, which we shall breach. Then we will penetrate the interior and locate Elizabeth."

"Well, that's real nice and all," Major Sixkiller interrupted, "but what if she doesn't feel like comin with us? Last I heard, she didn't much care for the Masters."

"Then the team members have orders to subdue her and take her into custody," Lady Anne answered, clearly irritated.

"And what of Mr. Grey?" I asked, my voice frosted with hatred.

"He is your secondary target," Colonel Ambrose supplied, "and if encountered, he is to be terminated with extreme prejudice."

Even if I had not been given this instruction, this would have been my aim. For what he had done to me, to the woman that I loved, and to my faction, he deserved to suffer an agonizing death, and I fully intended to be the one to give him his just deserts.

"Good," I said. "That satisfies me."

Sixkiller though, was not as contented as I. "Okay. So here's the hundred-dollar question; how'll we find her?"

"Nanoculons programmed to sniff out her DNA," the Colonel told her. "Once they have pinpointed her location, it will just be a simple matter of plucking her up."

"*Yeahhh*," Sixkiller drawled doubtfully. "With ten billion Lyrans and God knows what else standin in the way."

"That is what the commandos are for," Lady Anne informed her. "As for them, we will travel via Ebani to the 4th universe, and then rendezvous in the city of Apia, on the island of Upolu. Mr. Tidwell and Henry will be in charge of the strike force and they will see to it that we make our appointment with the submarine. That said, do either of you have any other questions?"

I certainly did. It had been vexing me ever since the operation against Project Blue Beam, and the requirement for a submersible had only heightened my concern.

"However did the Lyrans manage to overcome our stealth technology in the first place?" I queried.

"A good question," Colonel Ambrose said, "And the answer is simple, though I warn you that you will not care for it; we have Elizabeth and the *White Rose* to blame. With her assistance, and a working Phaseship to examine, the Lyrans were able to ferret out our secrets.'

"Although this means that they now have the same capabilities as we do, they do not seem to have developed anything that surpasses our technology. Not yet at least--which makes it all the more important that your lady love be rescued; she is simply too valuable a resource for our enemies to exploit. Given enough time, who knows how many other secrets she might help them to uncover?"

I nodded in grim understanding. "Of course. Thank you, sir."

At this juncture, everyone rose, and I prepared to depart. But one final surprise awaited me. Louise entered the chamber, seeming somewhat out of breath.

"Did I miss the briefing? "she asked, "Oh I do apologize!"

"No matter, my dear, "Lady Anne replied. "You already know the details. There was nothing new discussed."

"Good," Louise returned with a relieved tone. "And Penny knows about me?"

This arrested my attention. "What *about* her?"

"She will be coming with us as well," Lady Anne disclosed. "Her talents will be of value, and besides which, she felt the same as I did; that she could not be left out."

I did not remark upon this unwelcome development. I merely glared at Louise, and took my leave. Elizabeth mattered more to me than my dislike of the woman, and I already knew from past experience that any protestations that I made would be ignored.

My only hope was that her tendency towards inebriation would not compromise us in some manner.

CHAPTER 7: The Island of Death

In which we infiltrate the terrible lair of Mr. Grey. The traitor meets his end at last, and Elizabeth is taken prisoner. Then, we return to Saurii, and after that, travel to London, and ultimately, Bedlam.

As planned, we departed the Jurassic in multiple Phaseships and via an Ebani; I in Blackbird, Lady Anne and the new Speaker in *The Duchess*, Major Sixkiller in her *Sun Arrow* and finally, Louise flying *Betty Boop*.

When we reached the 4th universe, we made for the Pacific Ocean, and thence to the city of Apia in German Samoa. There, at the Imperial naval base, we were met by Mr. Tidwell, Henry, and three teams of *KSK* commandos.

After instructing our respective Phaseships to abide there until called upon, we then boarded the U-476. Our captain, Herr Saltzwedel, got the vessel under weigh immediately, and in short order, we were headed for the Island of Death.

During this interval, I took the opportunity to inquire with Major Sixkiller about Mr. James Bond. Based on her earlier remarks, this seemed the perfect mission for him, and I had since wondered at why he had not been included.

I subsequently learned that he was an entirely fictional character and not a member of Special Section at all. However, when she went on to regale me about his imaginary exploits, I found myself becoming gladsome that he did not exist. He was far too flamboyant to serve effectively as any kind of spy, and I found his judgement to be rather questionable when it came to his operations. Of course, I did not share this with the Major, as it was clear that she admired him greatly.

As for the voyage itself, Captain Saltzwedel proved to be a very competent commander, and delivered us without incident to the waters just off of *Motu'o'le'oti*. It was also our good fortune that we arrived on a moonless night, which allowed us to launch our rafts from the submarine's deck, and slip ashore without our enemies ever realizing it.

Nonetheless, we were careful to conceal the boats, and as we wended our way up through the jungle to our objective, we were each of us mindful of the possibility of encountering hidden guard posts or detection devices. Thus, we took our time and placed every step with care.

In due course, we came to the foot of the volcano and the ventilation shaft. Though the screen covering it was quite robust, it was no match for the effects of a chronopistol aimed at it by Mr. Tidwell. A few focused bursts were all it took, and the steel simply crumbled away.

Here we paused, and Lady Anne opened a small container and shook out its contents into the vent. These were the nanoculons which had been mentioned during my briefing, and in half a heartbeat, they flew into the shaft and began their hunt for Elizbeth.

"Well, let us get to it then," she invited.

One by one, we crawled into the passage, and at the other end, encountered a second grate, which met the same fate as the first. Beyond this, we entered a well-lit corridor.

Thanks to initial data already received from the nanoculons, we knew to turn left—and also that a pair of sentries were positioned just ahead of us at an intersection. Bringing our suppressed weapons to the ready, we moved in silence towards our opposition, and I fully expected that when we made contact, it would only be a matter of putting a few bullets into them.

Lady Anne however, had another notion. "I shall deal with the guards," she whispered into her com. "They may be of use to us."

Passing her submachinegun to one of the Germans, she closed the distance on the sentries with all the stealth of a cat. Her targets (who were equipped exactly as Major Sixkiller had predicted, with hard-hats and automatic weapons) did not sense her at all. Then, when she was sufficiently close, she threw herself into a roll, coming up between them.

Before they could respond, she reached out and pinched the base of their necks. I could not see the exact grip that she employed, but whatever she had used caused them to drop to the floor like sacks of flour.

"What did you just do?" I asked as we joined her. In all of my martial training, both in my present iteration and the previous one spent in Shamballa, I had never encountered such a technique and I was astounded at its effectiveness.

"Oh, nothing special really," she replied airily. "Just a little trick that I picked up on my travels."

"Well, I daresay that I should like to learn it," I asserted.

"Same here!" Sixkiller declared. "Hell, that'd make a nice party trick!"

"And perchance I shall teach you," she answered, awarding the Major a pejorative look. "I am actually quite proud of it. Did you know that it was even featured in a popular science fiction television show in the 2nd universe?"

"Indeed?" I queried as I disarmed the unconscious sentries.

"Yes. Gene needed something amazing for Leonard to do whenever circumstances became too dire, so I disclosed it to him. Of course, I didn't share the *exact* method with the man, but just enough for the effect to seem realistic for the cameras."

"Hmm," Sixkiller commented. "Ya know, I think I might just know that show…Star somthinorother…"

"Yes," Lady Anne responded dryly. "Something-or-other."

The two sentries were then dragged off by our KSK partners and promptly bound and gagged. Then one of the commandos indicated that he would remain with them, which was exactly what Lady Anne had had in mind.

"When they come to, see what information they can provide," she instructed. In reply, the commando gave her a curt nod of understanding.

Satisfied that our fellow had things well in hand, she signaled that we should proceed. It was not overlong before we encountered another pair of sentries, and this time, when Lady Anne made to neutralize them, Louise objected.

"It is my turn, Anne," she insisted. "You had the last ones."

"Very well," Lady Anne whispered back. "Have at them then."

Myself, I readied my weapon, certain that she would muff the job—especially since she had produced her flask and was taking a deep drink from it.

Of course, she would take a drink, I thought disapprovingly. *What else could one expect from someone so dissolute?*

Meantime, Louise strode towards her targets as if she hadn't a care in the world, and when she stepped between them, she casually dropped her flask. It hit the floor with a loud clang, and both men turned their heads in her direction.

This was when she struck. Quite unexpectedly, she spat a mouthful of whatever vile substance she had been drinking straight into the eyes of the man to her left.

As he clawed at his face, she threw her arm around the neck of the man to her right and executed a hip-throw. The fact that his head was restrained whilst his body was in motion did not contribute to his well-being, for the snapping of his neck was quite audible.

This of course, left the first man, who had just recovered enough to witness the death of his partner. Louise handled this by sweeping him off his feet with a kick. Then, leaping atop him, she pulled the lapels of his jumpsuit tight against his neck, strangling him into unconsciousness.

Smiling, she released the body, retrieved her flask, and toasted us. Cheeky monkey that she was, she even had the spunk to help herself to another sip!

"Are we quite done?" Lady Anne asked impatiently. "I should think it is time that we attended to the rescue of Elizabeth with some semblance of seriousness."

"Quite right," Louise conceded.

At this, two of our KSK teams separated and departed for their own objectives, which lay elsewhere in the facility. Left as we were to our own devices, we pressed on, and in the process encountered several more sentries, though neither Lady Anne nor Louise resorted to any further demonstrations of their abilities.

Rather, the KSK commandos who had remained with us were given free rein to perform their jobs, and they used entirely conventional methods to accomplish them (employing knives, garrotes and the like).

By and by, we attained our objective. This was an observation deck overlooking the base's main control room. Crouching low and keeping close to the safety rails, we were able to view the going's on below us.

The control room itself was elliptical in shape, with row upon row of gleaming metal stations manned by busy-looking technicians. The focus of all their endeavors was being projected onto three large display screens, and my breath caught at the sight.

The middle-most showed a view of the planet Saturn, and a gigantic fleet of spacecraft parked in orbit around it. There were thousands of these vessels, and of all shapes and sizes, with more arriving with each passing second.

It was an armada the likes of which exceeded even the wildest imaginings of King Phillip of Spain, and every one of these ships bore the triskelion of the Lyrans. Moreover, I saw that the local time for Earth and what I presumed was for Saturn, was being presented in the upper right portion of the image.

So that is what I have been seeing in my dreams, I thought.

Next, I looked to the left-hand screen. This portrayed dozens of different broadcasts all playing at the same time. Some were entertainment flickers, whilst others seemed to be news programs, and still others, children's programming, or presentations whose purpose I could not puzzle out.

As for the third screen, it was dominated by one of the shows from its neighbor, and a man was speaking, though I could not tell what the thrust of his address was. What I did know was that the Lyrans were deeply involved in all of it, and therefore, evil was afoot.

Once we have found Elizabeth, this place will have to be forced to give up its secrets, I resolved, *and then be utterly destroyed.*

Taking my eyes away from the displays, I cast about the chamber, searching for any sign of my beloved. Though she was nowhere in evidence, someone else *was.* Seated in a strange chair that reminded me somewhat of a bubble, and dressed in a leaden colored, sherwani-style coat, was none other than Mr. Grey himself!

Instantly, my fangs grew out, and a low rumble arose in my throat. Then I felt the touch of a restraining hand upon my shoulder. It was Lady Anne.

"Control yourself," she ordered. "There will be an opportunity for *that* soon enough. Just now, the other teams are headed this way and we must abide here until they are in place."

Forcing myself back into a semblance of calm (though only a tad), I reluctantly complied.

Presently, Major Sixkiller nudged me and directed my attention to a spot just behind Mr. Grey's chair. A great red button resided there and above it was a sign which proclaimed it to be a "Self-Destruct Button!" along with the warning "Do Not Push!" I could hardly believe my eyes.

"Hot damn!" Cassie whispered excitedly. "I *knew* it! Hey, Lady Anne, as soon as Elizabeth's hog-tied and we're ready to fly the coop, ya'll gotta let me push it!"

"As Penelope previously stated, that will be your prerogative," Lady Anne assured her. "For the nonce though, let us concentrate on our work."

Sixkiller acquiesced to this and settled down, and as the Tigress and I began to fantasize about what we would do to Mr. Grey when we finally had him in our claws, there was a shout of alarm. It had come from a flight of stairs that connected the observation deck with the main control room. And turning, I saw that a trio of guards had just reached the top---and had spotted us in the process.

Not a single member of our party hesitated to bring their weapons to bear, or to fire at the newcomers. Though equipped with suppressors, our shots were still audible, for unlike their depiction in adventure 'flickers', such devices do not truly mask all sound, but merely lower its volume.

Further, the fellows that we were shooting at managed to let off bursts of their own, which were not reduced in any way. Thus, everyone in the control room was alerted to the fact that a gunfight was now in progress.

Sheer pandemonium ensued, with the technicians either fleeing or taking cover beneath their workstations, whilst security guards stationed among them opened fire on our position. Bullets struck the metal railings, or buzzed over our heads like angry bees as we returned the compliment.

Then of a sudden, Lady Anne barked out an order. "Cease fire!" The reason for this became apparent when our second and third teams entered the control room from ground level and then engaged the security forces at close range.

The battle between them was short lived; caught entirely by surprise, the guards fell in rapid succession, as did those technicians who were foolish enough to bolt from cover. In but seconds, the room was filled with the smell of burnt gunpowder and no one but our forces remained standing.

Straightaway, I searched for Mr. Grey, worried that I would behold his bullet-riddled corpse, and therefore be denied the satisfaction of killing him myself. Yet he was absent.

"Did anyone see Mr. Grey leave?" I demanded over the general com.

"Jahwoll," one of our commandos responded. *"Der Hurensohn* ran just as soon as your team started shooting."

"Which way did he go?"

"Down the corridor nearest his chair," the soldier answered. Ignoring Lady Anne's instruction to remain, I rose, and pelted down to the control room, and thence into the passage that Mr. Grey had fled through.

The tunnel was not long, and signs along the way indicated that I was headed for the submarine docks. Therefore, I was not surprised to find myself coming into an underground harbor, wherein submersibles of different sizes and shapes were anchored.

Nor was I disappointed by what I found there; Mr. Grey had not yet made good his escape but was standing on the dock before what I knew to be a personal submarine. It was suspended from the ceiling by heavy chains, and he was exhorting an underling to work with greater alacrity.

His assistant was without question one of the largest men that I had ever beheld, with a great muscular physique, and the fair hair and eyes that identified him as a pure Lyran. Just then, he was operating a control box, and the vessel was descending smoothly towards the water.

"Hurry, you fool," Mr. Grey insisted. "Get that machine into the water!"

Seeing the speed at which the craft was being delivered, I knew that in but moments, it would reach the surface. Desperate to prevent this, I paused, took careful aim with my chronopistol, and fired at the machinery that was lowering it. My shot hit true; the submersible jerked in its restraints and ceased moving.

Suddenly realizing that I was there, and what I had just done, Mr. Grey let out a high-pitched shriek of panic and pointed at me.

"Get her!"

Turning, the giant turned and grinned. Then he produced an equally gigantic knife.

"Fight me, Pleiadean," he growled, hefting the blade menacingly. "I will enjoy cutting you apart piece by piece."

I suppose that his sheer size and ferocity, should have cowed me into submission, or perchance, tempted me to succumb to overconfidence, and therefore engage him in hand-to-hand combat with a similar weapon.

But I was in no mood for either. So, I chose a third alternative. I simply raised my chronopistol and put a bolt between his eyes. Imposing as he was, he toppled immediately.

Mr. Grey meantime, had scurried over to a support pylon, where he was frantically attempting to work a manual release chain. Though far slower than the engine had been, the submarine was once again resuming its descent.

Of course, this was not at all satisfactory, and I solved the problem with the same economy as I had with the henchman. Taking aim at the vessel, I put several shots into it. Straightaway, the areas that I had hit corroded and crumbled away, creating rather serviceable holes in the craft's hull.

Despite this, and fueled by sheer desperation, Mr. Grey kept working at the chain, till at last the submersible was in the water. There, it did exactly what I had expected it would, and promptly began to sink.

Finally comprehending the full magnitude of his defeat, he let go of the chain and stood there, trembling in terror. The very sight of him inflamed me to madness, and I transformed, and padded forwards.

Craven that he was, Mr. Grey cowered before me and held out his hand in a useless effort to forestall the inevitable. "No!", he implored, "Spare me, Penelope. I beg you! I know things that the Masters will value greatly. I can tell them all about Saturn!"

But I was too far beyond rationality for his words to matter. Roaring in anger, I swatted at his outstretched hand, and exulted in the man's howl of pain as my claws made contact. Then I used my weight to force him to the ground, intent on clamping my jaws around his throat and shaking him 'til his spine snapped like a dry twig.

Here, the Tigress intervened, reminding me that what I intended would end his life far too quickly to quench my thirst for vengeance. So instead, I raked his front and sides with my claws. As his flesh was shredded into bloody gobbets before my eyes, the traitor shrieked in agony, and no other sound could have ever been sweeter to my ears.

Yes, I thought. *Feel the pain that you have visited upon Elizabeth and I! Upon my friends! Upon the Masters. Suffer for your crimes before you die.*

Wholly unfettered, I ripped, I tore, and I rended him. I wanted his torment to go on forever, and it was only when I realized that he had finally expired that I ceased my assault.

All that remained of Mr. Grey was a ruined hunk of flesh that would have made a butcher blanch. It was a fitting end to an evil man, and I sincerely wished him an eternity in hell.

Then I heard footsteps behind me, and wheeling about, snarled at the new arrivals. It was Mr. Tidwell and Henry, and the two of them stood there, stock still, and regarded the scene before them with a mixture of revulsion and wariness.

"Penny?" Mr. Tidwell asked me carefully. "Do you recognize us?"

In truth, it took me a moment to do that very thing. I was still in the embrace of my bloodlust, and I shook my great shaggy head, forcing myself to embrace the power of reason, and in so doing, returned to my human form.

"Yes," I answered, wiping some of the gore from my features. "I am sorry, but I need a moment in which to compose myself."

As I regained my equilibrium, I did not look back at the corpse but pointedly ignored it, for I had chosen to visit one final indignity upon its former owner. From this point onwards, I would never utter his name, nor suffer to hear it. And if it happened that his memory still managed to haunt me, I had decided that I would even have him erased from my mind by the refactor.

Mr. Grey would suffer the greatest punishment that could ever be visited upon the wicked; not to be despised, for such vile creatures actually revel in their notoriety, but to be completely forgotten as someone who had never existed.

My companions meantime, made no remark about the carnage, nor my nakedness, and Henry offered me a survival blanket from his pack.

"Have we any word yet as to Elizabeth's whereabouts?" I asked, using it to cover myself.

"Not as of yet," Mr. Tidwell advised, referencing a hologram. "However, the oculons have not surveyed the entirety of this installation. There is still a portion to the northwest that they are in the process of investigating. It is currently in enemy hands."

"Then we must go there," I declared. The two men nodded their agreement, and we left the chamber, pausing at a cross corridor so that I could strip the clothes from a dead Lyran.

Though large, a bit of rolling, tucking and the use of Velcro securement straps, managed to produce a serviceable enough outfit for me, although the dead man's shoes proved to be so gargantuan as to be completely useless.

I was not distressed by having to go bare of foot though; better items, including proper footwear, would come later, I assured myself, for it was a certainty that we would encounter more Lyran corpses, or failing this, manufacture them ourselves through the agency of armed combat.

Eventually, we came back into the command center. There, I availed myself of what clothing I could scavenge. In short order, I had managed to find a serviceable pair of shoes and pants which actually fit me, and after putting them on, rejoined Mr. Tidwell and Henry. Just then, they were in the process of conferring with a group of commandos who were preparing for the final push to the northwest. And better still, they had good news.

"The oculons have found her," Henry explained. "Elizabeth is with a contingent of Lyrans at the far end of the complex, no doubt aiding in the defense. There are four other groups that we shall have to fight our way through first, however."

My heart raced at this. "We shall have to be careful when we finally reach her," I cautioned. "She must not become a casualty."

"Do not be concerned," the KSK leader assured me, "We have trained in rescue scenarios where Stockholm syndrome is a factor. I assure you that we will do all that we can to isolate and capture her without incurring any lasting harm."

I was not entirely pleased with his use of the phrase 'lasting harm', as it implied that Elizabeth might suffer some injury during her rescue, but I was forced to accept it nonetheless. The men and women around me were professionals, I told myself, and would not do anything that was not absolutely necessary. However difficult, I would have to trust in their judgement and not impair their actions in any way.

There was a brief check of our equipment (including my submachinegun and chronopistol, which had been returned to me), and then we started off. Nary five minutes elapsed before we encountered the first enemy group.

They had positioned themselves at an intersection, using heavy furniture for barricades, and unleased a fusillade of energy bolts and bullets in our direction. We in turn, sought cover in nearby doorways or alcoves, and gave as good as we got.

The firefight concluded when Henry and Mr. Tidwell launched a pair of specially equipped oculons. These evaded the enemy's fire, located its source, and detonated, peppering the Lyran defenders with metal fragments.

Still, we remained behind cover, till a nanoculon was dispatched to confirm that our enemies were all dead. Stepping over their remains, I was pleased with myself for having the foresight of scavenging what I had in the Command Center. Even their boots were nothing but shreds.

And so it went; we engaged in three more battles very like the first, 'till at last Mr. Tidwell notified me that the group ahead of us included Elizabeth.

Of course, they too fired at us, but out of concern for my lover, none of our fellows answered them with shots of their own. Then to my alarm, I saw that Mr. Tidwell was preparing to launch another oculon.

"No!" I cried, certain that she was about to be blown to bits right along with her comrades. Before I could make any move to interfere however, Henry restrained me with his powerful arms and pulled me into an alcove. Thus, I could only watch helplessly as the little robot flew through the air, found its target, and let go with a brilliant flash and a loud report.

Certain that I had just witnessed my beloved's death, I fought free of Henry's gasp and ran to the Lyran position. Yet, when I came to stand over them, I realized that not a one of them had been injured but were merely stunned. Even then, some were groaning and attempting to rouse themselves.

Elizabeth was one such. She lay off to one side, blinking furiously, but from the emptiness in her eyes it was obvious that she was unable to see or comprehend what was taking place around her.

"Stun grenade," Henry explained as he pushed past. "Don't you worry Ms. Steele, she'll be just fine."

Without further ado, he and Mr. Tidwell rolled her over onto her stomach, and applied a pair of handcuffs to her wrists and plastic restraints to her ankles. Then, as a final touch, a length of 'duck tape' was pasted over her mouth.

By this point, she was regaining her wits, and began to thrash about quite wildly. Mr. Tidwell paid this no heed though, and pulled her to her feet, wherein Henry lifted her up and hoisted her over his shoulder as if she weighed nothing. Though she kicked at him and made terrible noises, she was no match for him in her state.

"Right!" Mr. Tidwell declared. "All trussed up and ready to go."

I grimaced to see her manhandled so. "Be careful with her," I warned, my eyes, ears and fangs having once more assumed a bestial appearance. "Do not let her suffer so much as a single scratch or you shall answer to me."

Wisely, neither man dared to brook any impertinence. Instead, Mr. Tidwell merely awarded me a jaunty two-fingered salute, and took the lead as our team began its trek back to the command center.

There, we were directed not to the ventilation shaft, but down a corridor that led to the base's main entrance. This we found open, and caught sight of a small landing area which the Lyrans had used to land their accursed discs, and the occasional helicopter. What craft there were had been moved aside and a pair of Gamels had taken pride of place.

A seat in the nearest of these had been reserved for Elizabeth's return to Saurii, and Mr. Tidwell and Henry worked together to secure her. I myself, did my best to ignore the look of pure hatred in her eyes, and I was gladsome that we would not be traveling together. Though an Ebani would see to it that the trip would be a short one, I had not relished the idea of spending my time with her within the close confines of Blackbird's cabin.

"We'll keep an eye on her during the flight and meet back up at the base," Mr. Tidwell informed me. "Don't you worry, Penny. Special Section will see to it that she'll be fixed up as good as new."

I was not nearly as sanguine as he, and as I left her in his care and stepped down the cargo ramp, I whispered a prayer that she would be fully restored to her former self.

Lady Anne met me at the bottom.

"I take it that you dealt with Mr. Grey?" she asked.

"I will not say that name ever again, nor do I wish to hear it from anyone's lips," I told her firmly. "But yes, and permanently."

She considered my command for a moment, and then nodded. "Yes, I fully understand. In your situation I would feel likewise."

"Now, if you would excuse me," I added, "I should like to accompany Elizabeth back to the Jurassic."

"Why yes, of course," she agreed. "She will need the comfort of your presence in the days and weeks to come. As it is, our work here is done, and we should all depart."

"Hey! What about my big red button?" It was Major Sixkiller.

"You may attend to that straightaway," Lady Anne informed her, which surprised me for I had expected our raid to be followed by a technical team, especially given the mysterious images on the display screens. But when I made to question this, she raised a silencing hand and gestured for the Major to carry on with her business.

Grinning from ear to ear, Cassie made straight for the aforementioned button, and we followed in train.

"But if this device actually works—?"I began, keeping my voice low so that only Lady Anne would hear this.

"Be not afraid," she replied, her own tone equally as subdued.

Presently, and with great ceremony, the Major looked to us and then pushed the button. However, nothing occurred.

"What the hell?" she exclaimed. "Is this darned thing broken?" She pushed it again, and again, achieved the same dismal result.

"Perhaps it is awaiting repairs?" Lady Anne suggested.

"Well shit!" Sixkiller cursed, slamming her fist down upon the thing. In response, it gave out a sad little beep, and flashed. Once.

As she proceeded to utter a string of curses, Lady Anne leaned into me.

"It was never intended to destroy the base," she advised in a whisper. "*He* had had the signs posted as some sort of jest. According to our prisoners, the button was only used to relieve his stress. I could have informed the Major of this, but she was so looking forwards to the experience that I hadn't the heart."

"What of the information that this place holds then?" I queried, pleased that she was honoring my recent prohibition.

"A technical team should be arriving shorty to ferret out what secrets it can. The Lyrans did not construct this place merely out of pure whimsey, and given that, it is a certainty that whatever is going on over Saturn cannot be anything but wicked."

I awarded the displays a final, sober glance. Then I took my leave of her. "I shall see you in Saurii, madame," I promised.

The instant that we touched down at our base, Elizabeth was taken from the Gamel and escorted into the dome, and thence to a room which had been prepared in advance. It was a makeshift holding cell and she was confined within it, with a pair of mechanica assigned to stand guard over her.

I, meantime, went to speak with the Professor in his laboratory.

"We have her, "I informed him. "How soon can we begin her treatment?"

"I will first need to examine her and determine the extent of the Lyran imprint," he stated, beckoning for Charles to accompany him with a refactor set and an instrument case.

"It would be best if you remained here or retired to your quarters, my dear. Rest assured that I will seek you out once I have made my determinations."

I complied, choosing to abide in my rooms. Though I subsequently attempted to distract myself with a book, I was so anxious that I could not manage to read even a single paragraph, and instead, resorted to pacing about impatiently.

A quarter of an hour passed in this fashion, and then there was a rapping at my door. It was the Professor, and he bore a doleful expression, warning me that something was terribly amiss.

"The stamp of her reprogramming runs far deeper than I had anticipated," he admitted, "and we simply do not possess the means to effectively treat her. What we require is located in London, in the 2nd universe. There is a hospital there that has all of the resources we will need."

"Then to London we must go!" I avowed. "Pray tell, what is the name of this marvelous institution?"

"The Bethlem Royal Hospital in Southwark," he disclosed.

"Bedlam?" I gasped. "The lunatic asylum?" I was mortified at the notion of my dearest being packed off to a madhouse. Elizabeth was mesmerized, not brainsick.

"No, no," he replied, waving away my concern. "Not the asylum itself, but an installation hidden deep within its heart, and well isolated from the rest of the hospital. It is maintained and staffed by Special Section and will provide Elizabeth with the best care that the Masters can provide."

"Yes," I responded in a small, doubt-laden voice. "I suppose so. After all, you know what is best."

"There's a girl," he beamed.

It was raining when we arrived in London, and the foul weather only underscored the unhappy nature of our errand. We did not loiter, but instead, flew straight to Hyde Park.

There, just north of the Serpentine, was a horse drawn ambulance and two men. They were attired in the white coats of hospital staff, and the ambulance itself was a sturdy affair, with the windows firmly barred against escape. On its sides, it bore the name "Bethlem Royal Hospital."

Frowning at the sight of it, I followed Major Sixkiller as she landed. Then I alighted from my Phaseship and stood by as the egress stair on the Major's craft descended.

But a moment later, Elizabeth was brought out by Mr. Tidwell and Henry. Seeing the ambulance, she refused to walk any further and dug in her heels. This compelled the commandos to carry her down the stairs, and then drag her across the sodden grass.

When they finally arrived at the wagon, the attendants, who had positioned themselves at the rear door, opened it wide and assisted them with getting her aboard. This was no mean feat, for she struggled against them with great vigor and braced her feet against the door frame. In the end though, their combined strength won out and she was compelled to enter.

But the very instant that the door was closed and locked, she tore off the duck tape, clutched at the bars, and fixed me with a terrifying expression.

"You bitch!" she snarled, "I will see you gutted from your cunt all the way to your throat! Mark me, I will!"

Pained, I looked to Major Sixkiller. "Please," I said, "tell me that this is going to be successful."

She took my hand in hers. "It will, Penny. She'll be set to rights. I know it."

In the interim, the driver and his partner had returned to their seats, and with a snap of the reins, the ambulance started off. All the while, Elizabeth continued to hurl obscenities at me, each one fouler than the last.

I watched the ambulance until it had disappeared in the mist and rain. Then, I took my leave of the Major and reboarded my Phaseship.

"Don't worry, Penny," Blackbird assured me. "The Major is right; Elizabeth will get well again."

"Thank you, my dearest," I said, fighting not to succumb to a bout of weeping. "Take us home to Charlotte Place. I am sorely in need of comfort, and Father and Aunt Veronica should know of this."

As it happened, when we arrived, there was no need to have either of my relatives summoned. Thanks to Lady Anne (who had preceded me), they had been warned of my coming, and already knew much of what had transpired with Elizabeth. Thus, I found the welcome and understanding that I had so desired. Moreover, they agreed to accompany me when the time came to visit the Asylum, and for that, I was eternally grateful.

That appointment did not come for several days, and when it did, it came by way of Mendel the Rag Man. But upon hearing this news, my courage suddenly failed me.

Was this cowardice? In a word, yes. Despite the fact that I was a were-tiger, a veteran pilot, and a warrior of the No-When, this was one instance where none of that held any significance.

Instead, I was a shamble, and utterly terrified of what I might encounter. It took all of my willpower just to dress for the journey (with no little chivvying by Ms. O'Toole) and to board our coach. But, as I mentioned previously, my Father and my Aunt were there for me, and frankly, I could not have managed without them.

The ride itself was mercifully brief, a mere half of an hour from Kensington, and across the Thames by way of Westminster Bridge.

And despite its fearsome reputation, when at last I laid eyes on it, I was pleased to find that the Royal Hospital was not the run-down horror that I had so envisioned, but a stately structure, with a great dome and a colonnaded entry.

The grounds which surrounded it were pleasant and hygienic, with a goodly number of the inmates taking in the fresh air under the management of nurses and orderly's who themselves, were well-turned out in crisp, professional uniforms. Rather than embodying the chaos which the name 'Bedlam' tended to evoke, I would later learn that what I was witnessing was the result of 'moral treatment', which had been instituted in the 1700's by the great visionary William Tuke. This revolutionary approach to mental illness had supplanted less humane practices and treated patients not as animals to be caged, but as children to be cared for.

I was much reassured.

Pulling up to the entrance, we were met by a senior nurse, who escorted us directly to the office of Dr. Daniel Hack Tuke, who was no less than William Tuke's great-grandson. He proved to be a man cut from the same cloth as Professor Merriweather; a wise and learned gentleman with an imposing presence, and when he displayed the Sign of Six to us in greeting, he also identified himself as a member of the Fellowship.

Dr. Tuke immediately excused the nurse and took us into the wards himself. Again, I was pleasantly surprised; the halls that we traversed were not the cramped corridors of a dungeon, but spacious and possessed large windows, filling the place with sunlight and offering a healthful view of the grounds. Patients who were not considered dangerous occupied the seats and couches to either side of us, and a handful of nurses supervised their activities.

It was when we had entered the women's section that a rather startling event occurred. Three inmates were sitting together, and as one, they looked up at me as I made to pass.

When we made eye contact, time around us halted. Then the nearest of them, a young woman in her early 20's with raven hair, and intense dark eyes, spoke to me in a strange, sing-song voice.

"A Lady of Steel, is she? Despite such a lofty title, we do not give our treasure to anyone simply because they crave it. Even Arcturus had to prove himself worthy."

The woman opposite her, a grizzled old hag, responded to this and pointed accusingly at me, "I smell the Gaul in her, and I challenge her right to the sword."

Then the woman in the middle, a heavyset redhead, suddenly stood up and raised her fist high, shouting, "Gather your strength my soldiers, and as you love God, follow me!"

And then, just as abruptly, she retook her seat, whereupon all three of them chanted in unison, "Death is not the only measure of virtue."

While I struggled to make sense of this peculiar performance, time resumed its normal state. No longer were the women fixated upon me, and presently, they seemed as normal as anyone afflicted with madness could ever aspire to be. Nor could I detect any sign that they had any memory of what had just transpired. Plainly, whatever had chosen to speak through them, had just departed.

As for Dr. Tuke and my relatives, they continued onwards, wholly unaware of my encounter, and perforce, I followed, saying nothing whatsoever about it. After some minutes, we came to a side corridor and a large wooden door. There, the doctor produced a set of keys, and unlocked it to reveal a lift.

This was no product of the 19th century though, but something hearkening to the Master's time, being made of polished steel and lit by a hidden source that managed to banish all the shadows. There were of course, no controls, and just as I had seen on many other occasions, a mere wave of Dr. Tuke's hand was all that was required for it to begin its descent. How far we travelled, I cannot say, save that I got the distinct impression that we were deep beneath the earth by the time that the doors opened.

Just as in all of our bases, the corridor that we stepped into was a plain, utilitarian affair, with the same advanced lighting, and broken only by doors marked with Atlantean characters. These I knew, would also open at a gesture, provided of course, that the petitioner had the clearance to be admitted within their precincts.

One of these portals did in fact allow us entrance and Dr. Tuke ushered us into another ward, but one that was quite different from those on the surface.

It was overseen by a sleek nurse's station and manned by staff members whose blouses and tunics bore a seven-pointed star embroidered in gold. Unlike their counterparts in the hospital proper, they did not labor under the light of gas lamps with paper or dip pens. Instead, they attended to holographic terminals and monitored their patients on virtual screens that floated in the air before them.

Noticing us, a rather comely blond woman who I knew to be a Pleiadean just by the perfection of her physique, rose and smiled pleasantly.

"Nefer'heru, Ur-Senu. Antu Grímsdóttir sto an t'cher hita-pechtiu", she said in a lovely *contralto*, "Good Morning, Chief Physician. Commander Grímsdóttir is awaiting you in viewing room seven."

"We will abide here," Father advised, and he and Aunt Veronica remained where they were.

Suddenly bereft of their support, I followed Dr. Tuke into the viewing room and as advertised, Kára Grímsdóttir was awaiting us. The Ostlander was standing before a window, whose glass was as dark as if it had been fashioned from the purest onyx. Yet, at her command, it became totally translucent.

Elizabeth was on the other side. Dressed in nothing more than a hospital gown, she was no longer the ferocious creature that I had endured in Hyde Park. Instead, she sat quietly on the edge of her bed as a nurse slipped a refactor headset onto her temples.

"She cannot see nor hear you," Dr. Tuke said. "which for the moment, is for the best."

"What has been done to her?" I asked, for she seemed more a mannequin to me than the woman that I had known and loved.

The Doctor explained. "Initially, we were forced to employ restraints and powerful tranquilizers, but as you can see, those steps are no longer required. Though she is still under the influence of light sedatives, her present state is the result of our having extracted all of her memories. She is a *tabula rasa* if you will, awaiting a stylus to make its mark upon her consciousness."

"As for that, we will utilize the last refactor recording from before her abduction, and then create new, artificial memories to splice her mind to the present. The process is very delicate, and it will take us some time to complete the task, but my associates and I are reasonably confident of our success."

I did not miss his cautionary tone, and I was reminded of Colonel Ambrose's warning on this score. However skilled Doctor Tuke and his colleagues were, Elizabeth's recovery was not a *fait accompli.*

Come back to me, I thought, touching my fingers to the glass. *I cannot live without you.*

Then, I turned away. "I have seen enough. Thank you for allowing me this visitation, Doctor."

"We will send word to you of her progress, Ms. Steele," he promised.

What followed this, you might wonder? I simply cannot remember, save that I returned to Charlotte Place and spent the rest of my time in a mindless purgatory, feigning interest in the mundane business of the household whilst my heart was far, far away.

It was only after many days and when Mendel came again, and asked after me, that my soul returned, and then, no force in Heaven or Earth could have restrained me.

You see, I had been invited to return to Bethlem, and to visit Elizabeth herself. Not below in the confines of the special ward, but in the sun-dappled gardens that surrounded the Royal Hospital.

Calling for Mr. Tidwell and Ms. O'Toole, I had the Victoria brought 'round straightaway, and hastily dressed. This time, only Father accompanied me (for my Aunt was involved in a meeting of her Suffragettes and undoubtably planning some great act of mischief). And had I been able, I would have had Mr. Tidwell urge the horses to maximum effort, but thankfully, he and Father possessed greater sense, and we made our journey at more a decorous pace.

We were met by Dr. Tuke, and he guided us through the gardens to Elizabeth, and although they were quite lovely, I paid them no heed. The only thing of importance was reaching my lover's side.

We found her near a pink rose bush, seated in a wheelchair and companioned by a nurse. For a moment, I feared that she was still in a catatonic state, so motionless was she.

"Elizabeth?"

At the sound of her name, she blinked, and I saw the first faint fires of recognition kindling in her eyes.

"I know you," she said, and after a long moment, she added, "you are---you are—*Penelope.*" Her smile widened and a look of child-like triumph came over her features. "Yes, Penelope. That is your name!"

Overcome, I knelt down, and took her hand in mine, kissing it and gazing up at her.

"Yes, my love, it is I, Penelope," I cried, my eyes welling up with tears of joy. "Oh my dearest one. How I have prayed for this moment."

Then I looked up to the Doctor, "I thank you, good sir, from the very bottom of my heart. I will be forever in your debt."

"There is still much that we have to do," he warned. "She will require more treatment with the refactor. The process is not something that can be done in one go. Moreover, the procedure takes its toll on the entire body, and she will need to rebuild her strength before she can return home."

I knew that he had spoken truly for Elizabeth's fatigue was graven on her features. The simple act of recognizing me had cost her greatly.

"Is there anything that I can do to aid in her recovery? Ask, and it is done."

"She would be well served by your continued presence," he advised. "As you yourself are aware, someone who is in a newly Awakened state, for this is exactly what is occurring here, benefits from gentle coaxing and constant reminders. Further, if you can bring certain things to her, so much the better."

"Such as?"

"A favorite book perhaps," he suggested, "or a beloved possession. Such items can help to jog the mind in a positive direction, but nothing is quite as salubrious as your time and attention."

I stood. "She will have all that and more."

And this is exactly what transpired. Father and I departed the hospital and once returned to Charlotte Place, I gathered up books from our library, and then retrieved a silver hairbrush that Elizabeth had always adored, and after that, her favorite nightgown, and more besides. In the space of only a half an hour, I was back in the carriage with my armload and on my way to Bethlem.

Thus, I took up residence at the Asylum, spending the entirety of my time in Elizabeth's presence. I read to her, brushed her hair and sang songs that she had heard as a child, strolled with her in the gardens, and attended to her every need. There was not a single moment of the day, save when she was receiving her treatments, that I was not with her, and when she slept, I watched over her, only sleeping myself when I knew that her respite would be untroubled.

Ultimately, her condition improved. Not only did her vitality return to her, but she was able to recall much of what had occurred before her imprisonment at Moberly. She was even able to gently correct me whenever I was mistaken about a detail from our past.

As for her time as a Lyran thrall, here Dr. Tuke had shown compassion, and had expunged the entire period from her mind; that it had been captured to a recording was enough, and again, I found myself in his debt.

Then at last, the day came when she was pronounced well enough to be discharged. Just as her betrayal had been one of the saddest in my life, the day that we left Bethlem together, and travelled back to Charlotte Place, was perhaps one of the happiest.

The entire staff was waiting at the entrance to receive us, along with Lady Anne and Colonel Ambrose, and although they dearly wanted to celebrate this momentous event, I expressly forbade it out of the fear that it would overtire my lover. Instead, I had her taken up to our rooms so that she could rest and reorient to her surroundings in peace.

Here, I am compelled to share a very personal detail that nonetheless sheds light on Elizabeth's ordeal. It was a full fortnight before she was truly her old self again, and out of concern, I had refrained from touching her. Yet when it became clear that her vitality (and her interest) had returned, we made love at last. And here, in the crucible of truth that comes only in the most intimate of moments, I finally noticed the subtle difference between the woman I had known before Moberly, and the one who had come after. It had escaped my attention until this, yet now it was apparent.

While she was still as passionate as ever, she gave more of herself to me, as if her conditioning had somehow prevented this. Mind you, it was not a terribly pronounced thing, but still I detected it, and in so doing, realized that she was in fact, truly healed. This Elizabeth was the woman I had always known and loved, free of any Lyran taint.

CHAPTER 8: Excalibur

*In which I dream again of Saturn and curb the Sibyl's excesses once and for all.
Then, I am conveyed through the looking glass to the grotto of X'Kallabar and
face the trial of the Blue People. After that, I learn the ways of the sword and
meet a challenge in the crypt of the Yellow Emperor.*

For a time, I enjoyed the peace and quiet of Charlotte Place,
with no greater concern than to see to Elizabeth's happiness.
That, and keeping my promise to see Amica installed in our garden.
Blackbird was greatly cheered by her friend's return, and her
improved mood only added to our idyllic situation.

As for the Lyran menace, my worries were relegated to the back
of my mind. Better still, we suffered no strange visitations from any
party, had no odd visions or occult events, nor were we ensnared in
any dark intrigues. The hours followed one another with such blissful
conventionality that I almost came to think of my life in normal
terms. But as Fate would have it, this halcyon period came to an end,
and my true existence reasserted itself in my slumbers.

I had fallen asleep in our bed whilst reading my copy of *"Le Morte
d' Arthur,"* and quite without realizing it. It was not until Saturn
appeared in my consciousness that I understood that I was dreaming.

As always, I was drawn towards the planet, my dread increasing
as the distance between us shortened. And again, this was overlaid
with the malicious giggling of children. This time though, the Sibyl
and Maggie allowed themselves to be seen, and they were positively
delighted by my terror.

By now, I was at the end of my temper. White hot anger flared
up within me and I shouted at them. "This is *MY* dream! "How dare
you molest me so!"

The force of my words had a powerful effect for they recoiled
from me and disappeared. Then a shadow fell over me from behind.

Turning to face its source, I was just able to make out an object
spinning towards me from the very heart of the Sun. The brilliance
of the light, unfettered as it was by the lack of an atmosphere, made
it difficult for me to make out what it was, but as it came closer, I
realized that it was a cross. A cross made of wood, and on it, was
Jesus of Nazareth himself.

Our eyes met, and I heard his voice in my mind. *Do not think that I came to bring peace on the earth,* he proclaimed, *I did not come to bring peace, but a sword.*

Without hesitation, I reached out and caught the crucifix, now somehow small enough to grasp. As my fingers closed around the wood, it changed again, becoming X'Kallabar. Moreover, my hand was no longer bare, but covered by a metal gauntlet. And when I looked, I saw that the rest of me had also undergone an alteration, for I was now clothed in gleaming armor.

Even as I comprehended this, X'Kallabar began to glow from within. Then its radiance flowed down the blade and into me until I too was fully illuminated. Our combined light filled the darkness around us and infused me with an overwhelming sense of power the likes of which I had never before experienced.

Filled with this heady sense of omnipotence, I returned my gaze to Saturn and the terrible things that lurked amongst its rings. Then, I raised my sword high and prepared to strike.

Alas, before I could smite my foes, the scene vanished, and I found myself once again in my bedchamber, looking to the foot of my bed and the figures standing there. It was my mother, as well as the Sibyl and Maggie.

"I see that you too have become a dreamer at last," my mother observed. But whatever pride I might have felt at this achievement was eclipsed by my incandescent anger.

"That *child*—" I snapped, stabbing a finger in her direction, "or whatever she really is--is sorely in need of a good paddling, madam, and I'm of a mind to turn her over my knee right now and deal it out to her in spades!"

To my immense satisfaction, the Sibyl and her partner retreated to a place of safety behind my mother.

"They only served our purposes," she explained. "Do not hold it against them."

Unmollified, I hissed at the little prophetess and her cohort, causing them to shrink away from me. "From this moment onwards, you will leave me in peace, or so help me, I shall seek you out wherever you abide and see you set to rights! Do you *hear* me?"

Prudently, they did not offer up any challenge, but nodded nervously and promptly dematerialized.

My mother shrugged. "I must admit that she deserved that. Perhaps now, the Sibyl will reexamine her ways and adopt a kinder policy towards those she teaches."

"She had damn well better," I bristled. Then, remembering where I was, I glanced over at Elizabeth, fully expecting to see her awake and ready to offer an apology. Yet, despite all of the commotion, she had not roused.

In the interim, my mother had wandered over to the full-length mirror that we used to inspect ourselves. There, she raised her hand to the glass, and it rippled as if it were not a solid, but a liquid.

"Despite the Sibyl's excesses, the vision that she imposed upon you had its purpose," she advised. "It is time, my daughter, to take another journey through the looking glass. You have an appointment to keep with the Blue People."

"Have they contacted us then?" I asked.

"Not in so many words," she answered, "but through an intermediary that you well know."

"I do?"

"Yes," she responded. "None other than little Maggie. She happens to descend from a very ancient line of Britons that hearkens back to the time when the Blue People were their partners.'

"Because of this ancient bond, the Blue People reached out to her through her dreams and told her that the time had come. She in turn, informed us. So, you see, nothing happens by accident and everything has a purpose, though it might not be apparent at the moment.'

"She also shared a prophesy that the Blue People disclosed to her, and I shall tell it to you now; *'The hero will only prove their worthiness by defeating a mighty army, rescuing a princess, and facing a dragon in its lair.'*"

"What does it mean?" I inquired.

"I know not," my mother replied. "Perhaps it is purely symbolic, and perhaps it warns of events yet to come. Only time will tell. I will, however, add my own wisdom to this and beg you to remember one thing. It is that death is not the only measure of virtue."

This caused me to shudder, for it was the very same thing that the madwomen had chanted at Bedlam. Somehow, and despite their mental infirmity, they had enjoyed a link to things far beyond their ken, just as the Oracle of Delphi had once conveyed the messages of the Gods. Amazed, and wondering greatly at what this portended, I rose, donned my flightsuit, and then joined my progenitrix at the mirror.

Though I could see the two of us in its reflection, Elizabeth and our bedroom were entirely absent. In their place was an eldritch forest unlike anything that I had ever beheld before.

The trees within it grew to fantastic heights, surpassing the great sequoias and the redwoods of the 3rd universe. Giant ferns and great mushrooms the size of carriages, grew in their shadows, and small, luminous balls of light that were colored every shade of the rainbow cavorted everywhere.

Moreover, a pair of figures were coming towards us, using a trail that meandered through the forest floor, and in a heartbeat, I knew them. One was my sister, Caroline, dressed as a Druid Priestess, and the other was her companion, the Chuchniya. Plainly, I was not about to make my trek to X'Kallabar alone.

At a nod from my mother, I stepped forwards.

Passing through the looking glass, I felt a fleeting sensation of cold as if I had entered an icy body of water, but then this was replaced by the milder climate of the woodland. Glancing back over my shoulder, I could still see the general outline of the mirror's glass, and within it, my bedroom. My mother, however, had disappeared.

Then one of the little orbs flitted over to me, all aglow with a xanthous light. Like the one that I had encountered aboard the Black Knight, I instinctively knew it to be sentient. And when it came near enough to make out its finer details, I gasped aloud in delighted wonder, for in the very center of this amber phosphorescence, I spied a diminutive figure.

No larger than the last joint of my littlest finger, she (for her curves made her sex quite obvious) was the perfect reproduction of a full-sized human being, save that she sported a pair of wings like that of a dragonfly. Our eyes met for no more than a heartbeat before she gave out a tiny little laugh and flew away, but it was enough for me to discern the intelligence in them.

I also realized that what I had just encountered was the genus of every tale ever told about the fairy-folk, and also the answer to an age-old mystery. Like the Chuchniya, these Lilliputian creatures were visitors to our worlds, crossing over when and where they willed.

"Friends," an impossibly deep voice stated. When I looked about, I realized that it had come from a wholly unexpected quarter.

Of all things, the Chuchniya had been the speaker! This astounded me even more than the little fairy woman, for I had never credited the creature with the capacity for speech.

In response, the Wild Man made a grunting noise, which I took for amusement, and then he gestured with his great hairy arm to indicate the entirety of the forest. "Our land," he said.

When he saw that I had comprehended him, he pointed upwards, and looking to the heavens, another wonderment revealed itself. Instead of the moon shining down at me through the branches, a great gas giant dominated the sky, and we, I realized, were in orbit around *it*. Further, I noted that there were other moons nearby, which were also Earth-like, having landmasses, seas and clouds.

What manner of beings must live on those satellites? I wondered, involuntarily conjuring up fantastical apparitions in my mind's eye. Given what currently surrounded me, absolutely anything seemed possible.

"Come," the Chuchniya invited. "Walk."

Immediately, I fell into step with my companions and as we continued down the trail, my sister spoke to me by way of her telepathic gift.

Though we could make our journey much more directly, the Wild Man has chosen to honor you with this detour, she elucidated. *He desired that you be awarded the opportunity to see what few beyond his kind, and those like myself have experienced—his home, and the place of his people. The Jump Worlds are not the only alternate dimensions that can shrink the distance between times and places, and as you can surely appreciate, some of them are actually quite pleasant.*

"Yes," I nodded. "They are at that. I am honored that he chose to share this with me."

In reply, the huge creature smiled. To be frank, it was not a very good smile, and really more of a grimace (giving me the distinct impression that his kind was unaccustomed to using such an expression to indicate pleasure), but out of politeness, I took great care to respond in kind.

"Thank you, sir," I told him.

After a time, we came to a spot populated by other Wild Men, as well as their females and children. The children in particular caught my eye, for like human young, they were playing at a game of chase.

But, in their case, this involved the participants disappearing as they ran and then rematerializing a dozen or so feet away. Aside from

176

the fact that this radically increased the challenge of the game, it was also equally clear that there was a serious purpose behind it, for it was teaching them the art of bio-location, a skill which they would eventually require as adults.

Looking to him, I noticed that the Chuchniya seemed quite interested in their contest, pausing to watch, and then grunting in approval at the more adept participants (which only reinforced my surmise about the game's educational qualities).

After a moment or so of this, we moved on, leaving the Wild Man's relatives behind us, and entering an uninhabited area. Even here we were not alone, for at one point, I glimpsed a slim figure out of the corner of my eye.

It was shaped like a woman, but with impossibly thin proportions and colored a light green from head to toe. She was visible for only an instant, peering at me from behind one of the giant trees, but when I attempted to look at her directly, I felt a pronounced sense of alarm radiating from her before she disappeared. Not behind the tree mind you, but right into it, and with no more difficulty than you or I might run through a door to escape from danger.

My sister explained. *She is frightened of you,* she told me. *She knows you to be an apex predator.*

"But I would never dream of harming her or anything here," I protested.

Nonetheless, beings as fragile as she will avoid you out of caution, Caroline warned. *It is the price that you must pay for possessing the power you have—and that which is soon to come.*

Seeing yet another dryad (for this is what I deduced the first one to be) fleeing from my presence, I frowned. Predation was not my intent, and it galled me to be considered a threat out of hand. Yet, as my sister had aptly stated, this was my lot, whether I wished it or not.

At last, we came to a spot that was colder than what had preceded it. In addition, the air seemed charged with static electricity, causing the hair on my arms and neck to rise up.

Here, the Wild Man paused only long enough to wave me to him, and I grasped his great hand and allowed him to pull me along, knowing what was to come. For an instant, I felt as if I were tumbling through the air, and in the next, I discovered that we had left the forest behind us for another realm altogether.

It was the complete opposite of the Wild Man's world; naught but a great dark plain composed of what seemed to be dark unbroken stone, or perchance, even meteoric nickel. Though the sky above me was dark and starless, a white glow on the horizon lent me just enough light to make my way.

This was not the most remarkable thing about this place, however. What stood out was the sudden and surprising sensation that here, the divine spark that I had first sensed aboard the Black Knight, and had since taken for granted, was completely absent. Wherever I was, I was in a realm where God simply did not exist.

Worse yet, something *else* did.

Though I could not see it, the presence of some great and terrible force registered in my consciousness. I could not give it any coherent shape beyond a wild vision of thousands of eyes and whipping black tentacles, but I was clear on one point; it was the very antithesis of all things, including evil. I also knew that it was impossibly ancient and that somehow, in an age before even time itself, it had been imprisoned in this awful realm by unguessable forces.

Of a sudden, my sister stepped in front of me and clasped my head in her hands. *You must not think so loudly here*, she cautioned. *IT will hear you.*

Chilled by this admonition, and feeling the presence of the nameless horror all the more, I summoned up every lesson I had learned in Shamballa about controlling the mind's ramblings, especially where they concerned moving meditation. With a few deep breaths (and no little willpower), I caused my inner dialogue to lessen. It was not a total cessation of thoughts, but enough that the sensation of menace diminished, as if the demonic entity lurking in the darkness had thought itself mistaken, and was returning to its fitful sleep.

Not long after, I felt the temperature plummet and as it did so, the Wild Man held out his hand once more. This time, I could not have been more eager to accept it—though out of caution, I deliberately suppressed my exuberance.

When again, the world spun, and reoriented itself, I was relieved to find myself in relatively familiar surroundings. Now, I was in the stone corridor which led directly to the grotto of X'Kallabar.

"What was that last place that we visited?" I asked my guides. "It was terrifying."

A short-cut, Caroline answered. *Like the world of the Wild Man, though not quite as convivial.* My sister, it seemed, either had a true talent for understatement, or a very dry sense of humor.

"Well, I certainly hope that we shall not have occasion to visit it again," I said.

Have no fear in that regard, she responded. *We will not need to do so. Now, prepare yourself, for the time of your testing is nigh.*

Nary two minutes passed before the nature of the passage changed. It no longer depended upon the luminosity of the mold clinging to its walls. Rather, torches had been set into the stones at regular intervals, and when at last, we entered the grotto itself, the twelve Priestess Guardians were awaiting us, each bearing flaming brands of their own.

They did not greet us, but regarded our presence with stoic silence. Save for the sound of our breathing and the crackle of the torches, the chamber was as noiseless as the tomb it resembled.

As for the stone, it was no longer empty, but bore a marvel which up until now I had only beheld in dreams. X'Kallabar was there, resembling a sword in shape, but lit from within by a caerulean light that pulsed like the beating of a human heart. Once more, I longed to hold it, though I restrained myself, knowing as I did, that I would be committing a grave offense. Accordingly, I abided with my friends and contented myself with merely gazing upon its magnificence and aching with desire.

Presently, a thirteenth figure arrived. She seemed to glide rather than walk across the paving, and while the other women were comely enough, she was more beautiful than them all.

Her hair was long, and a shade of blond that reminded me of the fabled metal, orichalcum, both gold and copper. It complimented her azure skin and offset her eyes to perfection. These were the deep green of a forest pool, and pregnant with an ageless wisdom. Even without the great golden torque that she wore about her neck, and the richness of her garments, I knew that I was looking upon none other than Nyneve, the Queen of the Blue People and the fabled Lady of the Lake.

Who is this that comes seeking Xkalla'bar? she asked telepathically. This was not to me, but to Caroline.

Penelope Victoria, Daughter of Steele, my sister answered.

Nyneve raised a delicate eyebrow in my direction. *A Lady of Steel, is she? Despite such a lofty title, we do not give our treasure to anyone simply because they crave it. Even Arcturus had to prove himself worthy. Is she ready to face the test?*

Once again, I recognized the words from my encounter with the inmates of Bethlem. *So this is what they meant,* I mused.

She is, I heard Caroline respond.

Then face it she shall, Nyneve answered. *And prove her mettle before the harshest judge of all.*

At this, another mental voice interposed itself, and the newcomer stepped from the shadows. Unlike the Queen, her face was hidden by a dark veil, yet despite this, I could tell that she appeared to be as old as Nyneve seemed young. Older even, if not Old Age itself.

She has not the blood of these isles in her veins, the hag declared, pointing a long bony finger at me in accusation. *I smell the Gaul in her, and I challenge her right to the sword.*

The Lady of the Lake smiled at this indictment. *That is your prerogative, Cailleach, and you are partially correct. She is French, but only on her mother's side.*

Ah hah! the Cailleach exclaimed. *Even that is more than enough to condemn her as an enemy! I say that we should slay her, and in such a manner as to give any foreign pretender pause before ever attempting the same.*

Hearing this, the amazon guards set their torches aside, raised their staffs and took up fighting stances against me. Myself, I readied for combat while wondering at the Cailleach's claim.

I am not French, I thought, *but as English as oak!*

Then I reminded myself that this was not actually so. According to my mother, I was Pleiadean (although I had little idea what this meant). Under normal circumstances, this would have been enough for me to dismiss the Cailleach's claim as so much falderal.

Yet, there was something in her words that rang true. Though I struggled to deny it, I could feel the veracity of it in the very marrow of my bones.

Then confusion took the reins entirely as a memory arose. Till now, the details of that event had been relegated to the back of my mind, but presently, they demanded my full recognition.

When I had kidnapped Dr. Anton Brandt, I had delivered him to a spot just outside of Paris. Though my mother had never explained this choice of location to me, I now realized that France, and not

England, had been her home. And Paris had been the place where she and my mana-father had worked and lived out their lives together.

Of course, I could have argued that she had simply preferred the city—but not now. Now I knew; however impossible, and however alien she was, France was *also* her native land, and by extension, mine as well.

France! As my readers might well imagine, I found this all to be rather disconcerting and the threatening demeanor of the amazon guards did nothing to calm me.

I remind you, oh Veiled One, Nyneve responded, *that while the sword was given into our care, it was not merely to protect what we call Shacsana and outsiders call England, but also the world in which our hallowed isles reside.*

We are of Shacsana, the Cailleach protested. *What care I for the rest?*

Without the rest, we are nothing, Nyneve countered. *After all, what is Shacsana at its very heart, if not the guardian of all that is good and worthy in Mankind? That is the true mission of Excalibur; to preserve what is sacred and pure no matter what corner of the world it springs from. There is no higher cause.*

Pah! the Cailleach spat, casting a malevolent glance in my direction. *What good has ever come from France?*

It is a shame that you have never forgotten the Hundred Years War, Nyneve observed dryly, *or that unfortunate incident at the Castle Aargh!*

No! the Cailleach snarled. *I have not forgotten. Save for Gaulish interference, the Grail would have been ours!*

Nyneve awarded her a sardonic smile. *There is another thing that you must know about this Lady of Steel, oh Veiled One. Though her flesh is French, a portion of her soul is English, and from her father. You cannot dispute that, any more than you can her mother's lineage. Moreover, there is precedent; did you not allow Lancelot du Lac to join Arcturus, even though he too was not of our shores?*

Yes, and see how that ended! my accuser retorted. *He betrayed his king!*

All men are weak, Nyneve riposted. *Even those as valorous as Lancelot. This one though, is not a man, and of a different bloodline. She must be judged on her own merits--if merit she has.*

The Cailleach finally conceded the argument, but with no little reluctance. *Then test she shall--but her trial must be as if she were two persons and of two lands, rather than one, for of two she is. Perchance even three, for there is a beast within her as well. I can see it plainly.*

We are agreed then, Nyneve nodded. *Let the trial begin.*

Flashing me a look of undiluted hatred, the Cailleach waved her hand over the floor, and with this, the stone beneath my feet began to swirl about and bubble as if it had suddenly become liquid. My ankles were held fast by the viscous substance, and unable to move, I watched as a whirlpool formed around me and drew me downwards. In but a breath, I had sunk to my knees, and then it claimed my hips and went on to embrace my waist and chest.

Seeing me thus, the Cailleach cackled with delight. *Into the cauldron, oh Lady of Steel, and we shall see what emerges once the waters of life and death have had their way with you.*

The last thing I saw was Caroline, looking at me with what seemed an expression of pity.

There is no more I can do for you my sister, she told me. *What remains is in your hands alone...*

...Seeing the grim towers of Le Tourelle looming before them the soldiers of France had faltered. The English were waiting for us behind defenses that seemed impregnable. Yet the holy mission to rid my country of these invaders could not be allowed to slow nor stop—not until God's will had been fulfilled.

Grasping my banner and holding it high, I rode before our forces, letting them see the image of God gracing its white expanse and the motto *Jésus Marie.*

"Our Lord has granted us a great victory," I cried, meeting their eyes. "But another victory awaits."

I could see it in my mind, every detail starkly clear; the hated English flag being struck down and the men of France taking the fortress in triumph.

Though not without sacrifice, for I had also been granted another vision. I would be wounded in the fight, and most grievously. The pain would be well worth it though, I told myself. Where it concerned France and seeing my beloved Dauphin crowned, no sacrifice was too great.

"Gather your strength my soldiers, and as you love God, follow me!"

At this, the fire rekindled in their hearts, and with a mighty roar that seemed to shake the very heavens, they surged forwards. Though waves of arrows rained down upon us and the English artillery thundered, they did not stop. Nor did I.

In what seemed a thousand years and but a flicker of time, we had reached the palisades, and then the walls, though the missiles of our enemy rained down on us without mercy.

"Press onwards, oh soldiers of France! In the name of the Lord, press on!" I shouted.

Then the men bearing the ladders came up from behind, and began to lay them against the ramparts. Many who charged up them were felled, but many more followed after, intrepid in their faith.

Up, up, thought I, *topple these unholy usurpers! Cast them down to the earth where they belong.*

Seeing a ladder nearby, I caught hold of it, and helped the men to raise it. Once more, my prophesy asserted itself, and I realized that the moment had come at last. God was about to exact his price.

Still, I did not hesitate, and waving my banner one final time, I took my first steps on the rungs, willingly, and just as Christ had ascended to meet his end on Calvary.

The promised bolt came like lightning, piercing my armor betwixt my shoulder and throat. It felt as if a great fist had slammed into me, knocking me backwards.

As I fell into the arms of the soldiers around me, I wept from the pain and the fear that threatened to overmaster me. In this, I was belike my blessed Lord who, faced with the mortality of his body, had his moment of doubt. Nay, I was even more terrified than he, for I was no Son of God, but small, and flawed in every respect.

But of a sudden, St. Catherine was at my side, comforting me, and promising that all would be well. So assured, I let myself be carried away from the battle to a tent where the physician treated my injury, and somewhere during this, I fell asleep with a smile upon my face. For France, I knew, would be free…

…Do you see how gleefully she urged the shedding of English blood? the Cailleach protested. *How willing she was to see murder done?*

Unruffled, Nyneve answered this charge. *It was war and Jehanne d'Arc loved her country and her king with all her heart. So much so, that in the end, she was made a saint that both sides came to honor.*

And I say that we stopped the test too soon, the Cailleach complained. *I would have wanted to see how 'devoted' she was when they burned her at Rouen. Methinks that the flames would have made a doubter of her.*

They did not, Nyneve answered. *To the end, and until the smoke stole her breath away, she cried out the name of Jesus over and over again. It was the men who watched this who were the ones that lost heart. 'We are lost,' they said. 'We have burned a saint.'*

Then weak and befuddled they were, the Cailleach snapped. *Joan was a demon and nothing more--and this challenger is no better than she. On to the next test then. She will surely fail...*

...Two Messerschmitts were hard on Henri's tail. *Hold on,* I thought, pitching hard over and diving for the *boche* fighters.

For a few moments, the fields of eastern England spun beneath me like a quilt being whirled through the air by a madman, yet it was I who was doing the spinning.

In seconds, I was on the nearest German, and let loose with my .303 Browning machineguns. Pieces of the invader's plane flew off in all directions and black smoke billowed out of the fuselage. Staying in the fight was no longer an option for the enemy pilot, and he descended, heading for the Channel and limping towards occupied France.

I did not feel any sense of triumph at his defeat however, nor hurl curses in his direction, for a fellow Frenchman was still in peril. If I did not act soon, he would soon join the others who had died fleeing Vichy to fight the Nazis, his grave marked by an assumed name to protect his family from reprisal.

My moment arrived but a second later. For less than half an eyeblink, the fascist aircraft was lined up with my sights and Henri was clear. Unhesitating, I fired, and this time, my bullets found their mark in the fuel tank, or perchance, severed a gas line. Whichever the case, the ME-109 exploded in a fireball that left no doubt whatsoever about the fate of its pilot.

Then Henri and I became the hunters, making for another pair of Germans that were engaged with an equal number of our countrymen. We soared upwards and attacked them, the sunlight making the Cross of Lorraine flash on our fuselages. The sight reminded me of the banner that the Maid herself had once used to rally her soldiers on the battlefield.

Oddly, I even thought that I could feel her, reaching out across the centuries to lend her strength, and had I not known better, I might have supposed that she was there with me in the cockpit, guiding my very hand.

With such an inspiration, and my own skill at flying, the outcome was all too clear. My target wobbled in midair under my onslaught, and then dipped sideways.

Although the canopy opened, and the pilot bailed out, I saw that his parachute was on fire. Instead of saving him, it only served to mark his fall like a hideous candle lit to honor Death itself.

Watching him drop, I told myself that he was an enemy of France, and of our ally, England, yet his end was a terrible thing to behold.

But there was more at stake here than the life of one man. The destiny of the entire world hung in the balance, and only God and his messenger, St. Joan, knew who would ultimately conquer...

...You cheated! the Cailleach whined. *She did not die as she ought to have! I would have seen her dropping to her death clothed in flames, not the German.*

Death is not the only measure of virtue, Nyneve refuted.

Then I ask you this, the Cailleach challenged. *Did she rescue her friend Henri because he was French, or because he fought for a just cause?*

You have to ask? Nyneve queried. *Was it not clear? She loved both England and France and hated the Nazis with equal vigor.*

I am not satisfied with that, the Cailleach spat. *She must be tested a third time. There, she shall truly show the weakness of her character. I am certain of it.*

Nyneve, smiled. *As you wish....*

...Ours was a small village, no more than a few rude homes, overlooking the Irish Sea. Though fierce storms sometimes arose from these waters, I had never been afraid of the ocean, for I had no reason to be. It had always provided us with sustenance, only demanding our respect in return.

This day though, I saw sails on the horizon, and as the ships drew nearer, I observed how low they rode upon the water, and then I perceived the dragons carved upon their prows.

These were no friends, I thought with a chill, but enemies. As quickly as my feet could carry me across the sands, I ran from the beach, up the hill, and sought out my mother.

"Raiders!" I cried. "The Northmen come!" Though I had never seen these fearsome devils myself, I had heard of their terrible deeds. And against them, we had no real defense.

My mother did not doubt my report in the least, but gathered my brother and sister to her, all the while yelling out a warning to our neighbors.

"We must hide ourselves," our village headman declared. "It is the only way."

"But our catch! Our stores! We will lose all," another man complained.

"Better that than our lives," my mother refuted. "Hurry or all is lost!"

Even then, the boats had reached the shore and men were clambering out. There would be no time for us to reach a hiding place, I realized. They would find us.

Before anyone could prevent me, I snatched up a spear and ran back towards the beach.

"Aerona! Stop!" I heard my mother exclaim.

"I will slow them down," I cried over my shoulder. "Run!"

I did not pause to see if she complied, but kept on, hurtling towards the raiders. They seemed like giants to me; great and tall and blond with huge axes, and large round shields. Still, I did not let my fear overmaster me. Instead, I planted my feet in the sand and brandished the spear.

Seeing me thus, the men laughed. After all, to them, I was naught but a skinny girl, barely 14 seasons old and clearly no warrior.

The largest of them stepped forwards, and uttered something to me with a grin on his face. Though I could not speak his language, I knew what he meant well enough. He was urging me to abandon my martial pretense, drop my weapon, and step aside.

This I could not do. If I obeyed him, then everyone I knew was lost. Only I stood between my loved ones and these invaders. With as fierce a yell as I could muster, I charged at him, intent on running him through.

Instantly, his smile disappeared, and he stepped neatly aside. Again, I came at him, and this time, as he dodged my weapon, and I stumbled past, he struck with his axe. The blade caught me between the shoulders, driving the air from my lungs and replacing it with fire.

Suddenly unable to remain erect, I dropped to the sands, coughing up blood.

The last thing that I saw, was the sea, but I was not affrighted, nor saddened. Thanks to me, my mother and my neighbors had fled to a place of safety where the Northmen would never find them. Compared to that, my death seemed a reasonable price...

...So, at last, you have had the death that you so craved, Nyneve announced, *drawn as it was from one of her former lives. And this time, the English were not the enemy, nor any Germans, but the Danes. Yet, despite impossible odds, she did not falter, did she?*

She was a fool for having stood against them, the Cailleach snarled.

Perchance, Nyneve agreed, *but her effort was a noble one, and sprang from a stalwart heart—as it ever will. I say enough of this trial. You have had your three challenges and she has proven herself worthy each and every time. X'Kallabar is hers 'till her purpose has been fulfilled.*

Then may she be damned! the Cailleach cursed. *Though the weapon will pass into her hands, in the end, it will be her undoing.*

Your words are without weight, the Lady of the Lake rebutted, *and as you well know. All who wield X'Kallabar are the subjects of Fate; blessed with glory 'till the time comes for them to fall, and in falling, returning it to its scabbard 'till another hero comes to claim it. So it has always been, and so it shall always be.*

Agreed, the Cailleach said. *That she dies in the end is enough to satisfy me.*

...the Cailleach's words faded and the grotto reappeared, and as it did so, the Lady of the Lake addressed me.

X'Kallabar is yours, hero, she stated. *You have passed our testing and have been found worthy. Wield it in the name of justice, 'till at last the time comes to return it to the stone.*

"I thank you, Lady," I said, briefly glancing in the direction of the Cailleach. But she was already backing away into the shadows with a malevolent hiss. Disregarding her hatred, I stepped up to X'Kallabar, and with a slight tremble in my hand, grasped its hilt and pulled it free of the stone.

Instantly, I felt a sensation akin to a mild electrical shock, and the aura that emanated from the blade spread upwards into my arm, and from there, into the rest of me. As it filled every corner of my being,

I felt a Presence. It was neither male, nor female, but both, and then as it settled itself within me, it became feminine as if it were adapting its consciousness to suit my own.

How do you do? thought I, for clearly, we were now being formally introduced.

It's reply came in a flood of images. They were of a thousand clashes waged against as many enemies, and spanning from times that mankind had long forgotten to those within recent memory. And always, X'Kallabar was there, in my hand, smiting down those who dared to oppress the weak or fomented injustice.

I was more than a mere spectator however. I was Arcturus himself, known as *Dux Bellorum*, the Leader of Battles, fighting against the Saxons 'til I was felled at Camlannis by my son, Modred.

Then I was Drake, raising the tempest against the Armada and shattering the ambitions of King Phillip. After that, I was Sir Thomas Blakesley, bending the will of Napoleon and turning him 'round towards his own doom. And then I was Dame Margaret Corbin, wielding X'Kallabar to dissuade Adolph Hitler from launching Operation Sea Lion. Finally, I was myself, fated to meet an as yet unnamed enemy, who like all the rest, threatened England, and all that was unsullied.

But the Presence was not finished with me, for it had still more to disclose. To my surprise, a world quite unlike anything that I had ever beheld before asserted itself in my mind's eye.

The sun which shone down upon it was positively gigantic, taking up nearly all of the heavens, and it radiated with a brilliant emerald-green light that oddly, did not cause my eyes any discomfort. There was also an ocean beneath this brilliant orb, although it was so placid that I could scarcely detect any waves upon its surface, and what land there was, consisted of small, rocky archipelagos, utterly devoid of vegetation, save a species of lichen.

Here, great smooth pieces of clear crystals sat on oddly shaped pedestals, and as I observed the nearest of these, a ball of light glided over and fused with it. But a moment later, the crystal became airborne, silently launching itself towards the jade-colored sky.

Then the scene shifted; now I was standing on the shore near one of the crystal vessels and a group of the strange light creatures had gathered around me. Some were amber in color, whilst others blue, or yellow, or red, and the radiance emanating from them fluctuated.

It brightened, and then it dimmed, and then brightened again in what seemed an intelligent pattern. At last, it dawned on me that they were communicating with one another, and in a language composed not of words such as I was accustomed to, but of pure illumination.

This was when I understood exactly who they were, for I had encountered one of their kind aboard the Black Knight. I also knew that just as they had cooperated with the Acahmu to create that ancient satellite, so too had they allied themselves with the Andromedans to fashion X'Kallabar. Moreover, I realized that in so doing, one of them had sacrificed its freedom in order to become one with the weapon forever, and that this same being now dwelt within me.

My understanding seemed to excite the Presence, as if I were a particularly dull student who had finally grasped their teacher's lesson at last, and accordingly, more pictures were communicated to me.

They were of the Andromedans themselves, working alongside their luminous partners in mighty laboratories that would have left the Professor dumbstruck with awe. Unlike the beings of light, the Andromedans possessed bodies. These were quite tall and very thin, with long, delicate limbs and features that somewhat reminded me of the Greys, though they were far more elegant in their proportions. And, just as I had expected, their smooth skin was the color of the purest lapis lazuli.

Moreover, I perceived the great intelligence that resided behind their eyes. It was as far above my own as I would have been to an amoeba, and it beggared me. Yet, I was not affronted by their obvious mental superiority. Nay, I was instead filled with the earnest hope that one day, my own species would possess such towering intellects. Millions of years would be required to accomplish this, I knew, but I was filled with the certainty that something truly wonderful awaited us, if only we could survive long enough to attain it.

At this, the images abruptly ceased, and I felt the spirit within X'Kallabar retreating into a tiny corner of my mind, as if it had revealed enough secrets for one day. And there it remained, quiescent and only just perceptible against the backdrop of my thoughts.

Still grappling with all that I had just experienced, I looked down and regarded the sword in my hand, wholly unsurprised to discover that it no longer shone. Instead, it seemed just like any other weapon.

Then one of the priestesses separated from her sisters and came to me. Her expression was solemn, and she bore a belt and a simple leather scabbard. There was only one decoration embossed onto the scabbard's ebon surface; the coiling spiral, signifying the physical path to the grotto.

But in a flash of insight, I also apprehended another meaning. For myself at least, it also embodied the spiritual path of the Ladder in my mother's print, and I was immediately minded of Maggie's role in this adventure, as well as my mother's words.

'Nothing happens by accident and everything has a purpose,' she had cautioned, *'though it might not be apparent at the moment."*

Nothing indeed, I mused. With that, I took the priestesses' offering and fastened it 'round my waist. Then I sheathed X'Kallabar, and in so doing, felt a profound sense of finality come over me. It was as if, until that very instant, the Tigress and I had been an unfinished creation, awaiting the third and final component of our being in order to become whole at last.

I also grasped the true nature of my previous incarnations. Rather than haphazard meanderings, they had always possessed a single purpose. This was to deliver me to this very time and place. I was now exactly where I was intended to be.

True to their word, Caroline and the Wild Man did not subject me to another visitation to the obsidian plane, or its demonic residents. Nor did we go back to the Chuchniya's forest, or even England for that matter. Rather, and after I had expressed my gratitude to Nyneve and taken my leave of her, I was conveyed to Shamballa.

Though I was disappointed that my return to Elizabeth would be delayed, I knew without having to ask what the reason for the detour was. Equipped as I was with an unfamiliar weapon, a certain amount of training would surely be in order. Fortunately, I already possessed some experience with classical fencing (thanks to my upbringing in the 3rd universe, and as befitted a lady of my station), as well as what I knew from my previous incarnations as a student of the Shamballan martial arts, so I was not overworried.

I was however, a bit taken aback when I was shown to my quarters to find a large cape awaiting me, draped over the chair. It was a duplicate of the one that Grímsdóttir favored; a great black piece of fabric trimmed with fur of the same color and equipped with a heavy silver clasp.

Reasoning that it had something to do with my education, I tried it on. Though it lent me a decidedly barbaric cast, I cannot say that I was displeased, for as my readers will recall from my adventure in Antarctica, I had considered the addition of such a garment to my ensemble for some while.

Satisfied, and not a little tired from my ordeal in the grotto, I returned it to the chair and sought out the comfort of my bed. And for once, I enjoyed a good night's sleep, free of nightmares.

The following morning, I rose early, and after eating a light breakfast, made my way out to the training grounds, the cape resting on my shoulders and X'Kallabar at my side.

My sister was there, costumed in the robes of a Shamballan nun (and making me wonder at how she managed to dress herself in so many varied costumes), along with the Chuchniya.

I was not however, expecting to encounter Louise, who lounged in a folding lawn chair off to one side. She was wearing a ridiculously large sun hat, outlandish sunglasses, and of course, had a beverage in her hand, which for some reason, sported a tiny paper umbrella (and this hardly an hour after sunrise!).

I was also equally surprised to see Kára Grímsdóttir. Like myself, she was wearing her cloak and had a sword belted on.

Eyeing me appraisingly, she nodded in approval. "Good. Now you are a proper warrior. Today we will practice fighting with that magnificent blade of yours. Prepare yourself for some bruises, champion."

I tilted my head at an imperial angle. "I welcome them."

"We shall see," the Ostlander replied, picking up a pair of wooden practice swords. "Perhaps you might even benefit from earning yourself a dueling scar. It compliments one's features and sends a warning to those who are stupid enough to challenge you."

Reflexively, my hand went to my unblemished cheek. "I—think not," I said.

Grímsdóttir chuckled at my reticence. "That is my decision. Not yours." Then she tossed me a practice sword, which I caught one-handed.

"Today, we will learn the basics of handling your sword," she said, "but first, I wanted to show you the value of your cape. One would think that it would only impede you in a fight, but this is not so."

At that, she saluted me, and the moment that I had reciprocated, she attacked. Of course, I parried and managed a decent riposte, and in return, she deflected my strike, and then leapt backwards and removed her cloak one-handed.

Before I quite realized her intent, she had cast the heavy fabric so that it landed on her wooden blade, and then used the weapon to toss the cape onto my own sword. Suddenly weighted down, I was slow to compensate, giving her the opportunity to come in with a quick thrust to my breastbone! Had her assault been in earnest and with a real blade, I would have surely been impaled. Fortunately, this was training, and she pulled her strike at the last second.

Grinning at my disbelief, she did not return her cloak to her shoulders, and instead invited me to attack her. Knowing full well that she planned some form of trickery, I complied, and I was not proven incorrect.

As I made to thrust, she simply flicked her wrist and suddenly the cape was in my face, obstructing my vision entirely. Then she followed through with a slash to my sword arm and landed a stout blow to my calves, knocking me off my feet. I landed hard on my buttocks, giving out a most ungracious exclamation of embarrassment and pain.

Having witnessed my humiliation, Louise toasted me with her glass. "Bravo Penelope!"

Awarding her a scathing look, I regained my feet. Of course, Louise ignored my disfavor in favor of her beverage.

"So," Grímsdóttir said, winding the fabric around her arm with another practiced twirl, "perhaps you can see why we Ostlanders prefer such garments. A good cloak will not only warm you on a cold winter's night, but can come in handy in battle. Wouldn't you agree?"

I nodded, but out of caution, kept my guard up.

"Now, let us examine how it can be used as improvised armor to deflect a weapon." She had left a goodly portion of the fabric free, I noted, and I wondered at this.

Over the next few minutes, I learned that the loose section allowed a swordsman to push aside an opponent's blade without sustaining injury to their hand. It also worked quite nicely when it came to tangling and deflecting an enemy's sword.

Moreover, I also discovered (again to my chagrin) that the cloak could be employed to trap a sword arm, as well as several rather devious methods by which one could restrain the swordsman and bring them to the ground without inflicting any injury—save to their pride that is.

The remainder of our session was spent focusing on the essentials; learning to cut and thrust with X'Kallabar (and discovering in the process that it was far heavier than the sabers I had fenced with and therefore required entirely different techniques), as well as other elementary drills. When at last, the sun had finally set, I retired to my quarters just as bruised as the Ostlander had pledged, but greatly increased in wisdom.

Of course, this was not to be our sole lesson. We met again the following day, and for many more after that, continuing with our drills, and exploring various fighting methods. As useful as all this was though, after a time, I began to wonder when our lessons would address X'Kallabar's special powers, and sensing my growing impatience, Grímsdóttir soon satisfied my curiosity.

As always, we met on the training ground, just after sunrise. However, on this particular occasion, she was companioned by Brother Dorje himself. Furthermore, a dozen targets had been emplaced on the sands.

The first three I recognized as *goza*, the thick roll of tatami which Japanese swordsmen employed in the art of *Tameshigiri*, or blade testing. The second were stout pieces of wood, and the third were constructed of metal.

"As you can see," the Lama explained, "the first targets are entirely conventional, and any skilled swordsman wielding a quality blade can cleave them in half. The second though, might well test or defeat such a sword. And the third..."

"...are nigh impossible," I finished, easily imagining them shattering even X'Kallabar.

"Not for you, Jian Bing," he corrected, "or what the Professor calls the Fire of X'Kallabar. Success begins with the spirit of the blade itself.'

"You must call for it to aid you whenever you face a target that no ordinary weapon can overcome, and the greater your need, the greater the Fire itself. We will practice this in stages however; please cut the first gozu without calling upon the blade-spirit in any way."

Obediently, I stepped up to the target, unsheathed my weapon and attacked it in a conventional manner. Just as I had expected, X'Kallabar parted it in twain without any difficulty at all.

"Again," he commanded, "but call to the blade's spirit before you make your cut."

I did as he asked, reaching within myself to the place where the Presence resided. It, in turn, responded, and I felt it joining with me. Not entirely, mind you, but as if it had merely extended a single mental finger and made the lightest of contacts. At the same time, a lambent glow began to surround X'Kallabar, and when I struck, the second gozu came apart with even greater ease than the first.

"Again please," Brother Dorje insisted.

At this, I opened myself even further to the Presence, and as our union increased in strength, the light coming from my blade brightened as well. As for the third tatami roll, it separated so easily under my assault, that for a moment I wondered if I had even managed to land a hit on it at all. It was only when the top fell away that I was entirely certain of my success.

"Excellent," he beamed. "Now for the wood—and ask the Presence to give you even more of itself."

I walked over to the first wooden target, and there paused. *Help me,* I thought, *lend me more of your power.*

In reply, the Presence asserted itself with even greater vigor, and I committed to my strike. The wood fell away just as easily as the tatami had, and with nary a scratch to X'Kallabar's gleaming surface.

"Very good," Brother Dorje complimented. "now to your greatest test; the metal."

I very nearly refused him, for the iron poles seemed far too stout to risk my sword on. But the Lama had anticipated my hesitation.

"It is doubt that stands in your way, Penelope, not the targets, nor your sword's capabilities," he admonished. "In reality, the metal is no greater than any of the other objectives that I have set for you. Trust, Jian Bing. *Believe.*"

Nodding, I closed my eyes and opened myself wide to the Presence. We merged fully, becoming one being, of which my arm was merely an extension. By now, the light coming from X'Kallabar had become so intense that I could no longer perceive the steel itself, merely its general outline. Taking in a breath, I raised my arm and then brought it down in a decisive arc.

There was only the slightest sensation of resistance, and then I saw the top of the pole falling and hitting the sand with a dull 'thunk'. Peering down at it, I found that it had been severed so neatly that it seemed as if a laser had been brought to bear against it.

And X'Kallabar? It was wholly unscathed. Understandably, I was deeply impressed.

"This is but a fraction of what X'Kallabar can accomplish," Brother Dorje proclaimed, coming over with Grímsdóttir to admire my achievement.

So, my curriculum changed. Though our drills with the wooden swords continued (for Grímsdóttir never allowed the essentials to be forsaken), I engaged in more cutting practice with the Presence till soon I thought nothing of attacking the metal targets and was able to defeat them with ease.

This was not all though; after some two weeks of cutting practice had elapsed, and I had walked onto the training grounds for the day's lesson, I found that the targets were not in the middle of the courtyard. Instead, they had been erected at the far end of the enclosure, and in successive rows, with the metal ones being the most distant.

"You are to cut the first row of the targets," Grímsdóttir indicated, and as I made to step towards them, she raised a restraining hand. "From *here.*"

I looked at her as if she had gone completely mad. "However will I manage that?" I asked. "They are well beyond my striking range."

"By harnessing the Fire of X'Kallabar of course", she replied, "and projecting it outwards. Begin by calling upon the Presence."

Having enjoyed as much practice with this as I had, I reached the optimal state of awareness and achieved union with the blade's spirit almost instantly.

"Now," she instructed, "make your cut as if the targets were standing directly before you. Do not allow the illusion of space to convince you otherwise."

Had this been an earlier point in my training, I would have considered such a request to be utterly nonsensical, but having witnessed as many miracles as I had thus far, I merely accepted her command, drew my blade, and executed a slash.

At first, nothing happened, and she urged me to greater effort. "Reach out to them *through* the blade, and across the space. Feel the targets, and feel the steel making contact."

Redoubling my concentration, I visualized that very thing, and to my pleasant surprise, the light of X'Kallabar not only brightened, but the tip of its luminous field had increased in length to nearly a meter.

"Better," the Ostlander observed. "But you must try even harder. *Push.*"

I did as she bade, and the luminous tip grew even longer, and as it did so, I experienced a rather odd sensation. It came to me through the sword's grip and I felt it in my palm; it was the unmistakable feeling that the blade had just touched something. Yet, many meters of empty air stood between myself and the first row of targets.

Moving the blade before me in a slow arc that passed across the gozu, I felt it again, and this time, it was as if my blade had lightly brushed against each and every one of them.

Thrilled by this, I brought back my arm, and executed a cut, 'pushing' as hard as I was able. This time, I could distinctly feel the steel biting through the mats, and then watched in delight as they fell at the other end of the training sands. Thus, I began to learn what had I would have previously considered to be an utter impossibility.

In the end, and after many more days of this, I found that X'Kallabar was capable of effectively attacking targets dozens of meters away from wherever I stood, and that even the hardest of metals posed no impediment to it at all.

Still more awaited me though. When they were satisfied with my progress, my trainers informed me that I had one final lesson to learn, and that afterwards, I would be required to pass a test which would signify my graduation. It was, they advised, a trifle really; I only had to face the Emperor's army, and then defeat it to the very last man.

Naturally, I found this proposition to be rather daunting and all the moreso when I was expressly forbidden to bring X'Kallabar along! Nor did they allow me a surfeit of time in which to wonder at this strange prohibition, but instead, commanded me to stow the sword in my quarters straightaway. And the very instant that I had done so, we departed the monastery on horseback.

Our trek lasted a full fortnight, and although I pressed them all along the way, they remained close-lipped about our destination and exactly what awaited me. My puzzlement was only magnified when at last, we reached a large plain and from there, travelled to the foot of a great grassy mound shaped like a truncated pyramid. Dismounting, we walked around its base to the eastern side, wherein we came to the mouth of a cave.

"The Emperor's army awaits within," Brother Dorje announced, gesturing for me to step inside. Doing so, I discovered that the interior was sheathed in dressed stone and went deep into the heart of the hill.

My footfalls also activated some hidden mechanism, for after only half a dozen steps, fires sprang to life in braziers that had been set at intervals all along the length of the passage. Their light revealed a stout metal door at the far end, decorated with fierce looking dragons. Yet, this imposing barrier had no knob, nor any other device with which to open it. The only feature that seemed a likely candidate was a circular depression set in its very center.

Some kind of key is required here, I concluded.

Brother Dorje confirmed this when he reached into his traveling bag and carefully unwrapped a silk-covered parcel. It contained a large disk made of jade, that like the door, was emblazoned with dragons. This he inserted into the depression and turned it clockwise.

Immediately, there was the sound of some great and ponderous mechanism stirring to life. It was followed by a pronounced 'click', after which the portal slid aside to admit us.

Beyond this, there was only inky darkness, but from the breeze that wafted out and caressed my cheek, I knew that we were standing at the verge of a capacious chamber. Its true extent was made plain when we stepped inside a moment later, and more braziers ignited.

It was in fact, positively enormous; being large enough to house several ocean liners of a size comparable to the *Great Eastern*, and with room to spare besides. And at its far end, I spied what seemed to be a grand tomb, constructed of marble and intricately worked metal. Though imposing, this edifice was not what arrested my attention, however. Rather, it was what occupied the space between myself and the crypt that did.

Thousands of life-sized figures stood before me, all brightly painted and arranged in orderly lines. To the last, they were armed with weapons. Some bore bronze swords, whilst others held spears, and still others, bows. I was looking at an entire army, rendered in clay.

"Behold the army of Huangdi, the Yellow Emperor," Brother Dorje proclaimed. "He is a myth in all other universes, but a reality here in the 8th and these soldiers were created to serve him in the afterlife. There are other terracotta armies, including one in the 2nd universe built for Qin Shi Huang, but none are as great, and only this one was created with our assistance. What you are gazing upon are no less than seven thousand clay warriors, as well as horsemen and chariots."

As he disclosed this, the metal door slid shut behind us, and locked.

"And this, I presume, is the army that I am intended to fight?" I asked him.

"It is," he answered.

"With what, pray tell?" I queried, spreading my hands wide so as to emphasize my unarmed state.

"Why with X'Kallabar, of course," he returned. "If you call it, it will come to you in your hour of need."

He did not expound on this, but instead, bade me to remain where I was while he walked to a point in the wall. There, another circular receptacle awaited, and again, he inserted the jade key whereupon I heard another apparatus coming to life.

Or should I say, several of them, for as I watched, the nearest of the clay warriors stirred, and stretched their necks and arms as if they were wringing the sleep from them. Then they assumed battle stances.

Mechanica, I thought in alarm. Knowing full well how deadly such robots could be from my misadventure with the Lyran cyborg, I did the only thing that I could think of; I reached out to the Presence (though it seemed but a faraway whisper of itself) and cried out for assistance.

To both my stupefaction and intense relief, I felt X'Kallabar filling my hand but a heartbeat later, and risking a glance, saw that it was indeed there! Somehow, it had transported itself through time and space to come to my rescue.

Hefting the blade, I readied myself for battle. "Come on, you bloody bastards!" I cried.

Save for the movement of their ceramic parts, my adversaries made not a sound as they charged at me in unison. I, in turn, called upon the Presence, and unleashed X'Kallabar's fire. It licked across at the unliving warriors and they shattered into bits.

But even as the fragments fell, a second group and then a third came for me. I cut. I slashed. I felled them all, but more replaced them. My battle, I realized, was a futile one; for every dozen that I destroyed, twice that number surged forwards to attack me.

Just then a voice reached me above the din of shattering pottery. It was Brother Dorje.

"Penelope!" he shouted, "You must fight your way through till you destroy the very last of them. Only then can you prevail!"

Taking his words to heart, the Tigress and I reached out to the Presence and beseeched it for its aid. In response, the light around us became near blinding in its intensity, and all the while, rank after rank of the terracotta soldiers shattered, their remnants joining a growing pile at my feet.

I did not gloat at this though but focused my attention on the very last line of warriors whose numbers I had yet to lay eyes upon. Everything between myself and that group meant nothing, and what fell before me only cleared the way to my objective.

Spears were thrust at me, arrows came, swords slashed, but all these I swatted aside as I walked into the soldiers, leaving naught but ruin and devastation in my wake. It was only when I reached the rear wall, and made to dispatch the final figure, a general on horseback, that one of his retainers managed to injure me, and this was only a glancing cut to my left cheek.

I overlooked the injury however, and brought my blade down upon the leader of the ceramic army, demolishing him. Of a sudden, there were no more attackers. My battle was over.

"It seems a great pity to have demolished such a remarkable collection," I said.

Neither Brother Dorje not Grímsdóttir seemed troubled by this wanton destruction though. Instead, the Lama merely smiled and turned the jade seal anti-clockwise.

It was then that I noticed that some of the smaller pieces nearest me were beginning to vibrate and skip about. Then, larger and larger pieces did likewise.

For an instant, I thought it to be an earthquake, but when I did not feel any vibration in my feet, I looked about me and realized that the walls and ceiling of the chamber were not being so affected. Only the terracotta shards were acting in this manner.

Then incredibly, the pieces began to move across the floor and join together, with each one finding its opposite, till they had reformed into the very figures that I had thought destroyed. In defiance of all reason, the entire clay army had been restored without so much as a single fragment left behind to testify against me.

"Not such a pity after all," Brother Dorje observed. "It seems that the Emperor's soldiers will still be able to serve him in the afterlife."

"Remarkable," I exclaimed. "Absolutely remarkable."

He laughed softly. "Not half as remarkable as your skill, Jian Bing. It has been an honor to instruct you."

I smiled and brushed the back of my hand over the wound on my left cheek. Though the nanobots in my bloodstream should have prevented it, I found to my surprise that it still bled.

"You will have a scar there," Grímsdóttir informed me. "The 'bots cannot heal such a wound completely. That feat is beyond their powers."

Immediately I was minded of the spiral mark that my sister had left on me during my dream-visit to the grotto. The one that I still bore on my chest.

"It is a mark of your passage of the test," Brother Dorje explained. "and also, a warning that will follow you for the rest of your life; no matter how powerful you might become, it will always remind you that you are not invincible. Only the force of change is immune to defeat."

Thus, I had earned the selfsame dueling scar that Grímsdóttir had promised me, and learned a valuable lesson in the process.

We were met at the entrance to the tunnel by Caroline and the Wild Man. This time, she had adorned herself in a fine silk gown such as a well-bred woman of the Yellow Emperor's court might have worn, and had arranged her hair in a similar manner. There was no communication between us, telepathic or otherwise, and yet I could sense that she and her companion were fully aware of my accomplishment, and equally proud of my success.

With a gesture, she directed my attention to a most astounding object. It was a large circular mirror, large enough in fact to have taken in the reflection of an entire carriage, and made of bronze. An ornate border depicting tigers in various attitudes of attack and repose framed its polished surface, and it shimmered in the same manner as the looking glass that had conveyed me to Shambala. To add to this wonderment, it had no base to support its great weight, and instead, floated several handbreadths above the ground in the same manner as a Phaseship.

I did not need to ask her if this was my way back to London, for I knew that my adventure was at an end. I had mastered X'Kallabar, and the time had come for me to return to the century which I called my home. Thus, and with a final respectful bow to all and sundry, I walked into the mirror.

Exactly as before, there was a sensation of intense cold and then of tumbling through the air, followed by the pleasing sight of my boudoir and of Elizabeth still abed, and fast asleep. One glance at the clock on our mantle told me the rest. Though I had spent many weeks at the monastery, I had, according to London time, been gone for only two minutes.

My body, however, lent no credence to this temporal incongruity; a great weariness overcame me. Laying X'Kallabar and my cloak aside, I made for my bed straightaway.

But then the clock stopped ticking, and a voice spoke from behind me. "The answer is Nuremburg, daughter."

Turning, I beheld my mother, who rewarded me with a warm smile.

"You have been wondering how it is that you are French, but also a Pleiadean," she guessed.

"I have," I confessed, for the conundrum had not left me, even with all that had transpired. "And it makes no sense whatsoever."

"It will," she assured me. "Do you perchance recall Mr. Laske's little book, and what he said about alien intervention in humanities' evolution?"

"Yes, I do," I nodded.

"Then perhaps you also remember the portion where he spoke of the Lyran bases in Europe, specifically the one sited in ancient Nuremburg?"

Again, I indicated my awareness.

"Once we Pleiadeans took over custody of the Earth, I was assigned to that very station, and my specialty was applied genetics. I and my fellow scientists were directly responsible for modifying the prehistoric humans that were living in Western Europe at the time, and later still, we guided them in their social development."

Now I thought I began to see. Yet I remained still, awaiting the details in their fullness.

"My specific cluster of humans were located in what is now France," she explained, "and as part of my work, I contributed my own genetic material to the project, binding it with our subjects, generation after generation. These particular humans became my children if you will, and even today, a part of me exists within them all.'

"And just as any mother, I never lost my fondness for my offspring. Thus, when the opportunity and the need arose, I chose Paris for a home. After all, I had, in a distant way, had a hand in building it. They even honored me; for at the time I called myself Marianne, and they made me the personification of liberty and reason.'

"Does that perchance clarify things for you, Penelope? You are in fact more French than any Frenchman, and at the same time very much an alien. The Cailleach was not exaggerating, but merely simplifying the matter."

So, it is as true as I thought, I reflected.

"You do not seem pleased by this disclosure," my mother observed.

"No," I admitted. "Not entirely."

She leaned in and kissed my forehead. "Give the Gallic culture a chance, my darling. It is one of my finest creations. Take in the opera, and sample the wonderful food. I suggest that you try *Carmen* and afterwards, dine at *Kettner's*. You and your beloved will not regret either choice."

"Very well," I agreed.

"Maintenant, en route pour le lit avec vous," she said *"Bien dormir!"* "On the road to bed with you. Sleep well!"

Then she vanished, and the gears of our clock resumed their normal movements. Attaining our bed and sliding under the covers at last, I curled against my lover and proceeded to sleep more soundly than even the Yellow Emperor in his tomb could have ever hoped to.

It was well past noon when my eyes finally reopened, and Elizabeth saw to it that a breakfast was brought in to greet my return to consciousness. It was only when she sat on the bed to join me that the sunlight streaming in through our windows made my scar plain to her.

"Oh my dearest," she exclaimed coming closer to examine it. "They did not tell me of your injury! We must attend to it right away."

"It would be fruitless," I told her. "It is of such a nature that it will never fade."

Her eyes travelled to the spiral mark etched on my chest, and she nodded dolefully. It had been kept from public view by my garments, but this imperfection was another matter entirely; though it was not deep, and scarcely more than a crimson line, it was plain enough that polite society would certainly remark upon it. Then her eyes brightened.

"A cosmetic is the answer," she suggested, rising and stepping over to our vanity. "I've just the thing."

It happened that in her early days at Maddenhill, my dearest had shown an interest in theatrical performances (not with any desire to become an actress, of course. Such a thing would *never* have been tolerated for a woman of her station) and she had learned the art of using make-up to heighten, or in this case, conceal one's features.

Accordingly, she produced a heavy facial crème which she carefully applied to my cheek, and then, with a bit of blending, managed to obscure my mark enough that it would be overlooked by

203

the casual observer. We were both of us heartily pleased by the end result.

Having no pressing engagements, we then finished our meal in a leisurely fashion, and spent the remainder of our morning abed, making love, and later still, conversing about all that had transpired in the grotto, and the tomb of the Yellow Emperor. Elizabeth was fascinated by my experience but equally concerned for me.

"Surely X'Kallabar was not given to you for any haphazard purpose" she observed. "Something truly dire must lie ahead which only it's presence will serve to remedy."

"Indubitably," said I, looking across our bedchamber to the Ladder. "Nor do I think that it will be overly long before we learn of its nature."

The image of myself as an armored knight was now clear and surrounded by light. It held its sword high as if meeting the challenge of some hidden adversary.

Elizabeth followed my gaze and her features clouded over with increased concern. "Oh, I fear for you, my darling!" she exclaimed, throwing her arms about me.

I gathered her in and kissed her. "Whatever proves the case, my love, I shall face it bravely and be ever mindful of my safety."

We both knew this for a tenuous promise, but it served to lend us both some badly needed reassurance.

That evening, and to dispel our mutual misgivings about the future, we decided to indulge ourselves in some distractions. Towards that end, Elizabeth gave me charge of the night's itinerary, and mindful of my mother's recommendations, I immediately chose the Royal Opera House (where it just so happened that *"Carmen"* was playing) and then *Kettner's* for a late supper.

Because Bizet did not exist in the 3rd universe, this opera proved to be the first time that either of us had ever heard his work. Yet I did more than simply listen to it; I set aside my prejudices and opened myself to the experience, trying as best I could to *feel* the spirit behind the performance and by extension, the culture that had engendered its composer.

The very summit of this came when the aria, 'Habanera' was performed. It moved me to tears of ecstasy, and when at last the performance ended, I decided that I would seek out more of Bizet's creations, if only to recapture that exquisite bliss.

Kettner's proved to be equally as sublime, though I had not expected it. Located in Soho, and frequented by some rather questionable clientele (Oscar Wilde being one), it still proved to be a restaurant of the very first caliber. Our meal was truly magnificent, and we were treated to some of the finest examples of French cooking to be had anywhere in London.

I would later learn that this had had everything to do with its founder, August Kettner, who had been no less than the personal chef to Napoleon III. Though Kettner had passed away, the standards of excellence that he had established had not lowered in the slightest.

Thus, I was afforded a chance to literally taste some of the culture that my mother was so proud of, and in the process, came to appreciate her reasons. For all of my prior disdain of everything French, the food that was served to us far outclassed the blander offerings of English cuisine, and I daresay, I emerged a changed woman. From then on, my palette would continuously remind me of that meal, and clamor for more.

We returned to Charlotte Place quite late, and fully expected to head straight to our rooms without delay. As it happened though, a package had been delivered in our absence.

"Lady Anne sent 'er footman round," Ms. O'Toole told me. "He came just after nine and left this fer ye."

I took the parcel from her and unwrapped it. It proved to be an exquisitely bound book whose gilded title proclaimed it to be *"The 120 Days of Sodom, or the School of Libertinage"*, by Donatien Alphonse François, the Marquis DeSade.

I knew this author. Early in our relationship, Lady Anne had mentioned him in connection to the practice of sadism. Accordingly, I cringed. But a gift was a gift, and with some reluctance, I opened it to read the inscription;

"To add warmth to your winter nights, with special sections bookmarked for your perusal. Should you care to experiment, be warned that a limber form and some mastery of gymnastics will be required.

But, before engaging in any such private exercise, please report to the following coordinates for your next mission; 45°30'54.2"N 25°22'01.8"E, 2ⁿᵈ universe, 1890 CE.'

"All the best, Lady Anne Pratt-Netherby."

I daresay that when I hazarded a look at one of the pages that our patroness had flagged for my attention, I colored to my eyes, for the plates left nothing to the imagination, and I was compelled to slam the volume shut. Then, and to my great unease, Elizabeth took it from me, and eyed the same section not with discomfort, but rather, keen interest.

"So, to bed then," I said, trying unsuccessfully to retrieve it from her.

"Of course," she agreed, her eyes asparkle. They had, I noted, never left the page.

CHAPTER 9: La Belle au Bois Dormant

In which we visit a Transylvanian castle and I discover the true genesis of the vampire legend. Then, a harrowing mission to the 7th universe on behalf of a new ally, wherein I gain a strong dislike for Mongolian Russia. After that, Moscow, and the daring rescue of a captive princess.

Since we had not been ordered to depart immediately, we availed ourselves of the opportunity to rest. Then, the following morning, as we lingered over our meal, I regarded the Ladder print.

Another change had occurred, for just beyond the image of Elizbeth and I, a figure that had once been one of the angels had now become a rather comely young woman in the very flower of her youth. She was made even more remarkable by the fact that she occupied some kind of sarcophagus and appeared to be in a deep slumber.

Stepping closer, I examined her so as to assure myself that her features were neither mine, nor my beloved's, and to my relief, I was able to confirm that they were not. Whoever she was, she was a total stranger.

Seeing me so occupied, Elizabeth joined me, and made her own inspection of the sleeping maiden.

"What do you think it means?"

"I know not," said I. "Perchance she is someone that we are soon to meet. Perchance not."

"Time will certainly tell," Elizabeth opined.

And with that, we turned our attention to the day's business, dressing in our flightsuits, and flying in Blackbird to the coordinates that Lady Anne had supplied.

That journey, which took three hours to complete, brought us to the very heart of Rumania, and the village of Bran, whereupon, Blackbird received an encrypted signal directing us to land at the foot of Castle Bran itself in the *Parcul Regal*, the Royal Park.

For those readers who are unacquainted with this landmark, it is purported by some to be the very one portrayed in Bram Stoker's classic *"Dracula"*. However, I must make mention of the fact that there is no definite link between the stronghold and Vlad the Impaler (upon whom Count Dracula was loosely based). Further, no evidence exists to prove that the author was even *aware* of Castle

Bran, having never visited Rumania at all. A more likely candidate, at least according to literary scholars, is the summit of Mount Izvorul Câlimanului near the Borgo Pass, and there is no evidence of any castle having ever stood there.

As for his terrifying tale (which I had read courtesy of Blackbird), its publication was still seven years distant. At the moment, Castle Bran was just another fortress raised against the Turks, and its current owners, the Hapsburgs, were blissfully unaware of Mr. Stoker, and just how dramatically his book would affect the reputation of their property.

None of this though, had any direct bearing on our particular situation, at least as far as I knew. Thus, I wondered at why we had been summoned there. Unfortunately, the landscape failed to provide any clues; while rugged and picturesque enough, it was a remote location, and I saw no indication of anything that might have been of interest to the Masters.

Moreover, no one was there to greet us and explain the matter, and perforce, we were compelled to walk up a long narrow walkway to the castle, and thence to a steep set of stairs which in turn, led to the main gate. This proved to be a stout wooden door of conventional size and equipped with a substantial iron knocker.

It was only when Elizabeth employed it to announce our presence, that the portal opened at last, and we were greeted by an elderly man, who by his humble attire, was clearly a caretaker.

"Bine ai venit!" he greeted in Rumanian. "The interviewers have already arrived and are awaiting you in the library."

This puzzled me greatly. "Interviewers?" Nothing of this nature had ever been required of me before.

"Da," he said. "They wanted to evaluate your fitness and the Masters agreed to this stipulation."

Confused, I gestured for Elizbeth to await me in the courtyard and followed the fellow. When we arrived at the door that I presumed led to the library, he opened it and stood aside.

But when I stepped across the threshold, I found myself entering not a repository of medieval books, but a rather conventional conference room that would not have been out of place in the 21st century. In fact, when I looked out of the large windows, I did not see the wilderness that surrounded Castle Bran. Rather, I spied the bland, rectangular forms of office towers. Nor was it daytime any longer, but night, and the illuminated buildings banished the starlight from the sky above them.

One glance behind me revealed that the door through which I had passed was no more. In its place was a plain wall, paneled in wood. Clearly, by passing through the portal, I had entered into another universe.

Besides all of this, there was another oddity that confronted me; a mysterious glyph made of bronze and mounted on the far wall. By my reckoning, it seemed to be a melding of the alchemical symbols for man and woman, but bisected by a horizontal line whose arms terminated in crescents. One pointed upwards, whilst the other, downwards. Overall, it resembled a stylized swastika, and I was immediately reminded of the Nazis and their overlords, the Lyrans, which did not please me in the least.

Presently, a door adjacent to the glyph opened, and seven figures filed into the chamber. Four were men, and three were women. To the last, they were all dressed in business attire, though not of the 19th century, but the 21st. And though they were all elegantly proportioned and quite handsome, they were unnaturally tall, the smallest of them being at least six feet in height and the largest, greater than eight. Further, their coloration was that of albinos, with snowy hair, and pale, translucent complexions.

All of this I took in in an instant, which was as well, for as they turned to regard me, a powerful, but invisible force drove me to my knees, and my head lowered quite by its own accord, compelling me to stare at the carpet. Though I struggled against it, something was preventing me from moving, or meeting the eyes of my hosts.

Thus, when three of these ghostly figures came to stand before me, I could only perceive the lower halves of their bodies. Yet by their attire, I could tell that one was male, and that he was flanked by two of the females.

"There is no need for this, Inanna" the male said with tired irritation.

"It suits me, Enki," the woman to his left snapped, and I had the distinct impression that she was tempted to kick me with her shiny leather pumps, if only out of contempt.

"Enki is correct," the other female argued. "She is no hairless ape. She is more akin to our kind than any human and should not be treated so."

"I disagree, Aya," the first retorted. "She is not of Niburu. Nor are her people as old as ours, being little more than children by comparison. Best that we establish a proper relationship at the outset, and have her show respect for her elders."

"Enough!" Enki interjected. "We waste precious time here." Then to me, "It has often been said that the *enemy of my enemy is my friend*, and that is certainly the case here. Our former allies, the Lyrans, have taken one whom we once called sister and now seek to use her to deprive us of what is rightfully ours. This perfidious deed cannot be allowed to go forwards unopposed."

I had no idea what this strange being was rambling on about, and when I attempted to request clarification from him, I found that I could not do so. My tongue, I had discovered, was as paralyzed as the rest of me.

Then, another set of feet joined the trio. The small black shoes with their tiny silver buckles, and the fact that their owner was floating above the floor, identified her immediately. The Sibyl had joined us.

"Do you find her suitable?" the seeress asked them.

"We do, Ambassador," Enki replied.

"We do *not*," the one calling herself Inanna hissed. "She is small and weak, and clearly rather feeble-minded. I think us fools for trusting her with such an important task."

"And I *disagree*," Aya exclaimed. "Her valor and resourcefulness have been proven beyond a doubt, and besides which, she wields the sword—as well you know, Inanna."

"So she does," Inanna conceded bitterly. "and although I would prefer it were otherwise, I must also accept this new *alliance* we have forged with the Masters. But mark me well; the day will come when you will all see that we were better off when they were still our enemies."

"Perhaps," Enki agreed. "Perhaps not. The present however is indisputable, and she will serve our mutual ends well enough."

"Then serve she shall," the Sibyl responded. This said, the group turned as one, and left me there, staring at the floor. It was only when I was once again the master of my own body, that I knew they had departed.

That, and the evidence of my eyes, for as I straightened, I found myself standing in the very library that I had expected when I had first entered. Gone were the 21st century trappings, along with the skyscrapers. Instead, the small leaded windows delivered a bucolic view of the castle and the trees beyond it.

"Well," a familiar voice remarked, "they seemed pleased enough with you." It was Colonel Ambrose. He was seated in a great leather chair by the fireplace, and Sigrun Nälkäinen stood nearby, leaning against the stone mantle, her arms folded.

"Who were they?" I demanded.

Ambrose smiled crookedly. "Why the landlords of Earth, my dear. They call themselves the Nibirai, but you would know them as the Anunnaki."

"That is impossible," I retorted. "The Anunnaki left mankind to its own devices thousands of years ago. Mr. Laske's book was quite clear on that point."

He shook his head. "Though Mr. Laske accurately reported many of the things that I disclosed to him, on this subject, he was entirely incorrect."

"Then you lied to him?" I asked.

"Sadly, yes," he admitted. "Humanity was not ready to learn the truth."

"And what truth would that be, sir?"

"That the Anunnaki never departed. As soon as humanity had established its first civilizations, they simply withdrew into the shadows, and continued to guide the world's leadership in directions that profited them the most."

"Profited?"

"Yes," he answered. "They can best be described as herdsmen. They came to Earth with the sole intention of improving the native hominids, and fostering their development until they evolved into true Homo Sapiens. Once this process was completed, it provided them with a steady food source, and one close enough to their home world, Nibiru, to make the effort economical."

"Food?"

"Yes, Penny. You heard me correctly; food. You see, the Anunnaki are blood drinkers; the very vampires of myth and legend. They derive their sustenance from the consumption of that vital fluid, and by modifying humans to meet their requirements, they created an abundant supply of it for themselves. Surely, you did not believe that they nurtured mankind's development simply out of pure altruism?"

In fact, I had, and I was duly mortified. Moreso because these fiends had actually declared themselves to be our allies! Naturally, the Colonel perceived my distress, for I made no effort to conceal it.

"Penny, my dear," he urged, "you really mustn't judge them so harshly. They are not wanton killers like the Lyrans, but more akin to wolves. They take only what they need and without disturbing the balance of nature. In fact, it was they who implanted the idea of transfusions and later, blood banks, into the human mind, which ultimately benefited both races, though admittedly in different ways."

"Oh, how utterly *philanthropic* of them," I sneered. "Pray tell, what drove them into the arms of the Lyrans?"

"Humanity's technological advances," he responded, "especially where it concerned its ability to wage wars of ever-increasing size and destruction. Then too, there was the impact felt by the Earth itself. Mankind had managed to populate nearly every corner of the globe and was not only depleting it of its natural resources, but choking it with garbage.'

"Of course, they tried to intervene through their human lackies, but eventually it became clear that their creations were well beyond their control.'

"And control is precisely what the Lyrans offered; they blamed the Masters for all the chaos, and portrayed them as weak and ineffectual. Then they proposed a partnership where their combined efforts would bring humanity to heel at long last and consign it to cages, where it could no longer harm itself, or the planet.'

"All they asked in return was access to certain technologies, a portion of the human herds for forced labor, and assistance in prosecuting their war against us."

"So they agreed to enslave humanity," I observed sourly.

"Yes," the Colonel admitted. "They did, and it was only when the Anunnaki realized that the Lyrans intended to take everything for themselves, that they chose to switch sides. That, and grant us the use of an artifact that they had denied the Lyrans."

"What is this artifact?" I asked.

Ambrose looked up to Sigrun who nodded her permission for him to answer.

"It is the other half of X'Kallabar, and also of Andromedin manufacture. They called it *X'alsalaar*, but humanity knows of it as the Sangreal, or the Grail, and only when the two components are united, is the full potential of the weapon realized.'

"Arthur understood this, and that is why he sent his knights off in search of it. It was no act of piety on his part, but sheer pragmatism. He knew that with both the Grail and the Sword in his possession, nothing could resist him."

This statement caught me quite unawares, for until then, I had thought X'Kallabar to be entirely complete. Yet as I considered it, I recalled that Professor Merriweather had once described the weapon as being potent enough to 'shatter planets', though I had never experienced anything approaching that level of power myself.

Now, I understood why. It was but one half of a pair, requiring its opposite in order to become an actualized whole, and without which, its possibilities were severely limited.

"There is one small condition however," he cautioned. "They will only release X'alsalaar to us if they are fully satisfied with your performance on the next mission. Given the nature of the relic and its destructive potential, I cannot say that I blame them for being so reticent."

"And in turn, we are offering them--what?"

Sigrun awarded me a wolfish grin that I had come to recognize as her hallmark. "That we leave them alone to do as they always have, without interference. In comparison to what the Lyrans intend, the cost to Mankind is both minimal and quite acceptable."

I was outraged. "Then we *allow* them to continue to prey upon humans?"

"We do," she responded evenly. "Conditions in the 21st century are such that no humans need suffer, nor die, nor even know that any of this is going on. Mankind retains its freedom from Lyran oppression, the Anunnaki survive, and the Masters emerge from the war triumphant. A good bargain all around, I think. All that is required is for you to do *your* job--which brings us to the particulars…"

That very night, I found myself in the 7th universe, standing with Lady Anne, Kára Grímsdóttir and Louise, in the military airfield of Utti, in eastern Finland. No more than 100 kilometers from the Russian border, it was impossible to ignore the steady 'krump!' 'krump!' of artillery, or the occasional bursts of small arms fire off in the distance.

Nor could any of us overlook the roar of jet aircraft streaking east, their wings laden with bombs. We were near the front line of the unceasing war between Ostlander Europe and Mongolian Russia, and in that conflict, Finland was at the very tip of the spear.

We had not been sent to fight in this conflict however, but rather, to prosecute my mission for the Anunnaki. Under normal circumstances, this would have simply entailed flying in via Phaseship, doing our bit, and departing forthwith.

Unfortunately, the Mongols enjoyed the services of Lyran detection technology, and although it had not been confirmed, they were also rumored to have access to advanced anti-air weapons.

Accordingly, our timeships had parked themselves well out over the arctic circle and were awaiting our signal to come and retrieve us. In the meantime, we would have to rely on the talents of the *Utin Jääkärirykmentti*, the Utti Jaeger Regiment. Four of these seasoned warriors had been assigned to us, and they were a formidable group indeed.

Their leader, *Kersantti* Aarne Korhonen, was the very essence of what I might have expected; a handsome, muscular man with the almond shaped eyes and the blond hair of a classic Finn (and I must privately admit, that like Professor Merriweather, had I not been inclined towards the fairer sex, I would have found him to be immensely attractive, so perfect a specimen of manhood was he).

But more important than his good looks, were the Sergeant's many years of experience as a battlefield commander, and especially where it concerned special operations.

His second in command, *Alikersantti* Helleena Virtanen, was nearly two heads shorter, with platinum hair, freckles and pixyish features. Yet I do not want my readers to think of her as being delicate, for the Under Sergeant was as hard muscled and as fit as one would hope a woman would be in such a profession. And like her Sergeant, she too had endured many years of danger, and was reputed to be a talented sniper.

214

The third member of the Finnish Team and our medic, *Korpral* Järvinen, while not quite as photogenic as the Sergeant, had an easy-going nature and a quiet confidence about him that left me with no doubt as to his skill under fire. The same held true of *Soldat* Mäkinen, a demolitions specialist, though he was a red head, which was quite uncommon among the Finns.

While they had been charged with the mission of keeping our entire group safe, each of them had also been assigned to watch over a specific member of our party. The Sergeant and Lady Anne had been partnered together, whilst Louise and Soldat Mäkinen had been paired with one another, and Ms. Grímsdóttir had Korpral Järvinen as her companion. As for myself, I was with Under Sergeant Virtanen. These partnerships would be especially critical in the first phase of our operation, which was no less than a HAHO, or high opening parachute drop, directly into enemy territory.

Lest my readers misconstrue, none of us Pleiadeans were actually going to undertake this activity by ourselves. Instead, we would be passengers, riding in tandem with our Special Forces counterparts. Therefore, it was Under Sergeant Virtanen's responsibility to see me delivered safely to the ground, and then act as my guide through hostile territory.

Given my past as an aviatrix, one might assume that I was entirely comfortable with this. Yet I was not. Though I had always adored flying, I had never had the occasion to use a parachute. The very idea of abandoning a perfectly serviceable aircraft and plummeting earthwards with nothing but a thin piece of fabric to arrest my fall, caused me to feel no little amount of trepidation. Thus, when she joined me, Under Sergeant Virtanen took special pains to soothe my nerves.

"Rentoutua," she advised, slapping me on the shoulder. "Relax. You'll do fine."

Then, with a wide smile pasted on her camouflaged face, she proceeded to check my gear, tugging on this and pulling on that 'till she was certain of my readiness.

The same ritual was taking place with my fellow Pleiadeans, though they did not seem nearly as fearful as I. Ms. Grímsdóttir in particular, appeared to be taking the whole thing in stride, (but then, she has never been given to displaying anything but absolute bravery in all circumstances, so I cannot say if this was mere bravado on her part, or that she was genuinely at ease).

Of course, I fully realize that I still have yet to explain the exact nature of our mission, and the reason why we had been selected to carry it out. Therefore, I shall briefly pause, and provide my readers with the details, which will make all of it seem quite sensible, albeit rather fantastic.

Decades earlier, a parallel event had occurred in both the 7th and 2nd universes, but with decidedly different outcomes. In each universe, a group of Russian miners in the Tisol District of the Kemerovo Oblast had unearthed a marble sarcophagus in a coal seam some 80 meters beneath the surface.

Reportedly, it had been fashioned in so fine a manner that it would have put modern craftsmen to shame. And, once they had freed it from the rock and opened the lid, the miners had found themselves gazing upon the features of a beautiful young woman.

She was lying in a blue fluid of unknown composition, and perfectly preserved. Moreover, the depth at which she had been discovered suggested that her burial had occurred some 233 million years in the past!

Mystified by this impossibility, the miners had promptly contacted their overlords. In the 7th universe, this had been the Mongols, and in the 2nd, the Soviets. Both had responded with a helicopter and a body of soldiers.

Yet, when they attempted to drain the coffin so as to lighten the strain on the aircraft, the body within it had begun to turn black and decompose, prompting them to refill it immediately. Stranger still, the very moment that this fluid was restored, the figure had regained her original, uncorrupted state.

So burdened, the helicopter had taken off with its cargo, and headed straight for Moscow, and for a time, nothing more was heard about it.

But here is where the two tales diverged from one another, for although the Soviets had left well enough alone, and the find had been allowed to fade into obscurity, the Mongols had pursued a far different course. Somehow, they had managed to rouse the Princess from her long slumber.

Moreover, they discovered that she bore an ancient virus, that while harmless to her and those of her era, proved to be both airborne and lethal to any modern human not protected by special equipment. This, it happened, had been part of the purpose behind the strange fluid. It had acted not only as a preservative, but as a barrier against accidental exposure, and only the fact that the contagion had resided within her lungs, and that she had not been breathing, had saved the miners from meeting their deaths.

Worse, the Great Khan had grown tired of fighting the Ostlanders, and plans were under way to use the Princess to create a biological weapon that would finish the war by laying waste to the entire West. At present, the Princess was being held for this purpose in the *Khaldvart övchin Sudlalyn Khüreelen*, or Infectious Disease Institute, located in the very heart of Moscow.

All of this brings me at last to the rationale behind my presence, and that of my fellow Pleiadeans. Being aliens, only we were immune to the disease that this carrier bore, and only we could be trusted to aid in her escape from captivity.

The more perceptive of my readers will instantly deduce the rest, yet for the sake of completeness, I shall still record it plainly; this same Princess, was in fact none other than the one Enki had referred to, and it was their desire that she be restored to her time-period. The only question which remained unanswered was the reason for her burial, and on this score, they had steadfastly refused to comment.

I myself entertained several theories. One was that she had been ill with another malady, and had been confined in the hope that a cure would someday be found for it.

Another was that she had in fact died but had been inadvertently Awakened through the unwitting agency of the Khan's scientists and some unknown quality of her marble container. Yet a third, was that she had been sealed in as a kind of living time capsule to be revived in the future.

Of course, none of these hypotheses had any facts to support them, and until we were face to face, I could only continue to speculate. In the interim, there was still the small matter of crossing an active war zone and then navigating our way through a hostile nation.

The first leg of our perilous endeavor was conducted by an Ostlander Air Force transport plane, and took us an hour to complete. Though a direct flight to our 'drop zone' would have been far shorter, several factors made that utterly impracticable.

For one, Mongolian armor units stationed in the area were equipped with surface-to-air missile batteries, and it was a given that they would not react graciously to our presence. Further, as we had no wish to advertise our ultimate destination, our aeroplane was compelled to fly in a meandering fashion along the Finnish border until we attained the proper location and altitude for the jump, this being a dizzying 9,144 meters.

Then there was the business of surviving the jump itself, which required us to breathe pure oxygen for thirty-five minutes so as to flush the nitrogen from our bloodstreams, and thereby prevent decompression sickness (something which even we Pleiadeans were vulnerable to).

Of course, all of these preparations only added to my unease, and by the time the rear cargo ramp opened, my nerves were near their breaking point. Consequently, as Under Sergeant Virtanen and I crab-walked together to the lip (for we were literally joined at the hip) she spoke to me over the microphone in her oxygen mask.

"Don't worry," she said, "We do this all the time."

As she told me this, the yellow standby light winked off and was replaced by a green one, which then proceeded to flash insistently. This was our signal. Whether I wished it or not, it was time to jump.

"Come on," the Finn urged, "we go together."

Whispering a prayer, I made my way with her to the edge of the ramp, and then we flung ourselves out into the moonless night. After that, there was nothing but the howl of the wind and the sensation of weightlessness.

I am quite proud to say that I did not scream at this juncture, and thereby prevented injury to the Under Sergeant's eardrums. And after a few moments of free fall, I even dared to open my eyes.

This was where wonder temporarily replaced fear, for I felt as if I were a bird, wholly unfettered, entirely free, and a part of the night sky itself. Were it not for the sensation of my passage to remind me that I was falling, I could have easily been convinced that I was flying under the power of my own wings.

A mere 15 seconds later, and having attained 8,200 meters, Under Sergeant Virtanen deployed our chute. I felt a terrific jolt, and this was immediately followed by the sensation of being pulled upwards. Looking past my guide, I saw the great black canopy of our parachute billowing outwards as it caught the air and began to slow our descent.

From our preflight briefing, I knew exactly why the Under Sergeant had done this as early as she had; parachutes made noise when they opened and exposed the chutist to detection from forces on the ground.

By attending to this task at high altitude, it was now a certainty that no sound would reach our enemies ears, and thereby betray us. Further, we would enjoy the ability to glide through the darkness for a great distance, thus bypassing the entirety of the front lines by many kilometers before arriving at our landing site.

Obviously, our ultimate success depended on Virtanen's skill at navigating, and the accuracy of her Global Positioning System. However, I entertained no serious concerns on either score. The GPS system, while primitive in comparison to Blackbird's software, was reliable enough, and the fact that her fellow operators trusted her to be the leader of our 'stick' argued vigorously in favor of her expertise. As for my part in all of this, I had nothing whatsoever to contribute, and did my utmost to simply relax, and not interfere.

Forty kilometers later, and as we approached our final destination, the features of the landscape beneath me became easily distinguishable, and the primal side of my brain attempted to reassert itself once again. Yet I did not allow this. I had had enough of terror, and instead, readied myself for what was to come next.

Legs out as you land, I reminded myself, *and then slide in. And the moment that you have stopped moving, help your jump partner to gather in the chute. Remember; the enemy could be nearby. The longer that you take to conceal your presence, the greater your chances of detection.*

Barely had I finished this mental recitation when I saw the earth rushing up to meet me and hastily positioned my legs. Then, of a sudden, Virtanen's feet touched the earth, and after only a few steps, she brought us to a gentle stop.

We were down, and to my relief, I found that I was still alive.

"Quickly," she ordered.

Immediately, I unhooked from my harness and we set straight to work, gathering in the lines and bundling up the canvas. Once Virtanen was confident that I had things well under control, she let me finish and unslung her carbine, ranging its barrel around us as she stood guard against hostiles.

Our landing site had been well chosen though, and no one came to challenge us. Consequently, I was able to bury the chute without interruption and then follow my guide in a search for our compatriots. Nary ten minutes later, we had managed to rendezvous with them and set off together across the moonless landscape. Our objective was a farm near the town of Tolokonnikovo, where a member of the Russian resistance resided.

Out of prudence, we kept to the woods and farmlands. This did not prevent us from encountering danger however, for at one point, whilst making our way through a small grove of trees, we suddenly came within sight of a road, and three military vehicles parked alongside it. Though one of the crewmen stood watch at his turret gun, the rest were standing around outside and stretching, and another had stepped over to the shoulder to relieve himself.

Instantly, Under Sergeant Virtanen shoved me to the snowy ground and as she took her place beside me, gestured me to silence. Everyone else had done likewise, and not a one of us made a sound, nor moved unnecessarily.

A long moment passed, and then to my relief, the Mongols returned to their vehicles, started the engines, and headed away to the west.

"BTR-80's" Virtanen informed me. "Nasty things--and we are lucky they didn't see us. If they had been using their thermal imagers, their heavy machine guns would have turned us into pink mist by now."

Oh, how delightful, I thought grimly. Thus far, I thoroughly detested Mongolian Russia, and felt a greater sympathy for Kára Grímsdóttir's inborn prejudice towards its conquerors.

"Probably on their way to the front," the Finnish woman added. "Too bad we can't call in an air strike on those *paskiaisets*."

"Whyever not?" I asked her.

Sergeant Korhonen explained. "Too much of a chance that the Mongols would figure out that someone was doing the spotting. We don't need that kind of attention."

After hiding ourselves from several more convoys of enemy vehicles (one of which numbered at least one hundred armored machines) we came within sight of the farm. We did not make straight for it though; rather we dropped to our stomachs at the edge of a field, and Sergeant Korhonen surveilled the place with a pair of binoculars.

It was only when he saw nothing untoward that he sent Soldat Mäkinen forwards to verify that it was indeed safe. That, and task Under Sergeant Virtanen with the job of protecting the man with her sniper rifle, which like his binoculars, could see into the thermal and infrared bands.

Several minutes passed until Mäkinen had reached the farmhouse itself, and then he signaled the all-clear with his infrared torch. Yet, neither I nor my fellow Pleiadeans were allowed to leave our positions, and none of the Finns moved from their places either.

Instead, we remained where we were, while Mäkinen knocked on the back door. When it opened and the farmer stepped out, I noticed that Under Sergeant Virtanen had adjusted her aim slightly, making it clear that she had the farmer squarely in her crosshairs. Plainly, if the Russian intended to betray us, she would see to it that it would cost him his life.

There was a brief exchange between the two men, although most of it was lost to me over the distance. But at last, Mäkinen relaxed, and waved us forwards.

Even at this juncture though, our team did not drop its guard. Weapons remained at the ready, and all eyes were on the night until we had reached the house and were safely inside.

Its owner was one Pyotir Kuznetsov, an elderly gentleman with a tall, thin frame, a long white beard, and eyes that bespoke of a careworn life. But he greeted us warmly, and made no comment about the startling resemblance that I and my fellow Pleiadeans had to one another. Nor did he ask the Finns about the nature of our mission. Instead, he simply offered us food and drink.

Ms. Virtanen and Soldat Mäkinen did not partake however. Rather, she situated herself on the second floor with her rifle, whilst he patrolled the exterior. So protected, the rest of us were able to take our ease as much as the situation permitted, which is to say that while we took advantage of the lull, none of us were truly comfortable, and kept ourselves ready for trouble.

In the interim, Sergeant Korhonen conferred with Kuznetsov at his dining table and explained our needs. This was done over glasses of vodka, which I subsequently learned, was an integral component of any negotiation carried on in Russia.

"We only need a ride and your help in making contact with our fellow once we get there," he informed the man. "Then your part in this is over."

"And where would you wish to go, *tovarishch?*" Kuznetsov asked, filling the Sergeant's glass as he did so.

Korhonen unfolded his map on the table and those of us who had not elected to sleep gathered 'round it. Then he pointed to another small village situated on the north banks of the Neva river. "Here."

The Russian leaned in, studied it carefully, and nodded. "I have a truck, and if we take the right route, we can avoid Nevagrad completely."

Seeing that city on the map, I recognized it, and also understood the reason for his desire to avoid it. In all of the universes save the 7th, it was known as St. Petersburg, but thanks to my conversations with Kára Grímsdóttir, I knew the cause for this temporal discrepancy.

Though Prince Dimitry of Moscow had won the Battle of Kulikovo in all of the other timelines, the exact opposite had occurred here. And with his inglorious defeat, Mongol rule over Russia had continued unabated, Peter the Great had never become Tsar, and the name of St. Peter was completely unknown to the city's inhabitants.

Even so, from its prominence on the Sergeant's chart, it was plain that like its other iterations, it had still managed to become a great population center. Moreover, it was a given that being as close as it was to the front, that it served as a major staging point for the Khan's armies. Risking a journey through its streets was pure suicide.

"That will do nicely," the Sergeant replied. It was only then that he toasted Kuznetsov's health and their business was concluded.

I myself, took a place on the floor near the fire, using my heavy parka for a pillow, and as the stresses of the night caught up with me, I fell asleep almost immediately.

When next I awoke, it was just past dawn, and I discovered that as a side-effect of the HAHO jump, that my body ached terribly. Not as much as it might have had I been human, but still, my joints and muscles forcefully reminded me of the shock that I had suffered when the chute had opened.

And from the stiff manner in which my fellow Pleiadeans were moving, it was plain that they were similarly uncomfortable. But we were augmented by nanobots, and would recover rapidly, whereas, our human guides were not so equipped, and I therefore felt great sympathy for their condition.

However, despite our state, we were all of us greatly cheered when Kuznetsov saw to it that we were served a generous Russian breakfast. It consisted of tea, sandwiches with kolbasa, and also something quite new to me; syrniki, or cheese dumplings garnished with sour cream. This hearty and agreeable fare helped to reinvigorate us all, and after it was over, we remained within the confines of the farmhouse while Kuznetsov tended to his farm.

We spent this hiatus tending to our weapons, inspecting our gear, conversing, or playing rounds of chess, which as it happened, was a game that Sergeant Korhonen excelled it.

It was during this interval, that I also learned something rather disquieting about Mr. Kuznetsov which both explained his ready assistance, and also the aura of sadness that surrounded him. Korhonen explained that he had read the Russian's dossier before the mission, and had learned that the man's wife had been raped and murdered by a drunken band of Mongolian *Tsereg*, or ordinary soldiers.

Though the blackguards had been punished by their commander, the penalty had been relatively light, leaving Kusentov alone and without having received any real justice. Thus, he had joined the ranks of the resistance and had since fought his country's oppressors in every way that his advanced age allowed.

It was a sobering portrayal of the universe that Ms. Grímsdóttir considered home, and when I mentioned the incident to her, she was not surprised in the least. Apparently, atrocities such as this, and worse, were quite commonplace.

223

Dusk arrived, and when he was certain that his neighbors were not observing him, Kuznetsov brought his lorry around and we piled into the back. Then he concealed our presence with crates of produce and covered them over with a carefully draped tarp.

And once we were on the road, he proved to be a skillful navigator, carefully avoiding the main highways in favor of lesser roads, and where these would not do, took us on dirt tracks that no map had ever recorded. Hence, we arrived some four hours later and without incident at the hamlet of Krasnaya Zara, and in sight of the Neva river. There, he bid us a hearty farewell, and left us in the custody of our new caretaker, Alexi Lebedev.

Lebedev was a fisherman by trade, who plied the Neva for smelt during warmer weather, whilst supplementing his income all the year-round with another skill that greatly recommended itself to our endeavor. This was smuggling, and in this, he was no beginner, but an old hand at outwitting the Mongols. Better still, he had aided the Ostlanders on numerous occasions, and both he and the Sergeant were personally acquainted.

"Alexi, you old pirate!" the Korhonen exclaimed, shaking his hand (as the Slavic custom of planting kisses on the cheek is only reserved for the closest of friends). "How have you been?"

"Nyaploko," the smuggler replied with a shrug. "Not bad. The Mongols haven't caught me yet. So, the usual then?"

The Sergeant nodded. "And the usual fee for all your troubles, with a bit extra for expenses—paid in *Tughriks* of course."

"I would rather have *Kronen* instead," Alexi said, "but I think that the Khan might be offended."

The two men laughed at this, and as Lebedev produced the inevitable bottle of vodka, they got straight to the heart of the matter.

"We need to go to Moscow," Korhonen said plainly.

"I can arrange that," the smuggler replied as if this were the simplest thing in the nine universes. "Coach or first class?"

"Arriving intact would be more than enough," the Finn answered with a dry chuckle. With that, he produced his map.

Lebedev eyed it carefully, stroking his chin. Then at last, he leaned back and downed his vodka.

"You will go first by truck," he informed the soldier. "then by train. Once you reach the railyards at the Krasnoselsky District though…"

"…we will be on our own," Korhonen surmised.

"Precisely," Lebedev told him. "Though I can give you a contact in the city once you make your way out of the yard."

Owing to the extreme cold, the Neva had completely frozen over. This made it possible for us to walk directly from one bank to the other, with an associate of Mr. Lebedev acting as our guide.

Once across, we were met by the lorry that the smuggler had promised us, and were conveyed to a spot some ten kilometers beyond Nevagrad's outermost limits. There, the railroad tracks that served the city passed through a long stretch of deserted countryside, and we secreted ourselves amongst the bushes and abided in silence.

It was not overlong before our vigil was rewarded by the distinctive wail of a train's horn, and then we spotted the light from the lead engine as it illuminated the rails. According to the information that the smuggler had provided, this particular train was headed directly to Moscow, and having already been scrutinized by the Mongols for contraband, would not see another such inspection before attaining its destination.

It would, however, suffer a slight delay, courtesy of Mr. Lebedev and his cohorts. This came in the form of a large and rather decrepit farm truck which drove up onto the track and parked. Straightaway, the driver exited his vehicle, opened up the hood, and then began to wave a battery-powered lantern at the oncoming locomotive. It's engineer (who was also in the employ of Mr. Lebedev) responded by applying the brakes.

This was our moment; the very instant that the train had come to a halt, we dashed from our concealment, and made for a freight car which had been marked out with chalk. It happened that the sliding door had been secured by the Mongols with a stout lock, but we were not deterred by this, having anticipated the measure. Instead,

we climbed up the ladder attached to the side of the car, with
Sergeant Korhonen in the lead.

Which was as well, for the rungs were icy, and as I ascended
behind him, my boot slipped, and I very nearly fell off. But the
Sergeant seized my wrist at the last second, and with a smile that
reached his eyes, the big blonde man pulled me upwards till I could
regain my footing and join him at the top. The others (who were
surer of foot than I) were right behind me, and together, we made
our way along the slippery roof and thence to a hatchway.

In milder weather, and with a more motivated guard force, such
an entrance might have been padlocked like the doors below us.
However, the combination of the bitter cold, the hazard posed by
moving atop the cars themselves, and the cooperation of railyard
workers (who had been handsomely bribed to overlook it), it was
entirely unsecured.

Without wasting an instant, the Sergeant pulled it open and we
filed past him and dropped into the interior. As soon as everyone
was within, he used a cargo box for a step, climbed up, and reclosed
the hatch, making sure to add a bit of wood into its jamb so as to
ensure that it would not completely seal, and thereby trap us.

Then it was all a matter of waiting. Though it took but a few
minutes for the Tsereg riding aboard the train to push the lorry off
the tracks, their leader ordered his men to walk the length of the train
so as to verify its security.

And check they did; as I listened in the darkness, I could hear the
snow crunching under the boots of a soldier as he walked by, pausing
only to test the padlock on the sliding door before moving on. That,
and the noise that he, or one of his associates, made as they ascended
the ladder.

Here, my breath caught, for I was certain that the man would
somehow detect our entry and raise the alarm. Yet, for the reasons
that I mentioned above, he did not ascend all the way, and although I
could see the light of his torch through the small gap in the hatch, it
did not linger there for more than a second.

Then to my relief, I heard the unmistakable sound of his descent,
followed by the footfalls of his fellows, and snatches of casual
conversation in Mongolian as they returned to the warmth of their
railcar. This was followed by the rumble of the mighty diesel engines

coming back to life, and then the cacophony of the boxcars clashing together at their couplings as it began to pull them along.

After that, there was only the staccato clicking of the rails as they passed beneath our wheels, accompanied by the rumble of the cars, and the occasional clamor of warning bells as we passed through road crossings.

Our journey eastwards had finally begun, and it was not overlong before the monotonous song of our passage lulled me to sleep. Naturally, I was not allowed to simply enjoy my nothingness, for as my readers will fully expect, Saturn came to plague me.

There was nothing about the dream that made it unique from the others, nor were the Sibyl and Maggie anywhere in evidence. Rather, it was a repetition of what I had already experienced, and for that reason, I shall not comment on it further, save to say that when I next awoke, I was not as well-rested as I might have wished.

As for my companions, I found them gathered about a small but rather ingenious portable heater, which despite its diminutive size, had done an excellent job of staving off the subzero weather. While it was still quite cold in the boxcar, it was not lethally so, and I found that there was even tea available.

"Sergeant Korhonen was just about to have me come and wake you," Under Sergeant Virtanen said over a steaming cup of her own beverage. "We are only an hour away from Moscow, and he wanted to go over that part of the plan."

Glancing in his direction, I saw that Korhonen had opened a map of the city, and was spreading it out on the metal floor. It was not a military chart, nor Finnish, but in Mongolian and Russian, and seemed to be intended for use by civilian motorists.

Once I had joined the others, he proceeded to detail the steps that we would follow once our train reached the railyard. I attended to his every word.

At length, the train came to a halt, and I knew that we had arrived at the railyard at last. Immediately, everyone gathered up their gear, and Sergeant Korhonen climbed up onto the roof, and then helped us to ascend. Having been cautioned in advance by Sergeant

Virtanen, when I attained the top, I took care to keep as low as possible so as to avoid 'sky-lining' myself.

Then I climbed down the ladder as swiftly and as quietly as I could, till I was on the ground with the others. Seeing that we were ready, the Sergeant signaled to us, and we started off. Our objective was the fence which separated the yard from the rest of the city, and then a light industrial area that neighbored it.

But being as large as it was, and with many tracks to cross, our extrication was not a rapid process by any means. The train had delivered us to the very center of the place, and being a major hub for rail transportation, including the Trans-Siberian Railway, it was a beehive of activity. Both workers and Mongol soldiers were to be found nearly everywhere.

Two factors worked in our favor though; the sky was still dark, and there were many cars in the yard, creating a plethora of shadows and places in which to hide ourselves. Thus, we were able to make our way without arousing any undue attention. But this success, and all those that we had enjoyed thus far, should have served as a warning that our luck was about to turn, however briefly.

When we were nary more than a track away from the fence, I caught something out of the corner of my eye. Turning towards it, I realized that I was looking upon a lone Mongol sentry. He was standing in the shadows between two rail cars, and perchance he had been using the space to shelter himself from the wind and the cold, or possibly for some other reason entirely.

Regardless, a look of surprise came over his features, for our sudden appearance was just as much a startlement to him as his was to us. His mouth opened, and he began to raise his rifle, but then there was a sharp 'pop', and I saw a circle of blood appear in the center of his forehead.

Instantly, his expression changed to that of puzzlement, as if he could not quite reconcile what had just happened. It was only as he slumped to the snowy ground that I took stock of the suppressed pistol in Corporal Virtannen's hand, it's barrel still smoking.

"Come on," she urged, hastily tucking the weapon away. "Let's get this body hidden. And don't worry--we do this all the time."

Admiring her coolness, I took one of the dead man's arms, whilst she took the other, and together, we dragged him towards a nearby flatcar. It was loaded with equipment covered in heavy tarps, and knowing what she intended, the Sergeant clambered atop the car's platform, and then helped us to raise the body upwards.

This was not easy, for we were all of us compelled to handle what was literally a dead weight, but once the corpse was aboard, and we had joined Korhonen on the car, we were able to secrete it rather neatly beneath one of the tarps. Though I was an amateur at this sort of thing, it was plain that unless someone conducted an inspection of what lay beneath the covering, the Mongol would not be discovered until he reached his final destination (wherever that might be).

With our murderous deed now concealed, we made for the fence, and in short order, found a place where rust and neglect had created a breach just large enough for our party to squeeze through.

By now, dawn had come, and as we passed by rows of warehouses, what few people that we encountered were all ethnic Russians. Moreover, when they spotted our party, they made a great show of finding something else to occupy their attention, or failing this, simply turned their backs on us to enjoy a cigarette, or chat with a co-worker.

I knew the reason for this behavior without having to ask my fellows; centuries of oppression had taught them not to needlessly involve themselves in trouble (for we were after all armed foreigners and clearly in the pursuit of some clandestine business). Moreover, they had no love for their Mongol overlords, and did not wish to aid them if it could be avoided. Therefore, by seeing nothing, they accomplished both objectives, and with little effort.

Even so, we did not take their passive assistance for granted, for there was always the chance that an informant lurked among them. Accordingly, we kept our pace brisk and purposeful.

After a short while, we came to a side street, which was deserted save for several lorries parked along the curb. At first, I thought them to be similarly unoccupied, but as we approached, a hand waved at us from the window of the nearest vehicle.

Sergeant Korhonen returned the gesture and led the way, and as I followed, I saw at last why he had been so incautious; someone had made chalk marks on the rear bumper that to most eyes would have seemed accidental. Yet they were not, for one was white, and the other blue, these being the colors of Finnish Ostland.

There was no conversation betwixt us and the driver, and after Under Sergeant Virtannen had carefully erased the marks, we loaded ourselves into the back. Then we were off.

Some minutes later, our transport came to a halt on another deserted street, and the driver opened the rear gate, waving for us to board a second lorry. Again, there was no tête-à-tête, and we were taken to what proved to be an empty warehouse, save that cots had been set up for us, along with a table and some chairs.

This was to be our base of operations while we were in Moscow, and our host proved to be none other than our first driver. A great bear of a man, Dmitri Ivanov was not only a seasoned teamster, but also the leader of the local resistance cell. Just as with Alexi Lebedev, the Sergeant and he were well acquainted, and as soon as we had set down our packs and gear, he saw to it that we were provided with a warm meal.

Then came the planning session. At this stage, Lady Anne and Kara Grímsdóttir were officially in charge of the mission, but the Sergeant and Ivanov willingly volunteered their expertise.

It happened that Ivanov had managed to obtain us a copy of the plans for the Institute where our prisoner was being held, and the four of them huddled over it and discussed our options for several hours.

The KOSK Institute occupied the grounds of what in other universes would have been Moscow State University. As one might expect, it was heavily guarded, and a number of stratagems were put forth to breach its formidable security. In the end, they managed to agree on the most promising of these, and Ivanov wholeheartedly offered up whatever material assistance that would be required.

All that remained, was to put the plan into action. That, and to say goodbye to the Finns. Having successfully delivered us to Moscow, their part in this adventure was over.

I must say that I was quite saddened by this. In the short while that we had been associated with one another, the Sergeant and his team had proven themselves to be people of the very highest caliber; loyal to a fault, resourceful, and unfailingly brave. Yet, given the nature of our objective, and that of the hostage herself, accompanying us, was of course, utterly impossible. So, the next evening they took their leave of us.

"Where will you go next?" I asked Under Sergeant Virtanen as they finished packing up the last of their gear.

"Back to *Suomi*, perhaps" she said with a shrug. "Then another mission into Russia. That is our life."

"Fare thee well, then," I said, clasping her arm in the Ostlander fashion.

"You also," she replied. "Stay safe."

"Don't worry," I answered. "We do this all the time." This earned me a laugh. Then I added, "Perchance, we shall meet again."

"Ehkä," she shrugged. "It is a big world, and an even bigger universe. Anything is possible, maybe even peace."

"But not today," Sergeant Korhonen put in. "Before we depart *Moskova*, we intend to leave a little gift for the Mongols that I think will also help you on your mission."

He did not elaborate on the specifics, and the Finns all grinned at one another conspiratorially. Whatever it was, I was certain that it would be pure mischief.

Three more days elapsed, during which Ivanov procured all of the resources that we required. This included a stolen Mongol army vehicle, military uniforms, cheap black wigs so as to cover over our blond hair, and access codes to various portions of the KOSK facility.

We were all of us deeply impressed by his resourcefulness, and when the time came for us to prosecute our mission, he invited us with no little pride to the rear of the Mongol lorry so as to inspect two final items. These consisted of a pair of metal pressure cookers wired together to a cellular phone, and concealed in a large box labeled as foodstuffs.

When I beheld this arrangement, I was a tad puzzled. Though our plan had called for explosives, the devices were not at all what I had expected (though I freely admit that my expertise in this area is quite limited).

"Are we perchance providing dinner for the Mongols?" I asked dryly.

"It is always polite to bring an offering to a feast," Ms. Grímsdóttir replied with equal sarcasm, "But this is one celebration that our hosts will come to regret." Then she explained their operation to me in detail.

Though they were not elegant weapons by any means, I was both impressed by their ingenuity, and horrified by their destructive potential. But this was war, I reminded myself, and ruthlessness is one of its mainstays.

Presently, the box was resealed, and after thanking him for his support, Lady Anne distributed crickets to our party. They were of the same kind that we had employed at the Vatican secret archive, and once we had synchronized them, we boarded the truck.

Here, Lady Anne served as our driver, and took us from the warehouse into the streets of Moscow (for it happened that she was a practiced motorist, having learned to drive during her visits to her New York gallery, and with the aid of an expensive collection of luxury vehicles).

Although we encountered many instances of the Mongolian military presence during this journey, there was only one that deserves particular mention as it exemplifies the nature of Russia's conquerors in the 7th universe.

We had come into Lubyanka square, wherein the headquarters of the EKTA or the *Ezen Khaany Tagnuulyn Alba*, the Imperial Intelligence Service, resided. The building was of the Neo-Baroque style and might have been considered tasteful by some, save for its occupants, and two other features which marred its appearance.

The first of these was a gigantic portrait of the current Khan, staring down at the passing vehicles with a stern, unforgiving expression, and the second were the bodies. Every lamppost surrounding the square had a corpse dangling from it. They were a warning to all of the fate that awaited any who dared to defy the will of the Great Horde.

Understandably, we did not linger in this dreadful place, but pressed on as fast as the traffic allowed. At length, we reached the KOSK Institute, and came within sight of its main gate, and here, my pulse quickened.

Bright lights illuminated the roadway, and I counted four armed guards stationed at the barrier. One held the leash of a rather fierce looking dog who began to bark at our presence right away, whilst another stepped forwards and signaled for us to halt. But before any of them could get close enough to realize that we were imposters, we activated our crickets.

Time froze, and everyone save ourselves, went as still as wax statues. Shedding our Mongol uniforms, we alit from the lorry and moved past this frozen assembly at a jog. In but a minute, we had reached the main building and then a loading dock. There, we encountered a door secured by a number pad, and using Ivanov's purloined codes, gained access to a freight receiving area, and beyond that, a hall which led deeper into the structure.

Guards and cameras were everywhere of course, but like the security measures at the gate, none of it prevented our progress. The only real impediment was the sheer size of the Institute itself, and it was well that we had been given a map or we would have easily become lost in its myriad passages.

But at length, and thanks to this precious gift, we reached the secure containment facility at last. There was no mistaking it for anything else; besides being guarded by even more inanimate sentries, a large airlock separated it from the rest of the facility. This barrier was festooned with signs in both Russian and Mongolian that not only declared its function, but added the dire warnings, *"Level 4 Containment!"* and *"Danger! Extreme Biohazard!"*

Here again, and thanks to Ivanov's efforts, we had no trouble gaining admittance. Time, however, was growing short. We had already expended ten minutes. Worse, we still had no idea of how long it would take us to find the Princess, and once we did, how we would free her.

As it happened, we encountered numerous chambers filled with laboratory animals, or facilities for experimenting on them, but not the woman that we sought, and I for one, began to worry that our intelligence was incorrect. However, when we once again encountered an airlock, my spirits were buoyed, for the small windows set in its doors revealed a larger chamber beyond it.

Passing through the barrier, we came into a space that under normal circumstances would have been called a warehouse, but it contained only one object within its precincts.

This was a group of transparent chambers, linked by passageways, and served by large hoses, which in turn, were joined to massive air-handling units. Thanks to the translucency of the walls, I could see everything inside, including all of the furnishings that one might have expected to encounter in a conventional residence, including a couch.

A woman sat upon it. Like all of the Anunnaki that I had met so far, she was very tall, with pale skin and even paler hair. There was also an alienness about her that bespoke of a being that while seemingly human, was not, but hearkened from another lineage altogether.

Odder still, she was not affected by the time-stoppage, but was as animated as we were, and watched our approach with a calm detachment, as if she had expected us all along.

As I wondered at this, we rushed to the entrance of her quarters. Unsurprisingly, it too was guarded by an airlock, and when we made to examine it, we found that its controls were the same as all the others; a simple number pad and a pair of lights. One of these was red and the other green, and at the moment, the red one was illuminated, indicating that it was locked.

There was only one small fly in the ointment though. While Ivanov's spies had provided us with a wealth of information, they had not discovered the code for this particular barrier.

"What think you?" I asked the others.

"Since we do not know the numerical sequence to open this door," Lady Anne responded, "I would venture to say that we are compelled to employ more brutish measures. Say explosives?"

"Oh, what a capitol idea!" Louise exclaimed. "And thanks to my dear friend, Soldat Mäkinen, I happen to have just the thing."

She then reached into her backpack and held up a small charge made from some form of plastic explosive. "One for each hinge should do it."

I regarded her with great mistrust, for I was not at all comfortable with her handling munitions (whilst simultaneously wondering at how she had managed to convince the Finn to part with them in the first place), but Lady Anne and Ms. Grímsdóttir did not seem as concerned as I.

Accordingly, I kept my reservations to myself, and when Louise had placed the charges and indicated that the time had come to retreat, I joined the others at a safe distance and waited.

The explosions which ensued were not at all as thunderous as I had anticipated, and it even seemed as if they had had no effect at all.

Exasperated, I was just about to castigate Louise, when of a sudden, the door groaned, and then toppled to the floor with a resounding crash.

This left only the inner door to stand athwart us, and it was assaulted in like manner. The very instant that the apartment had been breached, we rushed inside. In but moments, we were standing before the woman on the couch, and I resorted to the Anunnaki language file that we had been furnished with.

"Your Highness?" I asked in that tongue.

She seemed to find this honorific rather amusing. "Yes, I suppose that I am," she replied with a half-smile, "though I call myself Nanshe, and have no formal title. Have you come to rescue me?"

"We have indeed, madam," I answered. "If you will come with us, we will escort you back to your home in the Carboniferous."

"I should like that," the Princess replied, and then Lady Anne handed her a special breathing mask. It had been calibrated to match the atmosphere of the Carboniferous era. Thus, she would remain comfortable during the remainder of our exploit, and it would also lessen the amount of any contagion that she might exhale.

Nodding in gratitude, she put it on, and we made to depart. There were now but twelve minutes left to us to leave and get ourselves well away from the facility.

Urging the Princess to stay close, we escorted her back though the laboratory area, and went not to the main loading dock, but to a secondary one.

A number of motorcars were parked here, including vehicles reserved for the KOSK security force. But a quick inspection revealed that none of them had their keys in the ignition, and I must say that I felt a moment of panic at this unfortunate discovery.

Louise, however, was entirely unperturbed. "Ladies have no worries! I will just hot-wire one of them."

Without explaining exactly what the term 'hot-wire' meant, she went to the nearest patrol car, and opened up the driver's side door. Donning her combat gloves, she then leaned in, and pulled away a cover from beneath the steering wheel.

This in turn, exposed a group of wires, and selecting two of them, she stripped their ends with her battle knife and twisted them together. Then she bared the end of another wire and touched it to the conjoined pair. To my astonishment, there was a bright spark and the engine came to life.

"You see? Duck soup!" she beamed. Though I was loathe to admit it, her trick had been a clever one, and I resolved to commit it to memory—not that I would have admitted this, of course. She was full enough of herself as it was.

A moment later, my alarm reasserted itself when she sat down in the driver's seat. "Penelope, you're riding shotgun. I'm driving."

"I should think not!" I protested, looking entreatingly to Lady Anne, who had after all, driven the Mongol lorry in an acceptable fashion. The last thing that I desired was to trust our very lives to Louise's hand at the wheel—especially since she was just then helping herself to a sip from her flask.

It was Kara Grímsdóttir who interceded however, and not on my behalf. "Let her drive, Penelope. She has more experience behind the wheel than any of us." As for Lady Anne, she merely nodded in silent agreement.

"Yes, Penny," Louise put in with no little smugness. "Let *me* drive. I learned from the best wheelmen in the business how to shake the coppers. So, get in and let's blow this joint."

Seeing that I had no support, and that our time was rapidly expiring, I complied, though not without praying to God that this would not be the last night of my current existence.

Meantime, Louise was feeding gasoline to the engine, and causing its revolutions to increase. Before I realized what she was about, she let go of the brake and sent us hurtling at the fence that separated us from the outside world. Although it had been secured with a padlock and chain, these proved no match for the sheer mass of the motorcar, and we smashed our way through.

Simultaneously, our watches reached the zero mark, and Lady Anne calmly reached into her combat vest, wherein she produced a twin of the cell phone attached to the pressure cooker bombs. Powering it on, she made a brief call which was answered by a terrific explosion at the main gate. The abandoned lorry disintegrated in a huge fireball, and shrapnel tore into the guards, shredding them to pieces.

"That should purchase us some extra time," she said, rolling down her window and tossing the phone into the darkness. "But I daresay that it shall not be overlong before we will find ourselves being pursued."

Grímsdóttir nodded soberly at this and wrapped the sling of her submachinegun tight about her arm. "Yah, and we should get ready."

Inclining her head in understanding, Lady Anne fished about in her field kit until she found a survival blanket, which she then draped over the Princess's shoulders.

"If you would be so kind," she said to her, "I should like to ask that you bend over and remain low in your seat, Your Highness. This blanket will keep you warm and shield you from any stray glass fragments."

Nanshe complied, and seeing that she was protected, Grímsdóttir and Lady Anne fired short bursts into the rear window. This created small holes in the glass that were just large enough to accommodate the barrels of their rifles.

Their action proved timely, for but half a minute later, flashing lights appeared behind us, accompanied by the wail of sirens. By their speed, I calculated that our pursuers would be on us in seconds.

"Now we shall have some real fun!" Louise exulted, increasing our speed. Meantime, Lady Anne and Grímsdóttir used their improvised firing ports and let loose on the closest vehicle. Seeing the gunfire, its driver swerved wildly and then the car's lights spun as it lost control and went atumble.

Another machine was right behind it though, and the angry flash of an automatic weapon from the passenger's side made it plain that the shooter was intent on seeing us riddled with bullets.

My companions were not cowed by this however, and after a moment, they managed to score a hit on the driver. With no hand on the wheel, the car swerved off the road where it collided with a tree.

Thoroughly enjoying their misfortune, Louise waggled her fingers at the image in our rearview mirror. "Bye, bye, Blackbird!" Then to me, "No offense, Penny."

"None taken," I struggled to reply, my fingernails digging deeply into the dash. "Just you keep an eye on the road, I beg you!"

Laughing, Louise flipped a switch, activating our revolving lights as well as the siren. "I have always wanted to do that!" she exclaimed. "Oh, what great fun."

Meantime, more headlights were appearing behind us, and I for one, did not see what she found so amusing. Nor did I wish to prolong this ordeal any longer than necessary.

It was time to use my communications nanite. *Blackbird,* I thought. *We have the Princess safe. Begin your approach and provide us with rendezvous coordinates.*

Penny, proceed to 48 Ozyornaya Ulitsa, she replied. *There is a supermarket there with a dirt lot adjacent to it. We shall meet you at that location.*

"Thank you," said I aloud, already consulting the map in my data monocle.

Then, I turned to Louise, "Turn left up ahead. It is *Michurinsky Prospekt* and it will turn into Ozyomaya Ulitsa in 4.9 kilometers."

Though I expected her to cavil at this, or offer up some other difficulty, Louise merely inclined her head and concentrated on the road before us. At Michurinsky, she only slowed a little and made the turn with a great squealing of tires before straightening out and accelerating.

We were not alone for long however, for a police motorcar soon joined us and attempted to pass on our left, clearly intent on either ramming our vehicle, or cutting off our escape. To her credit, Louise realized this and dropped back just enough to bring our fender into line with its rear tire. Then with a hard jerk on the wheel, she slammed into the fellow, causing him to go into a spin which turned him completely around.

"So's your Old Man!" she exclaimed. "Next time, know your onions!"

As the police car struggled to right itself and resume the chase, she sped up. For the briefest of moments, I worried that it would continue to harry us, but even as the driver regained mastery over his vehicle, Grímsdóttir and Lady Anne peppered the machine with bullets, bringing whatever ambitions that he might have harbored utterly to naught.

Once again, we had the road entirely to ourselves.

Yet, our unfettered state was not long lived. We had just passed the EKTA Training Academy when we came upon two more police vehicles, parked nose to nose and obstructing our way. Worse yet, there were men behind them, their guns drawn, and to me, it seemed the perfect trap.

Or so I thought.

"You dumb saps!" Louise remarked contemptuously. And then, without any hesitation, she rammed straight through the barrier, sending the two motorcars sideways, and the men behind them, flying back as if they were only ragdolls.

"Penny, if you ever have to block a car," she said as we drove past them, "always park engine block to engine block, and not fender to fender. And certainly, do not stand directly behind the cars!"

I must say that having witnessed this demonstration of her expertise as a 'wheelman', that I was tempted to credit her with some admiration. But only for the briefest of moments, for as I reminded myself, she was after all, Louise, and most likely had enjoyed nothing but a run of pure luck. That she subsequently toasted her victory with more alcohol only hardened my opinion.

Meantime, the intersection of *Proyektiruyemyy Proyezd* and *Michurinsky* was coming up fast, and in seconds it became plain that the Mongols had no intention of simply allowing us to pass through it unmolested. They were done with mere police cars by now, and in their stead, the intersection was guarded by no less than three BTR-80's. All of their turret guns were pointed at us and someone was shouting over a loudspeaker in Mongolian, most likely ordering us to surrender. And behind us, I spied the lights of at least half a dozen police vehicles struggling to catch up and seal off the rear.

"Oh my," Louise exclaimed. "This is not good. Not good at all."

"Stop the car," I instructed, and the instant that she had applied the brakes, I leapt out of the passenger side, calling on X'Kallabar. I was not at all certain if its Fire was up to this situation, but there seemed to be no other option.

Lend me every bit of your strength, I thought to the Presence as it filled my hand. *For I need it now and greatly!*

In answer, the blade blazed to life, its glow becoming blindingly bright. As for the Mongolian commander, he yelled something else through his speaker, no doubt confused by this sudden turn of events and not a little concerned.

And it was well that he was, for I brought up my sword and visualized its flame reaching out and through the machines before me such as I had never done before. Then I made my cut, sweeping it before me and along the entire length of the armored assembly.

As I did so, an incandescent line of fire appeared wherever the blade had passed. Then gouts of fire blossomed all along this, and the machines began to explode from within, their upper halves rocketing into the air on great plumes of flame.

It was over in an instant, and all three of the metal behemoths were naught but flaming hulks. For my part, I was awestruck by the sheer power of the weapon that I possessed. Cleaving metal poles on the training sands and laying waste to a clay army were one thing, but this far exceeded it. As for the Tigress, she was positively delighted, and at her urging, I turned to face the oncoming police forces.

Having witnessed X'Kallabar's terrible effect, they skidded to an abrupt halt, but the Tigress and I were not inclined to allow them to pester us any further. Summoning the Fire once again, I raised my weapon and cut the nearest of the motorcars in half. Those who were behind it either threw their machines into reverse or abandoned them entirely so as to flee on foot.

The Mongols had been completely routed.

Sheathing my sword, I returned to our conveyance. "Drive on," I said, indicating a stretch of the shoulder that was just wide enough to let us by.

For once, Louise had nothing pithy to say, and took us onto the sidewalk and around the blazing wreckage. Though the heat was tremendous, we were moving fast enough that nothing caught, and then we were clear and racing onwards.

Not long after, we spotted the bright lights of the supermarket Blackbird had mentioned and turned in. A crowd had gathered in the car park to watch the conflagration in the distance, and a number of them remarked upon our vehicle, though none made any move to interfere.

Blackbird, I called. *we are here.*

As are we, Penny, she replied, making the people nearest us gasp and cry out as she and the Duchess decloaked and disgorged their mechanica. They had landed in the vacant lot and were now in plain sight.

"Take us straight to the Phaseships," Lady Anne said to Louise, "and keep us as far away from those onlookers as possible. As they are innocents, I would not wish for them to become infected."

"I can do one better," Blackbird volunteered, now speaking on our general Coms, and at her silent order, the mechanica marched straight towards the group of civilians.

Their glowing eyes, and their overall appearance was enough to do the trick. The spectators scattered in terror, no doubt certain that they were being attacked by alien monsters, when in truth their very lives were being saved.

In the interim, Louise had delivered us to the foot of Blackbird's egress ramp, and she and I guided the Princess aboard, whilst Lady Anne and Ms. Grímsdóttir made for the Duchess. Having done their duty, the mechanica turned about and hastily rejoined us. When they were both safely within their respective ships, we ascended.

Our last act before leaving was to fire a pair of rockets at the stolen security car, thus sterilizing it with fire. Then we proceeded back to the KOSK laboratory, and again discharged our ordinance.

This time, we employed Bennu missiles, equipped with high explosive warheads. These leveled the entire structure, completely destroying any records, as well as whatever biological weapon they had managed to develop.

As for our effect on the timeline, and whatever psychological trauma that we inadvertently inflicted on the citizens of Moscow, there was simply no help for it. The event would have to become another anomalous tale that one often encounters in the historical record; too strange not to be recorded, and too fantastical for anyone embracing reason to willingly accept.

After all, strange flying wings appearing out of the ether, fearsome robots, and a group of female commandos flying off into the night, simply strains credulity to its breaking point. The actions of swamp gas, mass hysteria, or the effect of the moon passing in front of the clouds, is a much easier pill for the average human to swallow.

Once beyond the range of Moscow's anti-aircraft defenses, we still had some ten minutes before we would reach the edge of the Earth's atmosphere and our Ebani. Perforce, and when I was completely certain that we had no interceptor craft pursuing us, I directed my attention to our guest's comfort.

"Are you hungry, Your Highness?" I queried. *I* was certainly famished, and I reasoned that anyone who had been asleep for 233 million years might be a bit peckish herself.

"I am," she responded.

Rising from my pilot's chair, I opened the compartment containing our food rations and brought out sandwiches, all of them labeled as chicken, as well as self-heating cups of tea.

Thanking me, the Princess took a bite and then eyed it speculatively. "This tastes just like Ophiacodon. What is it?"

"Chicken, Your Highness," I answered. "It does not exist in your time."

"Fascinating," she said. "But now I begin to wonder; if your chicken tastes like my Ophiacodon, then what pray tell, does Ophiacodon taste like? I see that I shall have to ponder this gastronomical question at great length. In the meantime, my many thanks to you for the sandwich."

I could think of no reply to make to all of this, but instead, kept silent and set to my meal. I also noted that she did not seem to prefer her tea, but had set it aside after only a sip, and with a grimace of distaste.

"I suppose that you must be wondering about me," the Princess went on as she finished the last of her sandwich. "It would only be natural for any intelligent being to question my strange circumstances."

"In fact, I have been," I admitted, turning in my seat to regard her. "I must say that I find your internment to be rather odd."

"I suppose that you would," she replied. "And mayhap you entertained some theories as to the reason for it. The truth is actually rather simple; I chose to be there."

This surprised me. "You *chose* to be encased in a sarcophagus for *millions* of years? Whyever for, madam?"

She eyed me with all of the serenity of a marble saint. "To dream the Great Dream of course."

At my look of incomprehension, she elaborated. "Your Sibyl is not the only being gifted with foresight, though the road that she follows is far different than that of my people.'

"I was entombed in order to have the opportunity to sleep undisturbed, and to dream visions of the future. I also knew that when my business was concluded, that I could compel humans to

242

come and find me. It was all a simple matter of reaching into their minds and then directing them to dig out that particular coal seam."

"And did you anticipate that they would then hold you prisoner?" I questioned.

"I did," she answered. "Just as I knew that once I had contacted my fellow Anunnaki, that they in turn would dispatch you and your doughty little band to come and rescue me. Which is as well, for the Mongolians were starting to become rather tedious."

"It was no trouble at all, Your Highness," Louise quipped. "We were simply in the neighborhood."

"And a gladsome thing that you were," the Princess smiled.

Then Louise held up her flask and jiggled it enticingly. "Since you do not seem to care for our tea, would you prefer some giggle water instead? It's the cat's meow, Your Highness!"

I was mortified at the possibility that Louise might manage to corrupt her, but to my relief, the Princess refused. "Thank you, but no," she said. "We are quite familiar with alcohol and our kind does not imbibe."

"Well said!" I cheered, giving a Louise a censorious look.

"Flat tire!" Louise pouted.

"There is one other thing that has puzzled me, Your Highness," I said, pointedly ignoring Louise's sulkiness. "Why was it that you were not affected by the time-stoppage?"

The Princess grinned. "We Anunnaki are not beings such as yourself. We have an extra sense, and this is the ability to perceive time as keenly as you might detect light, or sound. Moreover, this same sense allows us to influence the time around ourselves, bending it to our will, and reshaping it as we wish.'

"Thus, when I sensed your intentions, and felt the effects of your clever little devices, I merely altered my temporal state. But please, do not take any offense; your crickets are actually quite ingenious."

"I feel none, Your Highness," I reassured her.

Not long after this fascinating exchange, we reached outer space, and there, we were met by our Ebani. This time, the pilot carrying the Speaker hailed from El Dorado, and saw to it that we were transported without delay.

I found the Carboniferous Period to be even stranger to my eye than the Jurassic. Due to the great abundance of oxygen in the air, and the continuous forest fires that this tended to encourage, the sky possessed a decidedly bruised coloration.

And where it was not aflame, the land beneath it tended to be swampy, and choked with great, dense stands of giant ferns, where dragonflies with wingspans of a meter or more hunted alongside millipedes thrice as large.

Thus, finding ourselves a dry area in which to land proved to be somewhat of a challenge, especially one that was large enough to accommodate our two Phaseships. But eventually, we managed to locate a suitable spot and set ourselves down.

Once we had alit, the Princess removed her mask and took in a deep, contented breath. "Ah," she declared, "the sweet, sweet smell of home."

"I am pleased that we were able to convey you here safely," I said politely.

"Yes," she responded. "And I am glad for the opportunity that it provided me to observe the woman who shall be the next steward of the Grail."

I smiled at this, pleased that after all we had been through in the 7th universe, I had not been found wanting.

Presently, the Princess caught sight of something above the trees, and looking to the same quarter, I spotted a silver object that vaguely resembled a child's sled. It was of far greater size though, and flew through the humid air at a leisurely pace.

"My fellows have arrived," she explained. Then stepping away from us, she did something that I could never have anticipated; she began to grow, increasing in stature until she towered over us. Though I lacked the means by which to measure it, I gauged her final height to be no less than 6 meters tall. She had become a giantess.

"Ah, so much better!" the Princess declared with palpable relief. "You cannot imagine how wearisome it is to maintain a smaller form for any great length of time, but so many beings find our true dimensions to be distressing that it is a necessity. Please do forgive me if I have affected you adversely."

"No, Your Highness," I answered, now craning my neck to meet her gaze. "We were simply caught unawares is all."

The Princess smiled back down at me. "Then I shall take my leave and wish you the best of luck in your next adventure. Truly, I think that Enki chose well."

The sled meantime, had dipped below the trees, and awarding us a final wave of farewell, she set off through the ferns to meet it.

"Remarkable," Lady Anne commented. "After what we have just witnessed, I am compelled to wonder if the Anunnaki are in fact the progenitors of the race of giants. Though, if that is true, then the fabled Goliath, and those who created the city under Moberly, would rightly be considered dwarfs compared to those who sired them."

"That seems a reasonable conclusion," I agreed, watching as the sled ascended back into the sky and then headed southwards. "Shall we be off then? I for one, am eager to return to *our* home."

"A capitol suggestion," Lady Anne concurred.

At Saurii, we did not simply land and then traipse into the base without a care. Due to our highly infectious state, we were instead directed to set down at the far end of the tarmac, where a large tent, made of plastic, had been erected. It was linked by way of a tunnel (also composed of plastic) to a rather ordinary dome which I could not recall having ever seen before.

This, I learned, was to be our decontamination facility, and the moment that we had parked within its precincts, a group of mechanica drew its flaps closed, sealing our Phaseships within. Then the four of us were directed to exit, and we were met by the Professor, Charles, and Edward.

They were all of them dressed in exposure suits that covered their bodies from head to toe, and wore oxygen tanks that supplied them with breathable air, free of contagion.

Behind them stood a large white box, equipped with two airlocks; one to facilitate entrance, and the second to serve as an exit. Further, a tunnel depended from the second airlock, which led out of the tent to the dome that I had observed earlier.

From this, it became clear that the dome was intended to serve as our quarters while we were quarantined. How long this would last, however, I could not guess.

Meantime, the Professor gestured towards the box. "Please enter the decontamination unit one at a time. Once inside, remove all of your garments and every piece of equipment that you carry.'

"Then, place them in the plastic bag that you will find waiting for you, seal it, and put it in the collection receptacle. When you have done all this, the process itself will begin."

"What of our ships?" I asked, inclining my head in their direction.

"Even as we speak, they are bathing the interior of their cabins with high levels of gamma radiation," Merriweather answered. "And nanobots have been tasked with cleaning every possible surface. Soon your Phaseships will become more hygienic than ever, and lack any trace of the virus."

"And X'Kallabar?"

"Like the rest of your possessions, it must go into the plastic bag to be decontaminated," he stated.

I was not at all pleased with this requirement, for I worried that the sword might be damaged by whatever would be employed to purify it, especially if hard radiation were involved.

When I gave voice to this, the Professor did his level best to mollify me. "Penelope, I have researched the matter as diligently as possible, and I am confident that the sword will not be harmed in any way. The Andromedin science that fashioned X'Kallabar is far and above our own, and all of the sources that I consulted indicated that it will be totally impervious to anything that we might care to subject it to."

Of course, I could not gainsay the man. He was too great a scholar and commanded too much of my respect to do so. Besides which, it was either compliance, or being confined in isolation for an indefinite period of time. So, when at last my turn came, into the box I and X'Kallabar went.

Just as Merriweather had stated, I found a bag with my name inscribed upon it. Shedding everything that I wore, I then stuffed the lot of it inside, pausing only when it came to X'Kallabar (and this for but a heartbeat).

The moment that I had put the bag into the wall receptacle, it closed, and I heard the Professor's voice coming to me from over a speaker.

246

"Please hold your arms out at your sides, fingers spread wide" he directed. "and then spread your legs apart and splay your toes."

When I did so, the lighting in the chamber became violaceus, and then amber, causing me to feel an odd prickling sensation all over my body. This was followed by a fine mist that was discharged from tiny nozzles set in the corners of the chamber, and after that, I was subjected to more strange lights and curious sensations.

The final stage of the procedure proved to be a rather conventional shower, which came at me from the same nozzles that had delivered the mist. Once it had concluded, a niche opened up in the far wall, revealing a clean towel.

I promptly used this to dry myself, and just as I finished, the exit lock slid aside revealing the tunnel and the dome beyond. Charles was standing there, and he subjected me to several injections of what I presumed were anti-viral agents.

He then provided me with a blouse and a pair of pants that nurses in the 20th century called 'scrubs', along with slip-on shoes. It was only when I had donned this costume that I was free to proceed down the tunnel to join my sisters in the dome.

We remained within our shelter for a full week, during which time we underwent various tests. Perhaps the most irritating part of it all was not the medical procedures, nor the confinement.

Rather it was being forced to share my accommodations with Louise, who used every possible opportunity to annoy me, or shock my sensibilities. Indeed, by the time we were informed that we no longer posed a danger to our fellow Chrononauts, I had been seriously contemplating the idea of smothering her in her sleep!

Naturally, Louise declared that her first order of business was to obtain some spirits for herself, whilst Lady Anne and Ms. Grímsdóttir were of a mind to return to their quarters, and there relax. I though, was only intent on retrieving X'Kallabar.

As it happened, when I had it in my hand at last, I found that the Professor had been entirely correct; it had suffered no ill effects. I was of course, immensely relieved--and then surprised, for as I inventoried my other belongings, I discovered something that had not been there before. It was a post-card, which had been tucked in the top pocket of my flightsuit.

On it were several images of a great grassy hill, surrounded by farmland. The mount was not a smooth prominence, but had terraced sides, and a single gothic tower dominated its summit. The legend in the lower right-hand corner breathlessly proclaimed the place to be *Glastonbury Tor, Land of King Arthur!*

What in all of the nine universes is this? I wondered. Turning the card over, my question was answered immediately. A message had been written there, and in a man's hand;

"Well done, Penelope. Please meet me at Glastonbury Abbey, 2nd universe, 5 August 2020, 2050 hours. Yours, Enki."

Evidently, the Anunnaki had learned of my success, and now the time had come for me to collect my reward. Shedding my scrubs, I attired myself in my flightsuit, and went to the office of the Hamilkets. They were, as I had fully expected, hard at work, but greeted me warmly.

"Ah, Penelope!" Hamilket 1 exclaimed. "It is good to see you back." His clone nodded in accord.

"Thank you, sirs," I replied. Then I held out the postcard. "I have just received this."

Hamilket 1 took it and read it over before. "It would appear that you have an important errand to undertake."

"Then I have your leave to do so?"

"You do," he answered. "Blackbird is fully disinfected and ready for flight."

"Thank you both," I said, awarding them a salute. "I shall only need a short while to reunite with Elisabeth, and then I will be on my way."

Hamilket 1's smile widened. "She is awaiting you in the recreation center, and best of luck in Glastonbury."

CHAPTER 10: The Dragon's Heart

In which I visit Glastonbury Abbey and venture into the lair of the White Dragon. There, I face my ultimate adversary, and earn my right to the Grail itself. Then I make a wish.

Because of Zerodianism's triumph over religion, Glastonbury Abbey was an unknown in the 3rd universe, and although my London home was situated in the 2nd, I had never had occasion to visit the place (as other, more pressing matters--such as the Lyrans-- had occupied my full attention). Accordingly, I had little idea of what I might encounter there.

Once one of the wealthiest religious institutions of its kind in all England, centuries of neglect had transformed the Abbey into a great gothic ruin. Beholding it, I could easily envision some sinister supernatural creature skulking amongst its crumbling walls, or perhaps a beautiful young heroine, making her way in the moonlight to a forbidden tryst. That the Abbey was also purported to be the last resting place of King Arthur and his Queen, Guinevere, only added to this heady aura of romance and mystery.

Sited well within view of the great Tor, the ruins sat in the midst of a gentle park-like area, with many places from which to choose from for a landing place. I wasted no time in selecting one and setting Blackbird down.

Of Enki and his companions, I saw nothing and wondered at when and where they might choose to appear. After a time (and **inveigled** by the lure of the ruins), I grew tired of waiting, and elected to leave my craft in order to explore the area. Halfway to the roofless precinct of the Lady Chapel, I heard the sound of an aircraft approaching.

Looking to the Tor, I beheld a sleek helicopter coming towards me and descending rapidly. On its side was the same glyph that I had beheld during my first meeting with the Anunnaki, and next to this, the legend, '*Marduk Industries Ltd.*'.

Enki had arrived.

His conveyance settled down with all the delicacy of the dragonfly that it resembled, and the Nibirai alighted. Straightaway, I noted that he was not nearly as tall as I remembered him. In fact, he seemed shorter.

But thanks to my experience with the Princess, I now knew why this was so; he was attempting to put me at ease by keeping as close as he could to human proportions.

Nonetheless, I braced myself for another heavy-handed demonstration of his occult powers. However, this did not occur, and I was greeted instead with what seemed a genuine smile and a friendly wave of recognition!

"Penelope," he said warmly. "I am so very glad to see that you accepted my invitation. And before I say any more, Princess Nanshe sends her regards, and her eternal thanks. She informed me that you were quite gracious, and very brave."

"Please convey my best wishes to Her Highness in return," I answered. Then I abandoned propriety altogether. "So, what would you have of me, sir?"

"That you join me for a walk is all," he returned, proffering me his arm. "As we came in, I noticed that you were making for the Lady Chapel, which is precisely where I intended to take you. *Shall we?*"

Allowing him to guide me, we walked to the chapel, and there, the Anunnaki paused, and turning, looked back towards the Tor with a contemplative expression. I could not help but to follow his gaze.

Though the lands beneath the Tor were cloaked in the indigo and violet of dusk, the tower at its peak was still painted with the orange fires of the setting sun. It was a dramatic tableau, and the perfect setting for whatever mysterious business that the Anunnaki had in mind for me.

At last, Enki spoke. "The ancient humans who inhabited this area believed the dragon to be a sacred beast of the highest order," he said. "To these pre-Christian tribes, the energetic currents that course through the Earth itself were an expression of draconic power, and the Tor that you see before you was part of a great energetic network of sacred sites, spread throughout the length and breadth of England.'

"They also believed that two dragons guarded the Tor eternally. One was the Red, whose coils encircled the exterior, while the other was the White, who resided within its interior.'

"Physically, these two beasts represented the different paths that one could take; either the seven-terraced trail which leads to the summit, or the underground passage that delivers the traveler to the Dragon's Heart."

He paused, allowing me the opportunity to appreciate this imagery, and as I did so, I traced the trail up to the tower with my eyes. It was very easy for me to envision a mighty creature residing there, its great coils wrapped around the hill.

"But there are deeper layers of meaning as well," he went on. "The pagan priesthood understood that the two dragons were also symbolic of the great universal polarities. One was the sun, the other, the moon. One was the male, the other, the female, and so on.'

"Together, they embodied the inherent duality of human nature itself; that part of the soul that is a creature of the light, and that which is of the darkness. And just as the Red and White Dragons once battled one another in the ancient tale of King Vortirgen, the priests saw our daily lives as an eternal struggle between these two extremes for dominance of the self."

Then he turned to face me. "Your quest tonight will be to travel from here to the path of the White Dragon beneath the Tor. There, you will follow the tunnel until you reach the very center of the maze, and when you do so, you will meet your opposite number. Only one of you can ever hope to possess the Grail, and so, you must fight to the death, and whomsoever loses will be consumed.'

"If you are fortunate enough to emerge as the victor, the White Dragon will guide you to your prize. But know this, Penelope Victoria Steele; once you have it, you must not allow X'alsalaar to come in contact with X'Kallabar. The joining of the Sword and Chalice is an immensely powerful act and doing so will unleash forces that you cannot ever hope to survive. Is that clear?"

"It is," I nodded, my tone resolute.

Enki awarded me a half-smile and then gestured for me to follow him. He led us down a metal stair that took us below the ground level of the chapel (for the original floor had long since ceased to exist), and thence onto to newer course of masonry which had been fashioned to accommodate contemporary visitors.

At the far end of this space, benches had been set out for prayer and meditation, and beyond this, there was a simple stone that I took to be an altar. Here, Enki waved his hand, and the altar slid away, exposing a tunnel.

"This is the starting point of your journey," he announced. "I wish you the best of luck, hero. You will surely need it."

Taking my leave of him, I lowered myself into the passage, and found that two items awaited me there.

The first was a simple backpack such as day travelers might employ for a brief jaunt in the countryside. It was emblazoned with the same spiral design that the Blue People employed, and seeing this, I wondered at the collaboration between the Anunnaki and themselves.

The second object was not nearly as thought-provoking, being a small, battery-powered torch, whose head could be twisted to form an angled light, along with a clip to secure it to my clothing. Testing the device, I was gratified to find that it provided a very powerful beam, which was as well, for the way before me was as dark as the depths of Hades itself.

With a final glance back up to Enki, I attached the torch to my flightsuit and began my trek. The tunnel proved to be a rather cramped affair, and I was forced to crouch so as to avoid striking it with my head. Roots also posed an added nuisance, and I found myself continuously brushing them aside as I made my way through the darkness.

At one point, I heard the sound of rushing water somewhere above me, and reasoned that I was passing beneath an underground river, though being unfamiliar with the area's waterways, I could not gauge my progress based upon this finding. Finally, I came to a cross passage, and entering it, found to my relief that it was spacious enough for me to stand erect.

Furthermore, the masonry was quite different here. Instead of rough medieval stonework, the walls of this new tunnel were of finely worked basalt (or some similar rock) and cut in the manner that I had only seen before in the Grotto of X'Kallabar. It was plain that this was a place that the Blue People had fashioned, and I daresay that I moved with care, wholly uncertain of what might await me.

Some more minutes passed before I heard a dry, rasping sound up ahead of me. It was not constant, but came and went, and it seemed as I approached it, that it was retreating, or perchance, enticing me to follow it and venture deeper into the hill.

Where have I heard that sound before? I asked myself. It was strangely familiar.

At last, it came to me; it was the sound such as snakes made when their scales moved over stone. Though I do not suffer from ophidiophobia, I have never cared for the creatures overmuch, and was not at all pleased at the notion that one of their kind inhabited these tunnels.

Meanwhile, the passage was beginning to ascend and turn inwards towards what I reasoned was the center of the Tor. As I climbed, the rasping sound grew in volume, and seemed closer with every step. Then, as I came within sight of a particularly sharp turning, I caught a glimpse of a pale shape slithering around the corner, and my mind utterly refused to accept what my eyes had just reported.

It had not been the tail end of a serpent at all, but rather something resembling a giant, segmented worm, yet of such gargantuan proportions as to be utterly impossible. The largest species that I was acquainted with was the *Megascolides australis*, and that only attained a length of one meter. This specimen however, had had the look of a creature measuring some *eighteen* meters (or perhaps even more) and had been bigger around than a giant anaconda!

Perforce, I convinced myself that a combination of the shadows, and my fatigue, had conspired to create an optical illusion, and nothing more. Nonetheless, a chill went down my spine, and I proceeded with even greater caution.

Eventually, I happened upon a circular chamber with a number of smaller tunnels depending from it. The space seemed unoccupied, and as I entered, I was already in the process of deciding what to do next.

This proved unnecessary however, for the rasping had returned, even louder than before. Then to my absolute horror, the very worm that I had dismissed as nothing but a mirage came into the chamber. It was positively enormous, with a great, eyeless head that still seemed to sense my presence. As it turned in my direction, I gave out a little cry of both terror and revulsion and made to step back.

Yet I could not retreat, for in seconds, the monster had encircled the entire space, preventing me from exiting. Certain that I was about to be consumed, I reached for my sword.

Yet it did not appear, and the Presence was silent. In a moment of sheer panic, I realized that X'Kallabar had been denied to me. Worse, the Tigress was gone as well, though how, and why, and where, I knew not. Save for Ernst's dagger, I was totally unarmed.

Fortunately, the worm did not choose to attack me at this juncture. Rather, it began to circle around the walls, moving at greater and greater speed, 'till its segmented body was nearly a blur. At the same time, a mist began to fill the room, growing thicker by the moment.

Then of a sudden, the mist came together, forming the shape of another woman, who as I watched, assumed a coherent form. As if my circumstances were not fantastical enough, the apparition that finally manifested before me surpassed all that had come before, if only because it was so familiar.

To my astonishment, I found myself facing a perfect copy of--myself—save for the fact that her flightsuit did not bear the insignia of the Chrononauts. Rather, it was emblazoned with the triskelion of the Lyrans, and the knife that she wore at her side was unmistakably an *SS-Ehrendolch*, an SS 'honor' dagger.

In a flash, I understood exactly what was afoot here. *There, you will follow the tunnel until you reach the very center of the maze,'* Enki had warned, *'and when you do so, you will meet your opposite number.'*

Worse, I understood that this would be a knife fight, filled with short feints and lightning fast attacks. That I would be injured at some point was simply a given, for as I well knew from my training, such was the nature of this form of combat.

Simultaneously, the eyes of my alter ego narrowed, as she too grasped the situation in its fullness.

"So I am to fight *you*, am I?" she asked, a pitiless smile coming to her lips. "It will be a distinct pleasure, *sister*." This last came out with all of the bitterness of the profanity that it was intended to be.

Right away, her hand went across her body to her blade, and she pulled it from its sheath so that its point faced downwards. Most would have considered this to be an amateur grip, but I knew it for what it actually was; given our limited space, she intended to get in close, and such a grip was well-suited to that strategy.

Thus, I did likewise.

"*He* created you, didn't he?" I asked, keeping my free hand ready to parry as we circled one another.

"No," she said. "Not him, but you, yourself. I am the Penelope that *should* have been when you went to Mr. Grey in Utah. But you ruined all that, didn't you? He never had the chance to re-imprint you and make *me* the reality in this timeline."

Seeing my perplexity, she laughed. "Did you really think that Caroline occupied the only alternate future? That there were no other Penelopes? No other possibilities? I *am* that possibility, and when I kill you, only *I* shall remain."

With that, she slashed out at my empty hand, but I managed to pull away just in time to avoid the strike, though only by the narrowest of margins. Then I lunged.

In response, she pivoted, and struck out with her blade, dealing me a cut to my forearm before dancing away. While the wound did not cripple me, it still hurt like the very blazes, and I answered it with an attack of my own, hoping to deal her a similar hurt, but alas, I failed to hit my mark.

Again, we orbited one another, and then without warning, she came at me. I managed to turn aside and moved past her flashing blade, and in so doing, saw my chance and sliced her upper arm. This time, my dagger tasted blood, eliciting a wince of pain from her even as she replied with an elbow to my jaw.

Her blow caused stars to flood my vision, but I still had enough presence of mind to turn on my heels, and then drive her back with a series of furious slashes. Now forced to defend herself, she parried and backpedaled.

Maintaining the offense, I jabbed and thrust at her, seeking a vital place in which to bury my blade. But as I came close, she dealt a vicious heel kick to the side of my knee, toppling me.

But even as I hit the ground, I went into a reverse roll. It took me straight into the great worm's body, and rebounding, I tumbled again, this time moving forwards.

My twin was unprepared for this abrupt reversal, or that when I came back up on my feet, I had deflected her knife even as I thrust my own blade into her. It bit in just beneath the apex of her ribs, and she let out a tremendous gasp, dropping her knife and reflexively clutching at the weapon that had just killed her.

For a long moment, we simply stood there, and looked into one another's eyes. Then, summoning up all of my willpower, I shoved the knife in until it met resistance and could go no further.

My twin let out a little cry at this, and her expression changed from one of pained surprise, to that of sad resignation, and then her eyes fluttered shut, and she sagged against me.

As I lowered her body to the floor, I knew that what had just occurred would remain indelibly printed upon my soul. That was the true price of my victory; no matter how justified I had been in my actions, I had committed the greatest sin imaginable, for I had just killed myself.

Fate, however, did not allow me the opportunity to dwell upon the significance of this. The great worm, which had remained quiescent during the entire battle, had begun to stir.

Hastily, I pulled the knife free of my dead twin, and scrambled to my feet, ready to defend myself against the monster. Its great head had reappeared, and turning in my direction, it opened its mouth, revealing a fleshy maw lined with teeth, and wide enough to swallow me whole.

Fighting back a wave of nausea, I summoned up every ounce of my courage. If I were to die after all, I was determined to go down fighting, and as the worm's mouth came nearer, I tried to gauge where I might do it the most damage. Yet before I could instigate any action against it, it dipped down and fastened upon the ankles of my double.

Then it began to chew, drawing the corpse into itself in fits and starts like a great mindless machine. Bones popped and snapped with each mastication, and I desperately tried to look away.

But I could not. There are some things in the nine universes that are so absolute in their hideousness, that they command the viewer's full attention, and do not allow themselves to be ignored. This was one such.

The last thing that I saw of my former enemy was her face. Her eyes were still open, and they seemed to stare back at me in accusation before the jaws closed one final time, and then she was gone.

With its meal now complete, the worm circled the chamber 'till it found one of the side tunnels. There it entered, and with surprising speed for a thing of its size, disappeared down the passage.

I could not do anything more than gape at this, but then Enki's instructions asserted themselves; *"If you are fortunate enough to emerge as the victor, the White Dragon will guide you to your prize."*

I had no choice, I realized. I would have to follow the creature and hope that wherever we arrived, the Grail, and an end to this madness would await me. Numbly, I went to the tunnel, bent over and entered, crawling on my hands and knees.

For a time, there was only the darkness, the sound of the worm as it moved ahead of me, and naught else. Then at last, I came into another chamber and rose to my feet. Of the worm's whereabouts, I knew not; for it had vanished somehow, but I entertained no doubts whatsoever about my success.

This was because I beheld the Grail floating in the air before me. I was surprised to find that it was not a chalice, nor a container of any kind, but rather a round, polished stone.

As large as my fist, the gem possessed a scarlet hue that made even the purest of rubies seem pallid by comparison. Flames of the same color surrounded it, and I could feel their great heat even from where I stood. Though I briefly attempted to reach for the gem, the crimson fire was too much for me. Something else needed to occur here, but I knew not what.

Then a voice spoke, as if in answer. It was neither male, nor female. Nor was it coming from any single direction, but seemingly from everywhere.

"You have triumphed, hero," it said, "just like Galahad, and because of this accomplishment, you may make one wish. Ask, and whatever you desire shall be yours."

I did not wonder at the veracity of this, nor the source of the words. Just then I was too exhausted, and too overwhelmed to be bothered with reason. Instead, I merely stared down at my hands and my clothing, still bespattered with the blood of my twin and pondered the question with care.

What do I desire? I asked myself. *Of all things, what do I yearn for the most?*

With this, the whole of my life since becoming a Chrononaut flashed before me in a raging torrent of memories. I revisited it all; my death at the hands of Bookman Pierce, my loss of Elizabeth to a monoplane accident, the slaughter in Tibet, my fateful decision in New Berlin, and more besides. All of it paraded before me in stark, and unmerciful relief.

Then I recalled a tale from the ancient Greeks, wherein the souls of the dead, having been judged worthy enough by the Gods to be granted a new existence, were obligated to drink from the river Lethe. I also understood why Galahad, faced with the same challenge, had chosen to ascend to Heaven rather than to continue with his earthly pursuits.

"To forget," I replied wearily. "For a time at least, and to be as a child once again."

"So mote it be," came the reply. "But know this oh hero; you still have one more task to complete before your desire will be granted you. For now though, the Grail is yours for the taking."

The fire around the stone vanished at this, and I was able to reach out and take it in my hands without any deleterious effects. Mindful of Enki's directive, I stowed it in my rucksack right away, and in so doing, the chamber vanished, and I found myself standing amidst the ruins of the Abbey.

Moreover, I could feel the Tigress stirring within me, and also the Presence. And when I called for it, X'Kallabar came to me. My powers had been fully restored.

I did not celebrate this however, but longed for sleep, and had I been able, I would have lain down upon the grass, then and there and closed my eyes. Yet, as the voice had stated, another labor still awaited me. Thus, I trudged back to Blackbird and had her take us away.

A Phaseship, delivered by an Ebani, was awaiting us when we reached outer space. H'reep was its Speaker, and Major Sixkiller, it's pilot.

"Howdy, Penny!" she greeted. "Did ya'll find anything?"

"I did," I responded flatly, not wishing to share any of the details. "The Sangreal is ours."

"Nothin else?" she asked, her disappointment palpable.

"Such as?"

"Like the Davidson's Chili recipe," she explained.

"*Chili* recipe?"

"Well yeah. I mean the Grail's fine and all—but Con Aggro has been holdin on to that recipe since before the Flood. And as anyone who loves chili knows; *that's* the Holy Grail."

"I am so terribly sorry to disappoint you, Major," I apologized. "But I was only successful in retrieving the Grail and naught else."

"Well," she sighed, "that's somthin I 'spose. Let's get ya'll home then."

CHAPTER 11: In That Sleep of Death

Wherein I learn the fate of the Finns and then the true nature of the rings of Saturn. Perforce, I accept a vital mission.

Entering the main dome with the Major, I beheld a thoroughly unexpected figure. Of all the people in the nine universes, King Elvis was there, in the passageway, and hard at work with a push-broom (though I could not imagine what dust he found to sweep up, given the efficiency of the mechanica and our housekeeping robots).

"It seems that Elvis is in the building," I observed. "What pray tell, is he doing here?"

Cassie indicated that we should pause out of his earshot, and promptly enlightened me.

"Well, it didn't work out fer him in Vegas. He tried to make it as an Elvis-Impersonator, but all the critics said that he didn't do a good enough job of playin the King. So, I convinced the Masters to take him back as a charity case. They modified his mind so that he'd never take any Illuminati orders, and set him to work right here. It was the least the we could do fer him."

"More's the pity," I responded.

At this, we approached him. "Good afternoon, Your Majesty" I greeted. "How are you today?"

Elvis ceased his sweeping and turned to regard at me. "I'm all shook up. Uh-huh."

"Yes…I suppose that you must be," I replied. "Well, best of luck to you, Your Majesty."

Leaving him to his labors, we made our way to the Professor's laboratory, whereupon I surrendered the Grail to a special case designed to house it. Then I made for my quarters, weary to the very marrow of my bones.

But just as I was passing the mess hall, I happened to spot Ms. Grímsdóttir and Sigrun. They were seated together at a table. Both had drinking horns, and a bottle was stationed between them. Moreover, their expressions were grave, and assuming that theirs was a private conversation, I made to move on, but Grímsdóttir beckoned for me to join them.

"We have news from Ostland," she explained. "Sit. You will want to be seated once you hear it."

Now worried, I did as she bade, and Sigrun produced a third horn, pouring me a serving of what proved to be a strong mead.

"What is amiss?" I requested.

"The Finns," Grímsdóttir stated flatly. "They did not make it back."

"W-what?" I stammered.

"Something went wrong with their side mission," Sigrun elaborated. "The Mongols discovered them, and there was a firefight. They're all gone."

Hearing this, a great numbness overcame me. Of late, I had wept aplenty for the dead, and it seemed as if this was all that I had left in me to feel.

"We are toasting to their memories as good Ostlanders," Grímsdóttir stated, "for they are in Valhalla now with the Gods. To the heroes!"

With that, she raised her horn and downed its contents. Then she held it out to Sigrun, who promptly refilled it.

"To the heroes!" I echoed, taking a drink from my own vessel.

Although I normally avoided spirituous liquors, there was something comforting about the fiery liquid, as if the pain of it going down my throat was helping to exorcise my distress.

Even so (or perhaps because of it), I could not fend off the memories of those we had lost. Their faces swam before me, and perhaps the worst of these were of Under Sergeant Virtanen, and her carefree smile.

Such a waste, I reflected. *Such a terrible and meaningless waste.*

Then I drank again and added in a salute to Ernst von Knectenburg, who surely occupied the same hallowed realm. Another toast followed after this, and then many more besides.

Consequently, by the time I finally left the hall, I was quite foxed, and when I drunkenly explained the circumstances to her, Elizabeth did not offer up any censure, but took pity on me and guided me to our bed.

The very instant that my head touched the pillow, I lost consciousness, and in any fair universe, a deep, dreamless interlude should have followed. But such was not the nature of my existence and the specter of Saturn chose this as an opportunity to torment me anew. This time, my dream was populated with extremely vivid imagery, no doubt lent to it by my adventure in the volcano lair, and therefore all the more horrific.

Unsurprisingly, when at last I became wakeful again, I was in a wretched state and could not do more than quaff a restorative cup of tea (for my stomach would have rebelled at anything more substantial). Then I sought out the Professor in his quarters, for I was wholly done with mysteries and eager for answers.

Of course, he received me graciously (though he was still in his nightclothes and had been at table when I had come a' calling), and once I had recounted my vision, and all those that had come before it, he bade me to sit with him at his desk.

"Your mother and the Sibyl warned me that you were having these dreams and that you would eventually inquire about them," he disclosed. "And now that that time has arrived, we should discuss the subject at length."

He typed a command on his holographic keyboard and an image materialized in the air. It was the twin of the one that I had seen in the volcano lair, showing the Lyran fleet in all of its malevolence. Then, at another command, the collection of broadcasts and entertainment features appeared alongside it.

"What you have been dreaming about, and what you saw in the volcano, is the result of our actions against Project Blue Beam, and the chip factory on Mars," he stated. "After those losses, the Lyrans were forced to change their strategy."

"How so, sir?" I questioned, doing my level best to stave off the darkness that the subject of Mars engendered.

He lit his pipe, took a puff and answered. "As you might recall, the Illuminati became enmeshed in the entertainment industry. After the Blue Beam debacle, the Lyrans directed them to place the blame for it on key government officials, and then explain away the phony invasion as a purely human conspiracy.'

"Following that, they had them begin the process of transforming the image of extraterrestrial life from one of fearful, bug-eyed monsters, to benevolent beings, intent on saving Mankind from itself.'

"To this end, major movies and television shows were produced, along with many documentaries. Through these presentations and many more like them, the Illuminati finally accomplished their mission. They transformed humanity's attitude from one of dread, to a sense of welcome and acceptance. Then they took the next step; they had the space agencies of the world reveal the existence of alien life."

As he told me this, the broadcasts were replaced by an interview with the UN Secretary General. He was discussing the topic of full disclosure, and its positive effect on member nations. I was not listening to his twaddle though. Instead, I was fixated by the tape scrolling beneath his image.

ET is Real! it proclaimed. *We are Not Alone! NASA, ESA and Other Agencies Reveal the Truth at Last! Extraterrestrial Fleet Spotted Over Saturn! Space Visitors Bring Mankind a Message of Peace and Brotherhood* …and so on.

"Lies! Lies and of the blackest caliber!" I snarled. "Those are Lyrans. They mean us nothing but harm."

"*We* know that, but not the people of this Earth," Merriweather gently corrected. "To the teeming masses, the Lyrans are their 'space brothers', who will come and take them to a better life while the ecosystem of Earth is allowed to heal.'

"It should come as no surprise that cults have sprung up everywhere, heralding this as 'a new age of unparalleled glory', free of war, disease and strife. Even the Pope has urged his followers to embrace them when they arrive, declaring the Lyrans to be sent by no less than God Himself. Earth and its peoples are nearly ripe for the picking."

"But surely not everyone will step aboard their slave ships," I countered.

"No," he replied. "There are always those in a population that are loners, or keen to maintain their independence, not to mention the ones who are simply unwilling to abandon the familiar. '

"To these, the Lyrans have offered the privilege of being 'shepherds of the planet'; to remain behind and act as caretakers until the rest of the human race can return. Naturally this is all nonsense; once they have the majority of humanity stuffed into their cargo holds, they will simply come and take the rest by force, or just do away with them."

"Diabolical," I declared, my fangs emerging.

"In a word, yes," he agreed. "And so subtle as to be nearly undetectable until just recently."

"What would you have of me?" I asked, my voice made husky by the Tigress.

"That you fly a very special mission," another speaker said. It was Sigrun, who had just entered. "The likes of which has only been flown once before, and by the crew of a plane called the *Enola Gay*. Then as now, many lives hang in the balance, and our resources are limited to only one weapon; yourself and what you bear."

"X'Kallabar", I guessed, feeling the Presence stirring within my being even as I uttered its name. "And X'alsalaar."

"Yes," Sigrun confirmed. "As Enki warned, when the Sword and the Chalice are united, their combined energy is such that nothing can withstand it. The blast radius of such an event far exceeds anything that primitive nuclear weapons could ever manage to achieve, and it will surely destroy the entire invasion fleet in one blow."

A suicide mission then, I concluded.

"Is there no other option, madam?" I asked her. "Perchance a massed attack by the entirety of our forces?"

"We considered that very thing," Sigrun admitted, "and we ran many simulations through our AI's. We also had the Sibyl and Maggie view every possible future, but all of them resulted in our failure.'

"The simple fact is that the Lyran armada is simply too large for our forces to defeat in open battle. At present, it numbers some 10,912 vessels versus the five score that we can field against it—and that includes the Greys."

"In the end, the only scenario where we prevail involves you and a solo mission. Here, their very numbers and the overconfidence that this lends, will work against them, for like the *Enola Gay*, they will not consider that a single ship could pose them any meaningful threat."

"But even if I should succeed in this endeavor," I questioned, "what will prevent the Lyrans from simply going back in time and recreating their fleet?"

Sigrun grinned. "Because we can do likewise, and send you back with X'kallabar and the Grail, *ad infinitum*. Under such an assault, and with such terrible losses each and every time, they will eventually abandon their effort, if indeed our first attack is not enough to dissuade them.'

"That is exactly what occurred to the Japanese; after two atomic weapons were dropped on the cities of Hiroshima and Nagasaki, they lost the will to fight and surrendered, so great was the trauma that they had endured. I believe that that is what will occur here."

I nodded at this, and considered all that I had just heard. Then at last, I looked to the Professor, who now seemed even older and more careworn to me than ever.

"You can of course refuse, my dear," he stated gently. "We would not hold it against you."

Though I feared to utter the words that would set the wheels of my destiny into motion, I knew what my answer had to be.

"I shall do it," I said to the both of them. "I shall fly the mission."

Afterwards, I did not return to my quarters. Rather, I left the dome, and made my way to the pond where the dragonflies dwelt. And there, I considered the two women in my life who mattered to me the most; Blackbird my virtual companion, and Elizabeth, who held the keys to my heart.

I would have to find my way with each of them, I knew, and for a long while, I meditated on the best course of action to take. At last, and when I believed that I had found my answers, I went to Blackbird.

When her egress ramp opened, I confess that I entered the cabin with no little hesitation. She had received the mission file the very moment that I had accepted it and knew all of the particulars, especially where it concerned my chances of survival, so there was no concealing anything from her. And given that she had once threatened to commit suicide if I ever forgot her, I was unsure of what her reaction would be.

Yet she greeted me with noticeable calm. "Hello Penny."

"Hello, my darling," I said. "I have come to speak with you about the mission."

"Yes," she replied. "I have read the file, and I understand its grave nature. It must be flown, and I think that it was very brave of you to accept it."

"Then you are not cross with me?"

"I would rather that you did not go," she said, "But I understand why you must."

"But what of your concerns?" I asked. "About my forgetting you?"

"I have been thinking about that ever since the file came to me, and I searched my databases for any information that would help me to resolve the matter."

"And did you find anything?"

"Yes, I found many things," she told me. "For one, I learned about the frailty of memory, especially were it concerns beings of flesh and blood. Then I learned about old age, and its effects upon the mind, and about other conditions that can do likewise. I also learned that I was not the only being to ever fear so for a loved one, or to confront the worst.'

"There was one tale in particular that lent me great insight. It concerned a woman in the 2nd universe whose husband lost his memory to an accident. He did not know anything about their life together before that event, or even about the world at large.'

"Yet, she did not give up hope, nor forget her love for him, and although he never fully recovered, thanks to her devotion, they learned to care for one another anew. In a way, she was able to share two lives with him instead of only one."

"That is a beautiful story," I observed, "and a wise insight. Is there more?"

"Yes, Penelope," she said. "There is Elizabeth. Despite her memories being re-implanted and altered, she knew you, just as Ziva knew Manfred after she had been Awakened.'

"And lastly, there is a quote from William Penn; *Life is eternal, and love is immortal, and death is only a horizon, and a horizon is nothing save the limit of our sight.'*

She paused, giving me time to ponder this before she went on. "I know now that it was childish of me to threaten what I did, for no matter what, I love you, and love—real love--overcomes all, be it a flaw of the body, or of the mind, or even death itself.'

"So I will not stop you from doing your duty, or protest. Nor will I allow you to face it alone. I shall go with you and I will be there at the end."

Hearing this, I was instantly reminded of my encounter with Jesus in the Garden of Gethsemane. *"Be there at the end,"* he had asked.

Unwittingly, I had come full circle, and I realized that in my own small way, I was doing the same as he had done; I had chosen to give up my life for humanity's sake, and this was to be my crucifixion. That Blackbird had agreed to accompany me up to the summit of Golgotha humbled me, and I silently thanked God that I had been blessed with so wise and stalwart a companion.

We talked for several more minutes after this, during which time we came to a number of arrangements regarding the future, and I was greatly heartened by this. Then, when all that needed discussion had been said, I left her to face my second, and more formidable challenge.

Unlike Blackbird, I had decided that I would not disclose my mission to Elizabeth, nor tell her that in just a few hours, I would be undertaking it.

In the light of my conversation with my Phaseship, I realize that some of my readers might find this to be rather cruel and callous, or perhaps even cowardly. But I had chosen this course out of love for her, knowing that the revelation would have only brought her pain.

Granted, I knew that she would still suffer, but I also understood that her distress would be less severe if it were a sudden thing rather than an event that she was given time to dwell upon. In a sense, what I intended could be compared to a doctor's needle; unpleasant enough in a moment of surprise, but far worse when the patient knows that its bite is coming.

So, when I entered our quarters, I affected a light and carefree mood, and saw to it that our evening together was as perfect as I could contrive. We dined on the finest meal that our facility was able to provide us, and afterwards, I made love to her with all the care and tenderness that she deserved.

When at last, she had drifted off into a contented sleep, I rose from our bed and penned her a letter, explaining all, and begging her for her forgiveness. I also counseled her to seek out the support of our many friends, and not to fear for the future. And as soon as the ink had dried, I quietly dressed myself, pausing for but a moment before Jacob's Ladder.

This time, all of the angels, and even Jacob himself, were absent. Only one figure remained, and it stood at the very summit, but a footstep away from the radiance that symbolized God and eternity.

Though it was quite small, and I was compelled come close to make out the details, I had no trouble recognizing the figure at all. It was myself, and dressed exactly as I was.

Everything is there, I observed. The scar that I had earned during my battle with the terracotta army marked the image's cheek, the Iron Cross that Manfred had awarded me was pinned to its flightsuit, and it carried both X'Kallabar and Ernst's dagger on its hip.

What a terribly long road I have travelled and how unexpected every mile of it, I mused. Turning away at last, I went over to the bed, and planted a gentle kiss on Elizabeth's forehead.

"I love you, my darling," I said to her in a whisper too low to awaken her. "I shall always love you." Then I deposited the letter on my pillow and left the chamber.

I did not tarry, but went to Merriweather's laboratory, where I was met by Charles and the Professor. They showed me to a chair, and had a refactor headset at the ready. Now more than ever, my pre-mission recording was of the utmost importance, for I wanted nothing whatsoever to be left out of the record.

The session itself was brief, as I was up to date, and when it had concluded, I thanked Charles for all of his companionship, and then conversed with Merriweather so as to make certain that all of my arrangements would be attended to.

"Then everything will be as I wish it?"

"Yes," he said. "Exactly so."

"And Blackbird? She as well?" I inquired.

"I would not think of excluding her, my dearest," he replied. "I have already set to work in that regard, and I think that you will both find the end result to be quite satisfactory."

"Good," I told him, letting out a great sigh of relief. "Knowing that, I can go forwards without entertaining any concerns. Thank you, my dear, dear friend."

He gave me a gentle pat on the shoulder and then showed me to the door, wherein I proceeded to the tarmac. My friends were all there, and Cassie handed me the case containing X'alsalaar.

I took it and gave her a heartfelt embrace. "Help her to understand," I said.

"Ya'll don't need t'worry on that score, Penny," Sixkiller promised. "We'll get it across t'her, though I 'spect that Elizabeth'll be mad as a hornet once she's done a'cryin—and not just at ya'll either."

"Most likely, she will be," I agreed.

Next, I turned to Hamilket 1 and shook his hand. "Sir, it has been an honor serving under you."

"The honor has been all mine, Penelope," he replied. "And if Fate decrees that we should meet again, I will tell you all about yourself. After all, stories are the only things that anyone truly owns, and I would like to return your possessions to you if the chance arises."

"I should like that," I told him.

Then I left them and went out to Blackbird. Manfred 1 and Ziva 1 were there, along with a Speaker that I did not know. They had agreed to accompany me partway to my destination. In fact, they had insisted upon it.

As I had with the Major, I hugged them both. "You have been the greatest of friends to me. I thank you for everything."

Though he struggled mightily to maintain a façade of Prussian stoicism, Manfred's eyes misted over. "And the same to you, Penny," he replied.

A long pause followed this, and then he added, "Well? Shall we get on with it then?"

"Yes," said I, "but first, I must give you something. It is better that you have it now than it be destroyed with me." I had removed Ernst's dagger from my belt and offered it out to him.

He took it and wiped at his eyes. "I will take good care of it," he managed to croak.

With nothing more to say to one another, we donned our helmets and went to our respective ships. Blackbird acknowledged me as I took my seat.

"Hello, Penny," she said.

"Hello, my dearest," I said. "Are you ready?"

"I am," she replied. "All systems are optimal."

"Very well," I responded, beginning our startup sequence. "We should not keep our friends waiting."

"Penny?" she asked.

"Yes darling?"

"Will it hurt?"

A lump came into my throat. "No, my love. It will not. When X'Kallabar and X'alsalaar are joined, the Professor assured me that the effect will be instantaneous. We shall feel absolutely nothing when the end comes."

"That is good," she said. "I would not want you to suffer."

"Nor I, you," I replied.

Of the journey itself, there is not much to tell, save that we transited courtesy of an Ebani, and arrived in the 2nd universe in a timely fashion. From our point of entry (which was just outside of the orbit of Jupiter, and between the group of asteroids known of as the Trojans and the Greeks), we made our way towards the ringed planet.

There was little conversation between us during this, and at last, when we reached Comet 67P, I landed on its rugged surface and here, we wished each other farewell.

"Shalom, Penny," Ziva said. "I know that God will watch over you."

"Shalom, Ziva," I answered.

"Viel Glück, Penny," Manfred put in. "Good hunting."

And that was the whole of it. Without further ado, they turned about and flew back towards the Ebani. Thus, I found myself alone, and rather than dwelling on my situation, and allowing myself any chance to reconsider, I immediately attended to my work. This was to ascertain the exact location of the Lyran armada, and then determine the best avenue of attack.

They were quite easy to spot, so great were their numbers, and seeing them, I could readily appreciate the wisdom behind the decision to send me alone.

Had we done battle with a force such as this, defeat would have been an absolute certainty, I reflected. *There truly was no alternative.*

Noting the time, I carefully positioned the case containing X'alsalaar nearer to my seat, and then sent the order to Blackbird to take us into the No When. Our transit was brief, and we returned to the 2nd universe at a point half a minute in the future, and directly above the Lyran fleet.

We were immediately attacked, first by energy weapons, and then dozens of missiles were hurled at us. Suppressing the primitive instinct to flee and thus preserve myself, I sent us into a steep dive, aiming for one of the largest ships at the very center of the formation.

As we plummeted, an energy bolt struck Blackbird's starboard wing. "Penny, I am hit!" she exclaimed.

"Press on, my dearest!" I cried, adding power to the engines even as she discharged her counter measures. Meantime, the distance to our target was rapidly decreasing.

Only a second more, I prayed. *That is all I require.*

Then a missile detonated almost directly atop us, and the panel off to my right burst into flames. Alarms wailed, and straightaway, Old Fred unlimbered from his place and began to fight the blaze with his internal extinguishers.

But an energy bolt found us, and the blast sheared off our port wing, sending us into a tailspin. It was too late for the Lyrans though, for we were now well within range.

Letting go of the ship's controls, I unsheathed X'kallabar, and opened the case to take up X'alsalaar. With Elizabeth's name on my lips, I brought X'Kallabar's tip to the Grail.

Though it seemed solid in my hand, there was no resistance as I pushed the blade through. The two objects became one and a bright light followed this, coupled with the sensation of intense heat.

Then everything was replaced by the grey void of death, and the curious humming that fills that strange realm. Having died before, I did not scream...

EPILOGUE

In which I Awaken, and although much is explained, much is not.

For some while after my Awakening, I simply basked in the sunshine and reveled in the sound of the waterfalls around me.

I am, I thought. *Once again, I am.* Then I sensed a presence and opened my eyes.

A young woman stood before me. She was scarcely in her teens and as fair as I, and like myself, dressed in a loose, white robe. Yet she was not a corporeal being, but as transparent as a spirit.

A hologram., I recalled. *That is what such an apparition is called.*

"Who are you?" I asked her.

She answered this with a sweet and loving expression. "I am Blackbird. The Professor created this image so that I could be by your side and help you to recover from your Awakening. You and I were great friends in your last life, and when you are fully yourself again, we shall fly together and have many wonderful adventures."

"Fly?"

Again, she smiled, but there was a wistfulness to her expression that I could not account for, as if my query had somehow saddened her.

"Yes," she said at last. "Fly. It was something that you and I greatly enjoyed."

"I should like that very much," I told her, and this seemed to revivify her mood. Then she looked to her right, and I followed her gaze. A strikingly beautiful woman, with raven hair and darksome eyes, stood some distance away from us, and when our eyes met, she awarded me with a smile that seemed warmer than the sun shining down on us.

"Who is *that?*" I asked, my heart catching in my throat, for I felt a deep and visceral attraction to her.

"That is someone who loves you very, very much," Blackbird answered. "Her name is Elizabeth. For a time, she was quite angry with you. But with the help of your many friends, she has come to understand and accept what you did, and when the moment is right, she will reintroduce herself to you. For now, though, she would have it that you simply enjoy your rest."

As Blackbird disclosed this, the beautiful woman turned, and walked out of view.

No! Do not go, I thought. *Not yet.* But she had gone, and her absence caused me to feel as if a part of me had departed with her.

Yet, even as I felt a stab of sorrow at this, a figure approached us. He was perhaps no more than thirty years of age, and exceedingly handsome, with an athletic physique, and penetrating eyes that shone with a wisdom that far exceeded his youth. Moreover, his expression was a kindly one, and although he too seemed a stranger, I warmed to him immediately.

"Hello, Penny," he greeted. "I am Professor Thaddeus Merriweather, though you might not recognize me, for in your last iteration I inhabited a far older body.'

I regarded him quizzically, and he explained. "It was necessary for me to play the role of an elderly mentor, but once my task was complete, the Masters rewarded me with a younger form.'

"Rest assured that I will still offer you all of the guidance that I can though, even if I might wear a different face. In the meantime, I I have a present for you, to celebrate your 1034th iteration."

He held out a book, and I took it from him. It was quite old, and the title read: *"The Wisdom of Hypatia of Alexandria by Her Student Synesius of Cyrene."*

"Thank you, sir," I replied.

"I appropriated it during an adventure that we had in the Vatican Secret Archive," he revealed. "and it is the only copy that exists anywhere in the nine universes. In your last life, you admired this woman greatly, and when I saw it, I knew that it would make a fitting gift for your next Awakening."

Perceiving my confusion, he raised a hand. "No, do not bother to try and remember just now, my dear. You will have another date with the refactor soon enough, and then you will remember all. For the nonce, simply enjoy the book, and the bliss that ignorance bestows. After all that you have endured, you deserve your peace."

"Thank you, sir," I said. With that, he rewarded me with a dazzling smile, and walked away. Out of deference to his generosity, I opened the volume and read a passage from it at random.

"Life is an unfoldment," it said, *"and the further we travel, the more truth we can comprehend. To understand the things that are at our door is the best preparation for understanding those that lie beyond."*

Yes, I reflected, *I am at such a doorstep just now. What, I wonder, lies beyond it?*

As I pondered this, another visitor arrived. She seemed to be my twin in every respect, save that a hidden reservoir of memory insisted otherwise.

It was my mother, and from the radiant smile that she awarded me, I knew that my question was about to be answered.

But what she subsequently disclosed, I shall not say. That, dear reader, is for another tale, and another life…

THE END